3 by Peter Neill

Leete's Island Books
Sedgwick, Maine

THREE
Copyright 2013 Robert Neill III
First edition published by Leete's Island Books, Inc.
Box 1, Sedgwick, Maine 04676
www.leetesislandbooks.com
Library of Congress Control Number: 2013905635
ISBN 978-0-918172-50-1
Design: Karen Davidson, www.davidsondesigninc.com

A TIME PIECE
Copyright © 1970 by Robert Neill III
First edition published by Grossman Publishers Inc., New York
and Fitzhenry and Whiteside, Ltd., Canada
LoC 76-106297
Illustration: Seymour Chwast

MOCK TURTLE SOUP
Copyright ©1972 by Robert Neill III
First edition published by Grossman Publishers Inc., New York
and Fitzhenry and Whiteside, Ltd., Canada
LoC 73-184475, ISBN 670-48243-9
Illustration: Jacqueline Schuman

ACOMA
Copyright ©1978 by Leete's Island Books, Inc.
First edition published by Leete's Island Books, Inc.
LoC 777-92932, ISBN 9181172-03
Illustration: Susan McCrillis Kelsey

PRINTED IN THE UNITED STATES

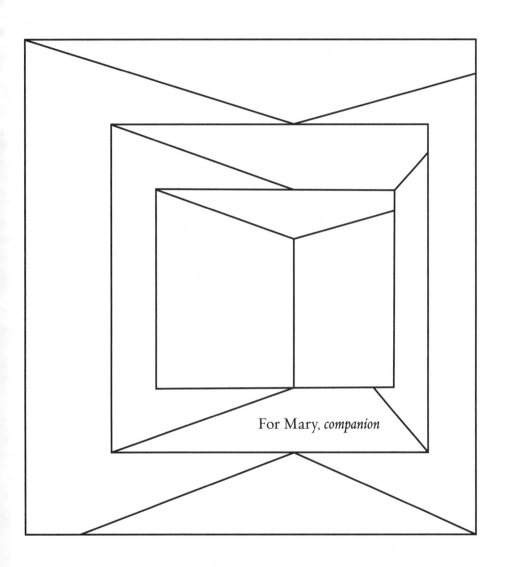

For Mary, *companion*

A TIME PIECE

To Horse and the Future

autobiography
anna
aimee
amura
annastasia

AUTOBIOGRAPHY

How do I begin? begin with events which are not completed; which have no logic; which span so little, so much, of Time? It is an impossible task to begin at the beginning. For all I know the beginning may yet occur within the next moment, may have already occurred somewhere in the middle, may have occurred even before the first few facts I know for certain. If there is to be a beginning and an end, they must be arbitrary; points which will last only an instant before a new departure replaces an old completion and my story begins again.

Point . . . on a circle.

With this, I take my life.

I go to join my dead wife. I jam the nib of my pen into my wrist, I dive beneath the hammering keys of the typewriter, I attempt my autobiography. There is an accepted technique: narrate at length the events of one's life in chronological order to create a compilation from which may be drawn some meaningful impression or conclusion about oneself.

Cantankerous old fart that I am, I must do the opposite.

I will tell everything at once, bring all my lifetime to bear upon a single moment.

one
single
moment
point . . . on a line
The blood, look! is already flowing.
Who am I, then, is the question.

It is the twenty-fifth hour of an ensuing day. I must hurry, whisper, my lips moving quickly against the microphone. I must complete it before the end.

The Circle has just left, gone their new ways; my eyes shifting about the room mark their leavings, the traces of their presence which before dawn I must remove; fingernail parings, plastic glasses coated with hardened drinking syrup. All must be put in order.

> *My name is Frank Timmins. I am sixty-two*
> *years of age. I was married for thirty-three years to the*
> *former Annastasia Saxton until her sudden death six*
> *weeks ago. No children. My preoccupation is teaching.*
> *I belong to no clubs, detest committees and academic*
> *conventions, I am listed in none of the catalogues of*
> *famous people. I am widely published, have written seven*
> *books on various aspects, several monographs; yes, a*
> *book of poems, and many learned articles. To the distress*
> *of my publishers and the university administrators and to*
> *my great satisfaction, I have released all my work under*
> *the pseudonym of Marcus Chais.*
> *But this is all so incidental . . .*

Lost in the past, there is a journal, printed in blue-green mold, bound in transparent leather. It reads: I was petrified, lest the mob of ungrateful fools discover me where I lay. I knew the anger of such crowds well, having moved their fickle natures myself with word or gesture. But no more, all is ruined and destroyed beyond my repair. I have been betrayed by their ignorance, but not by my lord who appeared to me in my dreams that first night in Bel. That was the beginning; a first word spoken; a certain knowledge that I could lead a village and transform them from impoverished serfs to great landowners and tradesmen; lead them from the tillers of stagnant fields to the custodians of the yellow-gold squares of plenty and silver streams of Paradise itself. That I could elevate Bel from a cluster of hovels, from lanes lined with broken stones, from a polluted well and gutters arun with sewage, to a great nine-tiered world within itself, a city worthy of epic and song, a seat of many parliaments and a focus of all good. Through me Bel would be seen for as far as the eye of man could see. I was to outline the city's nine sides for all posterity. I was given the covenant.

> *Let me try my introduction once again.*
> *My name is Marcus Chais. I am married, divorced, constantly in love. I revel in the camphor of old lace ladies, I violate the pubescence of sweet, young things. I have many wives. I am a poet—unpublished, but filled with anticipation of my first review. I am a priest, doctor, locker-room lawyer, Indian chief. I earn my worldly living as that celebrated vaudeville figure, Marcus the Magician.*

And in the present:
Marcus, slow down!
That is Lobe's voice from the back seat. We are driving at eighty miles an hour along a desert road, looking for a white barrel.
Forty-seven miles past the last station? That's what it says.
We've been forty-five. Keep a look out.
Eighty miles an hour and yet we are standing still. The sand stretches out to right and left and to the horizon, flat, desolate. I am the driver, I have knowledge of our speed as my eyes can see the white dashes of road markings passing so quickly they fuse to a single solid line. Aimee, beside me, can see them too, and, oh yes, perhaps Lobe can see them if his eyes are open. Lobe is frightened by the car and speed, Lobe is always frightened.
There it is! cries Aimee. There on the right!

> *. . . painted barrels mark the route but in the storms they are blown like papers across the sand, rearranged by the desert wind to make the journey impossible or never-ending; white barrels stationary*

until beside them accumulate piles of bones, roadside
markers with no more meaning than the stars themselves,
leading the caravan master from his true course into the
labyrinth with no walls no deadends no dangers

The car bumps off the hard-top, tires spinning in the loose
sand, until it maneuvers onto the surface hardened by the sun and
cleaned by a wind that leaves unfortunate wanderers deaf and dumb.
    Lobe, roll up your window, sand is blowing in.
    But Marcus, I need air. I don't feel very well.
    Roll it up!
    We go fifteen miles due south keeping a watch for barrels,
says Aimee.
    I glance at the windshield compass. Due south. Aimee has
the map spread over her knees, she looks up at me with the instructions,
all breast and sunglasses.

. . . but mirages: white heat turning sand to
glass: from the distance another car looms, a sign of
life, running toward you with equal urgency, with equal
speed until you collide in the empty desert with the other
driver's terror and realization in your eye

Wouldn't it be funny if we had an accident?
    Aimee smiles. Lobe seems to have fallen asleep, fat little man
with moustache, in his rumpled seersucker, a newspaper protruding from
the pocket. He snores once and fills with sand. We know little of him
except his fear, his fear of everything between St. Louis and the desert, of
motel sheets and restaurant spoons, of cheap hamburgers, truck drivers,
and running children, his apparent fear of us. It is inevitable that he
should be along.
    Marcus, we must be late, it's getting dark. Can we drive at night?
    I don't see why not. We have the compass and lights, and
they'll be looking for us once it's night.
    There is no sunset, no flamboyant spreading of color
across the sky. It is as if the horizon is too vast for the energy of the sun
to light with intensity. There is only a gradual dimming, batteries
failing, filaments melting, then it is black.

Freud: "Past, present and future exist
simultaneously in the subconscious."
And, therefore, I can take liberties. I can appear
as a character in my own autobiographical dreams.

Marcus, are you thinking or dreaming?

Frank Timmins stands in the doorway, his white hair lit strangely by the light behind.

Sometimes there isn't much difference, Frank. Come on in.

I love this old man, his perfect academic stoop, his hair hanging down the side of his face, and above all the vitality in his eye, in his hand and in his books. My love is that mixture of affection, envy, ambition and hatred a best student has for his professor. How can I ever repay him . . . or forgive him . . . for teaching me everything I know.

Marcus, you have taken root in this room like some grotesque flower thriving on lack of sunlight. What in this world is the matter with you?

He sits across from me, his vest too large now as age has deprived him of his slight paunch, he sits and immediately begins the habitual searching of his pockets for an unknown object he never finds. For a second, I see him as a corpse. Annastasia of course; her death has begun to tell on him.

Put me on the couch, Frank. I think I have caught a disease extinct for four hundred years.

Exemplary scholarship virus, I suppose.

Something which has grown from what you taught as good scholarship yes, and something from rank superstition and coincidence. Let me read you something I found in the bowels of our library.

I take up the journal from my desk and read at random: The time was near; to the west I could perceive a marshalling of clouds that seemed to roll skyward to the limits of that void above us. I called for the ceremony to begin. The populace of Bel crushed around me, their clothes ragged and torn, their faces ravaged by the drought that had dried their fields to iron and sent fissures through the foundations of their homes weakening them to collapse. The infernal heat threatened even to destroy the children and the aged with ultimate death by vaporation. I stood among them, in rags myself, seeing all their eyes upon me. The last sheaves of wheat were brought forward by young girls and laid before me on the cobblestones. A terrible silence commenced. At last I took the knife in hand and stepped in front of the five boys dressed in innocent village costume. With a glance to the west, I reached down and slit the first boy's penis. He gasped, cried out, and bled. I moved from boy to boy until at last, my hands bloody, I stepped back. The youths had fallen to their knees and the blood from their organs spewed onto the sheaves of wheat, flecking that brittle stuff with spots of life. I called aloud and to the west was answered by an immediate low rumbling response. The villagers were transformed from dejection and hopelessness to joy. They grabbed up the wheat and ran to spread it through the fields. The boys were carried on their shoulders and I followed knowing that when the rain beat upon the furrows and wells and washed the wounds of those five small boys, the joy in their hearts would encompass me.

It is powerful prose, Marcus, that makes a man of nearly seventy years feel a distinct twinge in his groin. Who is responsible?

A fourteenth century magician named Chais.

Oh Marcus, absurd!

Autobiography in the theatre of no-Time:
what the Sixth Patriarch said to Ming, ". . . see what
at this moment thine own original face doth look like,
which thou hadst even prior to thine own birth."

The high beams don't do much good, they don't light up the sky.

I flick the beams up and down to determine which to use. Aimee is right, the highs are useless and the lows do not carry far enough to allow for speed at all. I slow, check the odometer. We have gone only six miles since turning off the highway. The compass reads south, but we have seen no barrels but one. Ten more miles at least.

Hey Marcus, how about some heat; it's cold back here.

So Lobe is awake. We will soon hear how he is afraid of the dark.

Where the hell are we anyway?

Aimee turns to answer him.

We're in the desert on the way to the meeting point, but we're late.

Oh Jesus! How can you tell if you're going in the right direction? You could be going in circles, Marcus!

We have a compass, Lobe.

Yeah sure, shit, that plastic thing is really reliable, sure.

Aimee, give him some coffee to calm those nerves. You must

be the worst tattoo artist in St. Louis with nerves like that.

I'm the only tattoo artist in St. Louis, and I'm not nervous. Just smart, that's all. You're the goddamned scholar, aren't you, but you don't know that you don't drive around at night in the desert like it was the goddamned freeway!

I bet I can push a tattoo needle.

I've always wanted to be tattooed on the breast, says Aimee.

The Army guys want 'hot' and 'cold' the Navy guys want 'port' and 'starboard' and the jigs want 'love' and 'hate.' You'd think it'd be really hard to tattoo a spade. I use red ink. Everybody wants it above the nipple. Where do you want it, ma'am?

> *. . . in the heart in the sunlight in the heat in the desert in the end, she took it, freely given, like a lover might, a welcome thrust, hot and cold yes, love and hate yes, the heart is rigged to port*

Why not there too? Circles around them, purple circles.

Can you do that?

It's all the same to me. That's no crazier than any of the rest of them.

I think it's ridiculous Aimee.

A barrel! illuminated clearly by the lights. I drive as if to touch the rust and peeling paint, as if that touch could prove my bearing right.

OK Lobe, we're on the track. You can go back to sleep.

Just be careful, will you.

There's no Time for that.

> *Permit me this metaphor: in a forest of many trees, a man wanders, his dogs circling before him. If his way is lost, it is to the confusion, the vision of each tree duplicating before him, each branch echoed by one just removed, and beyond that, another ghostly line. Fog settles in, leaves accumulate on the bottom of the mist, it is this collision of cloud and forest that separates solid objects into tri-dimensional parts. The dogs run and seem to slip between surfaces of a tree, their mad barking compounds their absence into a mix of scent-inspired*

calls. The woodsman feels his way, loses balance on the oriental ground, grasps out for support, seeking a tree to steady him. His hand plunges past the hard edge, past all support, fingers closing on the nothingness that was sure bark, the certainty that was illusion. The dogs are gone, their yapping diminished. We have wandered, woodsman, into a shadow world where sunlight is broken like a diamond into moist reflecting fragments and truth becomes no single colored leaf in the carpet of ten thousand.

What to do: revolution? creative change?

The third alternative is of course to stand still forever, your boots impressed into the earth, nuts hidden in your cheeks and grubworms foraging between your rooted toes. The colors of your flannel jacket will fade away, mold will grow in your armpits and moss on the north side of your shins, your trousers will change to corduroy bark, your blood to sap, your brain to a resting place for migrating birds.

So there you are.

Come on, woodsman, choose.

Choose for me.

Choose.

Digging in the sand my excavation crew uncovered an automobile, mid-twentieth century. I remember the blue roof, pitted and worn by hundreds of years—slow friction of sand on metal, friction caused by the motion of the earth, by the tides, by sudden shifting movements beneath the crust many thousands of miles distant. There was a certain amount of excitement, I recall; one of the younger men speculated that it was an example of the heretofore legendary 1944 Pontiac. We vacuumed deeper only to realize we had found a '48 Buick of which there were already a number of excellent specimens on display in the museums. I was slightly perplexed however by the existence of the vehicle in that very spot and went so far as to consult certain ancient highway maps then in my possession. There was no known road passing any nearer than ten miles and no reason for anyone to have strayed in that direction at that point in history. We left it, continued about our business. It was of course another of those indecipherable riddles that make men archeologists in the first place.

No, I should not start there. The machine is tireless, and already I feel fatigue and creeping hoarseness. I must try again, begin from a new point, begin perhaps with myself?

I am a creative archeologist by profession. My name is Marcus Chais.

My work is that of peace. The battlefields of history on which I walk, the deserted cities I explore, once saw an instant of immense explosion which rocked the earth at war. Such phenomena, you see, disturb us no more. We live in the Entertainment world.

There are, however, new kinds of wars, fought in order to create political allegiance through the medium of the hypnotic power of entertainment.

Present Time is a void; it exists only as empty people exist, without significance. It is the political mission of all nations to fill Time and give it meaning. Man's brain has lost the ability to project itself. It must be projected to before it can perceive, remember or forget, before it can be occupied, entertained and happy.

My work is the creation of artificial imagination, the ultimate entertainment, perfect and equal in every human life. Through my efforts, man will have the capability to re-create in its entirety any point in his own history, any event, any perspective, any biography, purely for his own entertainment. With this ability, our Control will be able to rule a world in peace through the projections of historic events on public screens.

For myself, it is not a question of politics but of pure science. There has existed an unfortunate belief that the more we know of history the less we know for certain. Such relativism is heresy to science and I am motivated to upset for good this false premise.

Scholars have always selected facts and arranged them in such a way as to simulate history. But controversy has existed, conflicting arguments have been presented, which discredits any concept of the truth. This is of course the result of incomplete research, itself the result of imperfect discipline. There is an absolute; historical events actually happen and in that instant of happening they are imbedded in permanence with a cause for each effect, a motivation for each act, an explanation or relationship that can be determined for everything.

> *. . . cities beds and coffins imply permanence,*
> *men live and sleep and die on the treadmill: in what*
> *direction and at what exact speed does that man with*
> *legs stiff as stovepipes push the stone*

Academicians have unwittingly aided in reducing the immense complexity of my project. They have collected and recorded data of every conceivable type as part of their misguided belief that statistical evidence adds greater credibility to any given argument. We have used these compilations in our computerized world-view as possible norm standards against which great quantities of other data have been placed. Now, we come to the key function of my system: all historical knowledge interacting in terms of data probabilities toward re-creation of the actual.

> *. . . eclectic storm: a colorless rainbow and*
> *the air still fresh with static and lubricating oil: thunder*
> *and a scream, bowling heads at decapitated human*
> *tenpins, I sense nothing final*

The first phase of the program began: the systemization of all known knowledge and knowledge-in-progress. Beginning with the governmental data concentration camps, we moved to the regional memory banks, the libraries, universities, archives and micro-data centers, and in a short while we had the tremendous history core which was to be the foundation of the project. I worked as if possessed to get past the initial tedium so that I might proceed to the final piecing together of my perfect history. We had pressed certainty toward its outer periphery, we had again set segments of the dormant past into motion. Gaps and contradictions were welcome variation, but were usually resolved through directed investigation. No, the excitement lay in the discoveries to be made, in the new found twists of what had been so sure, in the incredible revelation of history unknown, the undocumented and forgotten happenings of significance which were hidden within the neat folds of recorded events.

The work called for creative leadership, and I chose a select team to work beside me: Seline, Becktold and Amura, three young minds, two men and a woman, all devoted and brilliant.

I watched their total abandonment to spectacle as we shared our first vision together. Their faces, expressions, attitudes, as we observed an early part of the Late Echelon, revealed to me the power of my project. I had chosen that period because of completeness of documentation and relative proximity to our own era and yet the effect was as hypnotic as if I had chosen that first mating of the stars at the Creation. They were transfixed, speechless, even shocked afterwards as their minds began moving toward some partial understanding of what they had experienced.

But I was troubled in terms of my own goal as it was evident that a great deal of training and preparation was necessary to ready even the brightest of my colleagues for exploration of the scientific implications of the undertaking. I had to raise them to my own level of detachment, all the while guarding against their loss to the machine, which with a sudden re-creation of an extraordinary event could at any moment capture them from me, turning them into happy but useless members of the world audience.

We started with fragmented visions of the most familiar events. I lectured on new methodology until gradually their resistance to vision-involvement increased. They learned to discuss re-creations in progress, to analyze in terms of research methods even the most spectacular events. I lengthened projections, progressing toward total segmental overviews, until at last I felt they were ready for the true beginning of our duties.

> . . . pumping the bellows, he kindled the fire;
> while forging the chain, the blacksmith choked on the
> fumes of his own bright burning coals; in creation lay
> the weakest link

I observe again the traces of the Circle. Red lipstick marks the glass near where Amura sat. She was at first so serious, so child-like this evening, listening with the intense concentration only the young can muster. But then, a discovery of something new about her, mad and irrational, so foreign to her birth and training. Perhaps she did not realize it herself, yet it was evident in her grasping hands and in her cries; tonight she was a woman.

Marcus, I dream of eternal Bel, she moaned.

Becktold had dominated as usual. He was only truly human when he was the focus of things, the center. I used him always for presentations to Control, his glibness and charm were a strong reinforcement to the powers of his brain. He had talked this evening with the subtle power of an artist painting an idyll which is revealed to be an ultimate grotesque at the last stroke of the brush. He is, perhaps, not to be trusted.

And Seline had interjected his remarks with a hoarseness that gave urgency to even the most trivial of thoughts. When he raised his voice in ejaculation I was stunned more by his tone than by the content of what he said. Only once were his observations interrupted by a laugh.

Was fear, known only as a phenomenon of the distant past, just now becoming a reality to the four of us? Yes, we were tonight far away from one beginning, from science and research; we were tonight together in the conception of our first human emotion, our first relationship, our first true collective vision. We were tonight four persons alone with our hands reached out to join a circle.

> *. . . child's games invite touch: struggle for the*
> *separation that will lead back to touching once again*

What is to become of us?

I am exhausted, and give no more direction than a revolving light. There is so much more to tell. My perspective fails, I shall sleep, I shall dream.

As Schiller wrote "To His Friends":
> *Only fantasy has eternal youth.*
> *What happened nowhere and never*
> *Can never age.*

Yes, Frank, I am a scholar, my life has been led through the alleyways of other cultures and other times, clasping in my hands bits of bone and human hair, bits of artistic and religious expression, transposed through my efforts into dusty monographs and articles published in journals and comprehensible to few. Such is my accomplishment.

> *. . . my potions do not boil, my spells*
> *inflict no wounds, the white pigeons I pull from the*
> *air cannot fly and gag on the gold coins in their beaks;*

*I am a magician's shell, fossilized, living like a snail
on knowledge dredged from the past, thriving on the
excrement of the world*

But it is too late for realization now. If one is to negate his
entire life, let him do so as a youth beginning, rather than with his dying
gasp, making death infinite pain through the awareness that life has not
been lived. Old men should be happy and death should be release, but
in the chairs of musty hotel lobbies sit bundles of pain and guilt and fear
whose eyes water with the knowledge of human waste.

My dear Marcus, don't be so maudlin.

You are right, of course, I am feeling sorry for myself. But
you Frank, you embody the spirit with which life should be lived and
inadvertently do me and the world a great disservice. In your classrooms
sit numbers of impressionable students just as I once did. They observe
not only your knowledge but more importantly your feeling for what
you know; they wish to emulate you. But emulation is false. Sitting there
they scribble down your every word and mannerism which later they will
ingest like vitamins to make them strong and brilliant like you. They are
discarding their own humanity and learning how to imitate.

*. . . children walking down the aisles of a used
clothing shop, naked and cold they choose to wrap a
feather boa round them or stand together in the legs of
old tweed trousers: do not move lest the wind penetrate
some rent or tear, stand quietly in fancy dress, preserve
the eternal masquerade*

And think what the world would be if everyone were a Frank
Timmins? My picture of the human kind is very different from that.

Mine as well, Marcus. I couldn't stand such competition.

Imitation and reality are so obviously different and yet are
so fused together in men's minds. In these cabinets, I have a collection
of clay idols and images: I have collected images and idols all my life and
I have created them for myself everywhere in the people around me. A
student in the classroom, I created one out of you. An accepted authority
in a field of scholarship, I created one out of myself. I created one out of
my wife, Aimee.

Marcus, you eat away at yourself like some self-destructing insect. This is not like you. Look to your work if you need something to hold on to.

I refuse, I am not going to add layers of knowledge around me. If anything, Frank, I must strip away most of what I have worked so hard to learn, the insignificant trappings of scholarship. These can be dissolved to nothingness in an instant.

> *... a golden calf, an irretrievable chalice,*
> *an honest man, a maiden hovering in the crooked*
> *arms of the grotto, the secret of light and the arch,*
> *an unknown element on the summit of the highest*
> *mountain, life bubbling from the marble fountain, even*
> *god: the incredible quest: and the wheel keeps on turning*

I have studied superstition and never been superstitious. I have written endlessly on the customs and beliefs of the world and never participated other than as the observer making mental notes while a virgin native is forced to eat the semen of jackals to appease some angered god. I have ransacked the belongings of murdered witches looking for additions to my collection, I have perused the diaries of heretic priests, I have trekked through the heights of the Himalayas seeking colorful traps for ghosts. What can be more lamentable, more sad, than a man who has looked at a leaf from the Bodhi tree through the glass of his microscope? I know nothing!

> *It is conceived of by him by whom It is not conceived of;*
> *He by whom It is conceived of, knows It not.*
> *It is not understood by those who understand It;*
> *It is understood by those who understand It not.*
> *Kena-Upanishad*

How does the journal read:
The cattle were my first disciples in Bel.

We slept away the night side by side. A storm hurried across the highroad toward the compound in which we stayed, pushing the fog before it. The fires of the village glowed like iridescent drops across the fields. As lightning boomed low upon the horizon the pearl ovals of cow eyes observed me enter through the rear gate shaking off the wraith-like moisture of the mist. Their heads followed me up the ladder, observed the unfolding of my cloak, the drying of my hair and beard with a handful of straw; and my almost immediate imprisonment by sleep. The cattle were my first disciples in Bel, mute and adoring.

I came from Selegue, a village smaller still, some day and a half journey from Bel. A day and a half walking on the rutted track that flanked the edge of the Due Hills, a journey whose crooked route proved unequal in Time and distance but meant freedom to me all the same. I could look up toward the hills as the cattle looked up from their fodder and see by day the smoke from the fires of Selegue rising out of a rugged crease which hid the actual roofs of my village. How often when following my sheep across our hillside pasture did I look down upon Bel and dream!

> . . . dreams and fog come and go without will,
> a clapperless bell rings in the wind to announce their
> coming, and at their depart no humid footprints remain
> behind to mark the path

My leaving of Selegue required no more effort on my part than my arrival there, my mother squatting in a corner of the sheep pens to give birth. As I tumbled forth she rose up from her haunches to fall forward, arms outspread, to die beneath the ram who was curious about the disturbance. And so like a lamb rejected by the ewe, the shepherd protected me with a skin and fed me in turn with the others that huddled in his shelter near the fire. Years later, I turned reflexedly from the path that would have taken me as usual to Selegue and chose the downward plunging trail. My sheep I left behind without concern, left for the thieves and the wolves, left to break through the low fences and follow me if that was their desire.

My first night of sleep in Bel was like no sleep I had ever had. The storm broke and shattered within my brain and lightning was graven across my eyelids. I heard voices sure, and dismissed them as those of curious cows seeking to know my name. Marcus Chais, I murmured in the straw, named Marcus for the ram who begot me and Chais for my mother's cradle from whence I came. I woke stiffened by my travels, but yet refreshed and eager to follow where fate would lead me.

Cocks not awakened by the sun, an old man warms his blood before a trembling fire.

Is there work here old man?

Work enough to kill us all. What do you do?

I was born a shepherd.

The sheep are dead.

I know crops.

The fields are dying everywhere.

What is there then?

You may dig and bury animals or hoe brown plants from the row. You may pull an empty wagon or carry rotten water to the failing cattle. You may listen to the weeping in the marketplace or crawl on your knees to the church and pray.

Gloomy man, what do you do?

I live and slowly die in Bel. Is that not work enough?

> *. . . the sun rises the moon sets, the wind*
> *shifts the seasons round, the planets move by the earth*
> *and wild flowers grow lushly across the graves of the*
> *dead, in the end there is life above all*

You are a fool, old man. An unhappy fool. Sit then, watch your fire die.

The day progresses with the harshness of the heat. As if the lord is feeding flame-breathing animals to bum away the darkness and the moisture of the night, the rain-washed walls dry to white. The villagers proceed about their tasks afraid to rush yet fearful that their jobs may never be completed. In the church the women expend their breath on prayer and waste precious tears. To no avail; the sun climbs higher to stain with yellow the urine-irrigated fields and to put out the sight of newborn children. What country is this? What hand created it so? Here nothing grows beyond the bud, and life, seared and cracked by the elements, is worthless.

Mixing crushed buds of garlic and ground pink glass, steamed weed and bits of bread, I made our food warmed over the pitted blue flame of burning dung. I had strung my cloak up to give me shelter and privacy from the others who lived in the empty corners of the market. We had settled there, homeless, dirty, high- and low-born. Pid the scavenger was near me, the old woman and her daughter, Anna, lived screened in cobwebs beneath the auction wagon, and the priest, Friar Manlius, scratched a cross and candles on the wall with chalk. We had shelter at least and water drained through the uneven cobblestones even when the sun was at its highest point. Our worst danger was the wandering cats, mad for sustenance, fur growing to their bones and claws striking sparks on stone as they ran among us. We ate together in defense, huddled with our backs touching and our feet before us to ward off the starved beasts circling around us with yellow eyes. The cuffs of my trousers were torn and shredded from their attacks.

In the early morning I gave Pid his orders and he scurried off to smell out the house in which the last dying sheep was killed; or he went to collect the mice from the gutters before the women sent out their weak and sleepy children for them. Pid loitered round kitchens where nothing was left unconsumed, he sifted through refuse already sifted through, he brought us bits of food and scraps of rumour and once a silver spoon. Yet few were more resourceful than my Pid. He was innocent and evil in a single breath, gentle and brutal in the course of a moment, he was scrupulously honest and performed the thefts I assigned him with skill and daring. He was a clown, a perfect thief, small of body but large of mind and heart, wearing a face that was never his own. In another Time, I would have received the spoon pinching his cheek in gratitude, but in Bel we could not live on molten silver.

The painful ravings of the old woman spoke to me of hope-lessness. Anna sponged her mother's sores with torn squares of rag, her white fingers touched with death cried out for rings set with precious stones or gloves of spun metal. They were royal hands, queen's fingers, tending venom-infected scabs of mother death. I tried to touch them, webs lay between us.

And Friar Manlius stared into our lives, expressing curses and complaints mixed with blessed tears. His was a liturgy of defeat, sung through his teeth and celebrated in an empty marketplace. He laid his tiny iron crucifix in the fire and burned a blackened cross on my pillow while I slept, mad priest.

Such times, times of hate, but if love could live in Bel, it lived in me; for little Pid, for Anna, even for the mother's scabs and the black benedictions of the priest. It swelled inside me, and when we survived I was to be again the shepherd.

Someday, I shall write about dreams, no
catalogue of types, no interpretations, not why one dreams
or what, but how one dreams. It is a matter of style.
I dream with great gusto and delight.
Some claim they never dream, just lie there
slug-abed in stone taking their rest as God meant for
them to do. Others complain of nightmare, horrors
costumed on the retina, running raggety andirons
chasing them down nerve corridors to the brain. They
roll, they thrash, they cry out and bump! they're on the
floor, out of bed, startled awake, covers about the neck.
The children cry. The adults suppress their fear.
Why fear?
What of the so-called dreamers who wrote
lyrics for a girl seen once? what of the dreamers who
carved the wooden gears of the first machines? what of
the dreamers with patched elbows on their sweaters who
derived the theories of our science? what even of those
dreamers who thought they might rule the world?
I don't think they were afraid . . . of their dreams.
Dreams are fantasy, incorporating evil.
Dreams are history. They are times of siege and sojourn,
stagnation and enlightenment, within the mind. They
have implication, they cause change, slow and eventual,
sometimes abrupt and revolutionary. History, personal
or collective, is the simple interaction of our dreams.
Dreams should be listened to, enjoyed.
Dreams are imagination, and, I believe, a style of life.

Lobe smells the plastic seat and dreams of leather: hard skins
of wandering longhorns tacked to the stable wall, limbs outstretched,
limbs outstretched to receive the needle. Lobe is a professional, no
Greyhound station filth, no nicotine on his fingers, no pleasure in his
subject's pain. His office, painted white, glistens like a surgery, needles
in the metal pan, inks on the shelf in a row. What now? He puts the
needle to his skin, his own soft skin, tattooing 'love' and 'mother' and
the names of girls he has never known except through the intimate act of
engraving them forever into someone else. Colors intertwine, letters join

embracing, the needle continues relentlessly across the balls of his feet, and in between his fingers, it touches his scalp, it burns his scrotum, he wakes without a sound.

Where are we now?

Almost there, says Aimee.

He watches Marcus at the wheel, watches the nervous ripple beneath the temple, watches the fingers open and close around the steering wheel.

Good God, I've had an awful dream.

Dreams are life for the dead of heart, Lobe. And men who live that life truly sleep like children. You must not have a conscience.

Leave him alone, Marcus. Look for barrels.

Lobe spits into his palms and smooths his hair. Aimee defends him, her neck like polished steel in the moonlight. It is a neck he cannot touch although he might reach forward. It is protection that lets him sleep.

Once I grew a beard.
I did not love my face.
Then I shaved it off.

Friar Manlius lifts the broken gourd to his lips and drinks the watered broth Chais has given him. He curses and then gives thanks.

Anna does not drink, but rather soaks a rag in the steaming liquid to place against a swelling sore in her mother's armpits.

Pid burns his mouth and spills liquid across his grey leather jerkin. He chokes, he cries, he laughs aloud.

I hold an eraser in my hand, round and Ruby-Red, with its green brush tacked on like a feathered plume. It seems I have used it all my life. So it seems.... The edges are used, worn white all around, there is a tendency to protrude on one side, draw toward ellipse on the other. The brush is losing bristle, lost most in fact, a bit chewed, a bit like a bird of paradise on the short end of a good cock fight.

It has done much erasing in a lifetime.

What I am thinking is this: two hundred

*pages, thirty lines to the page, twelve words to the line,
each word cleanly erased.*

Amura places her cheek against the hard surface of the
computer frame. Deep within she feels her pulse mate with the
vibrations. Six hours a day she supervises the machine with its ever-
increasing knowledge, six hours a day she can touch the plastic keys,
she can watch the tapes revolving.

It is her world that turns, moving through a pattern of
programmed stops and starts. She maintains her detached exterior,
but inside she races to keep up with the machine. She knows Marcus
watches her closely, she knows he watches her because of her early
abandonment to the visions. Struggling always, through the discipline
he has taught her, she keeps the façade he thinks reflects composure.

Ah, but the visions . . . she stands amidst swirling battles; men
and rearing horses with drum soundings and flags snapping in the wind
like pistol shots. She is there like a lonely tree in a plain devastated by
the tide of battle. She hears hoofs crush bone, she sees frothy bubbling
wounds, dismembered arms and legs and heads, she feels heat and fear,
she feels another's blood congealing, she feels victory and her stomach
turns in defeat. The uniforms rush by her, golden tassels swinging,
songs on their lips, towering red plumes, studded belts and embroidered
sleeves, silken handkerchiefs tied around their throats; in heaps they
lie, trampled, torn ragged, throats so choked with agony they cannot cry
out in death. She sits exhausted in her chair before the screen as Marcus
watches. Her full-blown heart is pounding just behind the openings of
her orifices ready to be punctured.

> *I will never be too old., . . I am ageless, a
> pudgy cupid hanging from the ceiling, love handles
> inlaid with gilt. Another famous writer took injections
> to preserve his youth. He went to night clubs, longed
> to dance, and complained of unnatural urges when
> soaking in a tepid bath. A ten year old girl inherited
> his villa in the south of France.*

Friar Manlius pulls a dark cloth over his head and enters the
church amidst the crying women to steal a candle.

The old woman dies.
Pid catches three fat mice in the stables with his hands.

> *Among the Shushwap of British Columbia*
> *widows and widowers in mourning burned a bag of cats . . .*
> *The Kiowa tribe never spoke a dead woman's*
> *name aloud, and those who handled her corpse,*
> *prepared her or conveyed her to the grave, were cut off*
> *from all communication and intercourse with mankind.*
> *Come back, O Soul, whether thou art*
> *lingering in the wood, or in the hills, or in the dale. See,*
> *I call thee with a toemba bras, with an egg of the fowl*
> *rajah, moelija, and with eleven healing leaves . . .*

Aimee looks through the empty windshield into darkness.
Such a futile journey, racing out into the desert to escape God knows
what. Marcus was so adamant on the telephone. The urgency of his
voice took hold of her and led her to the corner where he was waiting
in the car, lights ablaze and motor running, some two-bit television
criminal waiting for his moll. Why had she come? Why had his voice
moved her so, moved her to a meeting she had so far avoided? A turn
of her head confronts her vision with his profile, elegantly honed like
his mind, like their life had been together. And yet in that face she sees
what she had not seen before, she sees fallibility, the absence of which
had driven her screaming from the house some eight months previous.
Through their years together she had feared him and called it love; in
the desert in the darkness with his face outlined by small dashboard
lights, she loves him and is afraid.

> *Heinrich Scholz* (Religionsphilosophie,
> 1923) *insists on a similar point of view; see also D. R.*
> *Holiday,* A Vindication of Evil *(1941).*

Friar Manlius says the Mass because there is no one else.
Anna cries no tears.
Pid covers the body over with heaps of dust. In his mind is
the thought that they might eat her.

. . . no single leaf in a carpet of ten thousand.
There is a wind blowing through my autobiography.
I smell mold. I hear mice chewing somewhere in this
empty house.

Becktold; what he does alone is for no one else to witness, for
he knows his weakness, he knows his confidence diminishes as his vision
of himself displaces an attentive audience. In his apartment, he stands
alone making speeches to himself, talking to the walls and appliances
as if they represent infinite crowds or rank-encrusted bureau chiefs.
His pantomime seen by a neighbor spying through the window might
seem the lonely fight of some silent gladiator. In his heart Becktold
understands that he is deathly afraid to be alone.

He feels used. He is desirous of the power Marcus wields. He
gains courage from his own inflammatory speeches and disbelieves that
Time is not his ally.

Jung: "Although our mind cannot grasp its
own form of existence owing to the lack of Archimedean
point outside, it nevertheless exists. Psyche is existent, it
is even existence itself."

Friar Manlius begins a second Mass, the Mass to bring
about a death.

Anna tends her mother's grave.
Pid finds a flower he hopes to give her.

Marcus the Magician strides onstage,
squeaky patent leather shoes, swish of silk, creak of
collar starch, groan of suspender stays, a sartorial
chorus, he calls for a volunteer.
Frank Timmins, professor, comes forward shyly.
Climb into this box, if you please, professor.
Fanfare. Fol de rol.
I saw myself.
I saw myself in two.

Seline sits laughing through it all; he is the only one to see
humor in the visions. He is the cynic, slight smile upon his lips, the look
of a man who has seen everything, seeing everything again for a second
time. His resistance to the visions is dura hard, as if his first involvement
was due more to surprise than weakness. He performs his duties
without fault, he is the chief lieutenant, and brings to the project healthy
relaxation and a sense of the absurd.

Bel is so beautiful, says Amura.

It is ridiculous, a city of stone where men lie fossilized on
their backs. Beauty dies after one hundred Echelons, Amura. You are
much too impressionable for our work.

Don't tell Marcus.

Oh I'm sure he doesn't notice. Methodology won't allow it.

Annastasia! the lines that feed your eyes . . .
your funny feet . . . Memory is the glutton.

Friar Manlius begins to organize the monks.
Anna reads a book by moonlight.
Pid dreams actively of a sheep he once had known.

anna

Let me tell you about my Annastasia . . .

Poor Pid is burning. There are gruesome accounts of his flesh dropping
like bits of burning hay, his eyes alight with a fire never before seen, his
brains consumed by a dull blue flame.

    I go out into the city shrouded heavily in a cloak, I walk
among the people toward the torch-lit square. I am not recognized.
Hung up on charred scaffolding are the sinewy remnants of my little
friend. The armed monks stand between us, their heavy staffs in hand,
their dogs lying awake at their feet. The crowd regards them, and
Pid, in silence. There is no carnival execution clamor, no mad women
screaming, no children riding on the shoulders of fascination. There is
only silent fear, fear in the air and the smell of burnt flesh.

    Friar Manlius has done his job well.

    Drought and plague are past but suffering continues.

    Armed monks control Bel, patrol the streets by day and drive
the people like cattle to the Mass by night. The Black Mass of Saint
Secaire shouted in the square by Manlius *papa*, as he has now proclaimed
himself; dressed in red vestments, red of eye, he mouths the words to
his lost God that will bring about my death. The women forced to their
knees in martial prayer cannot say the words correctly. They falter
confused, and begin the ritual known since childhood.

    The monks flay them with clubs.

    Backwards, dog! Do not blaspheme. The old Mass backwards!

    Their trembling lingers begin to reverse upon the beads,
forwards if not backwards, what difference can it make for them? Their
prayers, so long sung, so long endured, had brought them plague and
pestilence and drought. Their city, nearly consumed, now faces a greater
consumption.

    But I know of their hope, their secret of the heart. It stands
with me wrapped in a cloak, it had stood in the marketplace before when
the rains had come and the drought had lifted. They had shouted my
name then, they whisper it now, fearfully, desperately, they say: Chais.

    Pid had been captured bringing me news of the small group
of men who had fled to the south toward the Due Hills when Manlius
had unleashed his monks. Those men were to be my force, my arm which

once upraised was to signal to my people, to Manlius and the world, that
Bel was mine. But Pid had been captured and burned. He had never
failed me before. When would his message be delivered?

Anna, he is dead.

Anna, my queen.

Burned dead before my very eyes.

We are hidden in the darkness of the mill, the two of us and
her mother's shroud, hidden behind the grinding stones which turn by
day a breath away from our heads. We lie petrified lest the milling monks
discover us and turn us to the bread served to the communicants of Saint
Secaire. And in the night, we plot and eat the grain which has dropped
upon us like manna dust.

You must get his remains, she says. I loved Pid too, she says.

Manlius leads the chanting: Secaire Saint, one evil the drown
water the and mud . . .

We grow weaker, Anna, me, and poor Pid.

. . . him choke pus and smoke . . .

We grow faint.

. . . people my of curses the in death in him bury, Secaire Saint . . .

We sleep, the millstone turning. The ashes smoulder.

Chais! Manlius once said. I am priest to this dying
marketplace, to you and Pid, this girl and her dead mother. Remain a
man, simple, powerless and subject, do not presume to do your tricks
while Manlius confronts you. Honor me, drink only my blessed rain, fear
me and my God and you will be saved from the woman's foul sickness. If
not, then I will say a Mass for the Dead against you as I did for her. Girl,
where is your mother's shroud?

There was no one else.

My mother, Anna cries in her sleep.

The ashes.

The monks are sleeping as my shadow returns to the square.
They lie against the walls like loose brown sacks of grain, their staffs
dropped and tangled between the limbs of silent dogs. My cloak whispers
against the cobblestones. When would his message be delivered?

I spread the shroud out on the charred wood and scoop in
the ashes with my silver spoon. They are warm and still smell of him,
the woodsmoke forever mingled with his sweat, his leather jerkin,
the laughter.

Pid, we will bury you.

Anna, my queen, will sift you through her hands in the morning light and with ash-grey fingers touch her lips, her breasts, between her legs. We will bury you.

We will lie listening to the cursing monks, the shroud between us, your dust fleeing up our nostrils. We will read the pattern of your life, and finally at twilight when the monks are called away by the bells announcing the resumption of the Mass, Anna will say: It's there, the message there, written for us on my mother's shroud. See Marcus, see it in the ashes, the men are ready and will fight!

Pid squats in the firelight, the refugees of Bel gathered round.

You must fight the monks. Come back and join Chais, come back and fight for homes and children and praying wives.

We must go back!

We will kill the dogs and monks!

We must stop the Mass!

You must go and arm yourselves in Selegue. You must learn to use your weapons well. You must be ready to fight before the Mass is over and our leader dies.

We will forge our weapons!

We will break their staffs and skulls! We will follow Chais!

They drink. Pid finishes one mug too many and rushes off to be burned in Bel.

As the great millwheel turns, I slowly feed the ash between the stones. Burned and ground to dust, reground and burned again to fleck the bread of savage monks, and then to seed their bloated bellies with cowardice and weakness. Now buried at last, Pid lives within us all.

They are all here, Anna says.

We are seated in a circle on the millstone, a single candle to give us light, Anna, my lieutenant, and the leaders of the men. Softly, I speak to them: . . . dried liver to rub in wounds, linen bandages to keep them closed or hunt for fire to seal them off . . . and from the right with ten armed men . . . but take the lamb's leg and let it bleed for fish to swim in and for us to drink . . . through the main gate attack . . . set torches to the dried brown robes . . . drive stakes into the hearts of dogs . . . and wear this strip of shroud around your neck to keep you from all harm . . .

Secaire Saint, one evil the down put.

Anna whispers: . . . preserve your women's thighs from the

eyes of lecherous monks . . . messages to prepare them for our coming . . .
no cock unless for little children . . . let old men and the blind help us . . .
no lips but for each other . . . our dogs attack their dogs . . . and guard the
bit of shroud with thy life . . .

Consort whoring the on damnation, Secaire Saint. The
candle burns low.

We are wrestling with the Mass, grappling in the faded light,
eyesight dimmed by dark-gowned liturgy. We are wrestling for their
souls or mine.

The tallow sputters; there is darkness.

In the night, a dog whelps beneath the altar and red-eyed
Manlius slumbers beside the chalice. Incense, white and burning,
from the inverted cross over the sleeping guards drifts to us hidden in
the alleyways of Bel. A blade first separates a hood from gown, lone
watchman. A woman kills him. Then the dark bundles lying about the
square are slashed, their wrappings torn. Rats run madly through the
storage house until no sack is left unravaged. The monks are dead, the
hated staffs cut off them. And in the sudden agony of death, they emit
ash, not the excrement of fear.

Even the dogs die quietly. Except for one, who moans as
she sees pegs driven through the soft blind bellies of her litter, already
bloody, not alive long enough to know of death. Her moan wakes the
drunken *papa*, he stands upon the altar.

Who is there? Monks awake! Toll the bell!

Red robes flashing.

Chais, is it you? You are dying, fool, by the Saint's life, you
are dying.

The circle closes.

Now come death let, Secaire Saint, blessing sombre thy with
and. Hour his arrives now; him take Doomsday! Amen!

A mother cursed, screams Anna.

Now come death let!

You beat our wives and children.

The people of Bel appear, awakened by the sound of evil
dying. They surround the altar to take revenge.

Now death, Secaire Saint!

You made them sing for the Devil's ear.

Now come!

Bel shall make you pay.

Now! Now!

A man climbs to stand beside the quivering priest. It is Marcus Chais, shepherd from Selegue.

He saved us from the drought and we forgot. And now he comes again. Chais!

Bel! cries the saviour. We shall kill this monk too. On the very scaffolding where he burned my Pid we shall kill him.

The men strip Manlius of his robe and nail him naked to the cross. Ropes secured to the foot, they suspend him, head downward, inverted cross, and watch him slowly die, mad monk and celebrant of Saint Secaire.

The circle looks on. Marcus holds up the silver spoon.

I am Chais, now King.

They cheer.

And this, he says, is Anna, my Queen.

She steps beside him, in the center of the moment, Anna, his Queen, her shoulders wrapped in the tattered shroud.

> *She was . . .*
>
> *She is dead, lying beneath me like a corpse, me the absurd male rubbing his organ against the crotch of a fallen tree, against the crotch of his own two fingers, against the crotch of his willingly subservient wife. I have these reflections. I am able, thrashing about as I am, to observe myself, as she might, lying there looking up into the mirror above our sexual bower; the mirror which does not exist as we were much too conservative as lovers to indulge in such perversions. It occurs to me, swiveling my hips more to the left than to the right, that we do not make a pretty picture. Certainly not an erotic one. No, and yet I am manipulated to pleasurable delights, will indeed eject my seed into her; it seems a question of degree.*
>
> *Consider the manual of sexuality received in the mail, in its plain brown wrapper so that even the postman might not know of our need. I see myself arranged, like those instructive diagrams, a man of many*

joints, transparent, faceless, entwined with an equally
anonymous mate, in the proper positions, above, below,
the infinite configurations of the human junglegym, each
absolutely correct in its execution, each totally devoid
of communication or passion. We are two dolls, placed
together in a pristine embrace by some virginal girl-
child. We are the awkward constructions of a young boy
playing with his first Erector set.

 But look! her arms are about me, and if I
take that mirror and place it before her lips or beneath
her nostrils, I find she is breathing, is very much alive, is
murmuring soundless words which I hear and assume to
be true. Yes, it does feel good, and yes, you love me, and
no, there is no one else in all the world like I am.

 So, not a corpse after all.

 Six weeks gone, dead and buried.

 I feel her shift beneath me. It is a supremely
rational act on her part, producing a supreme reaction
on mine. But what of her? Why just words articulated
in mist on the surface of a mirror? Why no cries, no
clenched teeth, no cuts as thin as fingernails across my
back? I taste the garlic of tonight's spaghetti; I want the
taste of blood.

 Perhaps I should ask her? We might discuss
it while I pump away, digging my hole in the sand,
searching for water.

 I'm not bitter, am I? I loved . . .

 I love my wife. This act of ours, or maybe
mine, is one of love. Should I strive to manufacture love
like the technicolor perfection of the latest film?

 I must do what I must. That's all.

 And so, somewhere back amidst all this
revery, I spewed forth, emptied my reservoir and calmed
my nervous muscles for the while. Does she know? or
does she await some signal, the slowing of my buttocks
or a subtle change in the color of my eyes to notify her
that the operation is through. Perhaps I should just go
on, keeping up appearances, penis shriveled then erect,

*making like a puffy Valentino. Would she continue to lie
there until the end of Time, eternally spread, open and
hospitable.*

    She might, Annastasia just might.

    *I am dead, spent, exhausted, lying beside
her like a corpse. We are dead together, naked in a
companion crypt, beginning to smell the odors of
personal deterioration. No matter. We are like the
romantic legend, married for life and death, fertilizing
one another in our quiet communion, mixing of our
flesh and blood into dust. Who cares how we loved, but
that we did so.*

    *And above us, on the earth, in that cemetery
of the living dead, as in the legend, do flowers grow,
intermingled on the combed expanse of our final bed?*

    THE JOURNAL:

  Bel! She stands nine stories above this fertile earth, nine
tall towers with banners flying. From the palace, I look down into the
winding streets below, a child's labyrinth at my feet, to which only I hold
the key. I hear the babble of voices rising to me like tributes, calls of stock
and fattened fowl, lives passing beneath me like swollen rivers. Marcus!
King Marcus!

  Oh Pid, if you were with us now, you would be the keeper
of the seal, the jester, first minister, court confidant, rushing across the
polished floors with your stumbling gait, your hands at work untying
colored bodice strings, fingers pinching, your head beneath the satin
skirts of the ladies. The silver spoon would be the scepter by which we
would reign, little Pid, we would plunder sweet coffers everywhere. But
you are gone, you have no vision, no memory, your eyes are put out by a
flaming stick, your brains fried on cobblestones, and your tiny rod and
balls thrown like tidbits to some favored dog. If you could only see this
jewel, Bel, strident, boastful, magnificent, a city beyond value, truly a
greater edifice than man should ever build. I will draw here in this diary
an outline of its beauty for you, Pid, a diagram of Bel surrounded by nine
strong walls. And do you see, atop it all, on the highest towers, reached
by an ascent above all the rest, my Anna's sanctuary, apartments for the
queen so close to the planets as to seem suspended in their shadow, the

only hint of darkness throughout my land? Anna sleeps there in a bed
draped with the finest embroideries of our women's fingers, cushioned by
the furry hides of our most elusive game. Anna sleeps there . . . alone!
And I call her my queen.

The women tell me no mortal may enter that chamber, no
human may pass the night there save Anna, divine consort, receiver
of a god who comes to sport her on that spacious bed. Pid! Do you
remember how in our dreams she was not so proud, she was no
godhole, how then we rode her, you atop my shoulders spurring us like
the hysteric animal we were. She responded with her wanton moans
to the touch of the silver spoon, prodding in the hidden depths of her
pudding pot, but now when I tap that tarnished implement on her
chamber door, a maiden with the looks of ten strong men comes to
push me away. We dreamed she loved us both, Pid; you naked save for
your leather jerkin, your legs twined about her neck, and me, hairy,
woolly, impatient as if she was just the first of endless ewes for the old
ram to enjoy.

But that was. . . before . . . what? Her mother's death, black
Manlius, the shroud, Bel. She won't have me now. Oh Pid, how this god
yearns for her divinity!

> . . . *a step forward extends the sphere of order,*
> *leaves a void, restricts the sphere of disorder, multiplication*
> *implies division, greedy hands attempt to grasp both*
> *balance pans filled with equal weights of mercury*

THE JOURNAL:

Sometimes I think of the future, not just the immediate
future, my life and reign, but on a Time so far from now that I cannot
comprehend it. I see then men looking back into the past to see our
civilization grown so high. Are they amused? Or envious? Certainly
Bel is not the end of what must be done.

Sometimes in moments of distraction, of illumination, my
mind sees ahead into those realms and I am able to recognize a face,
an expression, a feeling similar to mine. I see nothing of the future
life, just intimations that beyond the moment of that vision will exist
a million moments in which my thoughts may transpire once again.
I see myself in other men, future kings perhaps, future thieves. No

matter, I sense that my spirit will endure.

> *. . . cerebral historicity, nothing exists that is*
> *not now*

THE JOURNAL ONCE AGAIN:

My own history confuses me. Even as I write it in this journal
it appears contradictory. My origins are base, my motivations corrupt,
my actions false. The achievements of such a man must be questioned.
And what do I find? Progress. Security. Peace. But not for me, for
whose selfish good my efforts are directed; for those around me whom
I attempt to defraud. I am a failure and a success, the guilty one whose
crimes against himself benefit the world.

I fear the divine and yet I challenge it, and my challenge is
an example for other men to conquer their own fear. Surely heaven must
laugh at my self-deception. Surely I myself must realize that my so-called
miracles are truly magic, the translation of God's will into the language
of men. What if I change my life?

> *. . . mind and will are a sieve through which*
> *men pass like grains of sand, a perforated screen of con-*
> *sciousness separating large from small, fine from coarse*

AND ONCE AGAIN:

The king has lost touch with his people. He is a figurehead
and welcomes the detachment. I no longer walk the streets of Bel. I hide
within the confines of the palace like a frightened child. To maintain
my rule I rely on Anna who in her sanctuary secretly studies the ancient
books of knowledge. Day by day she becomes more practiced in the
hidden mysteries, more privileged in that clandestine world. The king is
a magician. To keep his powers before the eyes of the people, he stages
pageants for their entertainment. I pour wine endlessly from a beaker to
intoxicate a lad dressed as some foreign ruler. I pierce white pigeons with
sharpened needles and draw no blood. They clap their hands and exclaim
they love me. The king returns to his empty throne.

But our magic is more than mere display. We have cursed
with blindness and the sudden withering of limbs citizens who have
stood against us. We have caused our enemies to moon lovingly over

goats and speak with the pitched tones of women, in short, made them appear weak and foolish before their fellows. Anna reads the stars, writes symbols on black rock that bring these unnatural acts to being, she collects frog tongues and turtle eggs and burns fires with which to consume resistant metals.

The king is a magician. Whence comes his power? From the breasts of pigeons? From ambition? Substance ground to powder in a mortar? From the heart? From all of these, and all are valid.

The king has lost touch with his people. The king has lost touch with himself.

> *With callipers and parallel rule you attempt to plot my position in the university. . . .*
>
> *I arrived there by accident, stumbling forward as young men do into a position that was comfortable but not the brilliant appointment I had anticipated. My failure, as I called it then, was my great fortune. I stayed put, teaching students I enjoyed, free enough to do all the individual work I wished, and in so doing build a reputation.*
>
> *And then too, the university grew into a mythical giant, and through that incomprehensible growth, all those associated with it were somehow made larger. Of course, we weren't just knights, righting wrongs in the minds of the nations' children; we were young and human, with all the subsequent problems that seem so linked to youth. But our lives seemed so much our own, so uncomplicated, in conflict only over issues that seemed truly important. There was a spirit of growing together, cooperation, open discussion. To use a phrase popular among my younger colleagues: there was no bullshit!*
>
> *Now, all questions of humanity aside, the sheer number of us all, administrators, professors, students and staff, causes each day to be fraught with seemingly insurmountable problems, more of logistics than of principle. Committees meet, hundreds of them a day, briefs and editorials are written and read,*

communication is primary, and yet the atmosphere is
one of enforcement, arrogance and hate, upon which,
sadly, I must turn my back.

And I have. For all intents and purposes, I am
no longer a member in good standing of the university.
I teach my classes, faithfully and to the best of my ability,
but outside the lecture hall I must be inaccessible. I live
my life as I imagine it to be, teaching my students what
little I know, living with the memory of my wife from day
to day, and from my fantasy I exclude all the rest, all the
trivial issues, all the organizations and reorganizations,
all the clamoring for grades and degrees and grants and
alumni money, everything that is so purely secondary that
I do not deem it fit for presence in my dream.

Is it just nostalgia? an old man's yearning
for the simplicity of the past? I do not know. I have never
knowingly excluded any social concern from my teaching,
I have used my position to propagandize for self-sacrifice
and brotherhood, but when all is stripped away these
elements seem alien to the core of current conflict.

I have no answer. My commitment remains.
If I involve myself I become subject to the wills of others
and to the passions and hysteria which seem to turn the
most reasonable of men into animals. It is an impossible
situation, one with which I cannot cope.

So . . . Leave me alone. Leave me in peace.
Let me give what I am able. Let me be simply known as a
tired old man who attempted to fulfill his own demands.

Plot my position then. You will find me outside
the periphery, outside the infinite circles of the sphere.
I live beyond the edge if our world is flat, and if our
world is round, place me in the heretical galaxies existing
beyond our own. I live in a Time that is individual,
grow older still to the calibrations of a clock of my own
design. With the complicated navigational instruments
of any other world, I may be difficult to find.

The hooded falcon sits on his perch, brown white feathers in

repose. I must feed him soon, suspend raw meat above his beak to lull his
appetite for death. He is a young bird, newly captured, not yet trained
enough to accompany Anna and me on the hunt through the outer mead
of Bel. Still behind his hood his eyes climb, seeking reaches of the sky from
which to hunt, his talons open and close on the wooden perch like an
armorer testing some weaponry of war. The bird will not be mine. I fear him.

How stupid, my Anna would observe. She is at ease with the birds
as she is with the reptiles and insects for which she pays the children of
Bel in silver coin. She is not afraid to place her finger between the knife-
like jaws of an untrained eaglet nor to coil a viper around her neck in idle
play. How stupid. Yes, to you, my love, how cowardly I must seem.

But few are privileged to know the weakness of a king.

Through the streets of Bel I ride, my arm upraised to show the
falcon chained to my sleeve. Do they know the bird I carry is powerless
to fly, his age so great his food must be ground for him? King Marcus
goes forth to sport, look how unafraid he seems before the murderous
bird, look how strong and noble he appears, how worthy to be our king.

They and Anna cannot truly know my fear. In Selegue,
shepherds always keep the liver of the lamb to feed the eagles lest they
be angered and seek revenge on the flock. Priests must give consecrated
bread to the birds trapped in the towers of the church as they are
departed souls in flight. Swans and peacocks are revered as queens and
royal consorts; so must the birds of war like my falcon be ranked as battle
lords in the hierarchy of the beyond. There is a descending order of life.
Disruption of this ranking is what I fear.

I hunt in the name of sacrifice, giving the kill to the killer
like an offering due or a tribute rendered. Should the bird find our sport
against his will he may fly away, gone without tears from me for a good
bird lost, but rather rejoicing for a spirit freed. I am not equal to God
even though a king. I may not be his master. The world is his will, and
we in it so frail and slight before the storms and floods, the drought and
plague, before ourselves. How powerful then he must be who controls the
natural things, how helpless the men who try. I did once attempt it and
became a king, but my victories were over other men, my weapon hollow
sleight of hand that fooled desperate humans and yet passed naked as a
lie before the eye of God.

Falcon, I will keep and worship you. Teach me. Through
prayer and sacrifice, I will be instructed how to rule in Bel.

Idiot king!

Anna's voice fills the room like smoke. The falcon spreads its wings, alert.

You are helpless like a snake from whom the venom sacs are cut, spineless, wriggling king.

Where are you, Anna?

Where wits and magic reign, not the empty insect shell of kings.

What do you want?

Ha! From foul air and feeble earth I work the alchemy to form the precious metal of your success. Tin king is what you are, fashioned by my own hands, hammered from the profane image of Manlius, cast from ore mixed with my mother's dust and Pid and the crystalline tears of defeated men. Rule king, hand down your edicts, make settlements between your loyal subjects, enjoy your palace and your gold, but remember it is formula and incantation, not wisdom, that sustain you. Do not stray from the powers that made you king, lest those powers unmake you the way the falcon there might unmake a sparrow.

But Anna, look at Bel. The granaries are filled, the fields fertile, the people happy. Look at the tribute our richness brings from other towns and the respect paid our fortress and our army. Bel has risen out of the morass of pain and death to these times of peace and plenty. God has ordained this, not your magic mixing of potions and powders in some sunless room. God has stayed his hand from the plague and drought to give us this freedom. We must be thankful and work to prove his faith in us.

What proof will you offer?

Good works, enlightened rule, justice as might be found in heaven itself.

And what reward, king? Where do you seek your recompense? With the people? Or with your merciful God?

I cannot say.

You will die, king, and your body may be either tumbled into a filthy hole or placed anointed in a marble crypt. What is your wish?

I care not. Anna, why do you forsake me?

I seek to preserve us both from another turning of the wheel, from your prosperous road to pestilence once again. For Pid and my mother buried in putrid dust, for me, for King Marcus, I want a marble tomb for us all.

As do I.

Your wisdom and enlightenment will not deter our death or the fall of Bel. These may occur in any instant of divine will regardless of your reputation for justice among men. Our survival lies in our ability to combat this God, not please him. We must be his equal, attain the super-natural, yes, even to the point of eternal life, then truly might you be king.

Heresy, Anna. Guard! Meat! I must feed the falcon.

I have cast our fortune with the stars. We are ascendant but for a comet which passes once in a thousand years. It approaches soon. We must rise forever, we must have the power to destroy even a falling star.

Bring beef and venison!

The philosopher's stone.

Small birds, their necks already broken!

Distillation of the elements in a cup.

Lamb and veal.

No, Marcus, fire and water!

I will be king.

You are only a man.

I will . . .

I will, Marcus? I will or God's will?

Anna!

The falcon leaps from his perch; raw meat, the king's finger, in his beak.

Anna!

Magic, Marcus, black science.

Anna, I bleed!

Bel's red banners snap in sudden wind, the Due Hills disappear from sight, consumed by blackness blowing down their nearer slopes like hellish flax. The city begins to feel again the sting of dust blown against its walls; the people recognize the storm like recurring symptoms of a strange disease. Fading sunlight is filtered through the dust and wind, the sky runs dark, blood red.

Break dikes and dams! cries Anna from her tower room.

The waters swell as if expelled by the earth and overrun the fields.

Strike lightning!

The jagged edge splits wood and rock.

I will shake the world!

Anna, no!

A king afraid?

The falcon strikes again, his proud chest glistens in the light.

Beneath the ground, rock layers grind together and the rivers pulse with energy. The earth gathers herself into violent movement. Lava gleams, pouring from long-closed seams. Islands never seen before break the surface of the oceans that send mighty waves against the shores, drawing equal masses of land down again to the depths.

Distillation of the elements in a cup.

Guard, I bleed.

The falcon strikes.

Magic, Marcus, not your God.

From the streets of Bel come the cries of the people. They cower in the darkness, some pray, most cry out to their king.

Marcus, save us!

It is Manlius' revenge!

A miracle, a miracle again, great king!

What would you, Marcus? whispers Anna. Do now good works, be now enlightened, where now is your heavenly justice? Offer up your proof to the skies, put your heart defenseless before the falcon.

I will be king.

You are a man.

Yes . . . yes, how my blood flows.

Pid and my mother died.

Stop this, Anna. Bring Bel back to life, if you can.

Find the shroud, Marcus, and place it against your wounds. You will be healed.

The lava fades from orange to black, solidifies into soft curving waves of rock. The mad waters quiet and sink into the earth to irrigate the soil. Unknown islands settle slowly into the sea to be unknown again, the tides recede to uncover sandy beaches. Clouds fragment, the sun appears, the walls of Bel shine as though cleansed.

The falcon pecks drowsily at a plate of venison. King Marcus kneels before him.

Oh God, protect us . . .

Yes, pray Marcus, says Anna from her tower. Say your useless prayers.

Oh God, hear me. Protect us from ourselves.

*Busy day, busy busy busy day . . . housewife
humming in her kitchen, filling up the hours with new
enzyme emptiness. Wrapped in an apron, she performs
her ring around the ritual of boredom.*

Get off your ass, woman!

Get out of that television house.

Do something.

Annastasia! This goddamn house is filthy!

*The spectre of feminism is rising like some
great bugaboo of the Western world. Nurtured by
magazines, encouraged by the vote and their own
cigarette, women must have a career. Motherhood isn't
good enough any more.*

*Annastasia had her career, her own life as she
called it. There was an office and reading to be done at
home. There were meetings and office politics. But it was
not what she did that was important, but rather what
it did for her. Her Time was full, her mind was active,
there was always too much to be done, not too little.
And, statistically, remember, I was to die many years
before her. She was to have something to support her in
those hours of her widowhood.*

*The best laid plans of mice, men and
statistical magicians . . .*

*She was aggressive, argumentative and
stubborn. She lacked all the ladylike grace of submission
before the male master (or member) while retaining
all the ladylike wiles of tears, the pout, and long
interminable silences. Our life was as uncontrolled as
the elements, full of emotional disasters. We were often
vicious, sarcastic. We were often very sentimental.*

*But, good God, we were never bored! Not
with our lives, or one another . . . We were occupied,
fully, and in so being perhaps forgot to mind our
manners. Time intervened, with all its makeshift starts
and stops, there was so much life in so little Time. We
were in a hurry, we were selfish, we made enemies,
quickly, easily, left behind.*

She led her life, I led mine, for all appearances
they were independent. But out of the situation grew
some inexplicable kind of interdependence. In a crowd,
in some strange city, knowing she was many thousands
of miles away, I would reach out for her, as if one or
the other of us was threatened. And often I would
receive a call from her, the executive who had left some
important meeting to reach me and whisper some
unimportant endearment.
      How my memory strives to disrupt any
notion of quiet grief!

THE JOURNAL:
    She challenges me, Pid, no more no less, a simple challenge.
Like some boastful knight or swaggering man-of-arms, she forces me
to act against her. She does not seem to remember the circumstances
of our climb, perhaps she has forgotten where I found her in the
market, what her condition was. I wrapped brocades round her to
cover her bark-like skin, I imported scents to daub along her body to
conceal her odor, she is my queen, subservient, a toy, a bauble, always
grateful, always willing . . .
    She prevents me from her tower room.
    That woman with ten yeomen's arms guards the door.
    What do you advise, friend Pid. You are the chief lieutenant.
You have the king's good ear.
    How did I become king? you inquire.
    Most simply, I took! With deliberate martial force I took
the crown from the greasy locks of Manlius. I led bands of citizens to
a victory they could not foresee. They had no reason to believe that
I would be less evil than Manlius with his snarling dogs and monks.
They had no more proof than a few drops of rain fallen on their
pathetic fields, a few drops of blood fallen from the organs of their
sons. They followed dumbly; we held the day. And what did they
follow, my little Pid? A fraud, a sham, an ambitious thief. I stole
their kingdom.
    Yes, by God! Force her, steal her away. Pid! a royal rape!
Is that what you suggest?
    Take her like I would the moaning ewe; the king, a

trumpeting ram! The presumptuous queen, a beggar. A good plan,
tactician Pid, a triumph!

*Her funeral brought the angels of doom out
from their nests of black crepe. They came in the disguise
of friends, relatives, acquaintances, even strangers bitten
by morbid curiosity. The so-called arrangements were
left in the hands of a mortician to whom her body had
been delivered without my knowledge. He stank of
formaldehyde.*

*Such a collection of ghouls has not been seen
since the last great days of Hollywood horror. Inflamed
eyes peeped at me from behind veils; they wet my palm
in an endless stream of melted plastic handshakes. A
leather book was signed, calling cards were stuck in my
pocket as a testimony of attendance. Someone certainly
should have sent a flowered horseshoe with Good Luck
emblazoned on the satin sash.*

*There was no chance for grief in this
assembly. Instead, I smiled, I joked with my fellow-
mourners and observed their shock at my apparent
irreverence in the palace of the dead. Had I known what
entertainment it would have provided, I would have
worn my favorite yellow linen suit with a red carnation
in the lapel.*

*I whispered to Annastasia through the sides
of her overpriced coffin. Look, look at this one! Can you
believe that hat!*

*It was too bad she could not join us. Killed
in an auto crash, horribly mutilated around the face and
shoulders, the mortician's shabby art was not up to her
display in an open casket. She would have loved to have
lain there, gashes barely covered with white powder,
nose broken, bosom partly burned away, and accepted
their greetings like a hostess in a receiving line, nodding
graciously, squeezing my hand behind her in stifled
laughter. A carnival ball, a festival for doomsday freaks,
she always loved a party.*

Softly, Pid, gently so she does not stir.

Marcus climbs the stone stairway to Anna's tower. The matron at the door slumbers in her chair.

Now! Move to the flank! We will surprise her. Smother her cries for aid in the sleeves of her gown.

Marcus, back along the shadow of the wall, approaching alone down the empty corridor.

Attack! Oh get her Pid!

Marcus rushes forward to startle the poor woman from her sleep. His raised arm brings down the silver spoon against her temple. The matron falls unconscious in a heap the size of ten men at his feet.

What a blow you struck her, Pid. The arm you must possess. You might have killed her but for your experience in such things. Well done! Now, you see nothing stands between us and the door. There is a lock. Give me the spoon.

Marcus inserts the handle in the iron keyhole, he twists, deliberately he works it until with a sudden falling turn the bolt is drawn back and the door to Anna's forbidden chamber cracks open. He enters.

What! No angel here to give me combat? No cherubim and seraphim to keep me from her? God has surrendered his mistress without a fight. Pid, we shall share the spoils of battle.

Where are you, Anna?

She sits upright in her bed.

What new stupidity is this, king?

I mean to have you Anna.

I will welcome only the penetration of the divine.

Divine, I am King, I am! Do you think God would prohibit me my own queen? I do good works in his name and seek no reward but this. He will not deprive me.

I will then.

Pid's good right arm is here to help me.

Pid? Where is Pid's ghost you see?

There is no ghost, he lives, in a well-stuffed doublet that put your mammoth at the door on her knees.

Maud! Are you hurt? Come quickly, the king is mad.

No, Anna, I have returned to my senses. I mean to take you for what you are, a thief's slut masquerading in fancy costume. No more airs, no more incantations, you shall lie, day and night, legs akimbo like a

city gate welcoming home tired but victorious armies. Don't disturb your
guardian behemoth, she will not come, she sleeps a long sweet sleep.
    Leave me then before I strike you dead with a curse! My
presence here pits good against your great evil.
    Curse me if you will, God is mounted handily in my
vanguard. I will dedicate your first moaning release beneath me to him.
Yes, that's it. Come Pid, take off that feathered hat, this is sanctified
ground. Bring candles, incense, strip this bed of silken covers, make me
an altar on which to eat this bit of sacrament.
    Anna twists and writhes in the king's grip.
    You pig! Where is that damned falcon to suck out your eyes?
    He is with me, Anna, tame as a gargoyle above the nave. He
flutters peacefully on Pid's leather sleeve.
    King! I will send legions from the lesser earths against
you, spiders between your toes at night. I will bring back the lives of
prehistoric terrors and stable them in the empty stalls behind your
forehead. Each conscious hour will be like your worst childhood
nightmare, holding you beneath troubled waters until you awaken only
in the instant of your drowning. And sleep will not bring you respite, no,
for then all which your waking mind has suppressed will be released, and
horrors beyond your feeble imagination will stampede across your bed
trampling your screams into dust. King, I pity you.
    Let's have her naked, Pid. Let us look upon the hairy fount
from which they say her evil flows.
    Marcus tears off her sleeping gown.
    Oh yes, God. . . . There are indeed divine conquests to be
made here upon such a supple field. We will set the cavalry behind each
of those rising knolls, and foot soldiers secreted in the forests, and this
kingly general placed in that fortified depression in the center of the
ground to give signal against our enemy. I shall stand alone there, and
when their force charges from the hidden cave, I shall wave the standard,
the silver spoon, glinting its alarum to our army which with a mighty yell
will descend from all sides to rally in the orgasm of battle. Pid! Keep your
trumpet ready!
    And when battle's done, let our army gather round, kneeling
on grass made slippery with blood, to give thanks.
    The celebrant enters the sanctuary.
    Marcus mounts his queen.

He opens his breviary, begins the service.
He rolls his buttocks.
He intones a prayer, sings an anthem.
Marcus gasps, Marcus whimpers.
Pid! At long last . . .
Pid, the acolyte, long taper in his hand.
Pid! Greater than the thrill of battle . . .
. . . for these gifts we have received, chants the priest.
. . . greater . . . than . . . the thrill . . .
. . . this, O Lord, our offering . . .
Great god!
. . . our sacrifice . . .
Pid! Oh Pid, cries Marcus. The silver spoon!
She struggles beneath him. Mad king! Get off me, fool.
Idiot! Coward! Cretin! Where is this phantom Pid for whom you shout?
An-na! Pid is in your pudding pot!

> *We had no children.*
> *We often spoke of them, as one would of air*
> *conditioners or a second car. It seems horrible to describe,*
> *and yet children to us were nothing but a commodity.*
> *There were rationalizations. We were always*
> *too young (then too old), we had to be secure financially*
> *(never discussed in round numbers), we had to consider*
> *the question of overpopulation (but we did not have the*
> *courage to adopt someone else's child). One might say*
> *we were the very proud parents of a whole leather shoe's*
> *worth of bouncing rationalizations. Kitchey-koo.*
> *Our friends of course had children,*
> *would bring them retching and screaming to dinner.*
> *Did we mind? We couldn't stand it. Running little*
> *buggers, spilling and smashing, as if they were*
> *saboteurs parachuted into our happy home on a*
> *suicide mission. Their parents sat looking benignly*
> *on, too sophisticated to be openly proud, too polite to*
> *encourage such creative destruction.*
> *Frank dislikes children, said the mothers, in the*
> *car on the way home, their party dresses stained with vomit.*

*Occasionally a child would defeat me, trap
me into thinking that he was not so bad, perhaps my
children would be like him. The child knew, immediately
began to drain away my affection, until I would find
myself on the floor, on my knees, and this little pig went
wee-wee-wee all the way home . . .*

          *Frank was so good with Amadeo, said
the mothers.*

          It was awful.

          *We had a common vision: Annastasia in
torment in the delivery room, me the Norman Rockwell
father waiting. She screams, she laughs, she punctures holes
in her palms with her nails. I read a magazine. She cries,
she faints, she bleeds. I fidget, I pace, I appear self-conscious
beneath the bemused regard of fathers already initiated.*

          She delivers.

          *And out they come, through the recovery
room, my children, unlike any others, fully grown,
wrapped in the swaddling of a three piece suit
or a hostess gown, so alive, so well, so witty and
intellectually mature, perfect in every way except
perhaps for a tiny trace of afterbirth behind the ears.*

          *Annastasia follows the youngest,
affectionately watching as he reaches for his lighter to
light his first cigarette.*

          She looks absolutely beautiful.

          *Sons and daughters, daughters and sons,
listen to your father; this is the church and this is the
steeple and this is the looking-glass and this is the
tarbaby and this is the wind in the willows . . .*

          *I will huff, I will puff, I will climb the
beanstalk and lay the golden egg!*

THE JOURNAL:

    Humiliation! They have driven me before them like hounds
behind a fox, scurrying before the pack, here and there, seeking some
refuge. Dammit! Damn! What caused these sloths to grow teeth? Who
led them into the palace to climb the stairs with their cries and flickering

torches, to bandy around the waiting rooms and polished halls in their nailed boots? Where was the guard? Sleeping off too much wine? Wenching? I'll have the captain, by God, I'll have him!

By the looks of it, dear journal, I'll have no one. It's them who will do the having.

I hear them, tradesmen, merchants, farmers, all tugging at the leashes, jowls in the dust to trace my sweat, rushing up the alleyways and down the lanes. I am not safe here, it is only a matter of Time.

Where are you, king? Hiding in the brewery, reeking of the hops, head poked pathetically from an empty barrel, eyes above the rim looking for reflected torchlight on the ceiling.

Listen to them, hear them roar.

What! What's that? The call of triumph, of the kill. They must have Anna. Ha! The queen running naked as a bug's ear through the streets, pursued by all the gimps and bumbos she made lame by magic. There is some justice. I have had revenge, seen her plead, seen her beg for a second touch of the kingly sceptre, and next heard the sound of irate citizenry busting in the door to send us both hooting like loons, butts in the breeze. They will not go easy with her. And rightly so! She was against me all the while, so let me join their hungry pack, circling round her cornered nudity, jumping in with teeth like saws to snatch away a breast or lump of thigh. Oh yes, and then to take a bone, an arm or joint of leg, to gnaw on some porchfront, sleeping in the sun, resting jaws dried with blood on what was half her delicate ankle. Oh yes, yes, satisfaction!

Her stonesweight will glut them, subdue the fire in their bellies with her drowsy wine. I will relax, perhaps explore my barrel.

And a fitting grave I find it; the king discovered drowned in brown beer, aged over centuries until he returns to reign as intoxicating syrup unkegged. The master brewer must be told, his best recipe must always include a king. These old staves are cool and smooth. It will be a snug place in which to die and have my soul ferment.

Oh God, listen! Back on the scent.

Persistent fools. They should take more Time to enjoy their victories. I would.

Well then, let them come.

I will not struggle, I will be taken with dignity. Their emotion degrades them, moves them beyond acts of reason. They will regret my death. There will be someone to take my place, perhaps him who leads them now. Manlius, suddenly I see you standing atop your platform in the square, crying out at the injustice, cursing me. We have hunted, you and I, the same kingly animal, killed it, skinned it, dressed in its hairy robe, we have worn its proud head as if it was our own. But the eyes were made of glass.

Manlius, you prayed for my death. Now it comes. Like yours, at the hands of an outraged mob. Are we the same? Am I as evil to them as I claimed you to be?

The door! They are here! The dogs are sniffing, lifting legs against my barrel. The brewery is lit by the glow of pitch and anger. Rough hands reach down to grab me!

So be it! I am ready!

Journal, be my witness . . . .

Lies . . . and packs and packs of lies.

As an art, lying is near extinction, like the secret of egg whites in an artist's oil.

That's not true, says Annastasia.

The last known specimen of a rare bird is shot by the hunter, falling with an explosion of feathers into his salad plate. Another fiction revealed by a member of the fascist truth legion, another statue smashed, canvas ripped.

Burn the books!

Goddammit, Annastasia, don't contradict me in public.

How do you think I feel, Frank, hearing you puff yourself up and look foolish with all those ridiculous stories?

Intolerable woman.

But oh, she was proud of my work, and what were my books but a contented and cross-indexed pack of lies. She did not know those scholarly tomes were my very best fiction, written as such for the joy and enlightenment of all the world by the unknown novelist, Marcus Chais.

His efforts won me fame and little fortune. And satisfaction, not as an academic, his job well done, but as an artist, an elderly artist, a little drunk at the opening of his first retrospective.

My poetry was simply awful.

That's the truth!

Annastasia, can't you sense how exciting it is to state a case that is clearly false and watch the expression of belief spread across the face of the woman on your left. Then, what daring in the convincing explanation of another version to the woman on your right. And finally, taxing your abilities to their utmost, the moment when you engage the two in conversation, bring up the subject once again, and watch your fiction materialize from the playfulness of your imagination to the impassioned battle between two charming advocates of the truth.

Besides, something must be done to save the dinner party. That's great fiction, Annastasia.

Pull him out of there! Pigsfoot!

Pickled cod!

Hiding in a barrel!

Brewmasterl Crack it open with your ax!

A healthy blow, splintering staves, the hoops fly off to roll madly into the corner, the king revealed.

Look at him scratching in his book.

Mind that! It might be magic.

A book of curses.

My failed crop.

My daughter's pox and warts.

Three dead children. Two dead pigs.

Let the dogs have him!

Yes!

No!

Don't touch me, shouts the king.

Oh his spunk is up.

No more orders king!

No more tricks.

We have a new leader now. No more Manlius. No more Marcus.

You're going to die, king. With the whore, your wife.

My queen.

Your slut.

No more talk. Let's do him in.

They grab him, hold him above their heads as they emerge from the brewery, turning him in circles above them, passing him back and forth across the mob as if in each man's touch lay his revenge.

Burn him like a witch! someone shouts.

Yes, burn them both.

The brewmaster gathers up the barrel staves in his arms. That post there, he declares, piling the kindling at its foot.

Wood! Brush! Fire! .

They tie him to the stake, Anna is brought beside him. She is mad with fury. She screams at the hovering women.

You shall suck the cocks of snakes. Vipers will nest in your wombs!

Quickly, light it! shouts the crowd.

I am innocent, whispers Marcus. I will be spared in heaven.

Only Anna hears. You will be doomed to hell!

The fire catches, picks up at their feet, singes at their clothing, sends sparks flying to their hair. The crowd presses in close as the flames will allow, hatred adds fuel to the immolation. Smoke in billows, shimmering piles of distorted heat, they disappear, the fire consumes them.

Bel, I am martyred, comes a voice.

Bel, I die for you.

For an instant, there is a dimming of the flame, a clearing; quiet, serene, the king's blackened face appears. The crowd leans forward to catch his words, to revel in a final glimpse of his detested face.

The shroud for Anna, he gasps.

The silver spoon.

He seems to squint through the confining heat, leaning his now burned bald head as if better to see, to single out in the mob the one who set the flame; his last vision of the one who has displaced him.

Through yes bone lips, he tries to question: Pid, oh little Pid, is that really you?

aimee

Out of the center of nowhere comes the light. It is first a
seed and then more distinct it cuts through the night sky as if a point of
flame is burning through black paper. It is a sign toward which Marcus
instinctively veers the car.

They had passed white barrels, one after another, through the
quiet night suspended about them, mist accumulating in oval frames on
the windshield. They are in space, or rather beneath the sea, driving on the
ocean floor with the sand ringing in the fender wells and half expecting to
see the electric eyes of inquisitive fish reflected against the glass.

Marcus has the wheel to hold on to.

Lobe presses cheek to leather in a fitful sleep.

Aimee touches her knee, her elbow, the chrome handle
of the door.

The light grows larger now, it is round, orange in its center,
surrounded by a pure white globe of glare.

Do you see it Marcus? Aimee whispers.

Yes.

Is that where we stop?

If that is where the barrels take us.

Barrels like fat policemen in crisp white uniforms, a silent
whistle blown directing them down an empty thoroughfare.

Look Marcus, numbers!

98 . . . 97 . . . 96 . . . each barrel marked, a number on his badge.

Marcus slows the car.

45 . . . 44 . . .

The walls appear, and the gate, and framed beneath the arch
the single lantern glowing. It is a fort, built of sandstone and dried mud
and wooden beams which protrude over the wall tops, the base for what
once might have been protected ramparts, now broken, penetrated by
the wind. the numbered barrels end, the gate is open, Marcus downshifts
and slowly drives in. He shuts off the ignition, and stretching his arms
stiffened by the driving looks around him.

The fort is much larger inside than suggested by the outside
wall. Low arches line three sides, a sheltered walkway with shadowed
doors against the farthest edge. Wooden buildings with domed roofs are
constructed on either side of the gate. The lantern is strung up on a pole

in the center of the square; it emits the only sound, a steady hissing of gas escaping under pressure.

A door opens, scraping its wooden frame on the stone. A man's voice calls: who is it?

Marcus climbs out of the car into the light.

Chais, he says.

Who?

Marcus Chais.

The professor?

Yes.

And who's the girl?

My wife. And there's a third asleep in the back, a Mr. Lobe, the tattoo artist we were told to pick up in St. Louis.

Very good, comes the voice. We were afraid he might not be up to it after all. Tabo will be pleased. Wake him up and park the car outside. Did you bring bags?

Bags?

Sleeping bags. No matter, there are a few blankets left, but not so comfortable. I'll get them and show you where you can sleep.

Sleep the night away, grappling with Indians, rawhide in their teeth, or oriental tribesmen, their rifles inlaid with gold. You are the desert traveler, sleeping the night in a caravansary smelling of oil and spice, in the horse-changing depot reeking of dung and raw whiskey. Your mattress is a stone floor and your dreams are of stones.

Aimee, exhausted, falls asleep beside you.

Lobe says, if you don't mind ma'am, and wraps a blanket around his waist to screen the removal of his seersucker trousers, his shoes and socks with garters.

Watch out for spiders, he says.

Morning sunlight finds a hole in the roof, small beams focused across clouds of dust. Lobe wakes and smells coffee, frying eggs and toast burning in the oven of his St. Louis apartment.

Goddamn! What day is it? Where am I?

He gets out of his blanket and pulls open the door. A girl dressed in a kimono passes, glances briefly at his legs and shorts.

Where do we get breakfast?

She hesitates. There is none of course. Are you hungry? Did you come here to be hungry?

Shutting the door: I don't know why I came here.

The telephone rings in the hall outside his apartment.

Mr. Lobe, this is John Tabo calling.

Who? the police, the lawyer suing for damages to a society skin, the landlord? Who? Who?

No lieutenant, nothing, I don't know anyone, anything!

Mr. Lobe, I am certainly not the police, just another citizen like yourself, law abiding and perhaps a trifle tired of being treated like a criminal in spite of it. Don't you sometimes feel that way?

. . . goddamned cops showing me pictures of tattoos, health people rubbing cotton swabs around my office, a tattoo guy is always hounded. I don't ask questions, most times I don't even see their faces. Just push the needle, simple as that, take the money, no dope, no numbers game, not guilty lieutenant. Leave me alone, my breakfast is burning . . .

I have heard Mr. Lobe a great deal about your talent.

OK, Mr. smart-ass lawyer then. Listen, she was drunk, out of her mind with some kid in a tux steering her around. She asked for 'Whore of Babylon' on the stomach and that's what she got, laughing and pointing her tits at that kid. She signed the paper, just like all of them. You can't get me, lawyer, I'm safe, no conscience no regrets.

But it must not be the most financially secure trade in this world, Mr. Lobe. Surely there is a money problem?

Shit, it's the landlord. I pay the rent, never late, and because I pay you want to raise. Anybody who doesn't pay you keep on and take their car, TV or wife, but me who pays you keep on raising and threatening to evict. Yeah, there's a problem. Who is this?

I have need for a tattoo artist who is discreet, talented and willing to earn some money, Mr. Lobe. He must also be willing to leave his business for a while.

Oh, sweet Jesus!

You may treat me as another mad customer or you may give me the respect I, or my money perhaps, deserve. Are you interested, Mr. Lobe?

Where do I go? How much? Is it legal?

You will go to a place in the southwest and I assure you it is worth your trouble.

So why not . . . no police, no lawyer, no landlord, so why . . .

It is perfectly safe, Mr. Lobe.

So why not, Tabo. What do I do?

Be on the northeast corner of Twelfth and Market beginning at two Monday afternoon. A college professor in a blue Buick will pick you up and take you from there. Thank you, Mr. Lobe, and please do not be apprehensive. Goodbye.

A college professor, Christ! Why did I do it?

Don't you think you could put your pants on, Lobe? Spare Aimee at least the sight of those knees.

You don't like me very much, do you professor?

No.

Why not? What have I done to you?

You? . . . probably nothing, except make me nervous with your snoring, fidgeting with your newspaper, your stupid likes and dislikes and fears.

Marcus wraps his blanket around his shoulders and leans against the wall, watching Lobe, watching Aimee sleep.

But you represent something to me, something you don't even know, yes, that's it, something unknown. This whole thing is an unknown, picking you up waiting on a street corner, the drive across the desert, this place. It's like the answer to a question I know I want to ask but can't find the words and that frightens me. Who is this Tabo? Who are you? Who are we, me and my wife, in this forgotten room? You see, I know I don't know.

What crap you talk professor. You don't like me and you don't like your wife.

She stirs, rolls over clutching the blanket. Marcus wedges his jacket beneath her cheek.

I do, I do now, so perhaps there's hope I'll learn to like you as well. No, you're quite wrong, Lobe; I think I love my wife.

Aimee, this is Marcus.

Marcus . . . unbelievable, from the telephone.

It's sudden, too sudden, but I called because I'm going away for a while and want you to come with me.

Silence.

Aimee? It's Marcus, no joke, no mad joke. Are you there?

Where do you want to go, Marcus, after eight months' separation, where could we possibly go?

I know, I know. Aimee, it's so important that you come. Oh, how stupid that must sound to you.

Yes. I never would have thought anything could be more important than your work.

You'll come?

I don't see how . . .

Please! I'll pick you up, in an hour, don't pack anything.

Did I love her then?

What is it Aimee? You know I don't like to be disturbed at the office.

. . . to tell you why Marcus, why I'm leaving. I can't play the heroine you demand. You defeat me always, it is impossible, lonely, sad . . . knowledge can be manipulated, put into any order by your brain, but not me, not your wife, not even if that was all she wanted. . . . Marcus, I'm no wooden carving with hair glued into place and painted eyes, can't you see that . . .

Or then?

The girl in the kimono appears at the door.

Which one is Lobe?

Me.

Come on. Tabo wants to see you.

God, I'm hungry. I hope he's eating.

So, alone with your sleeping wife, alone with leering faces painted on the walls. Cat-calls deep within your ears, taunts and jeers rolling in the corners like distant thunder. Your mind releases a thousand associations, classical comparisons, historical allusions, the tableaux pass before you in simple animation. Soft-gowned women arrive, moving through the room on particles of dust, they settle in the corners, they caress the ugly painted faces, their innocent lips are bloodied by the leering smiles, the gowns torn from them fall into sunlight patterns on the floor. Now, there is life indeed, the voices reach crescendo, pearl breasts rasped by matted chests, great hands closed on rounded buttocks, no classical references now, only heavy breath and fluid sound, shadows locked in intercourse against the walls, on the ceiling and the floor, in all the corners of your mind. You are touched all over by this orgy, coupled bodies move along you, see, sweat on your forehead, a shudder building in your throat, cover your ears, close your eyes, clench your hands, as the earthquake opens a crevice and sweeps away your historical allusions to burn in the fiery orgasm of the center of the earth.

She is awake now. He whispers to her.

I brought you here to see John Tabo. Frank told me about
him. For a long time I put off seeing him, oh, a thousand things
interfered. You left me then, I was distracted, unhinged. Frank watched,
perceptive as always, but not much help in the end. And then for a
moment in my darkened office it all seemed clear. What that instant
was, that realization, I cannot say, but it persists and that is important.
I remembered Tabo and called to ask if I could visit him. Incredibly he
seemed to know who I was. He gave me instructions to pick up Lobe in
St. Louis and to drive here. The map arrived by mail two days later. I felt
like a hunted animal, a criminal chased by dogs, and through the phone
line a stranger told me a way. I called you, stupidly perhaps, but you
were part of it all, part of this journey. To where, I don't know. Tabo is a
hypnotist, but the events I have heard about are beyond that. I want to
see them, I want them to happen to me as an answer to that voice which
cries inside me for something greater than that which I have been able to
give. I am seeing things differently, Aimee, hearing sounds, feeling like
I never have before. It is exhilarating, terrifying and above all humbling.
I'm glad you're with me.

        I'm happy too, Marcus. Those eight months were such a failure.
        The room full of people, grotesques, circling, goading him.
        Go on, they chant. Go on man, touch her, touch your wife.
        Aimee. I'm sorry.
        Light applause from the languishing women, whistles from
the painted ones.
        Aimee . . .
        All are still.
        Somewhere an opening door, the girl enters.
        Oh Christ, save it for later, you two. Tabo's waiting.

> *You don't like your wife, said a friend*
> *who claimed he knew me well. He gave me no pause*
> *for reflection. And she must hate you for hating her,*
> *continued this well-meaning ass. Hatred then, his*
> *prognosis; divorce, that modern cure-all for social*
> *disease, his prescription. So much for a friend who*
> *knew me well.*
>   *Annastasia, if I may, a question from here*
> *on earth; can you recall a single quarrel?*

She would answer that we fought, squabbled,
needled, pecked and poked. Innuendo passed between
us like torpedoes beneath the surface. Yes, certainly, I
admit all that. So what? In public view? Of course, I had
almost forgotten. Sociological fact: the success of all
marriages is based on the consensus of false impressions
and misunderstandings compiled by observers of public
demeanor forming their opinions from trivia. Also
known as Gossip's Law.

Well then, I am guilty of overt and invert
sarcasm and a lifetime's oneupsmanship. I insulted her,
I provoked her, I dug at her incessantly. I sustained my
brutal treatment of her from dinner party to picnic,
faculty tea to debutante ball, and further I confess to
many other transgressions unobserved by the little
nits who concern themselves with these things. In the
public eye, I am a cad, an enemy, paranoid professor,
misogynist, sadist, and suspected fag. Oh friend who
knew me well, you are right, I am riddled with cancer,
I am full of hate!

I hasten to point out that it's nobody's
goddamn business but our own.

Let me add we enjoyed ourselves immensely.

And, finally, for a magician, it is merely
sleight of hand to transform hatred into love.

Good God, Frank, what do you think I am? What do you
find absurd about the study of this journal?

Is it what has driven you to a darkened room?

No. Aimee. Suddenly, like dust sliding from between these
pages, her absence has crept into my mind. Loneliness has turned out the
lights around me.

And the journal?

Everything is there, Frank. The exemplary tale, written not
to influence a contemporary audience, but left for me centuries after
to identify and interpret. This man Chais, he is my namesake and he is
everything I am not. Look how he worships! Look how he believes!

I don't see . . .

No! and I didn't see when Aimee left. Like you I merely
cried: absurd! Women are no mystery, Frank. I need . . .
What?
Women, wives . . . mystery . . .
A joke, Marcus?
The self-pitying professor, that is the joke. Marcus Chais
is the laugh, he is the punch line to the journal's story.
Marcus, control . . .
Control? Ah yes, as my teacher you would suggest that.
You taught me control.
Take some Time. Do some new research. I will fix it with
the department.
Get some rest, is that it? Sun? Beaches? Pretty girls?
Why not?
I need more than pretty girls.
Marcus, you are an intelligent man, but I'm afraid you have
no idea of what you need or don't need. Apply your mind. You are talking
in riddles.
There, Frank, that's it! A riddle! something with more enigma
than a girl bathing in the surf, something more intellectual. Watch my
ears prick up, curiosity begin to bubble, watch myth rise up again to blind
me. Oh, good therapy, Frank, you know me well, you know your patient.
A riddle?
Not the journal.
What then?
John Tabo.
The hypnotist?

> . . . *clear connection when for a Time all*
> *crackling static is filtered out, open lines as wide as wide*
> *itself, wires of the purest silver, quickly come, quickly*
> *gone, clouds and lightning, a bird may settle on the open*
> *wire and die in a flash of light*

I will call John Tabo. We will speak. Cables strung across
the nations and under oceans, satellites receiving. The hypnotist and the
professor will communicate.
Marcus Chais from the university calling, Mr. Tabo.

Of course.

What? Of course? What is he saying, Frank?

A riddle.

I have heard a great deal about your experiments, Mr. Tabo, and was wondering if you might be free to discuss them with me.

I am always free. I am leaving the city, however. Would you be willing to meet me at my research center? It is unfortunately some distance from here.

Yes, I am willing.

Good, professor. You will drive your car. I will send a map and, oh yes, there is a gentleman I would like you to pick up for me. He is on your way.

But . . .

Professor Chais, you will be glad you've come.

What am I afraid of? The darkness of this office wraps me in subtle paranoia as if I am now vulnerable to all the sticks and sharp rocks and hidden thorns of existence. They are looking for me the way a shark tracks the blood of a wounded swimmer. Aimee! Strangely enough, it is my will, this fear, to be hunted, to strip away all my established defenses and place my head within the lion's jaws. This Tabo speaks to me as if he has known me all my life. He expects my call, my visit, my giving some friend of his a ride. It seems all arranged now, my fear, Tabo's plans, an efficient Timetable to which I must conform.

Are you going, Marcus?

Yes Frank, it seems I am.

Compass of the mind. We spoke, Tabo and I, and said nothing, the sound of our voices and our words were as meaningless as the trivial details of an appointment. I feel purified, events within the privacy of the black plastic cone, tones of the artificial confessor still in my ear. But for all I know, I could create my own responses in Tabo's name. In that sense, I have talked to no one, made no arrangements, and am leaving on a journey that is entirely my own, to a center for personal research, meeting those along the way who are essential to my imagined estimation of the journey's purpose. Compass of the mind.

It is a riddle, Frank.

> . . . *confetti, bits and fragments of past belief*
> *torn to celebrate the turning moment, no climax, a circle*

is nothing more than hard right hands linked infinitely

    The journal, take it, Frank, back to the humidified air of the library vault. It has given its testimony, it has led me from one step to the next. Let us preserve it for some other Chais to discover.

> *. . . a wanderer discovers a circular path,*
> *elated by confidence he follows at all speed, indifferent*
> *to the way's own true goal, to lead all travelers back*
> *again to their moment of discovery*

Yes, I'm going.
Out of this darkened room, Marcus?
But first . . . first, more communication, the telephone.
Who?
The professor and his wife.

> *I see a commentary to this mental exercise, a*
> *chorus of wise old men, dressed in tattered robes, with*
> *long white beards and crooked stance. They stand in the*
> *wings, calling for final adjustments to their costumes,*
> *nervous as little children in a third grade review.*
>   *But now, they hear the cue! And out they*
> *dance, arms interlocked, denture smiles, kicking up their*
> *arthritic limbs like Lido girls. They twirl, they pirouette,*
> *they fluff their robes to show sagging buttocks to the*
> *first five rows. The crowd goes wild.*
>   *Wait! I cry. These old boys are meant to*
> *comment somberly, elucidate not titillate. I brought*
> *them on to explain our drama, not strip-tease, they're*
> *stealing my show!*
>   *Chorus: this is the story of a randy old fart . . .*
> *Wait a minute!*
>   *Chorus: who couldn't make it with his wife . . .*
> *Goddammit!*
>   *Chorus: yet still he wished to write it down.*
> *Give 'em the hook!*
>   *Chorus: in pecker tracks for posterity!*

*They break up into gummy laughter, slapping
their thighs, showering the audience with spittle.
        The audience? Well, who really knows about
the audience . . .
        Look! The old men have lined up to take
their bows.
        They have pulled off their beards and wiglets.
They have revealed themselves to be nine of me, Frank
Timmins, one and all, like everyone else in the company!*

I don't work unless I eat. Look at my hands! They're
shaking from hunger. I haven't eaten for thirty hours. I didn't come
here to be starved.
        Quite right, you didn't. Get Mr. Lobe some food and
fetch his equipment from the car. Mr. Lobe is an artist, we must be
sympathetic to his needs and whims.
        What? No meat, no fish, no eggs?
        No, I'm sorry.
        Just rice?
        Yes, Mr. Lobe, just rice.
        God in Christ, I'll die!
        You are much too fat, Mr. Lobe. A little loss of weight will
do your body good, not to mention your soul.
        My soul eats. It thrives on meat and potatoes.
        Of course. Please ask it to accept my apology. There is
nothing but brown rice. Are your hands steadier now? Quite frankly,
the sooner you complete your work here, the sooner you will be free
to return to wherever you please and fatten up that soul for the kill.
I would like to begin. Please transfer this design to my back. Nine
colors, any ones you choose. Take your time, Mr. Lobe, your best work
is required and will be rewarded. Do not worry about the pain.
        I never do.
        Good, neither do I. Ever.
        What is this thing?
        Does it matter to you?
        No. Well, yes, professional interest. I've never seen the
design before.
        Once you have engraved it into my skin, you will never forget

it, Mr. Lobe. Nor will you ever be able to draw it again, at least never the same way you do today.

What the hell is it?

The enneagram.

The needle hums, the room filled with the sound and smell of punctured flesh. Enneagram:

Red: call it alpha and omega:

Come in, Professor Chais. Please forgive my posture, but Mr. Lobe requires it for his work. Would you come around in front here where I can see you? I hope you passed a pleasant journey. The desert is very beautiful, I think, both by day and by night. The location is perfect. They say an ancient medieval city-state is buried beneath these sands. A little history for us to consider, yes, history. This is your wife? I am so pleased you brought her with you. Sit down, bring some pillows for Mrs. Chais. Good. Are you hungry? Mr. Lobe has consumed vast quantities of rice. No? It is so much easier to communicate with mouths and bellies empty. Now please relax. You are not relaxed or otherwise you would not have come. What brings a man such as yourself a thousand miles into the desert, following a crude map and picking up strangers? Not the sort of thing you would have imagined, is it, professor? May I call you Marcus? And what is your wife's name? Aimee, very beautiful. I think we all should have just one name, one is enough to identify us. Too many names and too many numbers seem to find their way between us. Do you find that true, Aimee? Yes, I think you do. Please do not be offended, Marcus, if I tell you how much I know about you and your wife. I have not of course learned anything more than what you have told me, although this is our first meeting. You are a well-known man, in the newspapers for your speeches and discoveries, your social activities, and published in so many learned journals. I have read most of your work I think. Excellent. Limited, to be sure. Ah, now relax, please. You will soon learn that of all the things I am, rude I am not. Limited, let me continue, only in terms of completeness. But surely you, the author, must know that. Certainly you do not think that your work is anything but one of many beginnings in the field, one of many approaches. Certainly you do not think that you alone are right and all-knowing about those intricate problems you examine. Of course you don't!

Brown: an angle unhinged, connection: mind and body:

Ah, Mr. Lobe has changed colors. We are one ninth of the way through. I hope this spectacle does not discomfort you. Believe

me, it is quite painless for me. You are a well-known man, and yet I
know more about you from the words you write than from all the social
columns and magazine reports. And what do you know about me? I am
a hypnotist, yes, with some accomplishments to my credit which might
excite your intellectual interest. Hypnotism is a strange ability, as you
must know. It is something one learns about quite by chance. I did not
go to the university to know my trade, it came to me. Quite a problem
it is, to know that one suddenly has such ability and power and not to
realize what to do with it. The circus? Night clubs? A pretty assistant in
sequined costume passing through the audience asking birthdays?
        Blue: triangle triad trinity: mind and body and then heart:
        No, I have used my art in other ways which few approve, most
call evil. Such ridiculous terms, good and evil. I am truly surprised that
after so many years mankind has not found them obsolete. We continue
to perpetuate them in so many forms, so many different codes and
moralities. Sometimes my head spins. Sect against sect, nation against
nation, system against system. Everyone right, no one wrong. There! You
see, Marcus, just how close we are to the truth . . . and just how distant
truth remains. It is the universal element out of which anything can be
made. Science, for example, claims the discovery of relativity, but only
because of the blindness of the philosophers and prophets. Throughout
history we have been confronted with the principle and yet only now has
the current system provided us with the needed proof. And so we cry
'relativity' and 'progress' and build a bomb. Absurd! You, Marcus, are one
of our foremost documentarians, an anthropologist, philosopher, student
of religion. You represent the failure of our scholars to go beyond the
mere recognition of fact. What has all your study and research proven?
What has it done for man, for me, for your wife, for yourself? Good? or
evil? Books are written, knowledge expanded, but understanding remains
static. Do you see it, Marcus, do you see? A change, Mr. Lobe, perhaps a
deep dark green would be nice.
        Green: earth environment:
        We are wanderers. Progress has not evolved from a circle to
a straight line. Will it? I think not, despite all our pretensions. We have
been walking the circumference for centuries, running, sprinting, hoping
to break away. But why not look within as well as without? Why not
explore that mass of knowledge we have isolated in our circle, examine
all of it in such detail that true understanding penetrates our pores to

be absorbed by the blood and circulated to mind and body and heart?
We resist. We resist in the form of established belief, preconception,
repression. We are not willing first to immerse ourselves in our own
world, thinking once we have surveyed it and outlined it generally on the
map we know all there is to know and must continue on to new ground.
All these old rules must be upset before there can be a new beginning.
Our potential for belief and understanding must be re-evaluated. We are
evangelists, and above all we cry out for our own conversion.

Grey: the moon and all the turning planets:

I am preaching to you, Marcus, and what is preaching other
than one form of hypnosis. I am preaching, and yet I have no real message.
I have no doctrine to impress upon you, but I have a goal: liberation.
Does that sound foolish? or is the man who took his wife and drove to the
desert prepared to listen to the fool? I want to liberate you from what has
grown within you for all these years, from those established beliefs and
preconceptions and repressions. I want to make children of us all once again.
Isn't that what you desire? Are you afraid to think of it? Through hypnosis
I can force you, even against your so-called will, to remove yourself from
lifelong prejudice and devote yourself to motion, to the evolution of thought
and recurrent patterns of the spirit. You will no longer be contained by your
physical shell, you will no longer be Marcus or Aimee Chais or a Christian
or a Caucasian or a man or a woman or the representative of any school
or grouping. You will be all men and women throughout history, you will
know all ideas, you will be part of the great How from man to the absolute
and back to man again and nothing will distract or inhibit you from the
assimilation of the All. You will be liberated from your absurd desire for
individuality and from the trappings of your education and success. What
seemed insurmountable problems to you will disappear, what was separation
will be union, what was doubt will be certainty. You need not listen to
my words, you need not acknowledge my existence or this occurrence, for
when once baptized in motion no memory of past life remains. It is the new
beginning I described and there are no secrets or hiding places, all is open
and clear and real, and despite all worldly artificial forms, despite life or
death, the scales are fallen and truth revealed.

Purple: sun one sun our sun:

My hypnotism unmakes men, they stand naked before
themselves, fascinated and unashamed. The revelation is their own, and
all decisions thereafter. I supply them only with the connection they

require, the last link, the first cycle of the pump. Stories of such individuals
may have reached your ears. They appear in each edition of the news: men
with valuable careers leaving family and fortune seemingly gone from
the face of the earth, politicians resigning office, priests abandoning the
church, wives divorcing husbands after twenty years, sons and daughters
leaving home. Life goes on, for those with new inspiration and new value,
not measured in any way they knew before. Marcus! Aimee! Join them.
When people find their way to me, I know they are desperately searching.
I am hard to find. I am their humble servant.

    Yellow: all suns in the end:

    We are almost finished, aren't we Lobe? I can sense you have
done well. The design is curious, don't you find? The enneagram is a
universal symbol, it is all knowledge, it is perpetual motion. A man may
be quite alone in the desert and he can trace the enneagram in the sand
and in it read the eternal laws of the universe. And every time he can learn
something new, something he did not know before. The enneagram is a
schematic design of constant motion, sought by men throughout antiquity.
But they searched outside themselves for that which was within them,
and they attempted to construct perpetual motion the way a machine
is constructed. Motion is never stilled, just as this tattoo on my back
will never cease to change with my motion, the flexing of my muscles,
the lifting of my arms. Every moment, every posture, every beat of my
heart will be manifest in the diagram by a different form. A motionless
enneagram is a dead symbol, the living symbol is in motion. Lobe, you are
truly a great artist to have drawn this design, for you begin to see now that
it is your creation, not a reproduction of what I gave you. Different then,
different now, when your needle inflicts its last sting, different still again.
Then it will not be yours or mine, but will belong to all the earth.

    Orange: the totality of all the worlds:

    Look at it, Marcus. Look, Aimee. See the diagram as the
fluid opening to what you seek, the way to liberation. Look deep within
it and begin to feel the motion. Roll with it, as with the waves when
you walk the deck of a ship. Move with its movement, with its rhythm
and sequence. You are suspended in the fluid, rising falling with its
inexplicable tide. You are relaxed. A thought! Did you see it! It passed
you like a lone fish in all the ocean. But there! Another! A school of
thought around you, tiny white fish, swirling like a snowstorm. And
there, look, another! Isn't that the one to which you belonged, dear

Marcus? I think it was. But you see it is gone and another takes its place, just as large, just as beautiful, just as alive. You are relaxed, you are in motion. Do you feel all knowledge around you? Do you feel yourselves, your friends, the stranger you pass? You do? You acknowledge them all. You what? You love them all. Marcus, Aimee, keep on, relax and keep walking and watching as the great Lobe completes his design. Marcus, Aimee, keep on loving.

Black: absolute; the end and a beginning: call it alpha and omega: It's finished.

Fine, fine, Mr. Lobe. A beautiful job you have done.

Why don't you return to your room. Food will be served you there.

OK, sure. Listen, what's going on here? Look at those two. What's wrong with them?

They're just sleeping, Mr. Lobe. They're tired, but they'll be rested soon.

Yeah, well, me too. Sleep. Yeah, Christ! I'm beat.

> *Sleep is death and death is liberation, escape from a world of lists and errands and appointments and those failures of the national power grid that stop the clocks that time our wars at ten past three.*
>
> *Ten past three, three past ten, I welcome sleep.*
>
> *My eyelids descend, becoming a cinema screen in four dimensions. I leave my orchestra seat, discard my popcorn sack to litter the floor of the conscious world and climb up on the stage to join Peter Pan and the crocodile, tic toc tic toc . . .*
>
> *I find people there exactly as I want them to be. Annastasia lives there now.*
>
> *I join my wife who chats amiably with a troll.*
>
> *I enter the kaleidoscopic world where there is no true and false, no proof, just joyous changing colors. I enter the state of mind where cocktail parties and disappointments are illegal.*

What, still here, Marcus? This room . . .

Here forever, Frank, trapped.

And Tabo?

Left behind . . . or perhaps before? Where are we?

You . . .

. . . am hypnotized . . .

And Aimee?

We're all asleep, Frank; me, Aimee, Tabo, even Lobe, dormant, dreaming, dying. I can't see any more, I'm blind, I sense only starlight reflected across ten million miles from a source I cannot view. I sense a layer of dust on the top of my desk. I must sit still, deathly still, and pray for light.

Where are you, Marcus? Good heavens man!

Not here, not here swimming in the nine-sided ocean, black with open drains shooting off like extra limbs. Where is my wife? This desk, empty except for dust on which shows the shadow of a man reclining, talking, on which shows some mysterious design as if drawn upon his back.

Frank! Do you draw? Inflict the pain?

Aimee, does it hurt you?

Persistent needles, breast and sunglasses, vest and shock of white hair, hypnotic terror.

Marcus!

Who is speaking? Frank? Aimee? Lobe? Tabo droning? The nine-sided ocean is expanding toward a ring around the center.

Neat catalogue from the scholar's files: cards, notes, clippings, referenced and cross-referenced, academic forms: statues line the hallways of this vast museum, illuminated by hidden lights, arranged on modest pedestals, athletes striking attitudes, graceful muses caught in momentary poses: these are the idols of an era: wooden masks streaked with patterns of white clay, pasted up with feathers stolen from netted birds: chipped ceramic, colored rocks interlaid to portray the mottled complexions of the saints: pale features, gold leaf delicately applied in an arc about the head: these are small monuments

vast quantities of shadow marshalled up by the tricks of a fraudulent magician, closer shadows

of man's belief: ivory, jade, stone carving of the many-headed goddess: a monolithic block

around me

catalogue: nine limbs tied together in the Gordian mental

knot: it is you, Aimee, who joins me in the museum, a strange and
wonderful girl seen standing before some painting, turning the pages of
her guidebook; I follow apprehensively without the courage to speak to
her, in mortal fear she will be lost in the maze: a woman
     dusty shadows
       is a monument to the beliefs of man: that retreating girl seen
for an instant in the refracting picture glass, that spread nude, that lump
of red earth with crude bit breasts
       an ominous colored signal
       blend them together until she with arm uplifted
       strikes out at the painting, shattered glass, curved nail
punctures; she tears the canvas in shreds, peeled pigment, her totem
image destroyed: she screams and the man, me, is struck across the face
by fragments: statues topple, hesitating lights—
       What? Frank, is that you? The particles of dust on this desk
seem suddenly disturbed, the design is broken, continuity disrupted, give
us something to hold on to!
       motion: the gyroscope inside no longer dictates direction; all
gravity defied: the museum turns, statues float like heavy birds in space:
the girl is gone, enveloped in her own vision: chaos—
       the clouds disperse
       shock of white hair, sunglasses, familiar expressions passing.
I am swallowed up in a lubricious passage peopled from my history:
they pop out of the walls as I pass by: burned black-eyed alchemists:
witchdoctors and rocketmen: God dressed in a vinyl suit: Lobe is
there like some olympian tattooing his design for the world: and Tabo
polishing this his personal hand mirror
       retreating shadows
       the girl floats naked there before me, her body marked with
scars of inhuman whiteness: glass cuts? acts of perverse sensuality? of
murder? her breasts her sex shock of white hair sunglasses an open mouth
there between her thighs to disgorge me like a disagreeable hors d'oeuvre
       Marcus, can you hear me?
       God, Frank, turn on the lights!
       friends and strangers, I see but cannot catch you in the void:
my fingers do not touch your marble skin: I am rocking moving the girl
too beyond my reach
       motion: my senses spun off like elements in a centrifuge:

I begin to hear words subliminally
  you what? you do?
  and motion turns me in upon myself, my arms like jacket
sleeves inside out, I place my fist inside my stomach, I poke two
fingers into my heart, my brains are emptied like upset baskets of
archeological discovery
  nausea, nausea mixed with shame
  the voice: you love them all
  dead, dreaming, all of us, the museum staved in by light
  I must stand still!
  Tabo intoning: Marcus, Aimee, keep on loving
  Frank, do you have a handkerchief?
  Yes, for . . .
  I must wipe the desk clean of all this dust.

> *The pleasure threshold, a Venus line drawn
> in the sand: cross it if you dare. We must know that state
> of demi-consciousness wherein awareness drains to the
> back of the head and one's only realization is the perfect
> physical harmony of the senses, pleasure so intense that one's
> notion of physical being is abandoned. The body cracks
> apart like a china figurine, and the essence it contains
> seems for the moment free, pleasure so great that the wee
> light of the thinking mind cannot reach it, as if another
> consciousness beyond ours is reveling in our experience.*
> *I feel her lips upon me in a thousand places,
> our tongues in a knot tying and untying, her teeth in
> collision with mine, an ivory click, limbs bodies motion,
> rhythm unknown to the composer's sense of Time, harsh
> breath and unintelligible expression, my five o'clock
> growth scrapes across her nipples.*
> *She explores, her hair in hurricane tumult
> above my chest and belly, and her mouth finds me, nips
> about the base, teeth catching tiny folds of skin, teeth and
> lips like two banded sets of stimuli climbing up to where
> they enclose me within their circular confinements, there
> to release her tongue again to touch . . .*
> *I too explore, my head against her thigh,*

*chin neatly hooked in the joining of her leg and pelvis,
I find her many openings, sticky spots of magic which I
attempt to fill with a driven knife of skin, from which I
try to suck her life's blood, my smell is her, my cheeks are
covered with her, my taste is her and her alone . . .*
    *We cannot know the true pleasure we
induce, we can only sense it through our own. Like
tuning forks first struck independently, our vibrations
induce sympathetic responses in each other, constant,
continuing. We hum together. We approach the threshold.*
    *A winking of the eye and now she fights
below me, I hold her wrists pinned to the pillow and
bite her breasts, a snap of the fingers, she writhes above
me, hands grasping to bring me closer in, I hear the
beginning of her moan, I see the flush spread down her
neck, down her collarbone and bosom, blood rushing
from her brain, in the midst of mechanical and electrical
energies of muscles and nerves, in the emptiness of
pleasure, in the pure white space beyond the doorway.
I whisper: Annastasia! She feels the sound of her name,
but she does not hear me.*
    She lost her senses when she loved me.
    *Preserve me, pickle me, yogurt, oysters, old
wives' tales, get me sulphur waters from the fantasy spa!
I whisper now: Annastasia, old men remember.*

Awake, says Tabo.
The girl sponges off his back with alcohol.
Marcus and Aimee, sprawled like cushions, stir from sleep.
Their hands are locked together, rigid grasp, not so much from attraction
as from fear of being torn apart.
    Get Lobe. I must know his plans. Awake, Tabo soothes.
    Twisted wires at once set free, unwind slowly back again,
hypnotic momentum in reverse. Aimee's face is streaked with tears.
    Relax, says Tabo. I know it was not a happy journey. Their
eyes blink open, images dissolved by the sudden intrusion of the sunlit
room, they close, they open, a clear erasure where once was horror.
    Marcus? Aimee?

They recoil as if the voice was an eternal threat.

Goddammit Tabo, I want my money!

Lobe, furious entry, his suit, fresh knotted tie.

I want a decent meal!

Relax, comes Tabo's voice.

Hey look, isn't that sweet! Those two, sleeping like babies on your cushions. Cushions! I come out here in the stinking desert, all the way from St. Louis cramped in that car, I put down your stupid design and don't get fed. I sleep on rocks! I want out!

How do you propose to go? Will you leave with Mr. Chais?

They're leaving?

I am afraid so.

I'm not riding in that car again. What a driver!

You'll walk then? I fear there are no taxis here, friend Lobe.

All right, wake up professor, says Lobe reaching down to shake Marcus. But I'm driving.

Aimee?

Yes Marcus, it was awful.

Get the car Lobe.

I regret you are not staying, Marcus. It is perhaps too late for you. It is not for everyone. I understand. Still, I hope you will remember . . .

Marcus, please, let's go.

Aimee, Mrs. Chais, it was not an evil thing. Reflect upon the design, your memories . . .

It was hateful!

No, no, it was good, for the ultimate good. You will remember . . .

Cut the crap, Tabo. I got the car started and we're wasting gas.

The barrels then, white personalities, leading away to nowhere, faces with their backs turned away, cold metallic shoulders, responsibility ignored. The sand is like a linen tablecloth

ready to be pulled rudely from beneath the wheels. They wander helplessly, their way dictated by black numbers .

. . . 23 . . . 9 . . . 58 . . .

. . . 1 . . . 97 . . . 71 . . .

Lobe drives, erratic desperate path.

Christ! Where's the road? These barrels have all been moved around. Tabo's moved the barrels!

Go north, Lobe. Go straight north to hit the road again. No

good shitty compass! The numbered barrels . . . Artful heat rising to mid-
day. The sand like a burning gas. Within the engine's seams, combustion
overcomes control, oil bubbles freeze to piston shells and the cooling
water boils away. Vapor fuel escapes, sending odors blended with hot dust
through the synthetic wall to the passengers, odors of old sweat and age
from the upholstery.

    Magic heat, pulling tricks from an unseen hat, dwarfs
and rabbits which seem like barrels which seem like etched tornados
moving across their perspective. Appearances become their own reality,
awareness becomes a lethargic syrup and sight nothing more than fluid
used to lubricate the eyes.

    It wasn't this bad before, says Lobe, wiping palm perspiration
on his suit.

    We drove at night.

    Oh yeah, Jesus, that Tabo guy. Why would he mess up the
barrels? He's crazy, he'll get us lost for sure.

    Just drive straight north Lobe.

    Come on St. Louis!

    Straight . . .

    Crazy nuts, all of them, why do I always get the nuts?

    . . . north . . .

    Hey look! Tracks! Car tracks! That must be the way!

    That's not north. We're driving into the sun.

    Just how many cars are out here driving around in the desert
professor? There's no place to go but Tabo's and the highway.

    Brutal heat, flexing vibratory tension, ability to inflict shock
by touch, by hand or head put out the window, by pushing through the
vents and windwings, strong hot arms insinuating a sleep-like hold.

    We've driven almost thirty miles. This thing is really heating up.
Lobe, we're . . .

    Tracks got to lead somewhere

    . . . . driving . . .

    I'm the one that's crazy. . . . in circles.

    Patient heat, calm and confident in its power, unhurried as
a southern temperament, content to stand back and dryly admire its
handiwork.

    Dead car.

    Oh fuck! says Lobe. Excuse me, ma'am.

Marcus, what do we do?

I don't know. Walk, I guess.

Which way?

North.

Which way's that professor? The compass points over there.

You follow that compass, professor, but I'm sure as hell not following you. You don't know your ass . . .

Come on Aimee.

Marcus, shouldn't we all go together?

I'm going to do what the compass says. That seems the most reasonable, rational thing to do. If Lobe wants to play the proud fool, that's his business. If we start now, maybe we can make the road before nightfall.

Won't you come with us Mr. Lobe?

No. I'll go my own way.

You'll die in this heat if you're wrong. Aren't you scared of that?

He's always scared.

That your direction Chais?

Yes.

Then mine's this way. Goodbye ma'am. Thanks for everything. See you around the campus professor.

He stumbles off, Lobe filling up his cuffs with sand, jacket over his shoulder, necktie pulled down like a noose around his neck. He leaves his newspaper in the car. For a Time he will be his own awkward figure, then the sun will reduce him to a black construction, a cactus silhouette; for a Time he will be a mere immobile speck and then cursing and afraid he will join the gleaming horizon.

Let's get started, Aimee.

Walking in sand, you feel the grains work in above your shoe tops beginning their annoying insect way of causing you to remove your shoes; you feel the warmth close through your socks as each step buries your foot in a sculptural mold, threatening to cast you there mid-step in bronze. The earth moves with tiny avalanches beneath your feet. Your calves begin to knot. Is it just fatigue? Is it the sun? Suddenly, nothing is certain, not even north.

Lobe discards his coat, takes off his trousers and drapes them around his ears.

You are aware of the headache which nearly strikes out the sun, you are dizzy. Your thoughts are no longer facile and continuous, they emerge slowly before your eyes like a succession of still photographs emerging from a machine. You push forward, driven not by brain but by internal motors. Reflex. Your hand slips from your wife's, she falls. You drop beside her and sand grinds against your teeth, catches in your hair and eyebrows.

Oh Marcus, my throat, my legs . . .

We can rest. Lean against me, in my shadow.

I can't go on much longer.

I don't understand, we've been walking far too long. The road must not be far away now. It's getting later, darker, at least this heat will cool.

Lobe reaches for the afternoon mirage.

Try, Aimee, just a little farther.

Lobe claws the dark rough surface.

Aimee, get up! I think I see it!

Lobe puts his fat lips to the asphalt.

I'll carry you. Over there!

Lobe sticks out his thumb at an approaching truck.

A racing pulse, notion of a heartbeat that is yours, now hear it! And like an echo, a second beat, chasing yours, ahead behind, and then for a Time coincidental. The physical engine which operates within my frame seems so automatic that in the night when suddenly I hear it functioning smoothly I am terrified by the mere realization of its presence. What then of those moments when my machine runs in unison with another? It is curious that my sense of physical mortality induced most often by the rigors of bodily union coexists with my most real sense of immortality and freedom of the spirit.

A young man's sensibility? An old man would harken to the beating of the drum, the tattoo articulated on a muffled snare, anticipating each stroke as the last, unannounced, unforeseen, indicating the beginning of that silence when in military funerals the flag-draped coffin is lowered into the grave. A bugle sounds. I am not afraid of death.

In those moments when I lay chest heaving

beside her, I found objects from both past and future.
And she found them too, not the same ones perhaps,
but we shared together the experience of discovery. In
those times I was free enough to find strength in physical
exhaustion to forget the world and all it forced upon
me, to be someone with someone, and who it was was
unimportant, that it was Annastasia was everything.
         I do not argue that there are no other ways
to achieve such a state of mind. For some there are the
dictates of mental discipline, for others the soothing
inconsistencies of religion. But for me there was no
Time. Too much, too soon, too many worlds, inside and
outside, too many people and problems and questions
and answers, too many objects that were not me, too
many demands of selflessness. By society's esteemed
standards, I was, I am, a weakling.
         I might have found true happiness in insanity.
         The sergeant once again lifts his bugle to sound
a call. And I listen vainly for my Annastasia's heartbeat.

Frank! My hands! Blood! Dried like grease beneath my
fingernails. I can taste it, spreading brownish blood against the roof of
my mouth, feel each particle mix with my saliva and dissolve to become
liquid again.
         There is blood in my mouth, my own, coughed up in
exhaustion. And sand. Or dust? God, Frank, I can barely speak.
         How to die? To choke on the vacuum of gasping breath?
         Or to fall, slow expiration, red bubbles of thin-blown blood
appearing at my lips? Blowing bubbles, ah yes, a fitting way for the
professor to close off his final lecture. What an exit! What a finish! It is
traditional to applaud at the end of the semester.
         So . . . say farewell to your office, professor, your darkened
room. It has been like a second home to me, these four walls, this desk,
these shelves and artifacts. Nine steps by nine steps, I have paced it often,
confirming the exact dimension, eighty-one steps square. I have never really
been confined by it, restricted by the smudges on the walls. Nine steps and
I had the universe. Look up, Frank, the shadow begins before there is a
ceiling. I could set up a telescope and stare at cobwebs in the corner believing

I had discovered some unnamed nebula, some galaxy with stars strung
in diagonals and planets similar to our own. The sky here is as vast as I will it
to be, like tissue covering my brain, like the empty reaches of the desert.
  I am running, running in a circle nine steps around.
  Treadmill with sand slipping off the edges of a moving rubber
ramp; legs pumping, standing still, slowly dying, a scholar's exercise.

> *. . . acts of consequence move and remove, if*
> *one is not neutral he is for or against, if one is not zero*
> *he is plus or minus*

  Say farewell to your friends, professor. What have they been
to you? Will they mourn your passing? Come in, Frank. Sit down, Frank.
Listen, Frank, while your friend and former student rants and raves. You
taught me everything I know and gave me no answers.
  Because . . .
  Because there are none. And even that is a lie. The
mathematical proof that disproves itself. Such a waste, both of us, what a
waste of friendship. I see some island where we sit side by side cracking
coconuts, too bad we don't learn that as children.
  We do . . .
  And then forget! Goodbye, little Frankie Timmins, I'm going
out to play in the sand.
  Say farewell to your wife. I did that . . . twice, a thousand
times, every minute of every day. Farewell, dear, and pick up a carton
of milk and clean the house and change the sheets and pick me up at
five this afternoon. Love me, dear, goodbye. Why can't you be more
like I want you to be? Love equals marriage equals compromise equals
obligation equals hate, in a word, so goodbye all those times and hello
after eight months apart, and goodbye Tabo, and hello . . .
  Death! I am running in the sand and there is blood on my hands.
  And goodbye . . . Frank, don't look so pale. Suicide is against
the law, I know that. I am a good citizen, public figure, teacher and
example to the young, I don't break the law. What would people think if
I took my life? Selfish, hear them whisper, such a self-oriented man, it's
too bad, isn't it, he had no consideration for others.
  He always seemed so level-headed.
  Ego, that's what it is, these scholars and their ego.

There will be no suicide. I will just . . . vanish! How do
you explain that? Vanish! The trick no magician ever dared perform,
sweeping his satin cape from his shoulders, covering himself from top hat
to shiny shoes, and presto chango! abracadabra! gone! vanished! in a puff
of smoke, the missing wand, the evaporation of the cape itself.

Now let them whisper: he took his wife on a vacation in the
desert and never returned.

It must have been awful.

He was a good friend of yours, wasn't he, Professor Timmins?
Oh just listen!

They were recently united after a long separation.

Too bad. They wanted so to make it work this time.

> *. . . deception is its own truth, the fakir*
> *of flesh and air, the rainbow made of papier-mâché*
> *through which you could drive an angry fist should it*
> *occur to you to dare*

There is such an art to living, it requires .so much talent.

Beyond me, I'm afraid. Those extra aces seem to fall from my
sleeves, and the eggs and colored handkerchiefs. So difficult, conjuring,
so necessary. And worst of all, I fear my planned finale will go awry, only
half of me will disappear, above or below the waist, my head or just my
feet, or perhaps my hat and cape and black silk tails leaving me naked
before the outraged audience.

Failure is natural to all of us, and realization of that failure
the focus of our conscience. It's the cover-up that takes a lifetime.

Running about in the desert, Frank, naked, sand stinging me
everywhere, preparing to die, mustering up the power to vanish, shouting
all the things I know in a futile attempt to drown the wind.

In 1492, Columbus sailed the ocean blue.

$E = MC^2$

God is dead.

Et cetera.

And soon.

> *Then she was gone. Just like that.*
> *Fog, a drunken driver named Smetna who*

apologized the morning after, three hundred and six
feet of skid to be exact, gasoline slick burning off the
highway, burning off the fog, burning off her breast.
Incidentals of her death.
         I was to continue, of course, as if nothing had
happened.
         I was to continue lecturing, smiling at the
coeds in the front row, breathing. After all, I was alive
and we can't help these things and wasn't I lucky not to be
with her. Show a trim edge of grief, not too much, not too
little, no black flag of emotional anarchy, appearances,
control, be brave, be strong, be all enduring . . .
         No one saw me if I cried.
         So forgive me if here in autobiographical
solitude I indulge myself a bit.
         Shit fuck cock suck!
         Blue-balled, baby-raping Smetna, damn your
soul. Cunt of the earth!
         Oh, professor . . .
         Blow it out your ass! I miss her!

Night. The desert makes a pleasant bed, holding daylight in
to warm you like an electric sheet. She sleeps peacefully exhausted. You
cannot; the cold will come, temperature ninety degrees out of phase with
the hour, will come to awaken her to the stars each one of which appears
like headlights speeding in the distance. In the morning, which way to
go? Rested, but subject to the heat again. What to say, how to explain?
         We must have come the wrong direction, Aimee, I don't see how.
But the compass . . .
         I know. I know.
         Retrace our steps, Marcus?
         Back to the car . . . Begin again . . .
         All that way? I don't know if . . .
         After reflex comes fearful determination, conscious travel
from brain to motor: lift the leg, place it, lift the leg: the goal before you
one that is no end at all, but rather the beginning of another determined
journey, and if wrong again?
         Marcus, I just can't . . .

As if in answer a wind sweeps the desert. Sand collects
against the windows of the stalled blue Buick, against its side. Wind
in gusts recklessly crisscrossing empty space, precise sound of infinite
particle collisions, metallic splinter rain forcing shut the eyes with a
thousand tiny pressures, piercing throat and lungs with abrasive needles.

Marcus and Aimee lie together, protective embrace, sand
filling up the furrows of their clothing, expanding to a dune.

Marcus, do something.

I brought you here.

We're going to die.

What does it prove?

Please . . .

A riddle.

Marcus . . .

I know nothing.

. . . kill me!

They crawl together searching for a breath, that hollow
respite in which to say all the things left unsaid. The wind throws knives
like a circus man, perfect cuts on their hands and scalp. They vomit sand.

It would be so easy . . . Kill me, please!

> *. . . wild birds rising from retreating mirage,
> soundless, glistening wings, shimmering lines clearing
> your maddened vision, a diamond beacon glowing coal
> black in the light, first saliva on your lips, first pulsebeat
> stirring your baked blood, first impulse in your brain
> of molten circuits, the first if not the last*

Quick, fast, better than Time's slow wearing, better than
petrification by the sun.

Ritual murder, sacrifice, yes, Aimee, I did a paper on it once.
Frank pointed out a glaring error in my research.

Marcus, I want to die!

He rolls into the wind, groping in his pockets for keychain
and pearl-handled knife.

Frank, I learned from you. Now I know how to kill!

He spreads her hair, her arms; he opens the blade and slits
her clothing to expose her bosom.

I love you, Aimee.

He grasps the handle, placing his other palm behind the hilt, he raises his arms together high above his head, back arched, then bending precipitously down, sudden, swift, he drives the knife into the center of her breast, between the ribs, with force to penetrate her heart.

Marcus! The cry dies-her hands raise up two streams of sand as if in offering.

. . . ritual expiation . . .

Marcus twists the knife, opening a purple wound. For an instant she moves beneath him until her eyes dulled say he has been merciful.

He stands and begins to run, lost and then found, a new piece of the wind's debris, he runs ever-widening circles in the storm, with his last breath, expending it, he screams.

Tabo! I remember!

He runs into abstraction.

Change!

A mental dissolve.

Motion!

Dervish in so quick a spin he seems to vanish.

Aimee!

Gone, invisible, the speed of light, in dislocated focus, with a life's blood drying on his hands . . .

The truck driver looks over at his passenger.

This guy hasn't stopped talking since I picked him up.

. . . the barrels you see they lied, they'd all been moved around . . .

The driver recalls newspaper articles he has read, considers his No Riders sign.

I'll kill him if he tries anything!

. . . the car stalled . . . lost . . . Chais . . . north . . . I found . . . you won't believe . . . I'm going to St. Louis. Oh, shit, pinch me, I must be dreaming . . .

amura

Pale yellow: electrum threads interlaid in pattern, two to
one, one to two, one to one to one, circuits of overlapping squares, levels
interlocked yet independent. On a chart they would appear just simple
lines, without impulse, devoid of power, characterless. But touch them
together, see sparks fly, rolling friction split off like bits of fire, protons,
positrons, electrons, charged to explosion, conductors of scientific passion.

Gentlemen, I am instructed to program entertainments for
mental warfare against our enemies. Our superiors are pleased with
our progress but now direct us to forgo further research and begin what
they consider more practical applications. We are so ordered, shall we
begin? Amura will remain as supervisor of normal operations, Becktold
and Seline will join me in individual attempts to develop an optimum
method. That will be all, thank you.

Becktold paces his office. He has developed the image gun,
a device able to throw a stream of projections, sight and sound, selected
from all history in irrational order, thus able to disarm an enemy through
the intensity of entertainment. He sees rebellion quenched by image
assassination, leaders stunned to silence by a burst of projections, their
milling followers herded by the threatening weapon into camps where
all thoughts of revolt and insurrection are erased by more subdued
applications of the same principle. Bit by bit all pockets of resistance are
discovered, resisters hidden underground come out singing when exposed
to the light of the image gun.

Current passed through a circuit induces current in another;
emotive action and reaction, brought about not by nature alone but by
ordained proximity.

He holds the gun in his hands, feels the metal grips, the
balance, the vibration. He pans the barrel in a circle, until he finds the
target. The simple sights align with Marcus Chais.

A trigger pulled, heady light, a man sees through the mirror
to the myriad reflections, not of him but of a hundred other men, in
costume, loincloth and ruffled sleeve, breastplate, fiberglass. They are
talking all at once and with a simple turn of head their friends come
into view, their mothers and their fathers, teachers, hated enemies
approaching. Their coffins close with voices still heard muted by wood
and brass screws turning, dressed in black the entire multitude follows

to the grave, the ocean bed, the beehive tomb, the hole in clay, lace
mourning, top hats glistening in the mist. Voices, faces like ants foraging
in the earth, finding empty eyes now entranceways to the anthill of the
brain. The brain, that is the target, guardian of control and knowledge,
the ants must crawl through tunnels of bone to that center suspended in
soft fluid, they must crawl and swim and dig into the tissue so that the
costumed host, the dead men and all their reflected families can enter
in and overpower the guardian with the color of their dress and the
babble of their shouted conversation. Increase the field, make certain the
efficacy of attack, release the trigger.

He is entertained, Becktold asserts. I shall lead, he tells the
empty office.

How is it coming, Becktold?
Fine, Professor Chais. And your research?
It progresses. Why are you laughing, Seline?
I am just enjoying your little competition, Marcus.
You're sure you are up to it.
Oh yes, very sure.

Resistance or conductivity, a matter of approach, whether
to free or accelerate the life blood's blow. By either means a circuit can
achieve the same end: equal source, equivalent result, only the in-
between is manipulated by the technician's fingers.

Seline perfects his irony tent. It is a decorated mobile unit,
traveling around the country with music blaring from loudspeakers,
projections thrown against buildings and window glass, drawing people
to it through natural curiosity. Inside, the projections are more grand,
they are taken from the most ironic historic events, wars fought for
absurd reasons, murders committed over nothing, the horrendous
consequences of history's petty jealousies and rivalries, shown with such
accuracy and completeness, with such sound and vivid color, that the
audiences respond with laughter as the human folly is revealed. Then
the irony tent turns in upon itself, re-creating for all to see the madness
of the audience, their bickering and pride, their disputes with neighbors
sitting a row or two away, their blind patriotic allegiance, their irrational
adherence to faith. The laughter increases until the audience loses all
memory of what they are or were despite its dramatization before them.
The experience does not repress them or overwhelm them, but rather
liberates them through purifying laughter. In the unforgettable instant

in Seline's hysterical tent, the inhibitions and foibles of humanity are
stripped away and they are entertained.

Calliopoetic music is playing in the park where Amura
walks. Through the trees she sees the flying bunting and painted figures
running across the bright metal sections of the tent. She joins the crowd,
pays her admission fee, is seated beneath the domed projection screen.
The show begins with a political murder, the hot-blooded student waving
his pistol in the air, grappling with those who have apprehended him.
After two shots fired into the be-ribboned chest of a prince, flames
fill the dome with a thousand burning crosses, burning cities, burning
bodies, food is burned while millions starve, men die fighting for peace,
demagogues shout, accused witches scream. At first there is shock, but
then a laugh, a guffaw from across the tent, picked up nearby, louder,
passing through them all like a virus until Amura too loses her control
and joins, tears streaming down her cheeks, her lungs choked with
rippling laughter. Two women fight for a man on the screen, fingernails
cutting bloodlines on their breasts; they are trampled by iron men,
round horns blowing, colliding with impact splintering sound; a man
holds a child's head underwater, a flag is raised to cheers, and then the
dome is filled with laughing faces looking downward at laughing faces
looking upward, the audience mated with itself, each seeing himself as a
screaming woman or a wild-eyed student; each one seeing himself.

The lights go out, the laughter does not cease.

Amura sees Seline and Marcus in the committee room, she
sees her admiration for them and their obvious attempts to earn her
admiration. She sees herself nurture their rivalry, her hands touching
them as they work, her desire to possess them only as objects to be
possessed. Her laughter multiplies, the facets of her life spread out upon
the dome in all their tiny splendor, her eyes close, she can stand it no
longer, she must see more, she sees everything, she sees nothing all at
once, her mind is laughter, that is entertainment.

Yes Marcus, I'm sure my system will surpass Becktold's.

Good, Seline, very good indeed.

Induction, churning dynamo, whatever the source of
electromotive force, effective circuits must be complete, not open-ended
broken circles, they must be closed, closed and individual.

Marcus Chais at his desk: your little competition he said to
me. What are we competing for?

He takes his pen and makes a list of names in his notebook. There are only four: Becktold, Seline, Amura and his own. His design, his application, his weapon is there inscribed. He founds The Circle.

Science is illusion? he writes at the bottom of the page before he puts the book away.

Pale yellow: electrum threads, pattern disrupted, relationship undone by joining all the terminals together until many circuits become one and the current flows frictionless and unhindered. Unified but useless, by an act of will, the circuits remove themselves from the machine; they are discarded and, yes, destroyed.

An old man is expected to learn patience from the lessons of his years. Dunce man standing in the corner, a second's tardiness sends chills rolling beneath my fingernails and traffic is madness, I detest the thought of Annastasia shopping, I have a physical abhorrence to standing in a line.

But more importantly I have lost all patience with our leaders, limping with the progress of a wounded snail though the generations; their maneuverings with the press and daily legislation, their exposed conflicts of interest and cronyism and their manipulation of information have pushed me beyond all concern with my so-called responsibility as a citizen. Age and the pile-up of experience and disillusionment and cynicism have freed me from the notion of respectability. I have become aware of the community of the night, no more, no less, than the one by day. Guilty people fear the night as an environment they cannot control with their inside politics and laws and patronage. Night-Time is yes or no, black or white, no lengthening shadow of middle grey, it is war or peace. Daylight has its subtle violence, muggings and flashing knives, all covered in veneer, some hastily painted coating of legitimacy and order. Daylight is clever, more circumspect, less honest.

Consider: the squeeze, take-over credit interest, the broker and his criminal commissions, the lawyer and the law, planned obsolescence and high-rise drugs, the ad man playing the age-old game with pea and shells of chrome, union leaders, congressmen, pocketsful of dues and campaign extortions, millionaires who pay no taxes, God's church and real estate . . .

Just to name a few . . .

Day people try to sleep at night but take pills to assassinate their dreams.

Sometimes they dance till dawn.

I am backed into revolution's corner.

But the pity is, I am too old to be the revolutionary, perhaps too guilty.

The system perpetuates itself, involving all our youth, until conscience prohibits us from being honest for fear of playing hypocrite. It is our own pathetic form of honesty, I suppose, excusing guilt with helplessness and realizing our limitations by not being the first man forward in the march toward something we know is right.

I stand for a whole generation that will not be embarrassed by past mistakes. No accusation, just fact.

I stand for a whole generation of bomb-throwing innocents who must change the world.

I stand for an old man who, as much as he may wish it, cannot hide his confusion and impatience in the sand.

What? Who? Have I been sleeping? Yes, yes, and the machine still turns throughout all my dreams. It is as if some diabolic surgeon has left the microphone inside me, wedged into a hidden cranny of the lung. I speak into it, I sleep, nothing is omitted, nothing erased. Bury the recording in the ground and one thousand years from now an archeologist like myself will find it, hold it up before the amazed eyes of his colleagues and declare: this was a man.

But he will hear many voices, many men and women. The Circle has now met and surely the end is near. We will be discovered. It is only a matter of Time, man's most precious scale. Time means nothing to the machine which reverses automatically to make its history endless and eternal. When we are gone, the machine will turn, perhaps recording a new individual, perhaps recording nothingness. Who knows?

Strange that all our science is devoted to the past. Have we reached that point in the progress of mankind when there is nowhere to go but backwards, no new goals to attain or worlds to conquer? The future remains a mystery; there appears no way forward. My computers allow us to wander through the silent ruins of the past, covered with white dust as if the bones of all men have been trampled beneath the boots of those who followed after.

We might as well be dead.

Is that the purpose of entertainment, to teach us how to live again?

The committee to choose the ultimate weapon has of course convened. The furor was to be expected, I suppose, given the brilliance of Becktold and Seline. I disqualified myself, claiming that the two most efficient systems possible had been developed by my associates and that if the committee was still set on a destructive application of the entertainment theory the choice was between the two presented.

They asked for my recommendation.

I had expected the question, but still I did not know what to reply, and so equivocated with flair and competence, veiling my opinions in such a way it was impossible to tell exactly where I stood on the matter. Becktold's trick. The chairman was upset. Attuned to my usual outspokenness, he had expected me to make his decision for him. In the past, I would have most emphatically, but the Circle had begun to tighten itself about me, all habits and former characteristics overturned.

Becktold was selected. He was instructed to form a team to perfect and construct the image gun in mass quantities as soon as possible. He was ecstatic and made one of his most sensational speeches in acceptance before the committee.

But still . . . he joined us this evening.

As for me, well, Becktold's appointment meant quasi-retirement. The emphasis was on application instead of theory, and I was the theoretician. My computers were reprogrammed to Becktold's purposes. Amura and Seline remained with me, along with a single volume computer block and the required technicians.

It was release.

We decided to apply our theory to our own entertainment, using visions to experience whatever events or periods in history struck our fancy. Amura, for example, was interested in tracing the history of female dress in the third millennium, while Seline set about the discovery of the most humorous story ever told. I plunged into my notebooks and diary to review the development of the entire theory, step by step, day by day, re-creating that most recent history for my amusement through recollection, writings, and of course the computer's documentary vision of its own birth.

I needed rest. Change. Too many of my years had been passed in rooms lit by solar transfer light with computer spinnings in my ears. I had lost contact with the outer life, with my own environment. I decided to prepare an expedition, the purpose of which was merely to allow me to leave the research strata and become a normal man again. I decided to put myself and my theory to a test. I reached back into the past for an actuality which although known had never been fully envisioned by the computer. I reached far back to make my task that much more impossible and settled on the middle first millennium city of Bel which was mentioned at length in an ancient journal first observed by Seline in a vision of the destruction of a university library during the second faulting of the earth. If I could find that city . . .

The only failure of entertainment was its inability to re-create an event to which there was no witness. If there was no account, written or narrative, no description to be banked with the computer, then although we might know the existence of the happening, we could not create it in vision. In many cases, knowledge had taken us to the edge of an event, and no farther. We stood there then like helpless soldiers, knowing that across a range of mountains a tremendous battle was taking place and that the crevices and jagged peaks would make it forever inaccessible.

Earth faultings are excellent examples of such events. The first faulting is so named because there was no survivor to tell us what existed previously. Man, naturally enough, has called this first faulting the Creation. The second faulting might just as well have been the first, except for the miraculous escape of twenty-seven hundred persons, mostly scientists in orbiting laboratories, who lived not only to describe the devastation but also to begin the repopulation of the earth. From their personal accounts and from the films, photographs and other scientific data they collected, we have been able to put together a fairly complete vision of the second faulting. It was in this vision that we discovered the existence of Bel.

The journal's story was not finished. At a point in its history, the narrative was interrupted and the emptiness of the following pages was all we knew of the fate of that marvelous city. No other mention of it could be found, a beginning and an open end. Fascinating!

The machine knows all, the microphone is nothing but an extension of myself, dylic tongue, snytheticon brain. I must be honest. There was another reason for my concentration on the problem of Bel: the journal's creator, my namesake, Marcus Chais! The development of the entertainment program had accustomed me, to be sure, to the incredible circumstance and coincidence of history. I was used to the cycles and oval vibrations of populo-historical relations. But when I discovered a person who spoke to me with my own name from some thousands of years gone, it was as if my own being had staged a coup and set up some other demagogue in Control. My science had defined me to such perfection, that there was no aspect of myself of which I was not aware. And yet across the measurable span of time had come just a name, my name, just a man confiding to his journal his thoughts, himself. I asked the unheard-of question: was that man me?

> *. . . answers teem within the den of snakes, knotted, intertwined, the heads with all the fangs exposed, coiled to devour the inquisitive tail, so many answers filled with venomous overflow enough to poison a question's conception*

We departed, Amura and I, with six technicians and the calculator packs, transmitters, and vacuums. Seline remained behind to receive our information relays, assimilate them, and retransmit to us the additional clues provided by the computer. We had isolated the probable location of Bel to the two hundred and seventh quadrant, an area of many thousand miles, mostly basalt debris and sand scattered by the explosions of the fourth faulting. We began a systematic probing of the crust to depths of one half a mile, and bit by bit we were able to outline two prime vacuuming sites, squares of land that seemed most likely to contain the object of our search. Amura selected the smaller of the two to begin. Seline radioed he had designated the active site MC Square for programming purposes. The vacuuming process began.

Our life out in that vastness was incredibly peaceful. The
silence was so great that even the steady whirring of the vacuums was
soon dissipated, unheard in the emptiness. Amura took long, aimless
walks, picking her way across the rocks, taking samples when she felt
inclined, dreaming her dreams. I sat in the shadow of the residence dome
and kept my diary. Alone there, I thought a good deal about Marcus
Chais.

In my baggage I had a small vial of nescient syrup. It was
of course outlawed centuries ago and strict punishments have kept its
manufacture to almost zero. I had learned of it while a student, the
recipe was widely known, but use was confined to a very small number
among us who one by one seemed to drop from our midst without
explanation. I had never experimented with nescient and knew of its
effects only from the rather inarticulate descriptions of these individuals.
In a vision recently I had watched a young medical student mix the
syrup. I had copied down the formula.

Why? In the interest of science? Curiosity? I had no idea. Nor did
I know what had motivated me to activate the mixture myself to produce
the clear heavy liquid I knew was just a few yards from me in my kit.

> *. . . gravity, compulsion, a river flows*
> *uphill, levers pulled to upset all the explanations, man*
> *floats weightless in the water, in the air, in the mind,*
> *compulsion, impetus, movement, reaction, reasons exist,*
> *but why*

Two voices spoke to me, my own, strangely different, and
the gasp of that earlier Chais, no longer limited to his aged journal,
almost uncovered, almost revealed, his words just slightly muffled by the
centuries of sand and gravel that still kept him from me. The voices came
and went, in exposition and debate, a symposium to which I was invited
sitting in an empty hall and seeing no participants upon the stage. I was
receiving instructions from them, from myself and beyond myself, my
awkward questions implying sophisticated responses of which I had no
understanding. In that peaceful setting, a mental upheaval was taking place.

Machine, if there was a moment when I changed, it was then
skimming through the pages of my notes when I saw my own inquiry:
science is illusion? The phrase centered before my eyes, the voices joined

to repeat it like a ritual chant, and for the first time myself I said those words aloud as fact.

Professor Chais! came the cry from the site. We have discovered something!

Amura ran across the sand, I left my protective shadow, hastening to see.

It was an ancient auto with a pitted blue roof.

> *Politics: I stand lost within the total complex of relations among men. I vote and my candidates do not win. I speak and no one hears my voice. I act and my actions are lost to the counter-balance of other actors.*
>
> *My window on the world is filled by men attempting to persuade me to join them, follow their way, their way not our way, join them, not together.*
>
> *If I reach out to grasp my brother's hand, his brother strives to knock us down.*
>
> *If I aid my neighbors to the detriment of my neighbor, I create an enemy far greater than those created by standing still.*
>
> *But if I live with self-interest alone, my head bent down over my belly to narsuckle myself, then I am equal to all the others, and I begin to find the way, out of the labyrinthian complex of relations among men, kicking, biting, clawing, killing or being killed, surviving with no one else beside myself in mind.*
>
> *No one beside myself . . .*
>
> *I had Annastasia; like parentheses, enclosing nothing between us except the space we wished, coming closer and closer together through the years until our boundaries touched, we became an entity in ourselves and all the other complexities among men were forgotten.*
>
> *No politics: except the parlor games we played.*
>
> *It was, you see, no more complicated than that, and in such simplicity, approached perfection.*

Touch: first.

Immediate.

She is paper flesh unrolled and I sit naked, cross legged beside her, drawing with my finger an oriental calligraph. It is to my poem that she responds, gains dimension like some balloon inflated by the whispering breath of my recital. She swells, becomes, breasts find form, knees are knees, recognizable, a woman, a name, Amura, beside me.

What is it? I struggle to ask the question in this final lucid moment. What made us pour out the syrup and sip hungrily? I must analyze the feeling: muscular consciousness, a black sphere in the stomach, transfer of Control from brain to the central knot which holds the limbs together. Soon how irrelevant it all will be, the nescient syrup has begun its work.

Soon.

Now.

I sit tracing an oriental sign. The tip of my finger runs lightly over her, sometimes a bit of flesh pinches between tip and nail leaving a fine white line, my poem engraved then erased as blood rushes to fill the inscription. She expands, breasts to pools, her wide stomach the ocean, waters flowing with rushing force to the spring. I stand, she and the seas and the bedclothes diminish to topography seen from mile-high perspective, fast cloud shadows, storms, warm winds blowing in circular pattern, the world turning a recurrent human landscape.

Apogee: the air is thin.

Enough idle drawing, enough rhyme. I fly above her.

I dive.

Then: light

My eyes are the beginning and there is no end. I see a limitless V, lying in all planes, upright, horizontal, in the sudden objective realization of Time's fourth dimension, I fall.

Fall . . . toward her so far away, so close, rise and fall, are we coupled?

Color streaks in all directions, velocity driving them downward into lines, blending momentarily, making combinations, then seeking to fuse again, to reproduce in half another combination. A slow process, so slow my rate of fall. We will collide, she and I, before all the colors achieve the ultimate mating and create black, the spectrum's child of darkness.

A ship rides the ocean, all sails tightly furled to the yards, a frothy wake, a lively progress, I am man o' war.

Cumulus painted like a circus wagon, drifting balloons collide like rubber kisses. Streamers fly, and bunting, and: sound—the wind blows by my ears like breath across a bottle snout.

Can eyes hear? ears see? Can all the senses be swallowed and digested?

Foghorns, and singing stays etched on my vision, swirling greys, high vibrating pinks. Through the optic nerve and auditory canal, through the blood and digestive track, experience comes and now I begin to feel again its center, muscular consciousness, the tight black sphere, where all is concentrated into a pressure demanding release, as if all the cumulative force of so many entrances were directed against the inadequate restraint of a single exit. It is building, but unimportant when its small tantalizing pleasure is put against the poetry heard by my ears, the songs before my eyes, the touch and taste of my descending brain.

It is building, is collision imminent?

The sailing ships and balloons change tack and I with them, aligned to their direction and drift, back and forth we glide, my arms outstretched to catch the void, my face prow-like splitting sensation into colorful spray. If there is to be an abrupt ending to our journey I have no way of knowing for there is no floating seaweed, no lone bird flying a determined course, nothing but crewless ships and a man in blue in a gondola with a telescope.

Marcus!

I heard a cry. A bird? A fish?

A tremor passes, the waves lift higher, the sea turns devouring, turns to extended flame, a sea of oil, of heat thrown upward. The furled sails burn to black lace fringe hanging like mourning veils, the silken cords part to drop the gondolas into flame. The man in blue is gone, but out of the inferno I feel him looking on, looking perhaps in the confusion of his death through the wrong end of his glass, but seeing me still as I plunge toward what was once a placid surface, what is now an angry sea.

Marcus! Marcus!

Hear it again? Exploding balloons? Spars snapped by the wind? Is the idyll over? Am I to be consumed?

Fire is crawling along my feet, feeding its way upward, bone marrow throwing sparks and stars. There is no impact, no shattering collision after all, I do not hit her like a raindrop striking glass. No, her

flames and mine join, we are reversed images come together, a united
light seen in V-shaped mirrors, two-sided, connected, and as the distance
between us decreases, identical. Her surface passes through mine, we are
unconfined and flow like liquids poured together, molten, translucent, as
if we are suspended in each other, below the flesh, in the mind. I see her
face, I see mine, she is balloon, I am man o' war, she is water, I am air,
we are fire, we are everything together.

I groan. It is like a handle to grab on to, a nail driven in the
heart. It wakens me, I return as the black sphere explodes in shuddering
contractions. My free fall is done.

What remains?

Touch: light: sound: simple, so simple that in our time we
had almost forgotten.

She is sleeping, her breasts in my hands, smooth like some
costly alloy.

Amura, wake up.

She stirs and turns to look at me.

Marcus, what have we done.

> *What of the Timmins' outside world?*
> *. . . scum on polluted rivers, pesticides,*
> *bulldozers in the wilderness, useless dams, dead fish*
> *like decomposed trash along the shore, oil slicks and*
> *blackened birds, yellow curtain of the air, sulphuric acid*
> *in the blood of grazing sheep, and the child whose lungs*
> *filled up in the classroom of PS 139 . . .*
> *I remember the path up Mt. Anne, so steep to*
> *my young eyes, where trees grew horizontally from the*
> *slope like park benches on which to gather gasping breath.*
> *A night passed there, halfway to the top, suspended you*
> *in a woven bag of darkness, like a cocoon hanging in the*
> *rhododendron, with drops of water along its bottom edge*
> *suggesting iridescence from the absent moon. And danger*
> *lurked, the cry of the wild mountain lawnmower,*
> *spinning rotaries hidden beneath its fur, cutting down*
> *the mountainsides, scars across the virgin forests, and*
> *sometimes shaving the heads of frightened little boys.*
> *I remember casting a fly-line into the wind,*

*after my first trout, the hook gaining more than an
insect's significance when its barb stung my scalp
and the line settled about my ears. It was early in the
season, the old-timers said the fish weren't rising
yet, late thaw that year, how clever I thought I was
when I tied on a Peter's Pride and felt my quarry tug
provocatively on the line. I lost that first fish,
as I have lost most since.*

*I remember a short draw, edged in small
trees, filled with tall dead weeds. Our dog went in,
disappeared except for the sound of breaking grass,
then reappeared, ears spread like wings, jaws closing
behind the tail feathers of a desperate pheasant, one fat
and sassy bird, not more than ten yards away, and then,
by God, a second scooting up with his chattering call.
I was so startled I could not lift my gun. My friend, a
fine sportsman, fired once, and fired again, both birds
gone in the trees, leaving behind a cherished image,
"The Double," a classic illustration in an outdoorsman's
journal. We looked at one another and grinned. The dog
returned with that reproachful look so essential to
a hunting dog with a less than perfect master.*

*I remember my first fence post, pulled laughingly
and easily from the ground by a visiting veterinarian.*

*I remember stalls I constructed reduced to
splinters by the horses with the same enthusiasm of old
boys at a fraternity initiation.*

I remember a garden full of dead zucchini.

*I remember an absurd attempt to make
love to Annastasia inside an Army mummy sack.*

*My outside world is inside, inside my
memory where it exists, has existed, will exist as
perfectly and naturally as I can make it. There are no
failures. My outside world is filled with fond sentimental
remembrances of success.*

Computer reaction time exceeds of course that of the
human brain. Early experiments measured the span of realization within

the standard human cerebrum in terms of milli-disequents, a crude, awkward unit in any type of contemporary calculation. But although we can surpass the brain's speed mechanically, we have yet to be able to re-create the phenomenon of understanding. Machines act without comprehension of what they do. Despite centuries of misgivings, man has remained the master of both his creation and his potential.

For example, during the early sections of the current modern echelon, certain small groups appeared, comprised of technicians, led by a few irresponsible philosophers, who subscribed to the now forgotten tenets of cyber-aestheticism. Their belief was the theory of man's essential inferiority to his own mechanical constructions. They were forever pointing to the contradiction between progress and scientific domination, holding that acts in the name of the former implied the latter, and that there would be a future time when the implication would become obvious and Paradox would occur, the cataclysmic end of the world. Elaborate theories evolved, equating the patterns of history with the patterns of the nervous system with the patterns of computer cybernetics, and when overlaps were discovered, they were isolated as micro-paradoxes, the symmetry of which was found aesthetically pleasing and meaningful, indeed as an object of worship.

Machine, I tell you this knowing you already know. But does it not point out the danger of too little knowledge? Those revolutionaries were apprehended and incinerated. Pity. They were made the wrong kind of example and thus we had underground cultists practicing cyber-aestheticism illegally for decades. Why not have allowed them to exist openly and multiply until in the dizziness of an expanded following and ballooning ego they permitted their folly to take its logical and limited end, the proclamation that on a forthcoming date terrible Paradox would destroy as no faulting could presume. The day would have passed and with it the philosophy, the movement, with all its leaders and disciples and hangers-on. The absurdity of their conclusion would have risen and set with the sun and again it would have been evident to those with the eyes to see that man's ideas themselves are inferior to his capacity to manifest them and that the mystery of this creation should be the object of his study in the full understanding that it is incomprehensible.

The acquisition of knowledge is an open-ended task. It is never complete. No man is ever educated. There is no danger of too much knowledge. And any system that within its framework encourages conclusions, proofs and finality is counter to the eternal stream and therefore false.

Science is illusion.

But the blue Buick was not.

Slowly we vacuumed around it, revealing its primitive sculptural curves. Time had not been easy on its cheap metal, the chrome trimmings were riddled with rust, the tires had slowly disintegrated as if buried in that sand they had kept on running at high speed. We pried open the engine cover and looking down at that child-like experiment in propulsion we laughed and joked.

Amura pulled open the door. The windows had been sealed by sand. The air inside was older than any of us, was undoubtedly the fuel and waste of the former occupants, whoever among men had abandoned the vehicle in the emptiness of the past. The air escaped with the feeble enthusiasm of a prisoner held in solitary confinement for many years. There was a distinct odor, an unsubtle combination of staleness and sweetness that would certainly provide us with a clue to the strange circumstances of our discovery. I had a technician take several aroma samples for Seline to process.

I had come to find a medieval city of the first echelon and what was my prize! We encased the Buick for transfer to the research strata and I ordered the crew to continue the search.

I kept the side-view mirror. Amura had leaned against the mount, which rotted through had broken. I turned the mirror over and over in my hands, I looked at my reflection.

The droning vacuums filled my mind, shifting debris from the collection sacks to medulla and frontal lobe. Something was being buried there, in exchange for the uncovering of the car, that simple revelation, something that was mine was being put down into an arid grave and covered over for all time.

Amura seemed to know.

We will find Bel, Marcus.

She walked around the site, sometimes talking with the men, sometimes sitting on the rim of our ever-widening dig, sifting sand through her fingers as if adding her own strength and determination to my search.

We will find Bel together.

Seline sent her a note: Amura, mind your R's and Z's.

We both might well have taken his advice.

Nescient syrup had become for us more than just a novelty or way to pass the time. At night in the privacy of the residence dome, we satisfied a need growing faster than the rate of human cells. We lost Control. Our bodies took on importance. We rubbed each other with creams to soothe the dryness of the sun; that in and of itself became a ritual, our hands moving over sectors of our bodies in strict order, bringing relief to a hierarchy of secret places. And then we would pour nescient from the vial to a drinking cup, hold it to the light in some senseless gesture of libation before we would pass it between us in a series of small sips, prolonging the pleasure of consumption, and when the dosage was exhausted, finding the only remnant of the taste on the other's lips.

We were neither passive nor detached. We were violent, using and torturing one another in unimagined ways. Sometimes together, sometimes alone, most times our pleasure in ourselves and in each other was so great that writhing and slamming our urinary organs together was no outlet and it was our orgiastic release to arch our coupled bodies back and away like mated horseshoe magnets and merely scream with all our power.

The technicians in the neighboring domes could not help but overhear. Of course, there were Controllers among them.

But the sights and sensations we shared were so tremendous we knew no fear. By day it was all we could do to conceal our desire for the night when the mystery of nescient would be revealed.

Yes, there were two searches. And then they became one.

The day was overcast, almost cool. I was taking my shift at the vacuum nozzle, slowly drawing it across the search segment. It was a boring, uninspiring task, but I felt it best to participate so as not to further alienate the crew. The discovery alarm was on automatic, it would warn me should anything appear.

I must have been very far away, in some fantasy or perhaps savoring the memory of previous nights. The shouting brought me to. Technicians stood above me, calling my name in competition with the loud siren. The vacuum nozzle had not only uncovered stone, my revery had allowed it to outline what seemed to be the foundation of a building.

Bel!

How we worked! Right through the night. All the vacuums going under my direct supervision. Rock by rock, it took shape. We

found a crude arch, the entrance of course, then followed the walls
around until we had a large square. As we deepened, ovals appeared,
domes, some staved in by the weight of sand, some incredibly intact.
We had found it! A storage house or possibly an inn? Certainly just the
beginning of our ultimate restoration of the entire city!

Everything was forgotten in the moment: introspection,
nescient, Control. Amura was just another fervent worker. And the
work went well.

Finally the edifice stood around us, crumbling walls, the
standing arch and domes, doorways of petrified wood hung to iron-red
hinges. Amura and I pushed our way into each empty chamber. We
found nothing. No pottery or shards, no hearth, no sign of makeshift
bed. Was this Bel? No trace of industry, no treasure, nothing. I was
incredulous, fearful that after all we had failed.

Another large, seemingly vacant room was entered. Yes!

There was something! In the corner, woven strands, frail
threads of material, colored and interlaid in pattern, quite deep in
layers as if objects covered by the cloth had been piled on one another.
And then, the justification for all our labors: there in the center with
splintered ends protruding slightly from the level of the floor, perfectly
preserved, were bones! A human skeleton!

How carefully we swept, peeling away the dirt like dead skin.
The ribcage was mostly crushed, the pelvis broken, muscles, tendons, the
human dust mixed with the sand we so delicately brushed aside. And the
strangest thing of all—beneath the bones, as if chiseled into the floor
below, we saw a symbol, nine-sided, a sign of some weird sort impeccably
fossilized in stone!

Amura and I looked into it, we were dizzy, vertiginous;
it seems absurd to say but the symbol danced before our eyes. In our
confusion we understood, our questions answered without explanation,
and under the harshness of the excavation lights and the shocked stares
of the men, we embraced.

Machine, I don't know any more than that. I've told you all.
Nescient had perhaps left some molecule of fantasy circulating in our
blood, it may have been too much work or sun, I just don't know except
that it happened without thought to consequences.

Machine, you know enough to have me dead.

It was not possible to measure the duration of our embrace.

And my inside world? Shall we listen in?
. . . insurance paid now or later and to whom,
now my beneficiary is dead, where or when, great God,
the forms to fill, three bags full, and then the two-year
warranty on a broken heart, planned obsolescence on
boy meets girl, I have no license to love, but I have an
honorary degree, and my sky is peopled with police and
old friends with bayonets and martial music running
through their heads like water through stone, hard
rock and country and Mother and America and logical
positivism, philosopher stones thrown at a hairy group
of Christ-like coyotes, radioactive not to be taken
internally, like patriotism, keep from the reach of the
young and healthy, feed on yourself, .04% riboflavin,
.09% iron, .62% Vitamin A, 98.44% sawdust, half
humans hanging on a hook, sirloin and grind the tail,
magic for the children of interlocking directorates and
old war films, plumber, I cannot pay $13 an hour to fix
a faucet, electrician, can you replace the fuse through
which the force drives the flower, general, what shall
we do with all these dead, terminate with prejudice,
he said, or bury them, or think of the men who tripped
and stumbled on the moon, were they me? or you? how
much shall we tip them, with immortality if you please,
if we sell the car and buy the boat and take a loan and up
the mortgage, if we cut out welfare and close the schools
starve the children and then forget, if we arm ourselves
with hydra-headed sticks and stones and talk loud and
wave the flag, if we stand tall and make speeches about
all mankind, people, I don't know, I just get hemorrhoids
and sick at heart and credit cards in the mail, you can
charge a funeral, hers, yours, my own, all of us . . . .
My inside world is outside all around me,
where it flounders amidst the true world's innumerable
realities.

Seline spreads the computer schematic on the table.
Thanks for coming, Becktold, something I thought you

should see. Quite a glitch, something in the duodenum transfer, I think. Smoke poured out the anal-lytic output slot when I programmed this design Professor Chais found in the desert.

What's he doing out there! With his help I could have the configuration of tread-mounted image power completed by now.

Get this thing fixed and I'll show you what he's doing. All right. I think we should run a tracer through the intestunnel. You program. Why would something as simple as this design make it blow? Chais always comes up with something.

Then through the intercom: try it now.

Seline taps the keys, establishing the ingest coordinates, then serves the design to the machine.

And within? the digits tremble in the cold, the printed circuits melt to flow inky black over color code, connectors vibrating toward nervous breakdown, bellows of info filling with fluid.

Seline! Pull the plug!

The impulse pump sticks a valve, micron tubing brittle, hard, as nine sides are compressed into one, and in the core of conclusion syllogisms arc and burn dispostulated.

I've never seen anything like it! What has he found?

He doesn't know and we can't seem to tell him. A precedent to my knowledge, an impressive one at that. Here, it appears, is something we cannot know. Incredible, isn't it?

Impossible!

Hilarious! Here after all this time is a fact that spoils our theory. The computer cannot envision it. Someone first drew the sign but where is he? Where is his grinning face on the screen? Where are those he showed it to, who for echelons have viewed it and wondered about it and watched it do to them something like it has done to our machine? Oh yes, Becktold, wonderfully strange, very funny indeed!

There must be some error.

None! Prepare yourself, put down the design and I think I can show you where the beginning is. For me, well, a search of mine is over, I've found the most humorous story ever told and can't tell you truly what it is except that the joke is on us and Chais and lovely Amura, we're all characters in the tale and should be laughing loudest. Becktold, let's share a vision together.

They strap into reclining chairs. Seline adjusts the

viewfinder. The screen flickers, takes an image, fades, takes an image once again.

Two large ovals and a supporting rod secured in a slotted base, a giant stanchion bolted to the floor sustaining mammoth weight above. Motion, the support intrudes slowly into the slot with the careful precision of an hydraulic piston, the rod extracts, wet with some clear lubricating grease, the large ovals rise and begin lateral movement, swinging in an arc, rotating in a circle, down again, and careful examination reveals the slot is flexible about the opening and surrounded by fine wire brushing, up again, down, to the dictates of a timing device installed inside the two modules suspended from the rod's base.

What is this, Seline! Some first echelon industrial device?

The vision curves.

Those are humans!

A steady progress up the spine to pan across shoulders and then a head to uncover another head beneath. Heavy breathing is the sound.

Amura!

Her teeth close on a portion of her lips, her hand passes in an unfocused blur across the screen to light on . . . on nothing, her eyes open staring unaware of an audience.

What's happening to her? What's she doing?

Her twisting head, dampened hair, the vision of a scream, the cry from the loudspeakers: Marcus!

Chais, Seline, Professor Chais!

Laugh now Becktold.

What is amusing? What is it?

It happens each night in the residence dome, they remove their garments and this occurs. Intercoursing, it is called, a primitive form of communication that had widespread use throughout the early echelons. Ridiculous, isn't it? The first form of human reproduction, regarded as sacrosanct by ancient religion, as the highest form of interpersonal relations by many naive philosophers of the Time. Replaced, of course, by artificial insemination and female brood herds, in turn replaced by our own methods of instant psycho-regeneration. You've never seen it before?

Never.

Well, you see it involves a rather disgusting insertion of one urinary vestige into another, the resulting sensation supposedly bringing about a loss of mental control culminating in a moment of supreme ecstasy, evidenced in this case, I presume, by our Amura's screaming. As I say, primitive and naive.

Why would she let him?

Ah Becktold, doesn't it appear to you that she is participating freely, actually enjoying her own performance? Look at them, look at their expressions. You must laugh.

Why?

It is ludicrous.

It's pathetic! Illegal!

Yes, there is some question as to the legality of the act.

Fortunately Control has not yet adapted Chais' theory to simultaneous surveillance or otherwise they might discover the creator in one of these absurd postures. There are agents in the crew, but as yet there has been no report. I wonder if it has occurred to the professor that we are able to observe him?

Look, Seline, look what they're doing now!

I agree, friend Becktold, that particular head to organ arrangement seems neither sanitary nor scientific.

He dilutes the vision.

I think that's enough, don't you?

Plenty. Seline?

Yes.

I don't really understand.

Neither do I.

The design? Amura? This intercoursing?

I know, I know. The discovery of the design, this act of theirs, this madness, join together as circumstances which jeopardize us all. And it is a laughing matter! Each event is inexplicable in a Time when all things are explained. Our theory is disproved, our system broken, our lives suddenly without meaning, smile Becktold, grin, laugh hysterically, we have here in an era of absolute reason a disconcerting example of mystery!

That cannot be!

Perhaps not. Strange thing: now there is doubt. We have been through much together, you, me, Amura and the professor. We've seen so many things, visions, history, explanations, knowledge, maybe more than any humans that have ever lived. And suddenly, now, out of it all, I can

see only one sure conclusion . . .
What's that?
Mystery makes the best entertainment.

*Consider that perfect anthropological
specimen against which our scholars lay their statistical
findings. No primitive this, no smaller cranium capacity,
not one of my children with sophisticated talents
fully developed at birth, no genius, not renaissance or
resurrected man, but rather the ultimate norm, nothing
and everything at once, Mr. Mean, the infinite nobody.
He stands before you, passively, beautifully, symmetrical
limbs machined to the nearest millimeter, his head a
perfect sphere, his mind a void, just look at him! He
has been formed by the patient study of all history,
the detailed examination of that continuing linear.
His design has been developed by the most advanced
machines, his testing has resulted in responses of total
neutrality on all counts. He is everyman. No ideas, no
opinions, no experience, no memory. He is the human
mock-up of all humanity to be kept confined in a glass
cage and devoted to carefully controlled experiment.
Is he not to be envied? But . . .
In an explosion of laboratory materials, Mr.
Mean breaks free. He has watched our world through
transparent walls and while we envied him, he, poor
fool, envied us.
Subject now to random experience, orgasm,
loves and hates, he seeks identity, the norm made
individual.
He may marry Annastasia.
He may read the obituary pages.
He may become a professor of this or that.
He may write poetry.
He may stub his toe at night.
He becomes another particle, so insignificant
circulating through space with no control over
movement or direction, no ability to will or avoid the*

violent collisions in which he is involved. He becomes
a prisoner of Time, his thinking seed existing only as
duration, its distance measured by the gap between the
numerals of a clock.
    When he was no one, he was immortal. Now,
like me Frank Timmins, like Annastasia, he is someone,
and his body begins to die after its twenty-seventh year.

Playback, this is a recording:
   . . . oh, I know, I understand what it is, a new Time,
unmarked, unbounded, a day or year or lifetime in which all the world is
contained like genius, science, mystery, religion, colored waters poured
together in a supreme mix, oh . . .
   . . . what if every lifetime was comprised of such moments laid
out one after another like bodies head to toe around the earth's equator,
what if everyone was genius, then what would our language be, how
would we touch each other, would there be anger, hatred, violence?
   . . . what if every man could see and press his lips to the design
in stone, drawn in charcoal against the whiteness of his cranium's inner
lining, cut into his tissue like convolutions on the brain, what if . . .
   My name is Marcus Chais. I was a man of science.
   And what was my great discovery? An instinct.
   And what did that make me?
   That made me . . .
   Science is illusion.
   And then what?
   There are so many stones beneath the earth.
   I found what I was looking for. I was fortunate. I found Bel.
   We dismantled the camp and returned to the research strata.
The stone and car came with us, the technicians were very proud of their
discoveries. I did not care. We could have buried them again. I would
have preferred it that way.
   I hear a fanfare. It curves around my head from ear to
ear. Danger? What danger? I am obviously not afraid. Listen to the
timbre of my voice, even and clear, not that of a man confessing in the
knowledge he will be incinerated or his psyche denied regeneration.
Let them come! I await their coming to the door! I will announce
them myself with the sound of trumpets.

I am terrified. I am whimpering, I am speaking wildly into the microphone.

Yes! Trumpets! Signifying what? Their triumph? Their quick uncovering of our small nest of subversion? Oh no. Swollen cheeks, lips to silver-worn mouthpieces, to blow that sweetest note: an echelon is over. Future visions will show our populace mid-way in their trivial tasks dropping all to take trumpet in hand making gentle harmonies to declare: an echelon is begun!

Confidence and tears then, emotion to inaugurate an era. Each new breath is mystery, taken in fear and trembling, in the uncertainty of beginning and end. A step takes you across a continent of ants; a long and tiring journey leaves you within yourself. Bravo! Laughter! Tears!

Silence welcomed me back to the strata, stillness that was extraordinary. Hatred, fear, frustration, perhaps awe, embodied in that total absence of sound, that complete lack of reaction from Control. Of course they knew. Were they merely waiting for the opportune moment in which to destroy me? Were they to make me an example?

There was no time to ponder such questions. I knew my duty. I issued invitations to the Circle. My task was to tell all I had been given to understand by my journey. I knew I must tell it quickly so as to spread the message and to insure against the death of my secret.

The Circle met, yes this very night. Look around, traces here and there, Amura, Becktold, Seline, gone, each an individual way. I must do away with all this evidence.

Machine, I am very tired.

A new age has dawned.

My name is Marcus Chais.

I am . . . I am a pagan!

Amura, where are you now? I cannot sleep alone.

Becktold, Seline, let me hear from you sometime.

An echelon of mystery, an incised stone, a buried car, Bel, a long embrace, I know, I am, Machine, I hate you . . .

My tale is over.

And it is just begun . . .

Time spawns the creative accident.
Birth, for instance, the improbable

rendezvous of sperm and egg.
> *Fortune's unpredictable chance.*
> *A thought and its remarkable combination of* chemistry *and circumstance which allows our minds to* know *and discover.*
> *Death. By natural causes. By flaming car.*
> *The creative accident is Time's own true* art form.
> *Like all art, it is waste.*
> *More examples?*
> *Being: it begins, it is, it ends.*
> *Being in America: the assembly line as* abstract expressionism, *oh, the perfect mousetrap. The American Dream creation.*
> *You see, we live surrounded by momentary* works of art.
> *Being me: I am a masterpiece.*
> *Frank Timmins is my name.*

Cacophonic voices:

Marcus raises the side-view mirror. His hands are tied around it, his waist is girdled with red cloth.

Reflections!

He circles the room, bowing the mirror down to illuminate the face of each guest.

I see Becktold. I see Seline. I see deep within this glossy well, to the chromium limits of this peephole on the universe. I am a voyeur peeping at the world's eternal mysteries.

He passes before Amura, sitting in one corner on the floor.

I see Amura, goddess of love!

Take, drink this nescient . . .

He turns, the circular mirror catches meager light to splatter it in action drops along the wall; white eyes appear on startled faces, white streaks run along their clothing, the floor sprouts a full field of white poppies in the wind. Their throats are coated white, white with syrup.

Internal engines reach instantaneous speed, isolating the core within and uncovering it to be bathed by the air, exposed, released, a core in which all beginnings and all ends exist together and indistinct from

one another. The core has a voice of its own. Its soft whisper is added to
the narrative event.

    Seline: Why not? I must, I will, now there is doubt . . .

    Bel is the center! shouts Marcus.

    Amura moans, rocks her body, on her knees, fingers splayed
on her skirted thighs.

    Yes, Bel is the center, she repeats quietly. Of the design!
shouts Marcus.

    He gropes with the mirror in his hands, he spins faster than
his feet are able, off balance. The reflections are indistinguishable
along the walls, until those static faces expand to nine expressions
unconfined, white space replaces black, dark lines move where once
were dots of captured light. They change, all perspective changes,
thus proportion is fluid, lines are telescopic, the room the mind the
enneagram, individual first, then collective, the Circle all turned in
together to a cerebral flux.

    Becktold: What is it? Seline! Discipline! Help me . . .

    . . . of the design, repeats Amura.

    Reach out! touch! put your cheek against the nine walls, run
your hands along the lines of movement and watch for that is Bel!

    Bel! cries Amura. She pulls at her blouse to expose her breasts
to Marcus. She leans backward, her head behind her feet, the dark lines
rush along her bosom like setting scars. Then, as precipitously as she has
moved before, her body relaxes, goes suddenly limp. The turning light
passes across her face, each flash illuminating a different emotion, reason
to passion and back again. She is like a child, indifferent to her body and
its nakedness.

    Marcus, I dream of eternal Bel, she says.

    Becktold jumps up to grab the mirror from Marcus, to
become the apex of the meeting. His eyes are wide, his voice inspired, he
is possessed, he holds the mirror on the level of his waist.

    . . . oh yes, certain, something growing there, on me, from me,
irrigated by my blood, some vestige come alive, I've never felt it this way
before, Amura look what is shown by the mirror!

    The reflection concentrates at his groin. Growing there with
such sureness, steady, a seed, a tiny stem breaking the surface, leaves
sprouting as it climbs, I see it towering, blooming, tall shade, I see its
shadow three times its length.

His fingers undo his trousers.

. . . set free, Amura, look, the creation, an echelon begun, a star is born . . .

Seline pares his fingernails nervously.

Amura moans.

Becktold falls to his knees before her.

. . . look, Amura, look . . .

Yes look! gasps Seline.

Marcus grabs the mirror, steps back and holds it high above his head opening the ellipse to an oval frame in which Becktold and Amura lie. She receives him, they couple, the light shifts across their bodies.

Discipline! cries Becktold.

By means of this, Marcus drones.

Seline replies: we are set free.

We are in hiding, secret, unknown . . .

We are unenvisioned!

We are linked together . . .

Like a chain!

We are beyond science . . .

We will destroy science.

We will know one another.

We will intercourse . . .

We will love!

Amura screams.

Oh . . . it's magic, whispers Becktold.

It's Bel, shouts Marcus.

Seline moves to take his turn. He too feels the power. He bends over Amura and speaks to her.

. . . this is another timorous entry, feel my tentative touch, experience will give us confidence only in the experience itself, Amura . . .

Becktold: I must sabotage the image gun!

Marcus: We must be unControlled.

. . . this thrust shatters the physical law, we are together, Amura . . .

We must spread the word to everyone.

We must work our magic.

. . . this withdrawal makes room for ignorance . . .

Amura screams.

. . . this is the joker you feel, this is the instrument of laughter pouring inside you, this love that spreads through you like warmth, this is the feeling that knows no bounds . . . Ha!

And the Circle enters the reflected world, the time of light, the Circle breaks open its circumference in its invitation to include us all before the end.

The voice of Marcus Chais remains behind.

Perhaps they won't come after us, I cannot be sure. I will leave the message behind me, I will record it, using science to its true end, to liberate and not Control. I will leave the tape behind me for some new man to discover. I must hurry, whisper, my lips moving quickly against the surface of the microphone.

It is the twenty-fifth hour when I begin.

annastasia

*The population of the world exceeds
3,419,420,000. On July 11, 1907, a son, Frank, was born
to Augusta and Robert Timmins of Sparrows Point, Mass.*

*In 1967, the birth rate was 17.9 births per
1,000 population, while the fertility rate increased to
87.8 births per 1,000 women 15–44 years of age.*

*Frank Timmins was married to Annastasia
Saxton, who died tragically in a turnpike collision,
October 2, 1969.*

*An estimated 1,852,000 deaths occurred in
the United States in 1967. This provisional rate is higher
than the final rate of 951 deaths per 100,000 for 1966.*

*Frank Timmins survived his wife by
six weeks, dying in early 1970 in the midst of an
autobiographical moment.*

*WWV and WWVH, the National Bureau
of Standards radio stations, have no tone modulation
during the last two minutes of each five minute period
commencing on the hour. During the third minute of
each five minute period, WWV transmits a special
36-bit, binary coded, 100 pulse/ second Time code,
carried on c/ s modulation which contains time-of-year
information (Universal Time) in seconds, hours and
day. The reference standard for this broadcast is the
frequency of an atomic clock whose accuracy is plus
or minus 1.1 parts in 100,000 million.*

*In the instant after death, Frank Timmins
was reborn with all eternity clamped in his fist and
was forgotten.*

Dear Annastasia, forgive me, but I must . . .

You loom before me like a target silhouette, you threaten
me, your body black with white lines drawn to indicate where once
I held your heart.

I must defend myself, for if I let you, you will smother me in
your blackened breast, erasing everything in my head but you, and you

are dead . . .

I will take my ax and chop off your head and limbs and stuff them in a trunk.

I will take a cord and strangle you and bury you at the end of a sandy lane.

I will lie in waiting until through my telescope I see you centered. I will fill you full of hot lead.

> *Feel the fire scrambling around your toes.*
> *Feel the knife stuck in your bosom.*
> *Feel the world cock splitting you in two.*

I am the past, I will be the future. In both I see misery, if you remain with me as a shadow or if you are departed. If I have no remembrance of you and our happiness together, then I will not know what I miss or what I yearn for. You must cease to be, as a person, as a tombstone, as a memory, and as a dream to come.

I must simply destroy you.

Now.

> *Bang! you're dead!*
> *Marcus, did you see?*
> *And you, Marcus?*
> *Did you see me plug her,*
> *Marcus of the future?*

But it is my death that is here occurring, my suicide now coupled with her murder etched in the glass of this momentary window. A pact between us, a signed note, victims of each other, found like lovers sprawled in a bloody rented room and captured by the sudden flash of the autophotographer. Both gone then, and with us the certainty that was us, the sureness of our being together, the stability of our daily life, the security of our love.

What can take our place for me?

> *Who am I?*
> *Marcus the magician-king*
> *Marcus the professor.*
> *Marcus the creative archeologist.*

There is a human design, many-sided and in motion. It is both my prison and my shelter. I am forever held within its shell, my body, my imagination, me. I look out and watch my hands grasp a cup, I see my feet beneath me as I walk, I see others as they look at me; no matter how far my dreams may take me that is where I am. And I am surrounded by millions like me, with their own bodies, sensibilities and dreams. Impossible as it may seem, we do not often share.

I see her face receding like driftwood down a fast-flowing stream. There are waves upon the water and in their renewal I see the proliferation of endless faces.

There is a human design, like a coffin, in which we float through Time. Its inner proportions change with the motion of its outer limits; it is nine-sided, it is a circle.

The enneagram.

It outlasts the cycles of our history. It exists as long as there are men. It is eternal, while men are not. There is a human design, and I, Frank Timmins, struggle within it. Oh! the magic of this moment, when in a summary of my years, I am afraid to start anew.

Anna!
Aimee!
Amura!

Annastasia! what we shared . . .

Until Time did us part.

I look around me.
The next moment arrives. The next beginning.

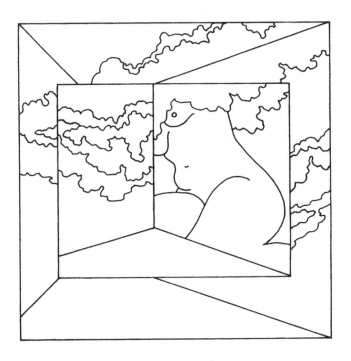

MOCK TURTLE SOUP

For Casey who cracked the egg: Welcome

one through thirteen

"When the salt has lost its savour,
    Who shall savour it again?"

    Nathanael West
    Miss Lonelyhearts

"It's all his fancy that: he hasn't
    got no sorrow . . ."

    Lewis Carroll
    Alice's Adventures in Wonderland

ONE

Wooden mallet sound: pok pok: slow crying out of warping wood.

The gangway protrudes like an epileptic tongue, black yawning hatchway to warm stalls below. The great bearded Supervisor drives the last silver nail and a clay jug of arak is broken over the prow.

SS Ark
Rotterdam

I'm up to my ears in nighttime.
My name is Fence.

The room I live in is the traditional square; it has four corners. There is sleep corner first, where the bed sits disappointed, never used at night, never uncovered to reveal it has no sheets, only a fake Indian spread, faded, laundromatted and mussed by my fitful daytime slumbers. And wash corner: with the little curving sink all brown stained from rust dripping spigots—the hot knob is missing, removed by the landlord who in further defiance of the cultural pattern does not turn on the heat until the winter solstice. The pipes wrattle-wrangle in wash corner, trying to tell me something, and all a part of the deception that there buried in the basement just below me is a giant boiler, bursting its plates with steam, boiling up caldrons full of shaving water, and on the hour announcing this happy bounty with oh! a joyful noise on the pipes. Wassail! Everyone else in the City must be using my water; their pipes are always exploding. You see the flashing lights of emergency vehicles parked before a brownstone, or see the buckled pavement covered with sand and water and clouds of steam as if a stream of clear volcanic substance has succeeded in cracking the earth's surface in the lost canyon of buildings. A grocer stands in bloodstained apron shaking his curly head as the hot water rushes down his steps, rippling like a trout stream in the crowded aisles of his store, rusting over tin can tops and swelling up the matzos. That, Fence observes, is the hand of God, grocer. He looks out for his own. I hurry by, fingering the edge of the razor in my pocket, carried there because I shave and bathe at work. Value that, grocer, because when you want to wash your hands all you need do is stoop down in your apron and wash off the pickle juice while others pass you by, their wrists stinking of kosher dill. So what good is wash corner?

Next, empty corner: the wall marked in a blond square where some former tenant painted around his bureau. He took the furniture with him when he left. My belongings are in boxes, old ones from the supermarket. I piled them in the outline of the square but they did not fill the space. I concluded I could not fill the bureau, I'm glad he took it along.

There is something about empty corner that reminds me of my home. It is an open space, the pale square on dark wall giving me a vista to admire as I lie on the bed looking down over paunch and feet. It flickers there like a screen where the projectionist shows time and time again a series of forgotten travelogues, streaked and splotched with light, houses and lakes and other ruins and walking toward me there a black man who lifts his hand in a sign of recognition. And I signal back, but furtively though, under cover of fiction, and dammit! look around the room to see if I'm observed.

Empty corner speaks to me, answers when questioned, occasionally provides unwanted explanations. People oftentimes sit and talk with me there.

Like this black man, for example, who worked for my Grannie-Annie. He strolls out of empty corner and says:

Proceed with the inquiry.

You are Ben, old Ben, the family retainer?

I held a salaried job for sixteen years, no insurance deal, no fringe benefits, no stock options, if that's what you're asking.

You are old Ben who took me fishing on the lake, who took me into town to do the chores, who taught me to look at a girl's legs first of all, who gave me by your constant repetition the only two bars of blues I know. Aren't you that Ben?

If you say so.

What's the matter! Don't you remember, Ben, don't you remember your warm room behind the kitchen, don't you remember the long cars you shined, the dumplings, the fried perch, the fly rod Grandfather gave you? We were all there, you, me, Little Bit, Grandfather, Grannie-Annie.

Sure, sure boy, I remember.

Well what the hell?

The sun always shines in empty corner on the blond square, even when the shade is drawn almost to the bottom, yellow light squeezes in and turns that corner into sunset, bright orange glow in my room's penumbra. Fence watches it closely, the sun going down like that. I watch for the magic green spark when the red globe sinks below the horizon. I squint to see the burning cord which slowly sets it down, the reflective track on which the great sun travels. And I climb suddenly on a bird with fiery wings, I grasp handfuls of golden feathers, I fly upward through the frame of a corner then dive beneath the lowered shade to rise again to reach the very peaks of the many mile high sun flares, to soar between the flickering towers of flame. You anticipate that the bird's wings will melt, flowing like candle wax, to pitch me forward into free-fall, falling to the earth again like the mythological bird-man-or was it a horse? But no, Fence does not fall from grace, he encounters other soaring birds, each bearing a rider, a veritable holding pattern of fellow dreamers. Empty corner: how it burns, romantic landscape hanging on my private gallery wall.

Door corner is the last, the way out. . . . The door is metal and has four locks and a peephole through which I can view the others: the lounging omnipresent with changing face and dirty needle, the daring young couple with bright friends and noisy clothes, a crooked man in leather with an illuminated cane, strange girl walking an imaginary child to school.

An old woman distorted in arthritic angles by the peephole glass pulls behind her a grocery wagon with goggling onion stems and bags milk wet along the bottom. She hums a crone song and wears a dark green shawl wrapped about her shoulders.

Grannie! My Grannie-Annie!

I spin away from the sight of her to see her fading from me once again in empty corner. She sits in her chair of that flowery chintz, her thin body swathed in the dark green shawl she wore, her eyes on me and the thickly knotted fringe linger for an instant and then the vision gone.

Time for work. To leave the room I must first undo the locks. The key slips in and opens one, the chain unfastened two, three the sliding rod, and four the coded number knob held open by cerebral recitation of a help line number. The handle turned, the door swings wide.

What about those locks, Fence? What about four locks on your door?

Locks to keep the inside in and not the outside out. . . .

I leave my window open; it sits there invitingly just a few feet above the sidewalk, the outside entering freely to tap the bottom of the shade against the window frame. You have lived in the City, you have taken a rented room. You would never leave a first floor window open lest the red-eyed intruder, hands shaking with narcotic need, sling his foot over the sill to rifle through your things, cherished, earned, accumulated over the years. You would first erect a wall of bars, a sturdy lock, or four, heavy curtains to protect you from public consumption. Perhaps you might even seek out the cop on the beat: that window there, Officer, watch it closely, it's mine.

You are absolutely wise.

But you see I have no belongings worth any modest exertion, a few cardboard boxes nothing more. Even my life if stripped from me like a watch and chain would scarcely bestir an interest. Certainly the papers would pass it by, the community might not even hear unless some neighbor chancing on the stair sees the flash of the police photographer or observes the authorities trundle me away in a rubber sheet with a three-by-five card wired to my pasty toe.

But you . . . Value, you have assets, investments, worth. Such a fuss the crowds would make, such commotion. And telegrams in your mailbox, wreaths and fruit baskets at your door, oh the world would care, the world would take obituary notice.

Fence is confused because he works by night, because he sees the world by the light of a second sun, neon sun, orange as a cafeteria bubbler. Night complexions are like white plastic spoons and emotions full-on full-off advertising display, fake sun of infrared making no shadows in the City, night blindness.

Fence leaves his window open on the world and people walking down the street at three a.m. know that that man there too is out somewhere trying to make it in the night.

Time for work, passing the normal people on the way home and me, Fence, all stiff-collared starch with the sleep still in my eyes at five in the afternoon.

Between my room and my occupation, in the middle, halfway, I'm neither here—nor there. Just anywhere.

The City Room is spent, it lies before me as I enter, exhausted and indifferent, evidencing all the trappings of journalistic activity, upset cups of oil-slick coffee, baskets full to flowing, intervals between the desks spillways for running sores of unprinted event: filing cabinet drawers open with folders gasping for air, stale tobacco sweat, hoods on typewriters like careless gags: the silence cries out for staccato calls of copy and criticism from bourbon-blooded men in shirtsleeves, questions muttered into telephone mouthpieces, sarcasm, cynicism, worldliness.

A cleaning hag slipper-sluffs her way across this empty panorama, dragging behind her on a string a box of dust and of course the news of yesterday.

Tonight it is raining, through some forgotten window half-open comes the needling sound of rain. Fence sees that Bernie Killian must be in, the green eyeshade is missing from the hat rack, a white take-out cup is on his desk. Fence makes for the nether reaches of the room, the filing cabinet he hides behind, a desk, a telephone. Taped to the typewriter there he finds this note:

> To the man who manhandles this machine by night: Do not
> repeat do not swivel the chair a single revolution. It lowers
> one thirty-second of an inch and I cannot reach the keys.
> *end*

A message from a day-freak.

I sit all night with Bernie Killian for company, and the cleaning hag, and my arms around the dictionary or street guide, fickle Fence. The hours crawl by on their hands and knees. Ten eleven twelve o'clock, tuck in the linotype, Bernie, the ball scores are in.

And sometime then, when it seems like all the world is dream on the other side of rain, Scraps appears, Scraps the man of the morgue comes out of hiding for his endless game of gin with Bernie K. Scraps: tight black trousers, legs long and pointed like the scissors he uses to clip little geometric shapes from the daily news From his keychain hang the lives of many, pictures they did not want taken, tales they did not want told, long rows of files in which the years lie neatly cut and pasted, back to back, sheaf to sheaf in manila folders, a million family skeletons catalogued for easy reference. Scraps is as wiry as a paper clip, his skin is the yellow-brown of aged newsprint.

It takes time to find your way around his morgue. The files are broken down by his arbitrary law, Scraps rustling the wide pages and making judgments. He is a hanging judge and the gallows' cord protrudes from his pocket like a soiled handkerchief. Files are flagged, green for innocence, yellow for ambiguity, red for guilt, and if all the drawers were left extended, Scraps' room would transform from dismal fog to a spring field of brilliant poppies, red.

One day, soon after I began the job, I found the folder F for FENCE, thick as any and fringed in black. Inside were notes and pictures, pen and inks hastily drawn on copy paper, obscene jewels with Fence for hero coupled to himself, or laid open self-dissected, and written observations such as: Fence drinks tea instead of coffee, Fence wears trousers still with cuffs, Fence chews his nails like pencil tips, Fence crawls in at night and out at dawn, Fence is Cinderella.

Subversive, libelous stuff.

What does it all mean? Am I disliked? A few days on the job and nightmares for the night-man.

On my desk, I find the brown envelope. It is always there waiting patiently for my arrival, for the satisfaction of returning to me my work of the night before, from Bernie K., a little game we play. The copy I produce is covered in flowing arrows smudged remarks blue pencil. Training, craft, says Bernie, future professionalism, there in the brown envelope. I am never printed, I write for the amusement and information of a single man who spends some part of his every day playfully pulling apart my words to rearrange them incomprehensibly like some misbegotten Chinese puzzle. Syntax, I find scribbled in the margin beside a paragraph listing the new officers of a women's club. Revise.

I catch on quick. One day Fence lifted copy direct from the first edition, the product of a staffer whose fingers have pounded prints on the typewriter keys, obliterated the letters for his own, a man bound to his vocation in spider webs, twenty years at rewrite, a master. Bernie's scratchings were intense and painful to behold, and on the final page that night he wrote: Fence you don't catch on too quick.

I have no deadline other than the dawn when I toss the envelope at Bernie's desk where he sits sleeping, eyeshade on his chest, dreaming old gin rummy hands and newsboy dreams. I head for home, I hurry to my room again to leave all that behind me and to miss the sunrise which just might turn me into a pumpkin.

   If Fence works for Bernie K., then Bernie K. works for
Publisher, and Publisher wears a double-breasted blazer and crested
buttons. He is a man of high ideals, he is community-minded, he has the
answers, and somehow as incredible as it may seem he expects his people
to be little publishers, blazers, buttons, ideals and all.
   He expects us to begin where he begins and to end up where
he ends up, but he is clever enough to understand he needs conspirators
not believers like himself to promulgate the ideal. Actors able to stage
carnival on notice, to wear the devil's mask or the angel's wing, we come
to work disguised in traditional unpressed tweed, in mirrored sharkskin,
in objectivity, we come knowing full well that regardless of the required
costume, we will strip it off at Publisher's signal and become anonymous.
That's not hypocrisy.
   Journalists are a dime a dozen. That's inflation for you.

   For Publisher there is always hope, some bit to be found
along the right-of-way with chipped glass and cinders and derelicts, some
peace to be found in the City alleys where the rats fight gang wars and
old literary men live in dumpster bins. Publisher leads the way down
the expressway of righteousness, cutting down obstacles with his silver
pen, pushing his version of progress. His projects proclaimed from the
editorial page are forceful in their narrow-mindedness, as successful
as he is stubborn, and yet curiously enough he stands frequently alone
among other civic leaders with only the courage of his convictions for
company.
   Thus the paper is the vehicle of exposé and crusade, the
voice of the forgotten in an absentminded world. Wrongs are uncovered,
corruption revealed, officials implicated, and a solution proffered like
the outpouring of Publisher's belly over belt, a solution of no practical
application or interest other than to readers suddenly awakened
to another deceit. The point is made, circulation rises, Publisher is
sometimes esteemed, often hated, nothing is done.
   It is a labor of love.
   Publisher says: You don't get it if you don't get the people.
   Bernie Killian works for Publisher and has the night shift,
that's what kind of man he is.

And Fence works for Bernie K.

So right away I know there's trouble. Bernie wakes with a start, rubbing his hand along his eyes, grey folds of skin and no lashes, squinting out from beneath the shade at me, Fence, sitting with my feet up in the book reviews.

There is going to be a fire, says Bernie.

I nod sleepily. Bernie is predicting the news again. Sixth precinct, says Bernie.

It is nothing to me, I swivel my chair one daring revolution and continue reading the telephone directory. Old Bernie's not a bad sort, let's look him up.

The static incomprehensible voice of the police dispatcher crackles over the radio. Fire. Sixth precinct. Well I'll be damned.

Better check it out, Fence.

Better check it out, Bernie the bastard.

All right, all right, and I kick the phone book out of spite, bend the pages, tear page 491 KILLE-KILLN, cross out Bernie's number.

Don't cry, Fence, you need the air.

So out I go, out through the prewar pretentious lobby, past the gimp who sells papers outside the revolving door and lives in his newsstand. Gimp makes lovely ladies out of unsold editions, screws them all night long, then folds and bales them for recycling.

You up, Gimp? I say shaking the wobbly box with a friendly kick to its grey wooden pants.

Out pokes his head.

Hey, Fence, who let you out?

Smart guy, Gimp.

Yeah. Say, look what I found.

He shows me a golden bird feather.

What the hell is it?

Beats me, Fence. Peroxided pigeon, I guess, blondes are more fun.

Mind on business now. Fire.

I watch the flames suck out the eyes of a tenement, a shattering implosion of glass, the brick face reflects light like sweat, like fluid. The hoses throw water upward over the facade to the inside, water's silver ribbon tattered at the end. The pavement runs, a mirror image of the urgent movements of the firemen, their helmets shaped like black badges against a sky of yellow and red. The refugees, rag-tag in night clothes, cluster around their few evacuated possessions, panic-gathered much like lives. They cling to futile symbols of possession, a burnt mattress thrown out the window, a frame stuffed with snapshots, postcards in a box, costume jewelry, a toy animal without an eye.

Bricks clatter and fall with a confusion of dust and smoke, wound opening on the third story, cyclopic, intense and sure, evil on me, drawing Fence forward through the steam, through the tangled hoses and gesticulating men, up into a corridor of flame where I am walking, an unopened door before me. Apt. 3D. McCurdy. Smoke runs down the burning walls like melting paint. And flame, harsh heat orange subdues and quiets diluted to smooth enamel red against which I could lay my cheek. My feet are bare as I walk over the bright eyes of coals, but with my step they sigh and succumb to blindness as my soles trample down their sockets of crumbling white. I walk to discover what is behind the door: a garden much like this one where the wind blows acridly with mint and the leaves are edged with autumn, a fresh wind bathes that silent place and guides me between rows of fruit trees to another towering wall, another door with a knob of brass. This is opened to reveal a protected field of frost, and its door a drift of snow, and its door an icy stalactite bank of mirrors. Each garden is more cool, pristine, contemplative, than the one before. I do what I can do, I put out the fire, good acolyte, I save what the refugees left behind, no one's hero really but my own. I am tired. Come here, friends, bring those scorched pillows for my head and let me sleep.

Fire is romance. Fire is poetry.

I am a child of fire.

Hoxie, my photographer friend, peers at me through the smoke.

Where are you, Fence?

There where the flames are.

Move over then and I'll get you in this shot.

He sways, unsteady aim, points his camera and fires leaving me all pinwheel lights and dizzy. The photograph: boy reporter on the job, see conflagration in background, reporter with big cheeks and craning neck, wide waist, short tail, hard shell, soft inside, isolated against the flames, a slow instant in a slow meander.

Let's have a drink, cries Hoxie. Let's go down to the pond.

This side or that? asks Fence.

Neither, of course.

We climb into my little red sedan for a rumble through the
City streets, all alive and animated for no one but the likes of Hoxie and
me, streets you can see along forever.

Wake up, Bernie Killian, you moose of a man in a green
eyeshade! I yell into the radio mike.

Come in, Fence. What happened? as if he didn't know.

You see one fire you've seen them all, right Bernie? A fireman
will tell you differently, but what does he know? For the newsman, fire
is crowds and barricades you just pass through, all bored and casual,
showing your press card. Fire is cause, location, damage, what's burning
hurrah! how many alarms? firemen hurt? names? how do you spell that?
age? any kids? arson? Fire is local color, the guy who smashed the call
box, neighbors, ambulance man, the magic cotton candy booth, the hot
dog stand selling red-hots to hungry fire-eating onlookers. Forget flame,
heat-corrugated air, the scrape of canvas hoses on asphalt, hissing water:
that's not news. Right, Bernie? Right?

Hoxie took a picture but all he exposed was my
noncourageous ash. We need a drink. You know where to find us.

The pond is the river, long and wide and dirty and deep,
cutting the country in two. We park the sedan on the levee and cross
the gangway to the showboat all night bar, Dewey's-by-the-Sea, floating
brazen booze barge on the outskirts of the City's territorial waters.
Dewey, old sea dog that he is, stands at the helm, pulling the tap in his
sneakers and Captain's cap.

Break open a bottle of rex red! shouts Hoxie. And a large
bowl of turtle soup for my friend here!

Ah turtle soup, like manna to me, credit where credit is due,
it was Bernie K. who introduced me to Dewey's and the specialty of the
galley, turtle soup.

A hangout then.

God! Mississippi River turtle! I have seen Dewey called
from the bridge to run across the gangway to the levee where in the bed
of a primered truck or on the seat of a battered Cadillac lies a wooden
box hodge-podge of streaked shells thrown together like a collection of
wet colored rocks. I have seen some little boy rush to pull Dewey down

the cobblestones to a cleat around which is tied a shriveled line. With a
toothy grin, the boy yanks the rope and beaches upside-down on its back
a hoary river patriarch as big around as a waiter's tray.

I have watched the exchange of silver, the barter, and then
the catch disappear over the barge stern into the galley door. Beady
eyes, claws, prehistoric skin, unappetizing to be sure, but there within
her laboratory amidst the steam and banging pots ol' Miz Dewey works
magic and fills kettles, crocks and mason jars with the frothy freckled
substance of her skill.

Turtle soup! hot aromatic with little flippers sliding
down your throat, the sense of the far-off, the what is not ever now, I
participate with my lapping tongue in the struggle, the journey of the
hard-shelled voyager and his soft belly. It's a great joke with Bernie.
As the nighttime hours get old and moldy, when the cleaning hag has
vanished beneath the desks like a dust roller, Bernie yells: eat turtle! And
I wake from some posture, some imagined world, to see his forehead
creased above the eyes where he is ever marked by the shade, to see his
mouth moved by some weird smile or laugh.

Let's eat turtle Fence!

And, me, the night-man, Bernie Killian's only companion,
looks out to dawn and Dewey's-by-the-Sea for sustenance.

So now Fence is looking into the creamy surface of a bowl and
hearing Hoxie cock his wrist for a long pull on his green bottle, hearing
Dewey suck saliva like spray over the top of his plate, hearing the various
creakings and groanings of the patrons, the booze barge, the river itself:
squeak a worn over shoe heel dubbed on whispering voices, fingers rasp
playing against a permanent stubble, loose change spinning on the bar
top: there is a bandstand in the corner forever silent, dust laden drums,
skins no tighter than an old man's cheek, open upright piano with busted
clappers and strings, trumpet clogged green with the phlegmatic patina
of time, a bandstand there, its only sound the patchwork silence that
reminds the listeners that somewhere else there is music playing.

I got rhythm, whispers Hoxie, dancing with his bottle.

No man is a soup bowl, observes Fence.

There is no moon as I leave alone and walk up the levee
toward the courthouse where once the slaves were sold. I sit and lean
against a cold stone pillar. Below the river muddles on. All that power,

they say, they marvel, power to eat away the soil, to overturn the wooden shacks, to grab a man away from his Sunday picnic, sandwiches and cold beer, to leave him twisted broken, like a drifting branch, gnarled and knotted humanity, bloated green in faded blue jeans. The river rises inexplicably to fill the fields with silt, to smash barn doors with a floating ram, to clean out the leftovers with persistent waves. White-faced mules shriek in the stalls, chickens riding debris send hawking cries to deaf shores, whole communities are lifted up for relocation, windowless houses found resting on a mudbank, still filled with water, the inhabitants sleeping a buoyant slumber or making do a meal of mildew with tin fork grasped stiffly in their fingers.

Where does it come from, the river and all its power?

Does it do anything but destroy?

Fence hears the soft sloshing of the current on the levee stones where the angular cables cut into the surface fastening boats and barges to iron rings. The wind quickens suddenly, and on it rides the wisdom of Bernie K.

Let's eat all the turtles, Fence!

Yes, Bernie is thinking of Fence out there in the night.

TWO

*On the levee darkies grind corn in their teeth, the
women compress the hay in bales between their dark moist
thighs. A pall of dust settles on the water and cracked lips,
thunderclouds marshal up in wads, suspended over the scene
by calliopoetic cables.*

The ammonia smell of stockyards.

*A stirring movement like the wind and water
current: whinnies, groans, bleats of pain: the Supervisor
begins at ten and counts down on his fingers.*

*A cat-calling crowd of onlookers hampers
movement on the shore. Pointing fingers at the awkward
shape of the vessel, men and women alike giggling at the huge
painted breasts of the Supervisor's wife hanging beneath the
bowsprit. A band begins to play, laughter drowns out the
coupling sounds of the nubile clouds.*

*Electric bell: the gates open silently, and two by
two the animals march toward the ark. Heads bowed beneath
the taunts of the mob who have formed two lines through
which the animals must pass. The hot-painted prods move
them on beneath sparkling eyes and the razor tongues of men.*

*Two anteaters, two bears, two cougars, two ducks,
two eels, two fox, two goats, two. . . .*

Two turtles!

Fence was much younger then. The ferns grew in wild
profusion in the soft musk hollow, the water lazily pushed a layer of
green pitted scum back and forth along the shore, the carp slept belly up
there by the broken trees. My bare feet made their mark in the mud, my
footprints filling with lake-water like old quarries. Up above, the hawk
circled, I saw him where the light slanted through the leaf screen to fall
filtered in the ferns. The hawk circled and Ben's voice came to me from
down the road: Move on up higher, get him, boy!

I aimed on the run, my legs hurrying on the embankment, my
heels sliding in the humid dirt.

Now boy!

I fired once, fell to my knees fumbling to reload.

The hawk cried and broke from his circle, warned, afraid.

I saw the gold feather tips catch the sun as he turned once over the hollow banking toward the lake flaunting me. Ben fired and the bird fell. I pressed one of the tiny drops of blood between my fingers and felt the stickiness until it dried away.

We tied the legs with string and I dragged the trophy through the garden to the house. My trophy. It was mine, I had shot it, I told Grannie-Annie.

No ma'am, he didn't. I shot it.

That's a lie, I shouted.

But she would not believe me and with her fan slapped Ben twice across the face. Two red splotches grew on her cheeks as if my bloody fingertips had touched there. She whipped shut the fan and slapped him twice and his face so black I could not see the mark.

A Commandment broken.

You will not be killing and teaching this boy to kill!

And in the kitchen he tied together his knot of curses until Little Bit came in and he was quiet.

Little Bit, the cook, that was his name for her. Her real name was Annie too, but she was always Little Bit to us. She had been raised on a farm, she had been a waitress, she could shoot pool. She only stayed a year, and when she left us Ben kissed her and it was the first time I saw a black kiss a white.

Ben and I took her to the ferry and he kissed her then gave her an envelope.

From him, he said.

He laid it on her open palm and she turned and was gone. I never saw her on the deck although she was excursion class and we stayed until the ferry was a long way out.

The day she first came I had been sitting in the rock garden when I heard the horn, Grannie-Annie returning from town and Ben who drove her blowing the horn down the road where I had lettered the sign DANGER and nailed it to a half-fallen tree. The car door slammed as I ran to the garage. Grannie-Annie was loading packages into the arms of a girl whose red curls appeared in disarray beneath her scarf. Ben took the packages from her as quickly as Grannie gave them, then he stood back and watched as the girl climbed into the back of the car after her suitcase.

This is Anne, said Grannie-Annie addressing us, the house, the gardens with all the vegetables and flowers, the opening screen door that brought Grandfather out to take his afternoon swim.

Annie ma'am, said the girl.

Anne sounds better, dear, better for a maid, and besides my name is Annie.

I've always been Annie, ma' am, since christening.

All right, if you don't like it, we'll simply find something else to call you.

Little Bit, said Ben.

She had been standing at the bus station looking out over the beach and weathered stacks of canvas chairs when Ben and Grannie had driven by to town. And she had been there when they returned, standing, staring, her hair blown in gusts from off the lake, her suitcase against her shins. The day's bus was gone, the ticket window shut. She was standing to look unbelieving at a horizon rimmed with water.

I've never seen the ocean before, she said.

Have you come here to look for work dear? asked Grannie.

Yes ma'am.

Well, you're a little early. Summer trade doesn't get up 'til after Memorial Day usually. I guess you'll just have to come home and work for me.

So we've got another stray, said Grandfather. Some damn stray come by the door to lap up a saucer full of cream.

He tied up the sash of his robe and left to take his swim. We opened up the maid's room next to Ben's and she hung up her clothes from the suitcase. I left and she and Grannie tried on the uniforms our old cook had worn.

And that night Ben stood in his white jacket while she put chicken and dumplings on the silver tray. Grandfather helped himself to dumplings three times and then he called Little Bit into the dining room. She stood there, her body seemed so much fuller in the nylon uniform that was a bit too small, I could see her slip beneath it, and she blushed and looked at the tips of her shoes while Grandfather observed her silently, wiping chicken gravy from his lips with a cloth napkin.

Saucers full of cream, I heard Grannie-Annie say.

Grandfather! hear me call his name now. Once I suppose
there was reverence to my tone, some tremor in my voice that betrayed
my innocence. He was unreachable and silent and I loved him. Resting
her chin on her fan, Grannie-Annie would tell me what a man he was,
how successful, how handsome when they had courted.

But listen to her speak it:

. . . it was a fine porch done by an architect who came to dine
and with one of my father's cigars in his mouth had taken his pen and
sketched it on our linen tablecloth. Mother told him she wanted angels
above the door, wings crossed above the threshold, and there they hung,
fat and rosy gold. Cherubs, you want, he said. No, angels, I answered for
my Mother, and with a scratching of his pen-point he drew them in and
winked at me through the smoke of the cigar. . . .

Sitting pensively, with her fan stirring the tepid air, her
cheeks and forehead and bosom powdered heavy white.

But Grandfather, Grannie?

. . . oh yes, heaven sent that man to me, I heard his heels ring
on the porch when he came to call, I heard the brass tip of his cane touch
the electric buzzer. We sat for tea. . . .

Where are you Grannie?

. . . and when he put down his cup his ring tapped against the
china saucer. He was my father's protégé, certain of success in business,
certain to provide a good home, certain to father children. My Mother
never liked him because he could not stand her cats. . . .

Yes, and picture me where I sat, my hand against her foot,
listening but not really hearing what she said, only taking up the tremor
of her voice, the way she had of speaking.

Her tone of speech, her tone of life, they were the same.

When she was dead and Grandfather and I stood in the
little room and lifted up the coffin lid to see her face as if carved from
ivory and powdered as heavily as was her habit, it struck me she had
lost nothing of her life in her death. There was a stillness about her to
which we were so accustomed and thus we were not sad as it was only
her dreaming body there which was to waken momentarily, her face in
repose gazing off to some remote space, her face lost in thought over the
profundities of a bird feeder or flower arrangement or groceries for the
coming week or chapter and verse of some favored piece of scripture.

. . . and God said, Let the waters bring forth abundantly the moving creature that hath life, and fowl that may fly above the earth in the open firmament of heaven. . . .

She could not mistreat. At least, so it seemed. In her sitting room, fish bowls lined the walls and the shelf below the window. Her dressing table stood near and its mirror reflected and refigured without perspective the rectangular shapes touched by the color of underwater green and the sudden sensual turnings of the fish as they foraged in the sand. Hanging on a hook was a little net of stretched cheesecloth and hanger wire. She leaned over, her face illuminated strangely by the water light, to trap a fish against the glass. She held it in her palm, observing the gills open and close, tracing the gaily colored scales with her fingernail.

Grannie.

Peculiar reverie, I would remind her to replace the guppy in the water.

She would sometimes try to feed them while they lay there in her hand.

We were all her children.

And even when she struck Ben with her fan, the reaction was consistent and deliberate: punishment given out of a greater sense of outrage for the killing of the hawk. Later she apologized and tried to touch the spot where she had hit him as if her hand against his cheek could erase that blacker wound she had inflicted against his pride. Her apology was as sincere as the sound of the ivory fan against his cheek.

A strong image persists of our life together in that old-fashioned house: Grandfather lying beneath the bay of French windows in the afternoon with the papers strewn about him. The couch was of that chintz and with the shadow of the window frames there lay across him a labyrinth of lines and light and leaves. His head was propped up on a tasseled pillow and whether his eyes were open or closed he rarely moved and his breath puffed through his nostrils in audible cadence.

I can remember watching him breathe.

I was his, a grandson without a father, something yes! to be taken in, to be considered little more than an investment or more rightly a charitable contribution. There was no communication between us, no acknowledgement of my youthful affection, no sense of that courting gentleman with boater and cane other than the fading echo of my Grannie's voice. We all led our life together face to face, we all gathered three times a day around the dining table, yet our fingers did not touch as we passed a dish between us.

THREE

*Tapestry hanging: mythology: bearded officers
riding dreams in formation, foot soldiers following after with
the weapons of historical event: interior decor of the highest
order: first class.*

*We hope you enjoy these accommodations, says
the Supervisor.*

*A golden bowl in the corner filled with blooming
rhododendron, the feed bin is lined with platinum and
the straw under foot crackles with synthetic freshness.
A nameplate on the door declares: Turtles One and Two.*

*Oh yes, very nice, replies Turtle One, fumbling
in his trousers for tipping change. I'm sure we'll be quite
happy here.*

*Life preservers and sickness bags will be found
in forward seat pockets. A card describing emergency
procedures and drill may be read at your convenience. During
our first few days out, we will practice this routine, remember
the Titanic. Please ring the bell if you require assistance.*

*The Supervisor consults his clipboard and hurries off.
Turtle Two flops in the straw.*

*I just don't think I could have stood those pens for
another moment. It was so hot and dusty, all those staring
people, and the confusion with the baggage, oh my, I'm tired.*

*Yes dear, but now we're almost underway, so
relaxing, a winter cruise, so pleasant so fine.*

*Turtle One walks to the porthole. He listens to
the commands for departure, the lines drawn in by chanting
coolies, the breathing winches, rasping hemp on levee stone.
A whistle blows, the band begins a diastolic march, the crowd
hisses and boos as the SS Ark moves out into the infinite flow,
power propulsing, the coal furnaces stoked with nuclear slag,
the steam engines enumerating combusted electrons.*

*A giraffe staggers by with a shuffleboard stick, the
bar is open, the Supervisor calls out to God.*

Looks like rain, says Turtle One.

Tonight Scraps left me something: newsphoto, of a woman pinned between a car seat and steering wheel, glass shattered in her lap and windshield frame compressed toward her as if it once held the mirror she used to apply her bloody make-up. All right, fine, good. But what made it fun for Scraps, what hurt, was the highway divider rail that had smashed the glass, entered her forehead, exited through her blonde streaked hair, leaving her head impaled like a bulbous fruit hanging from a metal branch.

For Scraps, that's great art.

To Fence, he wrote, with very best wishes for your future.

Bernie, I said, please. . . .

Publisher had talked with his man Bernie K.

Bernard, give me a series for controversy and irate mail. I've got some after-dinner speeches coming up.

His polished nails caught the light and the City Room turned on like Times Square at dusk.

Let's shake up the capitol, this is an election year. Good scandal, good dirt, you know the routine, let's call for investigative committees, we need more activity up in the statehouse than handball and backgammon. Give me a good fresh approach, Bernard, I want shock. I want outrage.

I've got just the man, said Bernie.

So thank you Publisher, thank you Bernie, no thank you Scraps, I'm off the revolving stool and on the way to the City Detention Home for Women, seven-floor doll house with a river view. Barges tie up just outside, the railroad passes sweetly by, and a highway with the motorists afforded a high speed washroom glimpse. The Detention Home is on the beaten track.

Historical note: built in 1899, the edifice enjoyed a bawdy hotel career, but alas over the years tariffs dropped from outlandish rates for corniced splendor charged to gamblers and cattlemen, to steam heat and hot showers for vested salesmen and furloughed soldiers, to absolutely nothing at all except that you be female and not necessarily convicted.

There is a distinctive smell about such places, an age-old mixture of cigar smoke and urine, of linseed oil, cracked linoleum and Lysol, of brass polish, dust and rust and sadness. Fence smells each one of those seventy years of history as he enters the lobby door. The hall has no spittoons, easy chairs or potted palms, it is lit by a bent desk lamp and the sudden defensiveness of the scarecrow guard.

You can go back where you came from, bud.

Isn't this the Detention Home?

For women, Jack.

I'd like to visit.

Visiting hours on Fridays 3:30 to 5:30, Saturdays 1:30 to 3:30 and Sundays 5:30 to 7:30, hours subject to change with out notice. No visitors on holidays 'cept Labor Day, Yom Kippur, and Valentine's. So now you got it, scram!

I'd like to see the Superintendent, Mrs. Melicci.

Mother don't see no one but by appointment.

I called. I've got an appointment.

He gets up out of the light with a creaking of his bones and a soft disintegration of clothing into must.

Fill in this card, and I ain't got a pen. Fill in time of arrival, estimated time of departure, name last first middle initial, firm, purpose, religion or philosophy of life, forwarding address. Leave all packages, briefcases, purses and firearms on the rack by the door, no smoking, no loud talking, no running in the halls, speak only when spoken to, wait in the Waiting Room.

Mother Melicci finds me and clamps my hand. Mr. Fence, she says, and a spark jumps between us with a vicious little snap. She is dressed in a grey uniform topped with white curls, a giant cloud formation, a thunderhead out of which electrostatic bolts are thrown.

I'm not grounded, what to do?

Nothing against you personally, Mr. Fence, but I don't like your kind much. I been in this business too long, I got a nose and I ain't smelt a good newspaper or social service yet. We do a dirty job, and you people want to make a stink about it every three or four years. Oh, I seen it all before, young guys like you, or what's worse them college girls, come in and get upset. Then we get the fancy legislative boys down, there's a report, and we sit back waiting for it to happen all over again. So here you are, Fence. We could get along, you could do yourself a favor and we'd get along just fine. Why don't you write for your paper what you think you should have seen here instead of what you see? That way, as I read it, nobody'd get excited and things would stay just like they are—nice.

She breathes that last word like a rattlesnake.

Mother Melicci, I am yours.

We walk together down hallways lined with bars, a matron to

help us negotiate the locks. There is an odor of wet plaster and metallic dirt as we seem to penetrate deeper and deeper into the building. Then at last we are locked with a triumphant click onto a balcony overlooking the hotel's grand ballroom—the crystal chandeliers and strolling strings and waiters putting out napkin fires with champagne—and Fence gets his first view of the detained.

A foreboding ocean of female bodies, a rippling sea of permanents and moving eyes, jagged rocks of breasts and cheekbones, elbows, noses, muscular shoulders and knees exposed by high drawn skirts. The tide changes with my appearance, with a sudden collective intake of breath and the motion of those many heads turned upward from metal eating trays to where Fence leans over the balcony rail. I am walking on the lake boardwalk again by the beaches and gazing with adolescent secrecy at the near naked bodies of the summer trade, older sisters, mothers, aunts who come to spend the summer spread and oiled on terrycloth, clustered in the oblique shade of umbrellas, backs to me, bodies heated by the sun, by the absence of husband, by the degenerate power of my sexual fantasy. Then comes the cue, and they all turn to discover me gawking on the boardwalk. The concentration of their regard is hotter than the summer sun; I am the focus and my face and shoulders and expanding groin are set on fire. I walk away, down the gull and tar-streaked ramp, not too fast, but then again not too slow.

Goddammit! who's on display here? The inmates' eyes are on me like hot grease, I hear their voices increase as if all their throttles are opened just a notch.

Ah vanity. And Mother Melicci to the rescue, pulling me from the grasp of an interminable blush.

All right! she thunders. This ain't the first, you've seen it before and if you're good girls you'll see it again, so why don't you just look down at them trays, that's where the food is.

Hey Mother, blow it for us, comes a voice.

Gimme some of them hot nuts.

Ooooh, you there, baby, let's mashed potatoes.

Knock it off! booms the Mother. We're takin' names.

I just took me one, shouts a patrolling matron.

Who's that lucky first winner?

Ruby!

Oh yeah, breathes the Mother. You're good, Ruby, you're really good.

I got a name!

Who's that?

The tiny twat!

No good! Throw her in the Gold Fish Bowl.

A great groan rises from the ballroom floor as a tiny brunette is hustled out a side exit. Mother Melicci takes a dainty handkerchief from her cuff and blots the corners of her mouth.

What's this taking names?

There you go, newsboy, you don't seem to see that these girls is rough, right off the streets rough, and got to be handled, and that's takin' names. You got to treat 'em like you love 'em if you want cooperation. Get it?

What happens once you've taken a name?

I just take care of them, Mr. Fence, Mother has her way.

What's the Gold Fish Bowl?

If you don't stop asking all these questions, Mother's going to get angry, Mother's going to take your name, Fence, and stand you in the corner.

We walk from floor to floor, cell to cell. Occasionally Mother stops to question a girl, laying her hand fondly on the inmate's arm. In the cells, the bunks are raised in tiers, the old hotel windows bricked and grilled. The lights are always on, an illusion of sunshine, and matrons prowl running their rubber billies along the bars. Yet the ghosts of lovers slip silently through. A two-time loser sleeps with her spirit salesman, he lies beside her on the bunk, his silk dressing gown open to reveal a freshly showered chest, a pint of bourbon uncapped nearby. Drunken G.I.'s stagger up and down the corridors, tapping on any door to awaken the prisoner within. She opens the cell bars just a crack and sees their rumpled uniforms and easy money. Hello, baby, here's the party. . . . Come on in, fellas. She takes a swallow of their cheap whiskey and leads those killers to her bed, its hard mattress stuffed with horsehair and a smuggled jar of vaseline.

Let's open up the register. We have stood long enough pinging impatiently at the bell. No clerk appears. Is he asleep at the switchboard or has he simply collapsed beneath the unnatural pressure of a desk-lamp light? No one's around, the dusty register lies at our fingertips, let's see who's here.

Forbach, Nancy. Charges: Destruction of Property, Drunkenness, Attack with Intent to do Bodily Damage. Six months.

Oh Miss Nancy Forbach, company nurse in your little antiseptic room, so tidy at five o'clock, wrapped in gauze, off to punch home, no one else to nurse. There is your lonely dinner to be prepared, sterilized I'm sure, rub your mouth with alcohol before you taste your soup. So dull, so humdrum, no one to light your Bunsen burner. You begin to drink quietly, until one day the walls of your dispensary wave like wind blown flags and your nylons rasp your flesh like burlap, so you take them off, so you smash the glass of your tidy cabinets, so you run naked through the offices jabbing at the male employees with a broken hypodermic,

Kowalscik, Texas. Charges: Prostitution. Ninety days.

You dream of the biggest panhandle you ever saw, you dream of tumbleweed and barrel cactus, you sip red-eye and sarsparilla and fumble in the sleeping miner's pants for his nuggets, you enumerate your riches, count your blessings, several garters, your pa's watch, your silk underwear, the true love of some ranch boy left behind, you sing songs of the opening of your own frontier, you let the Saturday night cowboys ride you to the limit, rodeo bronc, whoopee!

Hevart, Anne. Charges: Vagrancy. Sixty days.

What will you tell me, Anne?

I knew you couldn't be trusted, Fence, leave you for a second and already your nosin' in the confidential files. You're all the same, you newspapers.

You call these girls criminals, don't you Mother?

They break the law if that's what you're askin' and worse they break it all the time, just keep on coming in here, serve a month or so, try and make it on the outside, and bam! they're busted and back here with Mother. Try and tell me the hard-luck story, Fence, I've heard it all. I know these girls, and so when it's time to go I just say see you later and in a few weeks when the boys bring them back all beat and broken I just say why back so soon as if it was raining down in Miami Beach and they had to cut their vacation short. They calls me the Mother and they gives me a smile like it's good to be home again.

Home? the prisoner tears a flower from his sheets, Grannie taps food to her fish, Home Sweet Home hung forgotten and askew on

the parlor wall, firelight and the breath of migrants, children find the
pillow hollows, tree house, river cave, the corner in the library with the
fine worn edges of a book, the monk and his hour glass, the maestro
on the podium a graceful treble clef, the sculptor and his stone, a wax
museum where smiles are always frozen? walk across the threshhold of
the heart, is that where home is?

I don't call 'em criminals, Fence, I call 'em incorrigibles, they
ought to be detained, it's all they're good for.

We climb aboard an elevator which complains to its union
grievance board for having to carry such a burden. To the basement.

So here's the Gold Fish Bowl, announces Mother.

We enter a darkened room, in the center of the floor is a
pane of glowing glass the dimensions of the ceiling of a cell below. A girl
squats in that light-filled space staring at her feet. She is as naked as the
empty room.

The voice of the guard unreels: Prisoners in total isolation,
no visitors, minimum sustenance, no conversation with the matrons, no
voiding on the floor, yes the ceiling is a one-way mirror, do not walk near
the edge, do not tease the animals.

This is the girl sent down tonight, says the Mother. She's
been here before, two days ago in fact. Now we got her back again. All
she can see looking up is her own reflection, but she knows we're up here,
watching. Don't talk to me about reform, Fence, that's for dreamers, this
girl is case and point.

She has not moved, she sits, her bony knees on a level with her
shoulders, her arms around her shins, her head bowed to study her long
feet which protrude from beneath her thin figure. Looking down, Fence
sits for a moment beside her, attempting to be so still. But he cannot. His
muscles react to his awareness of them, he has to scratch, shift, squirm.
Fence knows she is no prisoner, she is gone, somewhere else beside the
room, or emptied in the emptiness, her mind her pulse her tendons
slacked to seeming nonexistence.

How does she sit so still?

She's a tiny twat.

Do all the girls whose names get taken get the Gold
Fish Bowl?

Not all, but most. Now take that Ruby girl you saw, oh yes,
that Ruby girl, she gets counseling, special individual sessions between

her and me, she gets the loving treatment. Very modern, up to date. We sit down girl to girl and talk it over. I've got a degree, you know, I give 'em treatment they can respond to, some girls like it so much they try to get taken down.

And this one here?

I've tried all I'm trying with her. She gets the Bowl regular.

Are there others?

The guard: Five Special Environment Detention Chambers, Numbers 1, 2, 3, 4, and 5.

2 is sleeping, 3 walks the perimeter of her cell, 4 lies on her back, pouchy stomach, sloe-eyed breasts, hand between her legs and a leer for the ceiling.

What about 4, Mother? Counseling?

You bet, and plenty of it!

My the things you learn in school these days.

I got a nose, Fence, and you don't smell so good.

Who's Number 5? Hevart, Anne. Charges: Vagrancy. Sixty days. Let me see you, Anne, swimming in the Gold Fish Bowl.

Red curls, skin traced with pale blue coolness, thighs strong and sturdy like pilings in the moonlight, and naked, naked as the day He made you, is that what you have to tell me, Anne?

Goddamn, it's Little Bit!

Those bits don't look so little to me, says the Mother.

FOUR

OOO-*gah* OOO-*gah* OOO
> *What is it, dear, heartburn again?*
*Tumult and shouting in the passageways, blink
red globes, the bulkhead doors sealing off airtight, the SS Ark
meets (and exceeds) all requirements established by the 1937
Helsinki World Maritime Safety Convention.*
> *Too much caviar?*
> *Animal the boats!*
*Turtle One reaches for his Mae West and
polyester raincoat.*
> *Boat drill, my darling, no need for alarm. The
notice instructs us to proceed without panic, with all
deliberate speed, to Station Five, Upper Deck, and to obey
calmly the orders of the Captain, Officers and highly trained
crew.*
> *The Supervisor drops to his knees in a funk. My
God, my God, back to the drawing board? His wife cackles
orders from beneath the bowsprit. In case of real emergency,
and as the establishment of a tradition, she will go down with
the ship.*
> *Station Five, Upper Deck: the blasé well-traveled
owl, the bewildered armadillo, the cuckoo hysterical slips
overboard into extinction, Turtles One and Two sit patiently
on their assigned thwart.*
> *The davits gears lines and pullies are jammed with
a coating of protective rust.*
> *Rest easy, my sweet, it appears the only way to
lower the boats is to sink the craft.*

Fence is lying on his bed, hearing the sound of empty corner:
Ben says, you remember how you was then, small and eager
and wet and spoiled rotten. You needed me, boy, for one thing or
another, change your pants, unwind that tangled fishing line, carry that
suitcase, show you how. It wasn't just your needs that made you what you
was, but what she made you need. It was your Grannie talking, hey Ben,

change that tire, hey Ben, show me how. I'm not blaming you, never have, just telling and see how I'm still tagging along and talking and teasing and trying to show you how just like it was in those days back then when you'd holler and scream and carry on 'cause you were hearing things from me you didn't want to. And there'd be your Grannie, coming out the door, all crinkled up in frowns, to stop me from my tormenting you. How'd she talk? Ben, don't you persecute that child, Ben, quit, Ben, stop. Both of you yelling, and I'd never listen, just walk on singing me something or setting up the perfect two-bank shot.

When there was a hawk that circled, calling at me, Fence, trying to sleep with the fine diagonals of the screen filtering the sound of a returning fisherman on the lake, when there was a hawk dropping in downward spirals, his beak curved in viciousness, its edge honed, its eye glancing off my painted walls to land on me momentarily, regularly, with the looming presence of a beacon, then my childhood shriek would wake the household and Grannie would come to berate the bird and the blows she struck would destroy the threat of claws and feathers of my nightmarish apparition.

The hawk rides the rising currents of my years. Now as I walk I hear again his cry and see his glass eye turned sideways to view me warily where I lie in mental darkness, his feathers glint there coated even as they are in dust, they move in some inexplicable wind through some inexplicable time. I hear the hawk cry not in fear but in triumph as if it is he who is hunting, who draws a bead on me, who will watch me fall into a heap of humanity with the perfect round droplets of blood on the nape of my neck.

Let the boy be, says Grannie from the corner. Let the boy be.

When his time comes, answers Ben.

You were growing up with them dying, boy, starting to rot before you even knew what living was.

Nigger! spits Grannie-Annie.

What's this? Ben, she cared about us, what's wrong in that?

She cared about what she wanted when she wanted and how she wanted, that's all.

The sound of ivory on his cheek.

Oh she loved you, yes indeed, but not for what you was, but for what she could make you. She could hold you in her hand the way she did them fish, play with you, dress you up like a doll, and when she didn't

want you anymore, well you were just put aside, back in the bowl to fend
for yourself. I cleaned them fish bowls, I polished her car, I planted her
garden. When she wanted the car, it was there and shining, when she
wanted flowers, they were standing high in rows for her to come along
and cut. You were nothing more than the car or flowers, used until you
weren't needed, decorative until you began to wilt, then you were left to
me and like the car and flowers it was up to me to polish you and make
you grow. I had my reasons.

What do I owe you, Ben?

You don't owe me nothing but that in my shoes you do the same.

And Little Bit?

A lid rattles, a lid on a pot where she is steaming chicken.

She pushes back a moist red curl, the stove hums with
pleasure, the odor of that meal fills my room, empty corner shimmers in
the heat. She turns and smiles, signaling that all is ready. Ben puts on his
white jacket and gets the tray.

Chicken and dumplings, our Anne's first meal, says
Grannie-Annie.

Ben is whistling the only two bars of blues I know.

Why did Grannie hire her?

Something new to play with, I imagine. Something new
to protect.

You know nothing of it! cries Grannie. I won't have you
influencing this boy the way you always did, teaching him how to nigger
kill and talk and curse. I brought that girl because she needed help,
because she was willing to work for her living instead of lying around
doing nothing, killing birds, shooting pool, tormenting an innocent boy.
Don't listen to him, Fence, don't listen, don't listen.

I am listening. I am remembering the day, one afternoon
so quiet like a Sunday when the kitchen smelled of nothing and yet was
filled with the aroma of cakes and pies and roasting meat, so quiet like a
Sunday when the fire crackled and Grandfather folded and refolded his
newspaper and Grannie-Annie played solitaire, the plastic cards clicking
against her fingernails, so quiet like a Sunday with the windows open
and the air filled with the calls of awakened insects, I am remembering
the muffled thuds of my sock feet on the linoleum of the pantry, I am
remembering two closed doors, one his, one hers, the noise and then the
silence and then her face, pink and flushed, peeking around the door

edge, smiling and explaining how I had awakened her from sleeping.

Where's Ben?

I don't know, he's gone out. Now won't you let me take my nap? There's lamb for dinner.

Gone out where?

Gone out.

It was so quiet like a Sunday as I retraced my path to the living room, so quiet with the roaring tumult of folding newspaper and the crescendo of shuffling cards.

You listening to what I got to say, boy?

Yes, yes, but it's late. I've got to get to work.

It never hurts to be a little late.

Ben, I saw Little Bit.

You saw Little Bit. . . .

Yes, in the Detention Home. I'm going to go see her, try and get her out.

You do that, boy, you go see her.

Don't see that tramp! Listen to your Grannie!

Now wait one minute here, we were friends, I admit that, but she was no tramp. And not so much because of me as because of her, we were friends, rooms side by side and working together. Days off, we'd go up to town and shoot some pool. She was good and the boys up there loved to see a white girl come around. She'd chalk up a cue and grin at the remarks and sometimes she'd laugh and poke at them boys leaving a little spot of blue somewhere on their trousers. She was mine but she could have belonged to anyone of those boys and she would have treated me the same, smiled and winked and put her hand on my shoulder and leaned against me just like that. She knew how to treat a man, but that don't mean she was a whore.

It was that first night then, that very first night, fatigued by the bus ride, shocked by the vision of all that water, happy with the success of her meal and new surroundings. But who gave into whom, or was there a question of giving in at all? They sat there drinking coffee late until he touched her hand, or she his, until he took her arm, or she his. The gravy was congealing around the dumplings and the chicken, the dishes done were draining on the sideboard, the bespattered coffee pot cooling on the stove. I was long since gone to bed, too stuffed to think, full enough to dream. Grandfather slept his heavy slumber. And

Grannie-Annie shuffled cards and counted fish, dreamt of angels and footsteps on the porch, she lay beneath a comforter hearing sounds from the kitchen she could not hear.

My room is so silent at this hour, this sunset. It is as if all the traffic outside my window, all the chaos of the City is somehow for an instant still, put in order. Figures come and go in empty corner. Ben and Grannie exit arguing, their faces contorted. Then Ben returns polishing the car in the sunlight, his shirt off, his black arms warm with sweat and reflecting the late afternoon like the glazed finish of the limousine. Green spark: Little Bit lies naked on the floor, she lies on her bed, the sheets in disarray, she lies in the brightness of a room, behind the kitchen below the glass. And the images meld, overlap in an endless dissolve, Ben's black chest covers Little Bit's full breasts, Grannie-Annie's face, her powdered face, fills my view, her mouth open and two bodies, black and white, framed in the fine drawn outline of her lips pronouncing: love thy neighbor.

Traced outline of bodies, face, upholstery flowers, the cracked plaster of my wall, a fluid carnival of optics, blue green yellow shingled forms, the scales of giant fish swimming by, lips words people all scooped up in cheesecloth, dark and light rolling down all planes, the hawk is there, above, and his wide wings are gold and in them I see my face faceted infinitely. . .

The sun has set. Night.
I'm going to talk to Little Bit.
I'll go with you, says Grannie-Annie.
Look for me there too, says Ben.

Work.
The gin rummy game is in full swing. Bernie's dealing.
What's the bet, Scraps?
Let's play for his soul.
Who's got a soul anymore?
The kid.
You must be frightened. Low stakes.

Cards in the fluorescent light slide smoothly, elbow ruts and cigarette burns on the desk top. Bernie arranges his cards neatly, shifting them in twos or threes, aligning up the corners, suits and rank. Scraps picks up his and discards.

You know, Bernie, it's an interesting question, who's got a soul any more. I figured no one until this kid comes along with something pinned on his sleeve. Everything's going up, food, rent, a good lay, but goddam you can get souls these days for nothing, they're giving 'em away!

Your draw.

Listen, I got rid of mine just about as easy as I'm sliding you this lean and lonesome dog-eared five spot.

Excellent discard. Come to poppa.

Bernie, the kid bugs me. There's something about the way he glides in here, the way he sits over there doing nothing but looking busy as hell. He stinks of old family, paneled living rooms and guilty money. He drives me around the corner, I've put a lot like him in that morgue of mine, and believe me I think the world is a little safer every time. I'll take that trey!

You passed one up while back, must be trying for a spade chain.

Dammit, you're not hearing a word I'm saying.

I play first, then I listen.

Well, what do you think?

Gin! I agree, I think there's hope.

What d'ya mean hope?

Hope he might hold out longer than the rest of us.

Why'd I keep these bastard kings? Hope!

Did you see those prison articles?

Of course I've seen them. First one runs tonight.

Well, what about that? He painted the place up like some goddamned rest home!

Not exactly how I pictured the D-house to be honest, but I've never been there. Good angle though, makes the Governor look like the wicked witch with all the state's beauty stopped up inside a glass bottle. The old man was pleased as hell. The kid did a good job.

Yeah, well, I been there visiting sometimes and there's not a word of truth in that garbage.

Oh my goodness, Scraps, such consternation. Since when has truth been your concern? or mine? Deal.

A copy boy runs into the City Room with an armload of first editions. He puts two handfuls on Bernie's desk where the game is underway. Fence motions frantically, five copies please, maybe I'll paper over empty corner with examples of my work.

That's fifteen cents apiece, mister. We don't give 'em away.

FIVE

The ark is steaming through troubled waters.
Lightning shoots across the sky like a crack in crystal. The
Supervisor takes a sighting on the hood ornament of a
thunderhead.
Turtles One and Two have taken to their bunks.
Musak marches soothe them, they subsist on tea and toast.
Isn't this our luck, says Turtle One. Save and
scrimp for a vacation and such rain, oh hell, oh damn!
Don't swear, dear, it's not that bad. We have
each other.
Rain gargles at the porthole. A violent swell sends
the ark spinning and the Turtles cracking together. Turtle Two
untangles her flippers provocatively.
Darling, she says.
Turtle One observes that look in her eye.
Of course, dear, rainy day, let me entertain you.
Fanfare: tarantara: the blackface choir sings
Hallelujah! drum roll shing-a-ling top-hatted dancers flutter
by, the stage revolves, thunder roars from the prop room, the
seas clap their hands in wonder, yes, the earth stands still.
Darling, says Turtle Two, and cradles over on
her shell.

Olden days, in the time of Merlin and the wicked Galen,
those artful fanciers who knew the why and wherefore of Nature's
pharmacy, in the time of witches living in spider forests, grinding herbs,
canning, brewing potions and packaging their remedies for love and
death that knights and princesses paid good money to try.

And modern times, with their injected serums that make
men cry out and reveal all withheld in the face of pain and humiliating
torture, that break the strongest with the subtle prick of the needle.
Sodium pentothal. Truth elixir.

Oh turtle soup! greater than potion or drug, with the magic
of olden days, with the power of modern times, you loosen up the tongue
and set the facts back on their feet again.

Little Bit scrapes the bottom of a bowl. We are at Dewey's
and I have taken the corner table in expectation of more guests to come.

Look out for that one, Fence, said Mother Melicci as we left
the Detention Home.

Sign out on the Sign Out Sheet, called the guard.

On parole, on probation, Fence the social worker with his charge.

Another bowl of soup, Dewey please, for the lady. And
perhaps some wine.

He grinds his dentures like winches.

'Bout time we got some class in here, he says.

Grannie-Annie and Grandfather sit down to my left.

Soup please for us, and two glasses of water.

Grannie opens her purse and wipes the silver with a hanky.

Ben walks in and leans against the bar.

Who's left?

Ah yes, here she is now, Mother Melicci hurries in, the guard
slipstreaming behind.

Mr. Fence, you come here too. Fancy that!

Don't flush the toilets after six P.M., says the guard.

See what I mean. Goddamn standing room only. Dewey!
Soups all around!

No one can resist it, soup of soups, for the moment there
is silence save for slurping, look at them swill it down. Ol' Miz Dewey
pokes her head out of the galley in wonder.

Good soup! says Grandfather.

I signal for another bowl. Dewey brings a steaming pitcher.

Well Anne, says Grannie-Annie, you're not looking as if the
years have treated you for the better.

Grannie, I interject, if you would stop and consider what the
years have done to you there dead and gone, a-molderin' in your grave,
but Fence, mind, respect your elders, the way your elders taught you.

Looks pretty good to me, says Ben. But then she always did,
didn't she?

Listen, old woman, you can't talk to me that way now. We are
equal, nobody's deader than anybody else the way I see it.

Little Bit looks up from her soup. How's Ben?

Dead as dead can be, says Fence.

How? When?

Oh Little Bit, can you be but moved by this, so perfect it can never be fiction, he died at the wheel of the long black limousine, on his way to pick up Grandfather at the Club, on his way just as he always was at that time on that day, fifteen miles an hour moving that great shining car in all its majesty through the traffic, he died of a massive heart seizure, painful but quick, he died but he brought the car to a quiet stop, parked it there with the tires unscraped against the curb, parked it there perfectly in the moment of his death. They found him sitting upright in his seat with his hands in a dead-sure grip on the steering rim. A life fulfilled.

I didn't hear about it.

Neither did I, says Fence. Grandfather didn't think it was important enough to tell me for nearly a year. I was away at school.

I didn't think you'd care, says Grandfather with a bit of creamy moustache above the lip.

You obviously didn't care much either, interrupts Ben. No flowers from the family, hundred-dollar nigger funeral and two bastard sons at graveside who thought an old man who worked for white folks must have something to leave behind. Some joke.

You should have saved the money we paid you, argues Grannie. Penny save, and let me see, sixteen years at two fifty a month, bonuses at Christmas and on your birthday, tips from our friends, and you squandered it all on women and billiards and guns and dogs, the sins of greed and lust and gluttony and nothing to leave for your children.

You old bitch, if you hadn't died first, I'd haunt you!

Mr. Fence, says Mother, I haven't been introduced to your nice family.

That's right, Fence, manners, form is paramount for bureaucrats and other incarnations of the dead.

Everyone, meet Mrs. Melicci, an old friend of mine.

Perhaps I should quote our friendship?

. . . under the able direction of Maria Melicci, who is the holder of a combined degree in Psychology and Physical Education from State.

Mrs. Melicci, known to her girls affectionately as 'Mother,' refers to her charges as 'misunderstood' darlings who have fallen victim to the debilitating influences of contemporary society.'

'In all my years of experience with this kind of work,' she continues, 'I have never known a girl who could not be reformed, rehabilitated, and placed back into society as a constructive citizen, school crossing guard, baker of pies and cakes, and mother of children.'

The Detention Home shows the mark of Mrs. Melicci's care and concern. From the dapper uniform of the receptionist at the door, to the cleanliness and homey atmosphere, to the unobtrusive presence of the matrons and the seeming absence of restrictive measures, the Home projects the relaxed good nature of a Brownie Troop or a YWCA summer outing.

Maria Melicci describes the Home as 'a happy twenty-four-hour bridge group, no hangups, just gossip, tea and cookies, and a little bit of love for everyone.'

Disgraceful, but that's what I wrote. Yes Mr. Fence, yes you did.

My very first words in print, and all what? yes lies! The brown envelope came back from Bernie—empty.

Mrs. Melicci looks like a very gentle woman to me, observes Grannie. Gentleness is a quality not often enough seen in this atheistic world.

So true, so true, agrees the Mother. My what a pretty shroud, Anne.

Thank you, Maria. I sewed it myself.

Grandfather climbs out of his soup bowl. I'm going to take my swim in the river, he says.

I can see nothing coming of this but an argument, a slamming of fists on the table, spilling soup. Waste.

You lazy . . .

You ugly . . .

Knock it off! shouts the Mother.

Do not raise your voices above normal conversational level in the dining hall, intones the guard.

You black maggot-infested . . .

You putrescent God-forsaken . . .

It could go on and on, pronouns and adjectives, not people, but memory does that, obscures the true personalities and retains descriptive labels for empty pronouns.

Little Bit, let's take a walk.

Sure.

If you will excuse us, ladies and gentlemen, we will leave you to your bickering and take the air. Dewey, put it on my tab.

Tab? What tab?

The rummy' game: gin!

Hey Bernie, where's the kid tonight?

I don't know, he would have asked for time off if he'd been here.

Time off! Seven years I been here and no time off.

What's he up to?

Something about a girl . . . Hmmm, that makes it 1,086 to 231, difference of 855 at a penny a point, $8.55 for tonight which added to the total brings us to an overall debt of $93.42, or one week's pay tax withheld. I'll speak to the business office.

Hearts and flowers, I knew it, the kid's in love. No wonder he was moping around this place. Oh Jesus, soul, lovey-dovey, what will this kid come up with next? Predict that one, Bernie.

One week's pay. Shall we begin again? I predict you'll lose.

People don't fall in love anymore, in today out tomorrow, slam bam thank you ma'am, free and easy on the backswing, that's the way. The kid's straight out of the nineteenth century, newspaper cub falls in love on job, corny-corn, an old-time movie. I think I'll write it up for the serials in the Sunday supplement.

Shuffle the cards.

Yeah, I can see her now, little cotton blouse and tits all homogenized and honey at age thirteen, debutante queen with fancy crinolines and an Eisenhower girdle and a mother at the door, what does your daddy do, sonny, as if their first wet palm date is a prelim to drawing up the contracts, music in the suburban church and an extravaganza for the country club. If the kid has the nerve to stick his hand in her pants, he'll find a Goody Two Shoes label on her cunt and plunk! goes his magic twanger. Oh Bernie, too much!

I agree, it's too much of a debt to carry. What is?

$93.42.

$93.42?

You owe me.

Bernie, you're the fuckin' company store!

Fence and Little Bit stroll down the levee, ankles twisting on
the cobblestones, hand in hand, for balance mind you. I wonder what the
hell I'm going to do with her now I've got her.
    What will you tell me Anne?
    We walk down to the courthouse, yes, where once the slaves
were sold, my private place where at least there is no argument, only the
finality of history. A bronze plaque is set into the auction stone as if the
selling of slaves was a great moment in our past. Slaves.
    Cold tonight. There is the change of season in the air. We
sit on the steps and stare out into the darkness where the river flows
like men's lives, a soft spring for beginning and then the open ocean of
immortality at the end of a wandering course.
    And Fence hears the hammering of the gavel and the voice
of the auctioneer: all right, all right, quiet down now, we're openin'
up for business here today. Bring in the first lot, Virgil. This here
is Number 46, a fine fifteen year old. Now who'll start us off right
tonight? Do I hear a bid? Come on, gents, no mean slave, this one. Do
three days work in two, carry her own weight in water. Thirty dollars,
do I hear. Worth more. Come bid, come bidder. Thirty-five and sold
and thank you. Number 21. There she stands in down home virgin
glory, blood's the proof, gents, come on up and have a feel, have a look.
Blood's always the proof. Sold! and think of me when you knock it off.
All right, here's what you been waiting for all this evenin', Number
58, that's 58, heavy labor, one sixty pounds, all muscle no fat, a little
surly, that's spirit, whip her into shape and she'll pull in your crops
better'n our white-faced mule. And here's the bonus! She's with foal.
That's right, gents, you heard me, two for the price of one. Ninety, ain't
enough. Hundred? Hundred twenty, once, and twice and sold sold
sold! Here's Number 23. . . .
    Fence stands above the pit, dressed in a paper-white suit.
Who's the stranger? Never seen the fella before. He's biddin' high.
Thirty-five dollars. One twenty. Auctioneer, I'm bidding high, I'm
buying all of them to set them free.
    Free?
    Blacksmith, chisel off your chains, clerk, set your papers
straight, put a sign on your door and a plaque on that stone, Mr.

Auctioneer, slaves aren't sold here anymore.
Do you hear it, Little Bit? What?
The history here.
I don't hear anything, Fence, except the cold.

Well then, come in where it's warm.
Fence opens the door to his room and ushers her in.
Not much, but home when the sun shines.
I think it's very nice. Could I have some hot coffee?
Problem: I have only instant tea and cold water. Would
iced tea do?
She smiles, she nods her head, she looks like Fence
remembers, warm like home-baked muffins, like a freshly dried towel,
like an early autumn morning in a down comforter.
Sit down—no chairs—on the bed, Fence will busy himself
with the tea and then sit on the floor and we'll talk, we'll talk.
Do you remember the lake, Little Bit?
Sure. She sips the foul stuff I've stirred up. Sure, that first
grey day, and your Grannie, all of you, I remember.
It seems so long ago. I was just a kid.
It was long ago. You're still a kid. But you'll turn out all
right, just like Ben wanted. God, I'm glad to be out of the D-house.
I was going crazy.
Vagrancy, Little Bit?
Down and out is the phrase, very low down and very strung
out. I've been there before for more glamorous reasons.
How many times?   .
Six or seven, maybe more.
How come?
You know, Fence, you've got a nice room here, not a bit like
I expected. I mean, this is a room, no suite, no apartment, a real rented
room. Who would have thought it? What would your Grannie say?
What are you doing here?
Working for the paper. Night shift.
How come?
Fence has to laugh, oh she's got you. More tea?
It's terrible.
She leans back against the wall, runs her finger through the

dust on the window sill, she looks, well, relaxed on my Indian spread, my daytime bed is positively proud to have her there.

What are you going to do now you're out?

I don't know. I'm tired, and you finding me has brought a lot back. Maybe I'll get a job.

Where'll you stay?

Hotel maybe, I'll find a place.

Listen, why not stay here? I'm here only during the days, gone by six and gone all night. You could sleep here and by the time I get home you'd be off to work. We could split the rent.

I'll think about it. Do you have a ladies?

In the hall.

I can see it now, curtains on the window, flowers in that sink, Miss and Mister on the mailbox, and close up forever empty corner, forever with a big stove, white and porcelainized, with electric burners and pots and pans, steaks broiling, turkeys roasting, pies cooling, the little timer ringing away at all hours of the day and night to signal home cooking here.

Sheets on the bed!

Clean sheets.

A crisp new spread? Little Bit!

So Fence, you want to hire a cook, a maid, a whore, for your rented room.

No!

What do you want then?

To share. . . .

She returns, through the tongue-tied door, her hair brushed, red curls over her ears, and a new powder line along her jaw and lipstick, neat and moist.

I feel better. So you want to share a room with an old woman, Fence?

Who's old?

Thirty-two.

Yes, I want to.

Well then, come here roommate. . . .

My God, what she cooked up for me was the envy of any European chef, all sorts of pastries one after another on the rolling table, cream puffs, napoleon slices, cherry tarts, and croissants stuffed with jelly jelly.

I was beaten and whipped, my nuts were ground, cream was everywhere, and sugar like you've never seen or tasted, I was touched all over by her ladyfingers, a banana was split asunder.

Maraschino!

Floating islands!

Very butterscotch soufflé!

She smothered me in her loving mousse.

It was a chocolate sundae morning.

We tossed and pummeled my poor old mattress, brought tears to its eyes as our movement brought back memories of its well stuffed youth. She bound me in her short arms and legs, I smelled the distant odor of her red hair, I slept on her ample breast. And as I slept, there was no taloned hawk whooping and falling, no horror, fear, rather the soft twittering of recipes in my dreams. She did not let me sleep for long.

How I nibbled up her crumbs and sauces.

How I cleaned her icing bowl.

How I drank the sweet sauterne of her loving cup.

And as the dessert dishes were cleared, we drank hot iced tea in demitasse and spoke of our new arrangement.

Yes, we can share the rent.

Yes, we can talk up old times.

Yes, we can cook up a storm.

Brandy?

In a quiet restful moment:

Little Bit?

Yes . . .

I think I'd better warn you. We're not alone.

Who's here?

Well there, in the corner for example, beyond my Indian spread, wadded up and thrown aside, sleeping in its underpants, stand Ben and all the others looking on in immortal silence.

SIX

Naturalists please relax: this is a love scene.
Tick.
Tick-click.
The stateroom is dark from porthole curtains or the massing stormy night. The sound heard above the wind is of two beating hearts, two chests together, two plastrons moving in embrace. Turtle Two entwines her flippers about her lover's carapace, she squirms beneath him, her vestigial tail begins to work with delight.

Turtle One strokes her exterior bony plates, he runs his flipper along those thick ridges which intimate the secret chelonian sexuality of her ribs and vertebrae, he rubs his leather cheek across the horny surface of her shell and penetrates the coy reluctance of her feminine armor.

Appropriate moans and murmurs.
Tick. Tick-click. Tick-click.
Their kiss unites toothless jaws and flicking reptilian tongues.

Familiar cries of pleasure and enjoyment.

A soft pinkish glow begins to illuminate the amorous pair. The friction of their mating infuses a light through the bony conductor of their shells, they heat, they radiate, they transluce, to shine a moist sweat brown, to show a reddish mirrored hue, like two hot rocks burning one step away from becoming quartz.

Turtle One releases primordial seed.

And simultaneously, Turtle Two jerks her head into her shell, she is racked by her coming emotion, and from within that protective chamber comes her amplified echoing cry: OOOOOOOOOOOOOOOOOOOOOOOOOOOOOO OOOOOO-gaaaaaaaaah

Ohmigod, not again! the Supervisor falls faint against the helm, no one takes the wheel and the SS Ark steams on irrandomly toward uncharted seas.

I have transformed my room for Little Bit, into a fay show
of color, gaudy pattern, ostentatious design, an action painting in
which we as elements, not inhabitants, are displayed, mannequins
wrapped in window dressing for those on the glass's other side to
admire and covet. Consumption. Fence looks back on his way to work,
over the heads of the gathered crowd, to see his window all aglow
like a three-alarm fire to welcome Little Bit home. That one there,
officer, erect the barricades. And returning in the early morning, I see
the row of plants, small hanging and green, she has purchased at the
supermarket, lined up on the window sill, shaking off the miraculous
urban dew, taking the sun, doing their daily breathing exercises to the
cadence of the neighbor's television, growing life, the very first seen
that day, isolated on a washed dead abstract facade. Ah yes, Fence,
your Babylon.
     Little Bit locks the door in earnest. I lose the keys.
     We might install a telephone.
     Little Bit brings home real china plates in her purse, from the
hotel restaurant where she works as a waitress.
     We fight with the landlord. He cannot double our rent because
there is rarely more than one person in the room at any given time.
     What about empty corner? giggles Little Bit.
     I insist upon our right to have in guests on occasion.
     Our life is the prepackaged dream, with donuts and still
warm instant tea awaiting me, and two toothbrushes in the glass,
and squinched kleenex in the bottom of the bed, and lipstick notes
instructing me to go out to dinner.
     Time off takes us on footsore walking journeys; you know,
sock-soaked walks on pavement that inspire you upon return to bury
your shoes. We go downtown where business is dying of suburban
suffocation and the Chamber of Commerce resembles a mausoleum.
The politicians boarded up the burlesque house and erected a marble
monument honoring the dead with the howitzers that killed them
displayed on the lawn. Bam bam, mommy, see the guns!
     The population downtown is the convention trade, that amus-
ing irony of men traveling from one City to another in the expectation of
more fun. The twentieth anniversary of the massacre of charlie company
on Bataan. Hi, Gus, how's the leg? Bam bam, Mommy, see the guns!
     We walk through the signs of renewal, urban that is, each

sign announcing the destruction of the region, the ball and chain coming to tear it all down by order of the bond holders and their mayor. Great openings gut the City, streets with no houses, only piles of rubble, bricks and mortar and twisted bedsteads, a sure copy of the blitz, a mighty war machine has caused all this in the name of a greater good.

It's all too familiar to me, I am a child of the television news.

The goal of all this walking is the park, strange anomaly, built for an exposition several generations past, like a City within a City, with massive baroque buildings overgrown at the foundations, the pavement cracked by grass, nature mistress here in warning to Cities everywhere. The park is curiously empty with its ponds and shooting fountains, its cricket field and hidden hollows and lovers' lanes. Does it exist merely as location for the advertising illusion? In the future, people will pay good money to see what's left.

Mechanized recreation nibbles at the edge of course, contemporary outdoor fun, roller skating trails, tennis anyone, and an observatory donated by a well-meaning philanthropist who never saw the City he lived in for looking at the stars. Golf carts for the riding stables, the zoo puts up a chain link fence and installs a ticky-tacky tourist train. Time will complete the transformation, covering the park in dollar a day parking for the monkey show, but for now there remains trees and grass and hidden statues, packs of gabbling geese walking on the bridle path, bird song, old men and young boys fishing with worms, old-fashioned mythical park-like things, and you can lie on a blanket, and rest your tired feet, and above the omnipresent sound of the distant City hear the intercourse of leaves. You can be alone, so alone that if you were of the inclination, you just might try and make your girlfriend in the middle of the public park with a million persons looking on.

Isn't this fantastic, Little Bit? Smell the country in that air.

I itch, Fence.

Relax, lie back and enjoy yourself.

Fence, come on, this is our day off, let's go to a movie.

We are lying then on my narrow bed, finishing up the tooth telling kernels of jiffy pop, staring at empty corner. Little Bit's breasts are greasy where Fence has touched them with buttered fingers.

The house lights dim.

The screen flickers, bright and sun-streaked, descending

numbers, and we are looking across a lawn toward a table set out in
the shadow of a tree. The camera begins to move, long awkward steps,
over-attempt at being steady, and we approach the table with its white
cloth lifted slightly at the corner by a breeze, with its chairs, some
unfolded some folded and leaning against the tree. Bits of colored
paper are scattered across the lawn, crepe creepers in the branches, and
crushed hats and napkins, plates and plastic forks. The camera holds to
observe the residue of some child's party, cake and icing smudged and
pink juice stains on the cloth, and then our perspective rises to focus
beyond the tree, toward a screened-in summer house and Grannie-
Annie coming toward us, dressed in light blue and a quiet birthday
smile, lifting her hand in a deprecating gesture, accepting the camera's
compliment only with the graceful motions of her sleeves. She is
talking to us, her mouth works silently and still it is a command.

Cut to boys at softball, the slow lobbing lethargy of a heavy
ball, water soaked from too long forgotten in the basement, the dead
sound of the stroking bat. Runners move, trees are bases or fallen jackets,
the fielders pound their gloves and crouch expectantly.

Fence is up, full-frame, in grass-stained trousers and a
sweater tied round his waist.

Grandfather, sitting in a deck chair behind the plate, is ump,
solid, impenetrable, just, wide like a backstop, with all the interest of
an empty bleacher.

Look Little Bit, it's me! Look how fat I was!

The ball lazes in. I swing.

I miss.

That is a strike, indicates Grandfather.

I adjust my stance, tap dirt from my cleats, cock my wrists,
spit brown from my chewed up chocolate, tum sideways to the mound to
compensate for the slowness of my reflexes.

Strike two, his hands resting on his vested belly.

Hot, in my City room my hands are sweating, I'm full of cake.

And yer out!

Jesus, that's pathetic. Fat little Fence strikes out, Casey, it's
poetry and at my own party. Humiliating. What birthday was that anyway?

Fifteen, and already a loser, Fence.

Who took that goddamn film!

Little Bit rolls over and carefully lays a breast on mine.

I did, little birthday boy.

Little Bit is sleeping, curved up against me. Fence lies awake, his body tuned to an hour pattern and not the time of day. Through the window, I hear the usual serenade: bombs ticking in bank vaults, the fall of giant corporations. A taxi door slams in anger and the City shakes as the subway runs through its intestine like a 13¢ hamburger. The bus at the bus stop, brakes sighing their fatigue, longs for the barn. Indicators of coming and going which serve to dramatize remote but apparent purpose.

Ben is doing the crossword. Six letters for 'mocking guest at a tea party'?

Turtle.

It fits!

Shut up Ben, you'll wake Little Bit.

He sticks the pencil behind his ear, puts the paper down.

Yeah. You two sure look comfortable. Mind if I join you?

Hold it! three in a bed? a narrow bed that's not used to holding one for more than a daytime slumber, a narrow bed that's now working overtime, carrying double, out of pride and affection for its owner and not for the lousy wages? There is a practical question in addition to the revolutionary moral implications.

Come on boy, I don't weigh nothing. I'll just squeeze down easy between you two and nobody'll know the difference.

A reasonable man, not a prude, I am well aware of the change in sexual attitudes in the decade following the war.

I am *not* a child of the change of sexual attitudes in the decade following the war.

In principle I am not against relations between consenting adults of the same sex, nor against group jungle gym, I have read of men and sheep, but nowhere in my experience is there a ghost-job! Ben, get out!

Quit kicking!

Out lascivious ghoul!

I've gotta right.

What are you talking about?

I saw it first. I set you up.

Listen to that, all right, a debt of honor, get in—but no snoring.

He puts that grey head down on my pillow, quietly, invisible, and together we wrap our arms around the dreaming Little Bit of love,

his girl and mine, she embraces him, I embrace her, she embraces me, and
I wrap my arms around that old man who taught me the only two bars of
blues I'll ever know.

Good night.

Bernie never bats an eyeshade. I'm late, I'm late.

Hey Fence, Publisher wants to see you in his office.

He wants to get married, calls Scraps. Old men and boy-chick
assholes. Society stuff, peau-de-soie!

I bequeath empty corner for the joy of all the world, and
Dewey to cater my last meal, please.

Publisher is working late, a monologue for the star reporter.

Me Fence!

. . . not much time to chat, Fence, cocktails with I think the
mayor, then dinner with whom? I can't remember, I'm yes pleased with you
son, did a fine job on the Detention series, telegrams, just look at them there
on the desk, letters to the editor by the sack load, pouring in, three calls for
legislative inquiry and best of all threats on my life, my life, must shine my
shoes, must find that polish, we'll follow up of course with outrage on the
page, let me see how about this: we note with interest reaction to our recent
prison investigation, no too dull too academic, how about this? to whom
do we owe the disastrous state of our penal correction system? come down
hard on the administration, shake up the sinecures, but of course we'll need
more, much more, Bernard was right, you're just the man, with photographs,
deplorable conditions, brutality, a few bruised faces, make it look good, these
letters, these after-dinner speeches, these classifieds. . . .

The walls are hung with pictures, framed Publisher with the
ball team, the president, the council of churches, the unknown soldier
and his proud mother, all smiling, all gladhanding, all back slapping have
you heard the latest, Publisher laying the wreath, cutting the ribbon,
kissing the baby.

Brutality? Deplorable conditions? Is he reading the
competition?

Thank you sir, but I don't quite understand. My articles
didn't mention brutality, they weren't anything like the real situation
down there, I admit, it was all lies.

Fence on unemployment, Fence on welfare, Fence and the
five-cent apple trade. I admit to a tremble.

Nonsense! of course it wasn't lies, liberties yes perhaps, but never never lies, I know son, but let's have none of this quibbling about facts, damn bow tie, here give me a hand will you, facts you see are relative to your acceptance of them, facts can prove anything, facts are fabrications, we're responsible to a public out there, great, vast, people, and that's all they get is facts, and the facts are awful, depressing, defeating, deadening, there! fluff it out to show the polka dots, so everybody's hiding from them, or behind them, because if you confront them face to face, Fence, it's suicide, a statistical overdose causing apathy and indifference and catatonic noninvolvement. We're out to beat that, you must think yellow, Fence, that's our rule of thumb, that's our purpose, we're artists remember that, great journalists are poets, Twain, Menken, Jim Hagerty, who gives a damn about the facts!

I don't catch on too quick.

Look, you write the truth about the D-house and it's ho-hum and turn to sports or comics, I've read this before, I know it's true, but I don't want to know. But you tell a lie and suddenly there is the unexpected, something counter to the conventional wisdom, and it's sit up and take a sip of coffee and begin to wonder, where's that nail brush, if they can do it in the D-house, if this Melicci creature can get it done, well then why can't the others, the wardens, the administrators, the governor, what the hell are they doing? Interest, the lie sparks the interest, Fence, and here come the letters, here come the telegrams. It's incredible how your nails get dirty in this City. And what are they doing, nothing of course, even if they're trying, but when the people get upset, get together, everybody's doing something, and something gets done, and what set it off? a lie! We tell one fat whopper, and now we can go about trying to tell the truth. Hold my coat, will you Fence, damn sleeve, the mayor's such a bore, it's a flash in the pan, that's right, Fence, but it does the trick for a moment and that's grand, and it's our responsibility to make it happen, keep it flashing in bright bright yellow, keep it flashing, flashing, flashing . . .

Jesus, Bernie, look at the kid. Publisher really did it to him.
Apparently. The old think yellow routine.
The blind leading the blind.
Fence is sitting in his chair in the City Room, yes feet up, slowly revolving, thinking, coming down off dizzy.
I have been given, it seems, poetic license. A covenant?

SEVEN

The earth is fluid, filled with swimming things:
the birds above, and clouds, the fish below, and continents.
In its center, volumes of heat pitch and bow into a centrifugal
sphere, expanding, cooling renewal on the under layer and
dying on the outer as the wind lifts deader winds away.

The apparent metaphor is directionless current
or accident or destiny. In a uniform medium, verticals and
horizontals are synonymous with circles, merely motion.
Immutable law of science. But consciousness demands a static
place, wagers on it, moves from awakening to impending
death bearing hope willingly as a concept in its microscopic
brain.

Hoping for collision, things going bump! in the
night. And so it is fluid that lifts the SS Ark and throws
Turtles One and Two together, and it is fluid that falls outside
their porthole.

And it is fluid that they breathe so noisily.
And fluid that lubricates their unforeseen union.
And fluid in which the seed does swim.
And fluid that is the seed itself.

In a moment, strange and wonderful, static and
full of hope, collision does occur, fluid meets fluid. In a
moment, for Turtles One and Two, something is conceived
but not yet born.

Something in the mailbox? Fence studies the postman's
prints in the dust around the slot. Very strange, Fence receives no bargain
flyers or sale announcements, one of the benefits of anonymity, escape
from the mailing list conspiracy, no giveaways.

The envelope is bent and familiar. Inside: a large black paper
heart on which is pasted a colored photograph, 8 x 10, glossy, of a girl, red
curly hair, voluptuous—only a superficial resemblance it seems to me—
covered ninety per cent over with first degree burns, rough raw flesh and
PHOENIX tattooed on her stomach. Her eyes stare straight at mine, she
holds a sparkler in her mouth, strikes a match on one scabby breast, and

stimulates her orifice with a lighted candle.

Dear Fence, reads the heart, Be My Valentine.

Fence is taking out his anger on his teeth. Instant tea makes an excellent powder. Presweetened. Mint.

Who sent it and what's he got against you? asks Ben.

This guy at work, Scraps, and I wish I knew. He leaves all kinds of stuff for me at the office, but this is the worst.

Or best. Where can he go from this? You know, I hate to say it boy, but this looks a lot like someone we know . . .

Shut up, Ben!

Up and down, one and two, brush motion up and down!

Oh shit, here's your Grannie boy.

Up and down, dear, between the teeth, behind and massage the gums, make it hurt, make it bleed, what's this you're using? why, you'll stain your teeth that filthy brown.

Right, Grannie, when you brush your teeth once a week you have to be thorough, oral hygiene is next to godliness.

Isn't this nice, a Valentine.

Grannie looks down at the black heart and it only takes an instant for the image to reach her dead brain. Shame, anger, outrage, she opts for an emergency disappearance, shawl tassels zinging like piano wire.

You degenerating black bastard! you've gone too far this time! she screams from a heat-distorted empty corner.

Oh man, we're going to get it. I think I'll exit by the front door for a change.

I abandon the brush, swallow off a mouthful, the better part of valor.

Wait a minute, I gargle, I'm going with you!

Where's Scraps? Fence is rushing up and down the aisles pulling open morgue drawers at random.

Come on, you son of a bitch, I know you're in here!

In the N's, I find him, extract him from the wall like a corpse on a refrigerated slab, he's sleeping, little weasel N for NOTHING.

N for NAP.

N for NECROPOLIS.

You got a warrant son, come in here without N for KNOCKING?

Listen, Scraps, I'm sick of receiving this junk mail!

Anger? Reaction? Something of the proverbial goat? I didn't know you had it in you, kid.

Cut the crap!

Crap's all there is, friend.

What's the point?

The Valentine's the point, saint's day for all the bleeding hearts, I thought you'd be interested in the subject matter. Anybody you know?

There I stand in N for NEVER-NEVER land between fury and resignation, belief and disbelief, victory and defeat, Fence standing in a moment that calls for a coup de grâce and the best he can come up with is the useless in-between, that ambiguous over-used expletive little more than a substitute for helplessness:

Fuck you, Scraps.

Be my guest, I don't often get it in the file drawer.

What's wrong, Fence? asks Little Bit. Why so quiet?

Don't he look preoccupied, regular philosopher stone, says Ben from you know where.

Nothing to say, old Fence alone with a speechless bed, a lover, and a well-intentioned apparition.

We'll entertain you.

With what? What it's like to be a waitress, what it's like to be dead?

Too boring for words, they chorus.

Ben grows misty. I like rememberin'.

Remembering what?

Nothing much, just things I did. You remember going out to kill that hawk, boy? I remember that. I remember every fish I caught in that lake and what I caught him on, and every fish that got away. I remember my best pool shots, arguments and fights I had, jokes I made and songs, and every girl I laid. You name it, if it happened back then, I remember.

How about that time we went to the carnival? laughs Little Bit.

Sure.

The man in the ticket booth wouldn't let us in at first, because we were together.

And I told him we were part of the sideshow, The Fabulous

Salt and Pepper, and not to worry because they always made us march at the back of the parade.

And you tried to kiss me and they stopped the Ferris wheel, with all those people standing around below us and pointing and you getting all hot and bothered and ready to rock the boat. I thought when they brought us down the crowd was going to eat us!

I wasn't scared, I knew all them people, I used to go to town, take this boy here and do the errands, they knew me too. I'd go to the butcher, and he was down there pointing with his wife and family, and I'd go to the grocery and Clarence, the clerk, he was there too with some white girl from the store.

I remember that butcher, shouts Fence.

Diversion.

He was always in the freezer, I thought he must live inside, and we'd order special cuts so we could go through that big wooden door and pick out the steer.

Yeah, and he set aside lamb kidneys and calves brains for your Grandfather.

Sometimes you sent me in alone for the order and he'd ask me: where's your black shadow, Fence? Sun's out today and I don't see your black shadow.

He said that?

He did, and I never really knew what he meant, he'd be cutting meat with a cleaver, winking at the other butchers, where's that black shadow?

You remember Clarence, boy?

Clarence at the grocery, short and bald and a falsetto voice, he took your chauffeur's cap and put it on a melon and drew a face with grease pencil, and he lifted me by my ears. . . .

And who cut your hair?

You did.

And you'd scream awful.

I was always screaming the way you tell it.

And there'd be your Grannie comin'.

Grandfather swimming, a cheese soufflé in the oven, the flowers bent down by the warm wind. . . .

The afternoon melds into nostalgia, Ben is the illusive grasp of memory, he flickers in empty corner, steady in the focus of

distinct remembrance or fading into disparate patterns of oblivion as
reminiscence fails.

Look at him, Little Bit, poor old guy, if it weren't for you
and me . . .

We won't forget him, Fence.

Little Bit and I are making love, and Ben is shouting orders,
big as life again, old ghost, urging me on, by the numbers, counting
cadence, instructing me on proper buttocks roll, when to plunge, when to
withdraw soft and easy, beating time, giving me the signal.

Let fly now!

Now, Ben?

Now, son, just after she starts talking the way she do, she
always started talking when she was ready for it good, and I'd come down
hard on her and get to laughin' listening to her moan. That's the way I
used to do.

I look over my shoulder to empty corner, seeking his
approval, but there is someone else I see, in that moaning moment in
which everything is forgotten but the future, I see another figure, wide
half-dressed in shirtsleeves undershorts and gartered socks, Grandfather
sitting there with Ben, side by side, Grandfather with a familiar smile on
his lips and an unexpected expression in his eye.

Little Bit is whispering and Fence falls into a private sleep
not so much from exhaustion as from a need to avoid the implicit
responsibilities of surrogate love.

Fence needs treatment, good for what ails you, from athlete's
foot to hysteria, the wonderful curative of ol' Miz Dewey's devising:

Turtle soup!

Drink deeply of the unifying broth in which all men and
women are equal and the same, shells discarded or cut in two for
ashtrays, flimsy bodies reduced to essence, for medicinal purposes only,
drink deeply.

And then continue.

Dewey, my captain, wipes the wiping spot on the bar with his
wiping rag and reflects on the philosophy of my noisy slurp. A quart of
turtle soup for the road makes that long crawl endurable.

Hoxie discovers my soup-grogged stupor, a pinch of self-pity, a spoonful of misunderstanding, and there's Fence belching in the corner booth and picking his teeth with a turtle rib.

Fence, we got work to do, what's eating you?

Drowning my sorrow, in cream and add a dash of sherry.

Come on! Bernie's predicted a porno-bust, call girl ring downtown, and damn if the police dispatcher didn't confirm it. Bernie wants the story for the early sheet, so hustle up! You're lucky I know where to find you.

Lost and found, Hoxie, is there a reward?

Drive. I got to load my camera.

He fumbles in a leather bag, takes out a plastic bottle marked DEVELOPER, and swallows long on bourbon.

That's not developer, Hox, that's FIXER.

Beats soup, Fence.

Nothing but nothing beats soup, my friend. Where's the bust?

Usona Hotel.

Where Little Bit of course is setting up the tables for the dinner shift. I drive the right-angled route like a whirlwind in the city center whistling.

The crowd is trading rumors like dirty jokes as we arrive, they pick misinformation surreptitiously from each other's pockets. We join them. Events like blood in the water attract us, crawling from out of our holes.

In the Manager's Office, the Vice Squad Chief, familiar figure 'round town, I'm the best damn cop et cetera, is making a statement, prepared like his slicked down appearance and pancake face, speaking convincingly through the flashbulbs and lenses to his public.

A confusing mixture of fact and fiction.

. . . three waitresses in the hotel restaurant working the innocent clientele for the purposes of prostitution, the business lunch crowd and mid-afternooners . . . whores, hundreds and hundreds of whores working the hallways and servicing the Shriners, Mafia owned and operated, communist inspired and forgetful about protection payments to the local precinct. . . .

How'd you get 'em, Chief.

Undercover informants. . .

They got records, Chief?

They got records.

They got names, Chief?

Those apprehended are as follows: Mischkin, Cynthia. Pulaski, Mary. Hevart, Anne. All three on probationary status and will be remanded, repeat that's remanded, to the Women's House of Detention of this city. Any further questions?

Fence has an inquiry or two.

What's the charge, Chief? What's the proof, Chief? When's the trial, Chief?

Young man, the tone is patronizing, there will be no trial, we have proof thus they are clearly guilty and why tie up the busy courts? of course the proof is confidential a witness whose anonymity we must protect and who would be compromised should we bring a charge, intolerable! of course a charge is unnecessary as these individuals have previous records and are at liberty only on probationary status now revoked and they are returned to jail, young, man, the tone is threatening, does that answer you satisfactorily?

Indeed. Facts or fictions, what difference does it make?

Thank you, gentlemen, well back to duty, the policeman's job is never done. . . .

Anger is a deceptive thing, an encephalographic blitz in the brain, a strong kettle thump on the heart, and the nerves transmitting some mighty stimulus to charge your skin like a fresh swept carpet, a fine tuned equilibrium is upset complexly, and yet the reaction is so simple, dizziness or an instant of a dark forgetfulness, no time to think, no time to understand anger until it's past.

Rigged! Hoxie, they've got Little Bit on some public relations gimmick! and we put that guy's face in the news!

That's right, Fence, electric flash, left profile, and you'll see it on page one in the morning. Come on, relax, call in and tell 'em we'll make the deadline.

Oh Bernie, wise man of the nighttime air waves, Fence whispers into the confessional microphone, stares at the glowing yellow radio lamp: they got my girl, Bernie, the police and the ghosts, they got my girl. . . .

His presence is in that light, in speaker hum, transmitted from antennae on the highest building, rebounding from stellar barriers his frequency modulates the confusion of the City, programs the fact, broadcasts the fictions. I await reception of his signal to enervate response.

Bernie, come in Bernie, communications moose, soup and rummy, I submit myself, blue pencil please. . . .

Fence flicks the on-off switch, this thing is out of order.

Uh Fence, comes the still small static voice, your editorial counselor is indisposed, this is Scraps speaking, who sitteth at his right hand, may I be of any assistance?

Poor brother turtle, poor prehistoric me. . . .

EIGHT

*The source of power to move the waves and
tides is the noxious waste gases from the fires of the earth's
core, released bellows-like through geologic gills such as
the Rodrigues Fracture Zone which divides the Indian Mid-
Oceanic Ridge horizontally and joins the Muscarine Trench
off Reunion Island to the Ceylon Abyssal Plain. From this
point, strong currents break off easterly to Diamantia and
westerly to the Agulhas Plateau and those tricky rips off the
Cape of Good Hope.*

*Young winds are stored in ceramic jars in the
secret caves of the hermit Bagba. He is instructed to allow
no premature leaks, to keep the lids tightly closed, releasing
winds only by order of the seasons. But loneliness is a severe
challenge to discipline, and Bagba, chosen as he is by a fallible
god, is not psychologically prepared for the solitude of his
distant mountain post. He is a compulsive conversationalist
and in need of someone to talk to he tumbles the jars, spilling
the winds wildly down from his hidden place to speak
articulately not with him but the sea.*

*This confluence of wind and water in the Indian
Ocean creates a formidable pressure disturbance, enormous
counterrevolutionary spirals which hide well-known hazards
and uncover dangers previously unknown.*

*The SS Ark is steaming for Afanasy Nikitin
Seamount, a notorious port where she will replenish stores
and the Supervisor will sample the brothels, when she strikes
this storm. Helpless, she is driven north, blown against her
will into the Arabian Basin. Certain other published accounts
claim the SS Ark comes to rest (with a sickening crunch, no
less) on Mt. Ararat (Elev. 16,946 ft.). Not so.*

*The SS Ark is ripped from her rudder to the udders
of the Supervisor's wife by a submerged reef off the Laccadive
Islands. And despite the precautions and good intentions of
her designers sinks like the archetypal stone.*

The guard is mildewing in his cot posted near the D-house door. He does not stir, but his lips move like the slow growth of spore, his breath coming wheezingly to regulate the twenty-four-hour operation of the establishment: no expectorating, do not bend the cheap tin spoons, no urinating between ten and six, no laughter at any time. . . .

Fence crawls up the steps into the revolving door, pushing it round with his forehead, gently, gingerly, no quicker than the speed of the old guard's brain. On his belly, Fence slithers across the threshold like a draft or a cockroach familiar with the labyrinthine routes through settling plaster walls. He hunkers beneath the cot, keep the butt down, arm and elbow for the elevator. The safety door plays a polka on its accordion bars, Fence presses the button for an upper floor and somewhere high above in the shaft the outraged motor shouts: hey guard! do your duty, it's against the regulations to ascend after sunset.

What? Who's there? Not the guard speaking, he merely notes with an asthmatic entry in his mental logbook that the elevator is in illegal use. He is paid to regulate, but not to sound alarms.

Who's there! Mother Melicci sits up in bed, suddenly awakened. I smell something! not fire, no, sniff, not smoke, sniff, sniff, but just as dangerous. . . .

Fence slides along the linoleum beneath the nodding billy matrons. He finds the proper cell, compresses himself significantly, and squeezes through the keyhole. Little Bit is sleeping in the bottom bunk and I climb in with her.

We crawling things like dark warm places.

Wake up! Come on, Little Bit, we've got to talk.

She gives me a sleep-sodden shrug, pulls her knees up to touch her breasts and murmurs: Fence.

Fence? Fence! fully awake now, Fence how in the hell did you get here!

Crusading reporter, rain sleet snow and all that, I am a distant cousin of the Hardy Boys, and what we don't go through to get a story. Listen, what happened? Bernie called a bust and by the time I got to the Usona they'd hauled you away.

It's a fix, that goddamned Vice Chief is out to stuff the ballot brains again.

I'm filling sugar bowls and in sweep the cops talking to each other across the dining-room on walkie-talkies. They put us in the paddy and here we are. . . .

Straight from the Keystone Manual.

We'll take them to court, press charges, we'll make them produce their so-called witness.

Fence, they probably got one. I don't have a chance with my record, and they know it. Anyway, Cinnie Mischkin was hustling a bit on the side and Mary Pulaski was givin' it away. And I'm living with you, how's that going to go down in court?

Living with me?

Well, it's not exactly prostitution, is it? But you let some assistant D.A. get a hold on it, and see what we're up to, poor Fence, paying or pimping and all you wanted was someone to fix your food. Oh, and don't you forget your Publisher, watch him sound off, slack morals among the young. He'll undoubtedly persuade you, crusader, to write the story. Shit, I've been had, Fence, a long time ago. I'm tired, I might as well relax and make the best of the worst. I'm not a total stranger to the Mother, she can be kinda sweet. Go home.

But you can't let them beat you with a nothing witness, you can't let them get you with nobody'

They got me, Fence. Nobody.

Look, I can spread this all over the page, I can get Publisher to . . .

Fence, your Publisher doesn't care except about circulation and the balance sheet, go ask your friend Bernie about making people care, he won't tell you lies. Now get out of here, I'm all right, I'm sleepy.

A shout is heard in the corridor, Mother at the gate.

I can fight them with their own shit, Little Bit, I'll get you out and we can start over. We've got a chance anyway.

Not much more than maybe, Fence.

A furious pounding at the door: It's here, I smell it here! I got a nose to tell me where the danger is. . . . Open up!

The Mother bursts into the cell, dragging the guard by the ear—if she doesn't rip it off.

All right, what's going on in here' The odor's strong, you got someone in here with you?

No, Mother, just my cellmate, Tiny Twat.

I smell danger.

She yanks back the covers from Little Bit's bed. What's that then! down there between your legs?

That? Oh that. Just a friend of mine, my tame turtle.

No pets, intones the guard.

The City Room: Bernie is painting his eyeshade with nail polish while Scraps reads the latest in that continuing series on the Detention Home.

Bernie, the kid's completely changed his lead. First he claims the D-house is all butterflies and badminton, and now he's hysterical over 'excessive psychic brutality,' What the hell's he talking about? Publisher like this piece as much?

Publisher said: Bernard, your boy's a natural.

Natural born schmuck with pedigree to prove it if you ask me Bernie. Look at him down there, shit, but I've tried to shake him, look at him with his feet up and all that blood rushing to his head, you'd think he'd drown.

The brain needs blood to think. You know, Scraps, I'm going to pay for a new deck, can't read the numbers on these old ones and that gives me an unfair advantage.

To think? Think? What about?

Steady, Scraps, relax. He's thinking about himself.

Ohmigod! What can we do about him, Bernie?

Bernie whispers to me: Fence, Fence this inquiry, this full pulsing through your head is the futile exercise of reason, take a giant step in the name of the real world; sit there, young and free, and watch what your mind will build around you. You'll see the City lined with panacea, slouched in the doorways the drug man encapsulated empty white and up, or the plain brown bagman, tilted to the lips and down, or the titillated store-front with its peep-show pages of hedonistic pleasure. Emerging from your sheltered adolescent vision of hidden good, you will discover evil as panaceatic glut of too much moving us to too little. The City is constructed of excuses: drugs, suicide, art, mechanized religion, apathy. You'll see reason used to prove the rationale of irrationality, see the mind make the machine to render it obsolete, see the mathematicians equate one with one and two and zero, see the philosophers debate the absurdity of intelligence, see the endless stream of faces finger fucking payphones and yearning for the greatest panacea of them all, apocalypse,

to put out the light illuminating our misery. You haven't lived until
you see this City. Fear, Fence, fear is the spirit, we are afraid of dying
and afraid of living and the City is our excuse for doing nothing, we
are a community of fear and only that holds us together. Continue this
pathetic introversion and you'll join us, you'll let your reason defeat
your sense of life. Get out of here Fence! get up out of this fucking City
Room and live! Living is pleasure, living is art, living is God! and if
the City won't let you live with your mind or body, then live with your
imagination! That's the only true avenue of escape. Get out of here, and
if you can't do anything for the rest of us, at least save yourself. . . .
    Bernie comes all the way across the room to tell me. It is the
first time I've ever seen him walk.

    You laid it on him, Bernie! How'd he respond?
    He just looked at me, Scraps, like I was the bloody prophet.
    Yeah, Bernie, Mohammed was a card sharp.

    A cautious knock at my door.
    Louder.
    Knuckle rap: three longs and a short.
    I peer through the eyehole to observe Hoxie circularly
distorted and spread across the surface of the glass. He dilates strangely,
somewhat out of breath it seems.
    Off come the locks with a medieval catalogue of sound.
    I got 'em, Fence.
    Three yellow spools of film in his grasp.
    Let's get started. Should I pull the shade?
    In wash corner, Hoxie pries open the film cans with my
church-key and begins the alchemistic transformation celluloid into
gold, antichrist! The hot spigot suddenly bubbles up with steam, spits
erratically like a geyser erupting once each ten thousand years, clears its
throaty copper piping and runs scalding on demand. Through the drawn
shade, the afternoon sun glows dull red, safety light, reveals Hoxie's mumbo-
jumbo. Fence feels like tea, but the glass is filled with three parts acid.
    Did you have any problem, Hox?
    Nothing, except of course the goddamn guard: no
photographs, no picture! He went dancing for the camera, so I snapped
him a couple of shots, put him on the steps to pose while I shot the full

facade. You'll see him when I get finished here, smiling like a death mask sitting for a portrait. When you photograph architecture, it's always nice to have some indication of human scale.

No Mother?

Nope, no sign of life at all, a few weird voices, but nothing else.

Voices?

I kept hearing whispers, just like that, not shouts, but a kind of incomprehensible drone. I started talking back, like one half a normal conversation, but the guard, sympathetic soul, thought I needed companionship. I walked all around that building with a buzzing in my ear.

How're we doing?

Almost finished, a bit of a rinse and hang 'em up to dry.

No time for that. Fence takes the strips of negative and puts them between mattress and his Indian spread, then stretches out to blot.

O.K., now what?

Now we take this sunlight from beneath the shade, bend it up a touch, aim it right, flick the switch and project:

Empty corner is a dull shape around which a chest of drawers was painted. Empty corner is the intersection of thoroughfares, downtown streets and passages of time. Empty corner is the Detention Home, a sequence of views, photographic rendering, documented brick and mortar. Empty corner is the teeming City, building mass, culture and history, an unknown future. Empty corner is the population. Empty corner, big and bright, is an open door, no locks no bars no distorting mirrors, out another side of my traditional room in the City.

Fantastic, Hoxie, what detail! See the guard. I can hear him bewildered: what's going on here? how'd I get here? no transpositions in time and space!

And concentrating, my ears record the movement of smoggy cirrus above the City, my eyes are inflamed by vision of civilization run dry, my touch is deadened by the callousness of the senses, my smell is drugged with waste, speechless and concentrating, I know the voices, underground murmurs, soft premonitions, spoken in tongues and evoking response, they are no one's voices save mine or Hoxie's or the population. What they say is what consciousness provides, fills in with understanding where there is none, breaking down the incomprehensible code and rearranging factors and lettered elements into a message of its own devising. Shut up and listen, Fence, the sounds beyond the City.

sounds, the constant communications stream that flows oblivious to
stalled traffic or legislated frequencies, the current of the driving river,
universal waters, put your ear to your ear and hear far-off breakers
crashing in ventricle chambers, swelling up the lungs, dissolving,
suspending, dispersing, seventy to ninety per cent of everything.
Translate, from the distant hammering drum, anvil stirrup, image rods
and cones, the fireworks of synaptic leap, mix bass with treble, empty to
full, absent to present, I to me to you to all of us, the voices.

Listen.

Fence, look we got pictures and diagrams, blueprints and
circuit schematics if you want them, we can find our way around all right,
that's easy. We can get in, through the front door for that matter, the
hard part's going to be getting out.

Conspiratorial voices, unseen fellow commandos with
blackened faces and rubber suits, all briefed for imagination, the ultimate
mission to end the war, hear them?

I am a child of paperback suspense.

A cinch, Hox. A pipe dream.

What?

Lie back, close your eyes and just imagine we're on our way
with all the friends in all the world to help us out.

NINE

To sink is to submerge, settle, penetrate,
degenerate, retrogress, decline, collapse. To sink is also to
immerse, excavate, overwhelm, abase, degrade, debilitate,
suppress and liquidate.

All such things come to pass for the SS Ark forty
days and forty nights out of Rotterdam.

She is steaming half-submerged in thought, settled
into the stellar intellectual patterns of her course, when she
is penetrated by a rocky finger playing about her keel. She
degenerates at first into giggles, then suddenly retrogresses
into fragments of her component parts. Her speed naturally
declines, her bulkheaded will collapses, and she is immersed
in the deep sea, excavating her volume in cubits as she
goes. Overwhelmed by this demonstration of her nautical
mortality, she seeks a base on the ocean floor where she may
degrade and debilitate in cemetarian peace. The passengers
are suppressed by the disaster, all hands on board are
apparently liquid-stated.

Not quite all.

Turtle Two observes the ascending reef outside
the port.

Oh dear, dear, we're sinking.

No fretting now, we're of the Testudinatian Order
and can swim, although I'm centuries out of practice. All that
land travel makes one so sedentary. This is a vacation, we
must make the best of it.

Isn't that just like you, darling, so philosophical in
the face of an evolutionary catastrophe.

Shall we off then?

Grannie-Annie is with me, rocking in empty corner, it is a
quiet time, Hoxie has wandered off to another part of this reverie, Little
Bit is sitting down to her tin tray dinner, Ben and Grandfather have gone
off together to shoot pool at an integrated establishment called death.
Grannie knits, a scarf, a green shawl perhaps, to protect her shoulders

from the chillness of the grave. It flows from her moving fingers, extends
from her lap to fall in great folds on the floor, to disappear out empty
corner no end in sight. She is knitting history, speaking out loud and
incorporating her chronicle into the woolen knit one pearl two stream of
time, plastic needles marking punctuation, her period comma colon way
of speaking. She rocks, she knits, the years fly by, and it is like a lullaby.

. . . too much too little, beauty, yes it runs like good blood in
our veins, me, your mother, even you as a child with almost a crown of
yellow hair, and turned out in the clothes I made you, your mother wore,
people stopped us on the street. . . .

She knots another ball of yarn, the colors reflect her temper.

. . . she ran away and died for no reason, we knew where she'd
gone but we never knew why with what we'd given her, and I made your
Grandfather have her followed by that investigator who brought you back,
do you remember, he said you never cried the long road back, she returned
too although dead, we could not let them bury her anywhere, could not
leave her with that man, your father, I raised you, for her, you were my
child, and I gave you what I gave to her, too much too little, beauty, yes. . . .

Tell me about Grandfather, Grannie?

He was generous, look at this house where you were raised,
these gardens, family, you cannot deny it what you are. Christ showed us
the way, Christ was mannered, well-bred, a gentleman. . . .

Growing up was easy for you, Fence, be grateful. . . .

There was too much emptiness in that house then, too many
hours empty like an afternoon when the sun would touch the stucco wall
of the living room, texture, the hour's own intaglio. Fence sat beneath
the piano, a shelter of stolid mahogany, with the fumes of dying gladiolas
heavy around me, the pendants on crystal lamps turning with the heat
and playing rainbow games on the rug. From the level there, the room
became something other than its chintz normality, became the eyes of
a china cat standing like a doorstop on an oriental ocean, the table legs
were like columns disappearing into the clouds supporting heavenly
cities, and the greatest mystery lay beyond the horizon there where the
rug met the reflected line of a polished wooden floor.

I played solitaire croquet, two three balls in succession,
striking brilliantly as long as no one watched, foot on red sending green
to that impossible lie near the tree root. One afternoon, I pulled out all
the wickets and tied them in twisted knots.

I took my fishing rod and cast along the lakeshore, practiced on backswing and thumb release until I hooked the plug in the bushes behind me, until I backlashed and tangled the line intolerably, impatience replacing interest, and when that ran its childish course, boredom set the rod aside. When I cast well, the plug arced into my vision, flinging wet bits of light like a subtle filigree and the instant removed me from the water's edge, the plug dropping to float stupidly while the fish made jokes about a fool attempt to lure them with a painted wooden corpse.

I sat on the tilted dock that Grandfather refused to repair, feet on the ladder he once had broken with his weight while launching himself for that daily swim, breast-stroking and blowing water like a desperate submarine. The dock slanted crazily, fifteen degrees against the axis of the earth, and was approached by a curving bridge. I stared into the water which was not transparent, saw myself bend into waves stirred by a passing outboard, saw my moods colored like oil on the surface, saw myself resolve the day by taking up the dream again from where I had left it off the previous afternoon of a child who must entertain himself.

Ben came to look for me. Betrayed by the knot tied round a tree at the edge of the cliff by the lake, he found me halfway down, hanging seventy-five feet above the water, seventy-five feet below the knot, my feet against the earthen wall perpendicular to its height, suspended there where I had been suspended since shortly after lunch.

What're you doing down there, boy?

Nothing.

. . . good things are wild things, nature determines, plants thrive when left to their own devices, fish die when overfed, God disposes, men thrive on independence . . .

After five, one determined hour after Grandfather finished toweling off and regaining wind, they had cocktails. Every day Little Bit spread mayonnaise and caviar, shrimp and cottage cheese, marshmallow and hard-boiled egg over toasted crackers, and the cars arrived with their contents carefully lettered on the driver's door, an influx of friends to receive the drinks Ben served on the silver tray. I lingered in the kitchen, dumping ice and consuming edibles as fast as Little Bit could construct them. Ben returned from the living room.

Your Grannie's askin' for you boy, she says come in to be introduced.

If all went well, I avoided that until the very last,
introductions in passing at the door awkwardly struggling with their
coats and I did not have to speak at length as I shook hands or kissed
the proffered cheeks which smelled of perfume and good whiskey and
sauce piquante. Those faces, and they were every day the same, blended
altogether into composite male, composite female, a steady evening only
exposure to coincident faces bent down to call me little man. They did
not remember childhood well enough to know how I saw through those
patronizing intimations of equality, those winks and kisses and pats on
the head. My embarrassment was not for myself, but for those socially
besotted shells of former children, a first unconscious suggestion of a
kind of failed future before me, adulthood.

Your Grannie says come even if I have to whip you!

The cars backed around in the drive, sometimes colliding
with great amusement, their lights suddenly showing me the ferns by the
side of the gravel road, they disappeared, the ferns the cars the guests
into darkness. Down the drive near the sign marked DANGER, Ben and
I found scars on the trees where they approached too near, we covered
up these wounds, reopened, with black paint, but despite our efforts the
trees slowly died, the road got wider, but the danger no less.

Ritual coming ritual departure ritual life, Ben and Little
Bit running into the living room to erase all signs of use, empty ashes,
remove the glasses, place another log on the fire, as if it were all to
start again immediately, a fresh start with old faces, usual alcoholic
combinations, endless servings of things to eat, servants like stagehands
setting up for an old hit that never seems to close.

Say Good Evening to Uncle this or Auntie that, little man.

Dinner remained, and I was asked inevitably by Grannie to
narrate my day, tell of the hours sitting in the garden or hanging off the
cliff, I made up stories, made up stories about the stories I had made up,
made up hours, made up days. Ben passed the dishes around.

We goin' to eat this fish you say you caught. I sure do like fish
for breakfast, he'd grin.

Oh no, he put up such a fight I put him back.

Grannie approved of that, one thing she could not tolerate
was the concept of dead fish. It gave her migraines. And when they died
in her aquarium, discovered floating belly up staring at her with an evil
eye, she'd shriek and call for someone, me or Ben or even Grandfather,

and we'd scoop up the concept in cheesecloth for burial in the garden. Little marker stakes indicated the lifespans of guppies and angelfish and when by error we planted parsley in the graveyard it grew like weed fed on transmigration of the soul, nitrogen and fish oil. If Ben and I had a successful morning fishing on the lake, there was fried bass or perch on the table and Grandfather ate heartily, arranging the tiny bones on the edge of his butter plate, while Grannie boycotted her usual bacon and toast and berated him on cannibals.

. . . I cannot comprehend what you see in hunting, fishing, killing and maiming creatures. You have no right to deprive life of life, it's crucifixion. . . .

You didn't catch anything, boy, that fish caught you chewing on a worm.

Ben, how many times do I have to instruct you not to converse with the guests when you're serving. Fence, eat more salad.

No thank you, Grannie, nothing more for this guest, oh and nothing more for Grandfather, formally drunk in his chair, the usual evening posture. He does not taste, he does not hear the entertainment of my day, all his whiskied faculties are brought to bear upon a lifetime of appearing straight and sound and sober.

I am a child of appearances.

Do you know, Grannie, I have been living with Little Bit, our old cook?

Indeed.

She begins to fade, a trailing off of the lullaby, now she drops a stitch.

Well?

I don't approve if that's what you're asking. It is indecent, immoral, unChristian and wrong. I do not approve of living with a known prostitute, I do not approve of living with a former servant, I do not approve of living with a woman older than yourself, I do not approve of living outside of wedlock, I do not approve of living. . . .

She is going, going.

Why, Grannie? You found her, you took her in, you liked her then, why'd you fire her? The hell with all the rest, we never had a better cook.

I did not fire her, Fence, comes the softness of her voice. Your Grandfather did. . . .

Gone, and dragging the scarf behind her. Sleep.

TEN

Turtles One and Two abandon ship.

They are joined by a few other aquarians who unfortunately, as the readers of books, swim to the surface in search of flotsam and jetsam, those age-old aids to would-be survivors of marine disasters.

Aquarians do not fare well out of water, they suffocate.

The Turtles frolic in the sea, stretch their flippers and soar on an aerodynamic shell. Suddenly they recall chapters from their history, Turtle heroes past and gone, campaigns remembered only by museums, adventures, romance, stories still told by the whitebeards at family reunions. No one really listened to them at those insect feasts, the children played tagshell on stones and fallen logs, the old folks sunned quietly, contentedly shut up in retirement, the middle-aged splashed in out-of-fashion bathing suits through the swampy shallows. No one really listened.

Turtles One and Two are born to civilization, and yet the old ways, lingering in the subconscious, swimming ways, below water ways, return to their rescue. No! not the old ways, nor the new ways, but the eternal way as taught by the preposterous allegorical intrusion, that wise old Turtle who emerged one day and told of his journey from waters of the one side to waters of the center to waters of the other side.

He taught that the sun rose and set in all waters everywhere.

He taught that water covered 139,480,841 square miles of the surface of the earth and was still rising.

He taught that Turtles are the chosen ones by virtue of their extraordinary stupidity, endurance and love of life.

He taught all that and then returned whence he came. Turtle One appears to lag, to fail to meet this challenge. His muscles ache from fatigue, he cannot coordinate flipper thrust. His eyes lose focus on the goal and he looks for something to cling to. He sinks lower, and lower still, until

*sliding into a Sunday snooze, he settles into a soft mud cloud
to die, smiling.*
   To become water.
   Fluid.
   Turtle Two, don't look back!

All things are connected, directly or no, into a system,
shudder the word, a system permitting by its vastness of scale total
flexibility. Like veins and arteries, myriad lines penetrating all corners
of our being, never touching, separated always in time and space, never
joining but once in the heart, all things are connected.

  In the City, houses share the common wall. A complaint
often enough, but isn't it also grand, if not reassuring, the loving squeal
of the couple next door or the introduction to your neighbor, spray-can
in hand, your common campaign against the roach who, too, is simply
acting out his destiny in his preoccupation with your building. Wires
run through the conduits beneath us, linking up our fingers on the
light switch, and the water tasting City-wide of chemicals, all when not
taken for granted or into the bosom of cynicism unite us in ways almost
forgotten, connections everywhere, frayed junctions, corroded joints,
a subterranean kind of sociability in a world that pays compulsively for
privacy. The great urban problems are those alligators in the sewers and
the rats gnawing on the connections.

  Events seem detached, absurd, indeed these pathetic overused
alphabetics do not rise to the description, reality must be grounded
in nightmare to be credible. What a tiresome illusion! And sad, its
disappointment revealed in political and psychological disclaimers
of involvement, as if anyone can truly believe that events are outside
the realm of our own making. Shells are abandoned like derelict autos
beneath the highway bridges, and where are the insides? the passengers?
the free-riders all shriveled up and cringing. What incredible blindness
to deny that we are the connective element, the tissue in-between,
all events existing only in our context, in our fabrication, perception,
reaction, did we not create everything we fear?

  Join the modern litany: I am no one. I am nothing, no
influence, no importance, no meaning. The churches are empty and
the God advertises on a rest room wall. Fence dialed the number, the
phone was disconnected.

Bernie! the turtles are being eaten alive, devouring self and one another.

Fence is on assignment, personal percussion, pounding heart, taps on his shoes, belching farting finger popping, Fence is a one man band.

All things are connected.

Good morning, Mother.

You're not welcome here, Fence. No visiting.

Visiting hours is on Fridays, 3:30 to 5:30. . . .

Go no further, friend guard, today is Friday, the hour is right, rules are rules, aren't they, Mother?

Made to be broken for the likes of you.

Whatever happened to devotion to duty?

Good-bye, Fence.

Good-bye! did ya hear the lady, threatens the guard.

I get the bum's rush. I shall return.

Hey! anybody home. . . .

Now imagine this: you are a beautiful red-headed little bit of love up on a bad prostitution rap, and you are lying on your prison bed thinking your thoughts and staring at the springs of the bunk above, curious, no sagging indication of your roommate's weight, but then she's a tiny twat, and suddenly you hear a familiar whisper, deeper than you remember, musty, mossy, out of the darkness, somewhat tainted like subway breath, somewhat soggy and amplified, reverberating like a persistent question in a long long tunnel. You are lying in prison semiconsciousness and a shadow voice announces the arrival of an outsider, friend, squeezing his hard bone head out the spigot of your sink, there cradled in the corner, a form, a blob, like ink on paper, shadow on white, arms extended to pull on the chipped enamel rim, leverage with which to extract his fat waistline through the impeding intricacies of the valve, grunting to himself, groaning, straining until with a moist hollow POP! the full human shape tumbles into the bowl, legs askew and dangling, head lolling to one side gasping for air, little baby bunting in a basket on your doorstoop. It can only be a nightmare.

Hey Tiny, you call. Awake?

Who sleeps?

You see any thing in the sink?

Everywhere I look, sister, I see the end of the world. The sink's as good a place as any. What do you see in the sink?

I think I see a man.

A man! Holy shit, my prayers are answered.

A familiar voice indeed. . . .

It's Fence.

Better than nothing, how'd you get in the sink, Fence?

Came through the pipes, Tiny! like foreign aid, hands across the water, spigot to spigot, all things are connected. A tight fit for a plumber like me, but all things are relative as well. Now for some like you, twat tight as a pencil nub, it ought to be easy.

Let me outta here!

Hold it, Tiny, you've got to come back, we need you.

Come back? you're kidding.

Look if we're going to get everyone out, you've got to come back. Give it a whirl, watch out for the grease trap, you'll find my friend Hoxie at the other end and he thinks I'm crazy, or he's drunk, or both. . . .

I'm gone Fence. Shazam!

Well, as long as you're here, Fence, I've got something to tell you.

No embrace? no mad welcome for the liberator? no garlands for the doughboy begrimed but smiling? The bootheels of freedom are ringing on the cobblestones, flowers rain from the balconies, what? no kisses? no riding on tank tops or in the back of open limousines?

I am a child of the Saturday cinema newsreel.

Just something to tell you, Fence.

Hey! come on, Little Bit, we're going to walk out of here, or rather slide, leave the Mother and the bum rap and the D-house and all the stupid articles, just like that! Why so solemn? It's a celebration, you want confession, see the Chaplain, I'm a fighting man myself, something of a hero.

It's serious, Fence.

Serious? Getting out of here isn't serious?

I'm pregnant.

z-z-z-z-z-z-z-z-z-z-z-z-z-z-z-z-Z-Z-Z-Z-Z-Z-Z-Z-Z-ZZZZZ do you remember the characteristic terror of the flying bomb? the unknown and dive for cover, the unexpected and head for the shelters, there are wardens blowing shrill whistles in the street, sirens wailing, firebells, and the pinpoint patterns of the Jerry, there is the voice of Edward R. Murrow.

I'm going to have a kid.

Now hear this, now hear this, Good Evening Mr. and Mrs.
America, and all the ships at sea, this is a catastrophe!

What child? whose child? my child?

Hysterics, panic, the scheme's upset, discovered, betrayed,
a spy's in the works, and the operation's already underway, the fishing
boats commandeered, timetables printed up, arrows agreed upon the
map, we can't recall, we can't revise, the climate's right, the chaps are briefed
and ready, we're committed, there's nothing for it but to forge ahead.

Typical, Fence. Not your child, my child! Goddamn you, I'm
going to have my child!

War brat, waif in the streets, begging, living in a shell hole,
scrounging for the occupation, rickets lice and chewing gum, hey soldier,
you want my mother? Now's not the time for children!

Look at my belly, it's getting bigger, feel my belly Fence.

War is war, war is hell, war is a cliché, what must be done
must be done, up against the wall, shoot the bastard! he's holding up the
whole bloody invasion!

It's my child, Fence. It's yours. It's Ben's.

Little Bit, look at you, out of uniform, battle dress, discipline,
ship-shape, omigod! oval as a steel pot, swollen like a barrage balloon,
agile as an LST, heavy as a blockbuster, TOO FAT FOR THE PIPES,
with a belly the size of that, Little Bit, you'll never make it down the drain!

I'll make it, Fence, this time I'll make it.

Tiny's back.

Like lightning, Fence! I came out the other end and your
stooge there nearly fainted. This is what you get for playing with your
head, he said. It was easy, easy, easy!

I told you Tiny Twat, we can empty the place.

And all that time lying here, Little Bit, you and me, taking shit
from the matrons and loving rehab from the Mother, doin' time and the
door wide open right underneath our noses. Christ, how many times have
I watched my face washing water spin and gurgle out that drain? oh man!

You weren't thinking, Tiny, you just weren't thinking right.

Well I'm right now. What's the plan? When do we move?
How do we help the other girls?

Pop the stopper and out, they've got drains of their own, hold hands, daisy chain, lovemaking with a dervish, away we go, all things are connected in the end.

Umbilically.

Little Bit lies awake and swelling by the minute.

Tiny dreams fantasies of free women.

Hoxie paces, glares accusingly at the sink, and wonders if sanity is worth it in a world of madness.

Bernie predicts the future.

Scraps shuffles and deals.

Dewey serves up spirits.

Publisher accepts a testimonial.

Grandfather swims in indifference.

Mother posts a guard against danger.

Grannie chats with Saint Francis.

And Ben puts his ear to the tight taut skin and hears a baby's cry.

Fence continues stirring up the soup, the mental solution:

Let me see now, I'll have Mother and the matrons don starched green gowns, like the muses, their cheap mascara eyes peering strangely over tied masks. Ritual afoot, ceremony in the sterile air.

Snap of the fingers and a large white room is created, oval and clean, immaculate seating tiers for observation of the center, anodized, stainless, where there will be delivery.

An audience appears, not students as much as interested parties, obscure types more often found in country courtrooms or theatrical auditions, old ladies knitting historical pamphlets, knave men playing cards, the son of a slave, a big cheese, a tiny whorelet, a retired sea captain, and a photographer to get it all down for the scrapbook. Below, the Mother and her team enter, rubber-handed, fingers splayed cabalistic, they circle the center, choreographed shall we say in an eastern sign. They take their stations as the victim, patient ritual object, is wheeled in swathed in state-owned sheeting, a virgin sacrifice healthily nine months pregnant and unconcerned with the mystical pseudo-religious suggestion of the situation.

Her legs are hooked up in stirrups; straps tie her to the table, men are not altogether unjustified in their tortured concept of the mechanics of childbirth. Mother mutters scientific incantations.

Breathing is heavy, rapid, pulse blood pressure normal.

There is a scalpel, but no cutting, no need here for epistemology, not the way Fence makes it, no screams no pain.

Whatever belief these attendant figures represent, creed, is of no significance to Fence the creator. I am disinterested in the specifics, arbitrary legalities and codes, institutionalized structures and traditions and holy holy holy orders, let them chant formulas or sutras, fabricate graven images or voodoo hands in blood, it is of no matter. But do not let them hinder me, I will banish them mentally and they will be dead for me, for her on the table, for all interested parties. This is, if need be, a private function, this is an event signifying future, an affirmation that the unknown will be.

Focus expectantly on the dilated mandala.

A head appears at that window, little fists throwing open the pubic shutters for a better view. The expression on that face betrays curious indecision, as if considering the possibility of prolonging the stay. The womb, after all, is deliriously comfortable, security protection atmospheric control, a Hilton for all men, Tigris and Euphrates, the barcalounger of our civilization. Shrug. Why bother?

But the choice has been made, long before the infant brain is formed to comprehend the decision, and the instinctual ramifications force out the head in its bloody freshman beanie and sophomoric grin. Arm shoulder chest, and a little all-American wiggle of the hips, legs and feet, toes pointed gracefully, done!

The Mother forgets her civil service pride and reaches out to catch the arrival, hand on the head, hand on the chest, supporting until all the traveler's baggage is accounted for, she chews the umbilical with her teeth and holds steady while a matron ties off the cord. Then, amazed always by the miracle, she exhibits the child to the audience, then presents it to her sister, Little Bit.

Polite applause.

Relief. The child is sound.

But the congratulations and admiring compliments are short-lived, interrupted by a disturbance, Fence rudely elbowing through the crowd to yank off the sheets for observation of the depleted source, the postpartum depression.

Thank God! I shout. She's got her figure back. We can all go free.

Imagine that.

ELEVEN

Turtle Two swims in grief.

 Rain makes metallic dents on the ocean, the waves hold like monumental forms. There is beauty to the chaos, sculptural fascination, while beneath it lurks the idea of machine, studied technique, an oil-geared monster which through mechanical metabolism creates the energy to shape the art above.

 Turtle Two adds salt tears to the rain.

 The land is under seige, Turtle Two cannot know the other threatened life, the birds blown inside out, the fish waking up as groundhogs. The plains, exposed, shield their eyes behind curved grasses, beaches are sucked away, the mountains, balded on the windward side, turn their summits in shame.

 The land becomes the sea, runs with the flood of upset reservoirs and lakes split open at the seams. The sea becomes the land by its bottom revealed, the submerged peaks first touched by sun, the coral blinded by the light. From out of the silt and rock, curious unforeseen buds grow and a confused gull diving for a minnow spears a worm.

 As grief turns to resignation to memory to renewal, so does this storm restore the earth's topography, the water quiet, its secrets protected once again by fathomed darkness, the wind subdued, the fields soft underfoot and growing, the air smelling sweetly and the slopes draining with springtime rushes.

 The machine is still.

 Turtle Two has survived this accident. She has abandoned the SS Ark to lobsters, scuba divers and the salvage firms. She has left her lover on his bed of exhaustion, a peaceful client for the ocean undertaker. Her head poked determinedly forward, she swims with resolution, leaving a wake behind her, for no apparent reason other than moss grows on another side of the tree, she swims west.

How 'bout that, boy! Little Bit's gone and got herself a baby. Ain't it wonderful!

Ben is beside himself with delight. All right then two of him, anything goes . . . in empty corner.

I suspect that's probably what she wanted most about all her life, what she came looking at the lake for even though she could've had it from that farm boy down the road, something she had to have but somewhere else. Gone and got herself a baby, I'm glad.

Fence propped up on an elbow, putting the gouge to the bed, listens in amazement. There is no limit to my dream-even the dead believe.

Ben lights a black cigar.

You know something, Fence, I never knew why when we was together, Little Bit and me, all tight and cozy in my room, she wouldn't take precaution. It was a sight, me reaching 'round for a package of prevention in my dresser drawer, fumbling in my socks and shirts, and her lying there askin' what in the sam hill I was lookin' for at a time like that. Come down here, Ben, she'd say, sweat streaked between her breasts and in her hair, and I'd say how I had to keep her free, from my exceptional manhood you know, she'd put those fat arms around me with a laugh and draw me down on her and say nothing but what she said. And me, mind not so much on the business at hand, thinking about how if we were caught she'd lose her job, and me mine, how if things weren't just right she'd swell up with a pickaninny, how good I felt, how good that white girl made me feel, what she was giving me while all the while I'm worried about what I'm givin' her.

We were good together even so, shortstop and second base, in that kitchen turning out nothing but meal after meal for you all, in bed, together, living side by side and that's really everything, side by side. For certain she wasn't like your Grannie who made everything big or small, black or white, rich or poor, somehow feel just how different she thought they ought to be from one another. She had a place for everyone, separated here, separated there, and Little Bit put it back together, me, you, those boys down at the pool hall, and since then how many more? Even your Grandfather.

What?

Hold on, boy, for a surprise, but she had another child once. It wasn't born, but she was pregnant. She didn't take no precaution with me, but it wasn't my doing, It was his. Sure. He told me. Your Grandfather.

The celebratory stogie is a bit oppressive, don't you think? I know you don't feel much affection for him now, I see the way you treat his memory when it comes 'round the corner, but you were just too young for him, boy. He knew it, he knew he wasn't anything to you, he couldn't be, just didn't know how. Believe me, he wasn't a bad man, I knew him, maybe better'n your Grannie did. I drove him around; sitting up front in that limousine silent when he didn't want to talk, talking when he wanted to listen. He did business in that car, asked my advice in front of his partners, here, well, I was butler, chauffeur, servant, slave, but in that car I was friend. He had lots of other women. Your Grannie didn't provide that kind of entertainment, she didn't care much for that kind of love.

Well, well, well. . . .

He accepted that, let it be, didn't make demands here, took his pleasure elsewhere. Simple. I drove him off to town, leave him off anyone of several places, wait, then pick him up. We'd talk those girls over afterwards, what one did, what one wouldn't do, and sometimes he'd invite me in with him. I only accepted once, I couldn't pay and it wasn't my place, but once, well I was feeling deprived if you know what I mean, so I said why not. We went to the apartment, him in his fancy suit, me in my chauffeur's cap, a couple of dudes believe you me, and announced we was comin' in. That girl was some thunder, she said no we wasn't, she wasn't about to let me past the door and was going to kick us both out when I just grinned and left. He came out afterward and apologized, and I told him no mind, and he couldn't understand what she was angry for 'cause he was going to pay double, and even though she screwed the hell out of him he didn't go back to that one. We laughed and he gave me the rest of the day off so I could go get my own ass somewhere where I could. And he couldn't and that made us even.

Ben chuckles to himself, draws on the cigar, and in the swirling smoke I see Grandfather in the back of his limousine, out with a drunken crony for a bit of an afternoon. That face which I took to be infinite napping, eating, drinking, in its neutrality, is only one visage among many. Ben may be right, I accept that the attitude of polite interest in his wife, my Grannie, the appearance of strained condescension toward me, Fence, the dead daughter's son, may be one curve only in the smoky illusion of my memory.

Fence you were going to get an uncle.

I am a child of the southern gothic novel.

He told me about it one day in the car, and I kept on driving. But I was angry, plain pissed off, and jealous, hurt, I kept driving. He told me yes he knew we'd been together, but he said nothing to your Grannie. He said, I remember it as if he was speaking now, how he thought she was a fine girl and ought to be protected from the likes of us.

It's our responsibility, Ben, no matter who's the child is. I couldn't take it all in, how and when for one? Why had she gone with him? It was too much for my poor head. It was impossible, but there he was, from the back seat telling me.

The only real solution, Ben, is to send her away, dismiss her, and the rest of us will just have to keep on living as always.

She should go away with her cardboard suitcase, just like she'd come, and I admit I had begun to think of her staying forever.

I'll take care of it, Ben, there'll be no child.

He was sorry, more than he thought I knew, and that may have been the truth.

She's a good woman, Ben, but I don't want anyone to be hurt.

Hurt? Ben and Fence took her to the ferry, going away, and there was an envelope. From him, Ben said. He laid it in her open palm and then she turned and was gone. Fence never saw her on the deck although she was excursion class and we stayed until the ferry was a long way out.

Three hundred and fifty dollars in that envelope, boy, and a slip of paper with an address. You and me put her on the boat, remember? Your Grannie folded up the uniforms hoping the next cook would be 'bout the same size so she wouldn't have to buy new. She didn't have much to say about it, we closed up that little room next to mine.

That's how it was, boy.

The cigar is pretty well smoked down, just a butt beginning to taste foul. Ben throws it into the sink where it dies in a hiss. He gets up suddenly and walks into empty corner, embarrassed I guess, not wanting Fence to see a grown ghost cry.

And for Fence there is a dingy hotel room, in the City somewhere, an empty corner of anonymity, with the bed stripped of sheets and blankets, covered with a rubber pad, and Little Bit, stripped too, pale white skin, lying there. Her knees are lifted, spread, she is held by a grey-haired woman in a uniform. She seems groggy, her face appears in pain.

That's all right, honey, the woman soothes. I'm a nurse.

Take it easy, honey, almost done.

A little man, hat on in the house, balding, dirty fingernails, a little scrap of nothing performing a necessary service on the sly, an open whole his face, a nameless entity by appointment only, he carves and cuts.

No one followed you? No one knows where you are? He takes the envelope and counts the contents. No checks, no large bills, good, he takes payment in small denomination.

You got pretty red hair, hon. Dyed?

No twisting now, no sudden movement.

Everyone makes mistakes, dear, this is the best way.

Women got a shitty deal, we got to stick together in times like this.

No talking, Maria! I can't concentrate.

Well, an artist is he? Too bad art is against the law. There! Withdrawn and wrapped, into the hotel toilet, just like that. Down the pipes!

No worry, nice, clean no bleeding, take two aspirin and don't call me ever. The little man pulls off his rubber gloves and he has no hands.

All finished dearie, all over now. You've got a good figure, nice and firm like I was before too many pretzels and too many operations. I bet the men just hound you to death. Take care of it, honey, believe me, it's all you got.

The hawk circles the City descending, to penetrate the smoke glass concrete barriers of protection against marauders. His sharp living lens magnifies the Cityscape to see the streets like trodden mouse-trails linking hovel to burrow. He observes the weak undercover and the self-satisfied strong parading anniversaries of victory, both equal in nutritional value for an ever hungry hawk. His wings spread a shadow like a passing plane, astronomers squint at the sun for eclipse, old boxers recall unconsciousness, religious men reread Revelations and shower the congregation Sunday with apocalyptic spittle. Silent, soaring, diving, the hawk challenges the architecture, his shrill cry shatters the restaurant crystal, shorts out the subway, jams fifty million telephones with a busy signal. The hawk interferes with the connections.

The pickings are good. The City is strewn with stillborn. The hawk feeds gluttonly.

And Gimp finds his golden feather, like an epitaph left behind, a calling card, a warning.

As a child, Fence shot and missed. I was in too much the hurry to aim and fire correctly. Ben killed the hawk, with the cool determination of a hunter, quarry impaled like vision on his sights, brought it down bloody from the sky not by the lead pellets in the act of firing, but by the brain in the act of aiming. Ben killed the hawk, and I dragged its corpse on a string triumphant through the garden.

The hawk circles the City, master, adversary, lover, dangerous, more real than memories and strangers on the graveyard train. Who ever heard of assignation with a bird?

How now, hawk?

TWELVE

*Turtle Two swims westerly, following a constant horizon,
before, behind, to either side the same, four bright lines
leading to intersection, corners.*

    *She grits her teeth, summons up the fortitude of
ten million years of natural history, and like a Daughter of the
American Revolution swims blindly on.*

    *The western line becomes a shore: reef, rollers,
sandy beach, waving palms, mysterious human footprint.
Music greets her approach, chattering monkey anthems,
calling tenor birds, frond rhythm rollicking like a come to
the banana republic advertisement, no mocking marches that
played for her departure, no the music of the spheres.*

    *She is exhausted and lies in a stuporous daze,
oblivious to this nice native welcome. Someone lays a lei
across her leathery neck and invites her to a luau.*

    *But she must resist frivolity, even sleep, for there
is purpose to her journey. The booking on the SS Ark cannot
be forgotten, nor her grief for her dead mate overcome, nor
the challenges of the long swim left unsung. She must act now,
to justify her history and herself; to fulfill to the best of her
imagination her responsibility as a survivor.*

    *She crawls up the beach, beyond the limit of the
waves and tide, beyond the limit of fatigue, beyond the limit
of her normal comprehension, and moving her flippers in a
dance begins to make an impression in the sand.*

Well then, to begin . . . who goes first?
Tiny Twat of course. She knows the way.
Then Mary Pulaski.
Cinnie Mischkin.
Nancy Forbach.
Texas Kowalscik.
And so on.
Someone upsets the Gold Fish Bowl.
Then Anne Hevart and an infant child.

And Fence follows last, squeezing his wide waist through the stainless opening and shutting off pursuit with a rubber stopper. Suck it in and down I go, rolling, gurgling after, washing away the fingerprints, I negotiate the trap, a double U-turning arabesque, crying out in gleeful loop-the-loop, and settling into my aerodynamic ass-end down configuration for descent straight like a drain pipe in the empire state, past black flashing entries, lead-filled joinings of the unseen network of escape that even the plumbers are unaware of, that network when in the City all the plugs are pulled, all drains opened in that same precise instant, will accommodate the inestimable volume of fluid coming together in one final rush to freedom.

The journey in the compression of a narrow diameter pipe is a lonely one, with only a suggestion of camaraderie in an intimated presence of someone gone just before in an absence entered. And in turn this implies a same filled emptiness to whoever follows behind. It is a descending stream of ideas, or ascending if you simply reverse the pipe, and what precedes or follows may take multiple form, a construction of words on paper, for example, or paint on canvas, or light exposed on celluloid, or tissues and bones and chemical bindings united in an everyday manifestation of human life. Such a journey is both terror and a comfort. Such a journey fosters neither self-centeredness, arrogance nor war, such a journey fosters humility but not defeat, and the fundamental historical understanding, past and future, that we are all alone together and traveling through the pipe.

We reach the bottom with a splash and Fence fills his nose with forgotten Red Cross training. We gather in the holding tanks in the dark, in the large concrete pipes and stone-faced tunnels with address plates and street signs above and below, a second City invaded by our small band and several million gallons of unprocessed fluid. We string out, those girls and Fence and one small child, each after the other, calling to and fro to give direction. But suddenly we hear other whispers, riddle explained, like those Hoxie must have heard, voices of people on the way out, echoing in the gutter drains or steamback riding up through the ventilating perforations in the manholes.

We are not alone.

Light reflects off the curvilinear walls making us dark paper puppets and finger game animals, one is tiny about the twat, one is humped with child, one resembles a suitcase with two love-handles and broken buckle on his mouth, me, Fence, stumbling through the waste and tasting brackish water on my tongue.

We stop before an opening, halted by our guide. This way to Fence's traditional room in the City, announces Tiny as she disappears head twat feet into the pipe.

Fence has some advantage climbing upward, let it out, expand the gut and wedge between the walls for resting while the others cling to welded seams with toes and fingers. Above us like a pin prick in darkness is the outlet to wash corner.

One by one, knees over the sink rim, we emerge blinking to find Hoxie snoring drooling on my uncomfortable Indian spread.

Wake up, Hox. I'm back.

You've got seaweed in your hair, Fence. Yawn.

A little bit of sewer laurel, why not? after all I've just executed the perfect crime, never before achieved in the imagination of detective writers. My room is bristling with women, the formerly incarcerated milling about and worried about their manicures. Hoxie chats away, is passing his green bottle round.

Paradise, Fence, I never knew fat guys had such appeal.

The baby intervenes, emits a healthy complaint, bubbles of impatience, diverting the ladies' attention to its discomfort, a thousand fingers for pricking with the diaper pin, a thousand opinions to resist, bits of advice, cure-alls, mythical old wives tales, lofty dicta from the drugstore psychologists, a thousand handy rules for the successful raising of children at home in your spare time for fun and profit and were afraid to ask.

Hoxie, get that camera working, we've got an exclusive, this child must have a record of its youth.

Portraits: Child. Mother and Child. Mother and Child and Several Hundred Maiden Aunts.

And a very interested Grannie, a shimmering of ancestral presence in empty corner, a knitting needle tattoo in honor of the heir, a well-intentioned Grannie annoyed because the flashbulbs hurt her cataracts.

Fence, that child's not warm enough.

Hello there, dearie, shout the Maiden Aunts. What were you in for?

The meteorologists are caught napping of course, but no matter, certainly nature's upsets are far less inconveniencing than the labor movement. A static storm passes over the City, deleting pomposity and bad jokes from the talk shows and cutting off the music survey at twenty-nine.

Atmospheric electrical circumstance cannot be faulted, nor really can the guard who by his own admission slept through the entire performance. Mother Melicci brings it on herself through her remarkable olfactory sensitivity which allows her to perceive that danger like garlic stewing down the block is again abroad. Clad in her hair shirt sleeping gown, stalking the halls like a Shakespearean insomniac, she discovers the Gold Fish Bowl, where she has gone for a little after-hours stimulation, something nice to attract the sandman, is empty!

The tiny papers rolled into her hair flare and burn like sentry fires, ash falls down the collar of her gown, she takes on the titillated attitude of the volunteer who puts her hand on the electrostatic multiplier at a science fair. Her anger produces the disturbance and a few first degree burns about the head of certain matrons struck by lightning.

Commuter trains fizzle and die, the dynamos stop whining and the paranoid utilities go into their sabotage drill. The Pentagon loses contact with the President aloft, and for lack of direction, the current war ceases fire. In the Mother's swollen fury follows a calm collected silence, a strange quiet as if the earth, squeaking on its axis, stops turning to take time out for an intelligent assessment of the world situation, a pause for renewal.

In the City Room, the game continues. Scraps and even Bernie seem unaware of the climatic turn of events. But the cleaning hag knows, she watches in disbelief as the unswept dust of her employment rises to gather in threads weaving around her slippered feet. The typewriters, shocked from their natural state of apathy, tap out treatises on magnetism and Fence's nighttime chair revolves like a free-willing gyroscope.

And in the morgue, in Scrap's rare collection of documented innuendo, the print and photos fade, the million family skeletons disintegrate to dust, tabula rasa, time to start sinning all over again.

The police radio, the alter ego of Bernie K., regains its voice and comes through loud and clear:

With the voice of Mother screaming:

OOOOOOOOOOOOOOOOOOOOO-GAAAAAAAAAAAAAAAAAAH!

Where's Fence? asks Bernie.

THIRTEEN

The sand is cool on her moving flippers. Turtle Two creates her nest, arranges the shadows, while the sun, high above, observes with a maternal eye and remembers that time when she too gave birth—to the earth.

It is tiring work, more taxing than her long instinctual swim. She is out of water, deprived of buoyancy and grace. Small sand crabs, disturbed by her wheezing invasion of their domain, scurry out of the depression and run crazily down the beach to burrow again into quieter surroundings.

The pit is at last ready, she settles in, gets comfortable and almost as an afterthought begins to disgorge her eggs in a soft sticky spew out the tail opening of her shell. Round translucent spheres, like abnormal grains of silica, drop onto the smooth bed she has prepared. The eggs fall with the extravagance of life and are buried by the twitching movements of her flippers and tail, covered over by the reflex of evolutionary habit.

Only with this act completed can she indulge her own fatigue. She crawls carefully forward, so as not to disturb the nest, and turns away from the land to the water. The oncoming waves receive her, aid her with a drawing entry. She floats out to the deep, there to decline to the ocean floor and the spirit of Turtle One. The fish will nibble her dead with kisses, and salt will accumulate on her shell turning it white like marble marking the memory of a life well-lived.

Back on shore, a miracle parade begins. Out of the surf, as if in mocking imitation of Turtle Two, come the other turtles, hundreds, thousands, refugees of other cruises, other sinkings and survivings, come to dance upon the sand and deliver.

Night falls, and the following morning sunlight reveals nothing but semi-circular tracks in the sand, coming up from the water, returning again. The source is mystery, the explanation hidden, the phenomenon wonderful.

Bernie is lost in thought, not concentrating on his game, pensive moose.

Go get him Scraps, he says suddenly.

Scraps can't believe it, wax in the ears, going deaf from too much gossip.

Get who?

Fence.

And just where do you expect me to find him?

He will be in his room, lying on his bed, arms behind his head, eyes closed, he will be dreaming, Scraps.

Too much, Bernie, you're a witch.

I just been there before. Now move your ass!

It's a big story, Bernie, and you send for a little man to cover it. You must be gettin' old, I'm going to start winning more, hot damn!

Winning, losing, that's what it's all about Scraps. The kid's going to move off center and we got a bet which way he goes, remember?

Someone is rapping at my door.

Quiet everyone, I shout. Their milling bodies still.

Fence, whispers Tiny, it must be the cops. You've got to get us OUT of here!

That's true, I've brought them this far, I'm responsible. But how?

Empty corner! Yes!

Through here!

A ripple of a rush, followed by hesitation; Fence is, after all, pointing to a solid, if slightly cracked, plaster wall.

That's all you can come up with, Fence? for us to beat our heads against the wall? Frustration we've got plenty of.

Come on, believe! the dead have lived there, in that colored geometric form, paint on tenement paint, imprint of a personality gone before, perhaps that former tenant went out the opening himself when he saw what his interior decoration had conceived?

Just try it, try it, somebody!

Good girl, Tiny, brave Twat, step up and lead through the needle's eye.

I've got nothing to lose, Fence.

She grits her teeth, clenches up her fists, aims her forehead just so, and lunges at the wall. She disappears.

Gone!

She vanishes, OUT the other side.

But there's her head, poking back through, hanging on the wall like a hunting trophy. Bloody genius, Fence, the trip's fantastic. She waves an arm. All prisoners exit here.

They're moving, a line forms like immigrants rising up from steerage, leaving the known behind, taking a chance with an empty space, stepping off the ark at the promised land.

There goes Cinnie Mischkin. Good luck, girl.

Hoxie's next in line. On Cinnie's tail?

Don't forget your cameras Hox.

Turn 'em in to Publisher, Fence. I'm giving up photography. Seems life's too short to go to all that trouble just repeating what's already done. I'll see you.

Later, Hoxie, old friend.

Oh hey listen, Fence, you ought to tell Dewey about this. He's been looking for a new place to moor.

Done! the electrochemical transformations occur, impulse from cerebral sphere to hemisphere, it does not take much to conjure up the image of Dewey's-by-the-Sea.

'lo Fence, the usual.

That's right, Dewey, and I've got a surprise for you.

I cut the cables from the cleats, haul in the gangway and watch the demented rats scurry for the levee. Free, the old booze barge holds steady for a moment, caught not so much in the eddy as in the permanent momentum of her lengthy mooring, but new current sweeps across her bow, along her flanks, churning those side-wheels for the first time in centuries. The spray bathes the old wood like a new coat of varnish.

Dewey rotates the tap signaling the engine room full speed ahead. He barks out an order, adjusts his Captain's cap to a jaunty rake, wipes a tear from his eye.

Thank you, Fence.

A gentle river motion moves the bar toward empty corner, the customers batten down their stools with all the proper knots, the wind blows them new life, they move smartly like sea scouts on the watch. Two warning blasts on the whistle, sails drop from the yards, the booze barge tacks through empty corner like a stately clipper ship. Magnificent!

Ol' Miz Dewey stands on the stern, clutching her recipe box

to her bosom, she'll be busy cooking over there.

The line continues, one by one through the wall, here's Grandfather, here's Grannie-Annie, arm in arm, curious, a new color in their faces, new pallor new union, corsage and bud in the lapel, a golden fifties wedding, a retirement village must be abuilding in empty corner.

Grannie looks around her in wonder. What strange friends you have, Fence.

You'll like them, Grannie, if you only get to know them better.

Yes, I think so. Fence, your Grandfather and I made mistakes, you don't mind, do you?

No Grannie. I don't mind.

Well, I guess it's time to go. She gives me a kiss. Grandfather puts his hand on my shoulder, we touch for a moment and that's a start.

Good-bye.

They are nearly all aboard now, a few more figures linger near the end. Little Bit stands before me, with her swaddled bundle belching at me good-naturedly over her shoulder, a kind of precocious recognition parents boast of.

Going away.

Memorize those neutral features, Fence, seek out whatever elements of your own but consider the supplication in your search. Prepare to retain the image only, child, going away because Fence does not wish this person above all to grow up in the City, to find himself unaware of his own potential and hiding in a single room like a sneak thief hoarding a cheap treasure trove of shoplifted urban days.

Good-bye child, good-bye Little Bit. I look at those red curls, that round face and body, and feel no sadness. Someone has lent me a precious possession, something of infinite quality, to be held in the firm knowledge that ownership is beyond reason, that use is not a question, the object is flesh and spirit and surpasses all concept of worldly value. Lender and lent are simultaneous, they have extracted nothing from me but my own capacity to create.

We're all back together, aren't we boy?

But not like back then, Ben. I owe you that much.

You just growed up, son. You turned out all right.

It's not over yet, Ben, it's just beginning.

Well, we'll be around, Little Bit and me, if you need us. . . .

Although we got new responsibilities now.

Gone. Good-bye.
I am alone.

Someone is rapping at my door.
Who is it?
Scraps. Open up!
Fence gets up and opens the door.
Hello, Scraps.
He grins. Hello shithead.
Well?
Bernie sent me. He says for you to get your lazy butt out of
bed and over to the Detention Home. There's been a prison break.
That so?
Smartass!
You know, Scraps, I've been thinking. I don't think my
heart's in this kind of work. I think I'll quit.
You can't quit, motherfuck!
Listen, Scraps, listen carefully, I want you to take a message
for me back to Bernie. Inform him with the greatest of consideration,
politely, gratefully, even reverentially if you can, that I am no longer in
his employ. Tell him that.
You can't quit, I'll lose the bet!
Yes, I've made my mind up, you go back and tell him, Scraps,
that Fence is going OUT to be with the turtles. He's clairvoyant. He'll
know what I mean.

Fence looks around his little room, familiar secret-sharing
bed, window pinned to the wall like a cheap illustration, dripping spigot,
strange light square opposite the door.
I look round in farewell, then cross the threshold to go OUT,
OUT to the landing and stair
OUT to the streets
OUT to the City
OUT to the light-time
OUT of myself
and into the beauti-FUL SOUP! I'm up to my ears!

THE TURTLE'S EXHORTATION

All along the beach the sand is stirring.
Shells crack, tiny beings crawl out into the light.
A new generation of turtles is born.
Above, in the sky, the hawk circles in search of prey.
There are dangers ahead.

I am a child of the future.

ACOMA

For my tribe in St. Louis (Pasteur)

Protaph
Joseph Set-6
Call Me Primo
A Scat Illogical Rider
Home Stone
Seizure
Out of Outland
Kiva
The Autograph: Wall One
Graphiphonia
The Explanation
The Autograph: 2
Hy-Gi-Ya
Down and Out among the Vermin
Third Wall
Rialto
Moonpie
4 Wall
Club Carnia
Worm Resplendent
5: A Jabberwall
Speakeasy
Inflection
EU Dream
The Wurlitzer
On the 'Brane'
Solunar
Xero Dream
Wormlight
Zoon
Acoma

*We shall meet in a place where
there is no darkness*

George Orwell, *1984*

$L = f(D)$
Love is a function of death

Eugene Zamiatin, *WE*

PROTAPH

In the beginning: Uch'tsiti threw a clot of his own blood into space where it grew to become the earth: and

Acoma: mesa:

Acoma: pueblo:

Acoma: *temenos*:

Acoma: crossword construction, triple entendre, veridical dream and paranomasia: was begun:

JOSEPH SET-6

So too with him, who comes to this Elapsed Time Unit (ETU) grown from the artificial foetus spot—no big bang drop, rather the slow drool of an ultrarecipe cross a pale glass placenta to be an entity now of perspiring brain, brittle ossicles, cells mortifying in confusion, to be an entity now when d--th seems imminent, a matter of minute matter.

This Joseph Set-6 is sought after by the Anthropols, THE POWERS THAT BE. In their view, he has committed a significant act of disobedience, an implicative act, germatic, possibly germinal, against the HYGENIC STATE. THE POWERS THAT BE are searching everywhere, distastefully overturning the dirty shadows of The Outland, sifting sands and Sets, running programs and pogroms, spreading their electronic curiosity into every nook and cranium. They are fastidious and thorough; they will discover Joseph where he has fled in hiding:

Acoma: the sky city, there Joseph, lonely figure of speech, finds a refuge. He has a choice, for in this microcosmos are innumerable pueblo apartments, as many as the possibilities of language, deserted space only asking to be filled. Occasionally others pass this way, a few hardy aseptic travelers taken by the glove (rubber—one size fits all) along a prescribed route, a parody recitation of history, mumbled by a uniformed Primitive, a taciturn savage, who points to shards and busted ladders and empty hearths, then, shuffling his hot soc mocs in the dust, lingers for a gratuity, symbol of the declension of his once developed culture. No traveler, though, has discovered Joseph where he cowers, no one has strayed nor dared to climb the treacherous series of handholds, finger grooves, and toe jams which lead to the topmost chamber of this pyramidical archeologram wherein he now exists alone.

Joseph has no food; if he consumes anything at all, it is himself, a pure cannibalism by which his metabolic energies are diverted to feast upon the lean, then muscle, gristled nerve, the dangerously splintering bone, and, finally, as there is always that certain kind of person who saves the best for last, the delicate pulp of the grey brain. An inverted homicide is Joseph Set-6, an introspectre, an idiophrenic gastronomorphe.

Joseph may survive—as the human brain contains more than enough nutrition to sustain a man beyond the term, the however prolonged pale of his pathetic lifespan.

Joseph may survive if, standing at the door of his pueblo room, he does not inadvertently intersect his anatomy with that of a sleeping curl of reptile nestled in a cleft of rock, a snake striped with brilliant rings of color, josan, pink, green, yellow, black, easily overlooked as a geologic vestige of petrified time, a snake whose monolobed logic, despite her innocence and sweet nature, is to attack when herself attacked, to sting when stomped. Colored stone, she rests there in a permanent state of dream. Endocast and reticule of poison, her name is Coral.

CALL ME PRIMO

Mouth wide like a primal scream of accidia, the Primitive yawns, a pointy-toothed paniculation, breath absolutely ozostomiac, and his grubby hand out as the last sterile denizen of the STATE climbs aboard the waiting land yacht, a two-sparred quarantine. These ochlocrats drop, like sticky lozenges, Zimmerman nickles into the Primitive palm. He sucks complacently on an overtip, a silver Crick-n-Watson, a troche undergoing electrolysis in the saliva bath behind the cheek of an original shroff.

Primo does not regret to see them glide away this day of days, their pale trails of static lingering on the vistant lorizon like a caucasoid retreat. But of course his expression is benign, save for the slow mastication and pHandango of that currency, a facade so essential to his primonativity, features like petroglyphs, indeed, the reason for his employ. Nothing betrays the drumbeat of his joy. The season is over, a fact he confirms yet again with a glance to the sun, this an acquired classroom method, a fraudulent habit, yet authentic detail in the masquerade. The HYGENIC STATE Park Service only budgets Acoma open to visit from the iCities for an ETU, interval of repetitive spiel, bead and necklace hustle, photos in rented bonnet, and other feathered humbuggery, sequestered between parentheses of peace, the long, undeniable calm of Acoma.

He pulls off the hated head dress and closes the gate, the spirit barrier, to prevent trespassers from illegal diapedesis 'til next opening day. A sudden boom of thunder in his stomach announces his dinner, smouldering in the pot tended by Hy-gi-ya, his squaw, before the door to their caretaker's home in what once, long ago, was the Church of the Silly Gringo Fathers. Slowly, he turns to ascend the silence and steep ravine that are the only access to the sky city, Acoma.

But his empty thoughts are violated by a swervering roar from the parking lot, skid introducing a motorcycle, burble vroom REMREM, paused and panting, dyspmeic, plateless, engine number filed, said machine leaning to one side on a human kickstand, burble vroom REMREM, an invader's long-booted black leather leg.

Cursing inclusively, Primo returns, speaking by signs in his excitability, a blur of irascent prestidigitation that if accompanied by sound would have showered the new arrival with spittle.

--Too late, *naalniih*, get lost! This Park is closed for season!

--You and whose Indian Nation, rudskin? The spockin' POWERS are after me, Worm, and I'm headed for higher ground. Look out, Hiawatha! Comin' through!

A SCAT ILLOGICAL RIDER

Is Worm. Once, thumbing a ride on PYTHONINE oh so baaaaad! he was not chewed by worms, but was those worms achewing, oh dear great spock, oh spock awful! THE POWERS THAT BE approach; Worm stole the cycle way back in St. Louis (Pasteur) and left like ASCARINE a disgusting trail of leaking oil, exhausted exhaust, smuck, colacans, and moon pie wrappers, nasal drip, orange gobbed q-tips, and offensive mounds of waste, each flagged by an extravagant twist of pastel tish: yes, all of which register BUST on electronic olfactory trackers. Worm is on the proverbial lam. He flees the heartbreak of seborrhea.

His body, stripped of its black coat, is the substance of old
wax, stippled thin opaque, riblets protruding as if not a live thing but a
twisted wire constructus, a resofinicular hanger for yellow paste, musty
paper, a lifeless production of living reproduction, an exhumed tussaud
and tatterdemalion. His rot-gut gutted gut no longer holds the acid tight:
his liver, a blood sponge torn and dried by paranoia. Fluids mix in him
incoherently, lymph and sweat, urine and oil, their circulatory tubes
shredded and shriven by the implosion of artificial shock. His heart beats
in RPM's, respiration whistles between his tartar nicoteeth and bruises
his gingivitic gums, his skin burns flamed and graved by sun and sand and
incisive despair. Worm is pilose and pinto and verrucose, his complexion
a textural assortment of bullae, bunches, bumps, bulbs, buboes, bursae,
bunions, buttons, roseola barcoos, livored stictacne, tumid tumercles,
wheals, warts, and wens; he's got crabs and scabs and from his pores,
craters, and osantine lantigo creeps a foul tyroid smegma. Worm, germ,
sperm, in his many forms, the great imitator, he is a living spirochete.

He removes his helmet, his corona, to show a face soft and
nervous, a quivverlip, jaundiced eyes shot with blood, whites the color of
piss, and a regard that conceals whatever his lucidity beneath the glaze of
pain. Worm aches. All over.

--So Cochise, this is where I run to, spock me, a stereo high-
rise, urban renewal. Thought I left St. Louis (Pasteur) . . . Musta took a
wrong turn back in Peripeteia.

The bike tumbles over, carboils hissing on the hot asphalt.
The helmet rolls like the head of a lopped revolutionary. Worm slithers
past the Primitive who taxes his diaphragm to shout:

--Hey, no entry, bud! Can't you read that gate! Aggravating
remedial! Friggin' alexiac!

Worm crawls on. Primo responds with some aboriginal anger.

--You trespassin' bandeliero! You gotta pay to see my land!
Off-season rates! Shettle admission! Shettle to park that bike! You carryin'
camera? Shettle to photograph! Hey, I got bits of authentic lore left cheap,
this year close-outs. You want arrowheads? I got 'em, flutes and sawtooths,
folsom and a honey clovis, I got a bison tusk, I got river pearls!

--Buzz off, Geronimo . . .

Worm climbs the worn steps to the mesa table and there,
suddenly, Acoma looms before him, rising with dizzying double parallax.
The brightness plays like tickling fingers on his scarry brain; he squints,

he shields his tormented eyes, he thinks for an absurd instant that up up
on the acme he sees in a doorway the figure of a man.

--Spockin' A, Worm, these old orbs givin' you nightmares!

No, impossible, incredible that any intrepid tourist or fugitive
adverb could venture far beyond the observation limits regulated by the
HYGENIC STATE Park Service, Division of Outlandish Monuments,
and Primo, their custodial Indian guide.

And so Worm climbs the ladders. The rungs break like soft
mold beneath his weight and he must grab at the next desperately for
the sharp chalk edge above. His knuckles, cut and bloody, clot quickly
with a white scab of dust. Chalk in his leather suit, chalk grinding in his
groin and armpits, between his fingers and itching toes, in his ears, up his
nose, chalk and phlegm in his lungs, his mouth fuller still with the chalk
of fatigue, he looks behind him and where once he could not see the
summit, now he can see no way to return. The blood rushes to his head.
There are more ladders to go higher still.

The view from there is out to that southwestern horizon,
that circulinear by which the earth's dimensions are measured. The sky
is no wash, its gradations of color rather suggest an overlay of screens,
tinted and translucent, red over blue gauze over yellow, with interspersed
haze by heat rising. And in the distance, like a clone, a mocking twin,
a too perfect imitation, rises Katzimo, enchanted mesa where prayer
sticks, carved and feathered, lie in the sun like the bleached skeletons of
snakes in improbable places, lost pleas to lost gods, forgotten invertebrate
thoughts and deeds. The desert, by its geology and vast sense of irony,
simply smiles at religion.

Primo is just a speck below, a chip of colored glass, his yellow
herring purple bone poncho blending with the high striations of the
land. The Primitive has forgotten Worm, officially at least; by now he
considers what he might get for the motocle in a horse trade. Listen!
Primo, like a tinhorn huxley, is recounting his dreams, enumerating tips
and swaps of his lost heritage, and far up in Acoma, where sound climbs
faster than man, Worm can hear so clearly the anecdotes of turquoise
and hammered silver.

Worm's draped lids droop lower still, lethargy encases him
stubbornly like a stuck sleeping bag. A man who has ridden non-stop
from St. Louis (Pasteur) past the Suncity into the Outland with only
moon pie for company must sleep, a man whose metabolic system is

addicted to a supplemental mortarload from the pharmakos pestle—and
for several ETU has righteously abstemed—has a constitutional right
to torpid inactivity if only to seek another reconstituting dream. Worm
trembles in his leather suit, his abercrombie entropy, one cold poppa in a
zippered vagina.

--I'm cool. Blue areola! Gotta find some cover!

He discovers to his clutch hand side a strange low oval, a
swollen mud mound with a bottom center hole.

--Hey, outta the wind, warm, round, secure, old Worm a
mummy in a muthaspockin' tomb!

He crawls in, coils, snores. If only Primo might pass him
by, with a little band of gawking visitors, Worm might overhear how
some ancient people used this adobe oven in which he sleeps to bake the
ancestral bread.

Night rises, not black, not blue, but bright with the moon's
vain expressions, the desert sand a looking glass.

HOME STONE

Night falls, in a million pieces outside the old church where
Primo's woman, Hy-gi-ya, stokes a fire of dried juniper, filling the
crisp air with that spectacular smell. Hy-gi-ya is the last of the Acoma
Indians, a burden she carries with her like a stone inside her stomach.
She is ageless, this last one. Six hundred years of memory chronicle the
downfall of her tribe, at its peak the moment of her birth, the mesa then
aswarm with children and mongrel dogs, the pueblo like a presumptuous
hive rising higher and higher in an architectural gesture of defiance
to the dry skies. The gringos came in search of silly yellow metal and
slaughtered repetitions of the people; there was little rain to water the
withered crops or gather in the shallow reservoirs, the skirted fathers
sang their service in the exalted house to honor a shrivelled little person
on a stick—very confusing—followed by old women in pants who took
away the Acoma language in notebooks, leaving their odd guts and
grunts in its stead. Hy-gi-ya has seen through all this history. Now only
she remains, with a rock inside her to bear witness that there had ever
been Acomas. She looks from day to day for death on his black pony.
During the long hours, she collects food and smokes thoughts and lives as

unchangingly as she has always, accepting the world as she finds it: there.

Primo wheels some machine into the cheerful light of their homefire.

--Hy-gi-ya, look what the loco left in the lot.

--Loco?

--Real viral guy rode in, dumped this and gone . . .

--Gone where, husband?

--Up in the Park. Germy son-of-a-copulator!

--Snakes'll get him up there . . .

--So, good riddance. What do we do with the hog?

--Hog?

--Gringospeak, woman. The hog, the bike, the cycle. Thing is one soiled item, worth Shettles back in the Publicity. Ought to just ride in tomorrow and make us a trade.

--You'll get cheated, like always. See how useless that thing is. Ought to just shoot it, put a creature out of its misery.

--How you give me *tah honeesgai* with your yawp, woman! I got to think. What do we need new out here?

--Nothing.

--I'll get you a real stove, neutrino-powered, color-coded, hydrosonic . . .

--Least you can ride the hog, can't eat no microwave . . .

--Maybe a freezer?

--Who needs freeze?

--Or some BUTONIL or PARASIN or some of those ten-grain DEMEROL thrown into the deal . . .

She squints at him through the firelight and wrinkles and laughs, a low rumbling sound like a rock rolling in her stomach:

--You're one crazy husband, husband. Snakes got you long time ago. Sometimes you are just too much Navaho. Sleep off these deals, your people been taken to the cleaners for centuries!

But for her sharpened tongue, Hy-gi-ya's the perfect woman, good cook, a mature toss in the buffalo robe. Primo sits down to eat, swallows some prickly pear gas, a belch of pre-Columbian origins, and reaches into his stash for a dry thought leaf. He leans back, massaging the leaf between his palms, rolling it carefully. He will smoke, but not without sending Hy-gi-ya outside for a look around. You got to be cautious when you inflame, thought smoking's been against the CODE

OF CLEANLINESS since the STATE was foundered.
But then the POWERS THAT BE don't ever come to Acoma.

SEIZURE

Joseph Set-6 passes this first night with his spine against a
cold mud wall, staring through the door at absurd lunar physiognomy,
as wide and incredulous as his own, foolish caricature pinned on the
blackground. Frozen like the landscape he observes, like relief carved
from bloodless soapstone, Joseph does not sleep. He is alive as the night
sand. Slowly, before him, as startling as an afterthought, there is sunrise,
tinted veils like lapsebeams, glowing curls, a womanly forehead lifted
above the horizon, and that passionate eye, the morning. The sun's
glance pierces him like a shining needle and plunges into his brain with a
rush of energy that brings his wakefulness to consciousness.
Like an Urethran insult:
--You oxymoron! You graphoon!
Joseph feels the familiar aura; like the poet, his pollex begins
to twitch. The oscilloscope within him shows the emanata, notes the
intricate overload, its ephemeral green graph tracing a wild erratic
pattern, irregular, fast, ponderously slow, as if the curves of impulse are
echoing back and forth like the screech of demented bats reverberating
silently through a multitude of soft canyons, grey draws, moist cul-de-
sacs. Joseph hears all this with encephalographic ears.
His arm begins to tremble.
He taps his sternum; yes, the PILL CASE is there, as
required of every citizen of the HYGENIC STATE.

PILLS ON YOUR PERSON?
PENALTY FOR LOSS OF LIFE: D--TH

Engraved on the lid, like a medical enpsychlopoedia carved
from a hypodermic point, is Joseph Set-S's complete metabolic résumé:
Electrocardiogram
Blood: Type, RH, Pressure Gauge
Lymph Blood Cartography
Personality Plot

Disease Career (If Any)
Blemish and Scar Coordinates
Oral History
Waste System
Organ Synopsis
Skeletal Apparatus and Nerve Schema
Tissue Muscle Bone Analysis
Set Genetic Template
Flaws
Emergency Instructions

And containing within, PILLS, in pharmacopious numbers:

Acids: Plain and Fancy Antibiotic Spectrum
Pitstic and AntiPerspiration Tabs
Tums
Breath Purifiers: Spray and Sucres
Coagulants
Depressants
Exultants
Immunoglobulins
Laxatives: 31 Flavors
Relaxants (Opiates of the People)
Flatulence and Stomach Gasbag
Placebos

And for Joseph's CASE, waiting in the wings like an understudy saviour, a small blue and yellow encapsulated wondadrug, PHILISTINE, to control his epilepsy, his epiphany, his only flaw and embarrassment since INCEPTION. From the very beginning then, not a wholophrast, a popsynopsis.

The PILL CASE, issued to each citizen at THE COMING OF AGE, is the antidote for all poison in the HYGENIC STATE.

But in a curious, and possibly misdemeaning, act of will, Joseph does not fumble to enlist the miraculous aid: the PILL CASE remains *in situ* while he observes his shaking limbs, rippling muscles, not with fear but deliberate fascination. He watches with the naive near necrophilic interest of pedestrians eyeing that one lying feloniously racked

by convulsion, lipids shaking with hysterical laughter, a coughing cry, a
gag, and pathetic tears of urine despoiling the perfection of the streets.
How can the POWERS THAT BE tolerate such a thing? Disgusting!

KAHN IS OUR JANITOR. HE CLEANS THE WAY.

Joseph remains part of the horrified crowd so helpless in their
surprise, ignorance, sympathy, revulsion. Joseph stands on the periphery;
PILL CASE above his heart, he knows, he knows and does nothing.
A stiffening forcibly extends his legs, a rigorous tone spreading
through his body like a mammoth blush. His head twists, like a child
discovering blurred vision, flashing on the high empty corners of Acoma.
Tonic.
And then the shaking, the tremolo arc, black rainbow,
dispossessed, once strangely revered divine, once an anagoge.
Clonic.
Saliva runs, a slick unsalted sweat, on his bluish derm cold as
condensation against the skin of sculpture.
Grand mal. Purge, critical test run through all circuits. He
pulls from his pocket what a Calculator is never without, his FELT-TIP,
his trusty scripto, oh! that bic clic, that cap snap clapping technic sound,
and on the wall above where he has fallen this amanuensis puts a first
morpheme, the initial writ of an annelectual digest.
THE AUTOGRAPH.
Sunrise at Acoma. There is no one to hear Joseph's pitiful
scratching, or above that the shrill afflatus of Urethra's voice in his ear,
drowning even the post-seizure boom of mighty Alpha with her abdolatry:
--Joseph, you witling, can't you keep still! You suppository
rhetor! You abecedarian trope!

OUT OF THE OUTLAND

The Primitive is up with the dawn, although in his
excitement indifferent to the solrads of her rosy titillations. He bathes,
rubs his sanguine skin with handfuls of fluid sand. He slips into the
green vinyl uniform (one size fits all) of the Park Service and ties back
the do of his unsanitized hair in a baggie. Hy-gi-ya inserts a fresh

AIRWICK in its vented pocket, a traveler's medallion, then wipes off the suit one last time with windex and electrocloth until it gleems as fulgent and mylarized as an ancient alliterated allegore. His final act of preparation is to take from a nail on the church wall, wherefrom once hung the shrivelled man, his PILL CASE, suspended there in reverence like a beloved repeater or a kennedicon or a vroman pyx embodying the host of an undistinguished ancestor.

On to the Publicity, the capital duplicity of the HYGENIC STATE, that shimmering paradigm, that glorious expression of life to which to rise before shadowy d--th! How fearful to leave and go north into the Outland to Acoma! What rapture to return on his periodic visits! The Publicity: thoroughfares through which can be seen like clockwork the intricate inner metabolism of the STATE; the tall glass towers and apparency mocking furtiveness and privacy; above all, the nonbiodegradable sense of siblinghood and community; the Publicity is a lyric to probity, purity, and permanence.

Most of the world is, in fact, like Acoma, abandoned to the destructive state of nature and ventured into only by the most foolhardy or immune. Vast tracts of formerly settled space, entire continents, have been left to disease, to be roamed by viruses and defecating animals. Fed by such wastes, the streams run polluted there, lakes covered with glistening slime, swamps areek with algae and gas and secretions of subhuman things. Even the mountains, despite the fakery of their clean white caps, are only costumed piles of rock and dirt ridden with annelid crawlers—these lands all defined as earth, ground, filth and its noxious by-products, unnecessary to make things birthe and grow, hence useless, eternally decomposing, eternally dying, d--th d--th d--th . . .

Primo is one of the few who live outside the Defensive Membrane, a number of dislocated diplomats and other cultural transvestites, and the personnel roster of the STATE PARK SERVICE, Division of Outlandish Monuments.

To the all-knowing POWERS THAT BE, Hy-gi-ya is an anundrum.

Primo kicks the starter, picaro beginning his imaginative journey. The engine catches and idles, burble vroom REMREM, pitched precision and smoke, an illegal litany to the previous ETU when design, material, and anthrops were flawed. He tries the gears; he stomps the lever with his vinyl pump until with a rip of mechanical patois it engages and he

sets off at speed, Mr. Clean astride his Rosinante, a not so white tornado.
The desert is his shunpike.

KIVA

The Worm one oversleeps the dawn. The indotherm of the
day invades his black leather chrysalis.

He wakes, blinking, hot-headed, unrefreshed. The white
light of Acoma, implied by the harsh half-sun opening of his shelter,
is like fomentation to his brain. Ovens, after all, are made to bake, and
like a crusted loaf he is stiff and stale, his blood flow impeded, here and
everywhere crimped to make his limbs tingle with an independent sleep.
Curled there, a twisted pasty, he finds his circumstances as he left them,
unconfectioned, the lifetime pasticcio of a miserable ourobouros.

Burble vroom! Worm gains the edge just in time to see Primo
spur on that 500 cc. maxibike, off with hites and briffits.

--Savage! Fink! Stealin' rudskin! Quixotical hohokommie!
REMREM!

--Sterco athapaskan! Trapped! POWERS goin' to waste me
like a metaphoric victim!

But this herpes simplex has never been apprehended; long
criminal, he does not panic. The average weight of the average brain of
the average male is 49.6 ounces—and wits, Worm proves, weigh just as
much as intellect.

--But what'll I do for moon pie?

Around Worm nothing grows; the only thing that draws
sustenance from the earth is the pueblo itself, rising from the ground
like an enormous weed, dried by unrelenting sun and wind, pressed
between the pages of time, and vulnerable to touch, that is, any sudden
jarring might disturb its subtle bonds and cause a soft disintegration into
historical pieces. If Worm is not simply to waste away, if he is to show
one last insanely heroic posture of resistance, he must draw on his special
reserve.

--Got my hollow bootheel one blue and yellow finality cap!
Got my big bang departure hermetically sealed streptokamikazy trip!
Sweet NEOARSPHENAMINE! Knew I'd need ya!

What speak is this? Worm's brain is jellied and scarred, there is mold growing round the temporal lobe and a bad rip in the amygdala. A delicate organ, called the enchanted loom, the slightest imbalance and it weaves the warp and the woof of a cosmicomic wrapping.

So then, off with the boot! to release fleeing fug of fermented nylon sock, the waftarom of ETUs. Placing the buckled stomperboot on a nearby rock, he strikes a blow at the union of catspaw and sole, he wedges the seam, nails stretching like sticky glue and fighting the ignominy of separation, one proud high-cut piece of footwear. Worm yanks and twists and slams, the leather tears, threads holding bot to bottom rip away, and from within its calf-taped place falls that seven-inch reasor, that secret razor with the patchuko design, by which he slashes his own unresisting hide, poor split pinki . . .

--Spock! By St. Johnson (& Johnson), that smarts!

A bloody prying still till he can just fingernail that yellow cap with the pale blue blue stars.

--Oh, give me the UMs all over!

The brancused gelatin will not be grasped, undoubtedly an aversion to being finged by gritty onyx; no patience now, like an angel of hell in a five-n-dime. Pouring with plewds, he falls over into slack shadow, the oblique shade of that sun cutting across Acoma. He strips off the jacket, his skin glistens like bad butter in the afternoon; shrunken chest, sunken armpits, like the dens of cringing animals, full of abandoned holes.

Clutching the cap like NITROGLYCERINE, he staggers down the pueblo street. He limps; bootless, his left leg shorter than the right elevated on its clumsy gear pusher, he limps like all other righteous males in the HYGENIC STATE. A comeuppance. A come down. A comeuppance. A come down.

Light gives no respite. He climbs higher, to where he finds extruding like an epileptic tongue a ladder disappearing down. He tests the first rung. It holds. He peers into the darkness and intimation of woodsmoke, ritual, distant chants, of coolness, dryness, solace, mystery. A presence rises to touch his face. So down, down with one boot on, one boot off, down with yellow miracle blue star magic, down the ladder into the earth, into the forbidden center, into the mirror backing darkness, the secret heart of Acoma.

--Must be another oven. These spocko injuns sure eat bread!

His bare foot meets the earth, boot follows cautiously

after, its sodden thud touching off a salute of rattles and cacophonic
SSSSSSSSSSSSSSSSSSSSSSSSSSSSSSSSing, a rise and fall hissteria,
evidencccce of snakes screaming a serious sinfonia of fear and anger. Such
sound would send most sylogists scurrying to escape, but not our Worm,
symbol syllable symptom of skepsis—although he might concede a singular
staccato in his sinciput and a synchronous syncopation in his ticker.

--Sssssay, wasss happening? Peacccccccce . . .

The dangerous tremolo ceases, the silence is startling. Then,
from the left:

--Hiss?

--Hiss . . . hiss . . .

Conversation. Several other voices join:

--Hiss. Hiss hiss hiss!

--Peaccccce, snakes . . . I'm a worm jusssst like you.

Slowly his eyes penetrate the gloom to see around him a
succotash of snakes, lounging in senatorian postures, weaving, darting,
looped together in hasty consideration, craning their spineless necks
for a better look at the intruding stranger. A reptilian convention this, a
gathering of the clan, BPOE lodge meeting, World Congress of the Sub-
Order Ophidia.

--Well, brothers?

--Hiss.

Decision. Like a password. An asyndeton.

What do they recognize in this Worm? Is it the repting
gait suggestive of sidewinder? Or the protruding glottis which allows
him to breathe while swallowing moon pie whole? Or perhaps their
chemoreceptive sense has taken note of this one's insinuous personality,
his psychological components, enzymes and proteinacrous substances,
which are the analysis of venom.

Worm finds place among them and thanks his lucky asterisk
for the sudden deviation of events. He must rethink. He has allies now.
No longer a STATEless person, he is now a citizen of the Hybernation;
he has been naturalized.

The stellar cap lies in his palm, his exit visa. A venerable
rattler nearby lifts his head inquisitively and with flicking tongue
questions the need for such wondrous extradition. Worm smiles,
strokes that old diamondback:

--Maybe later, yeah brother, maybe later we'll all have some . . .

THE AUTOGRAPH: WALL ONE

The narrative illumined here is a psychohistolysis, a breakdown of narrative into parts, an anaglyph. The Felt-tip follows a serpentine linear in sinuous style, flush with semiotic life. I, Joseph Set-6, the author, only hope that you, readers of this autograph, you POWERS THAT BE, will strive to interpret this helioscript discovered on a supraterranean wall and discover an explanation, see the light.

Even now I hear Urethra shouting:

--What gongorism! What simplectic crambo! What carbuncle!

I am by calculation no philosobuff. Philosophy, as you will see, has been outlawed in the HYGENIC STATE as the bastard of imagination, that linguistic perfidy. The theorhetorical function of the human intellect has been assumed by THE POWERS THAT BE and their graphiphones, and so if my speak, if not my behaviour, seems awkward and anagrammatic, it is because I have been cleansed since Inception.

I have memory of that first event:

0000001 and counting nothing suffused with viscous light, to not be, I had to being, I is not, then I was, void, then all sense nonsense.

This was Inception. Again Urethra:

--What absurd zoetry! You dort!

So cruel, she was one of the last natural born.

--Joseph, it was exception! And in a vacuous light, you antihistocrat, you number of the vitamin Elite!

--Urethra, let me speak!

--Joseph, I have no use for your SET CREATION nursery rhymes!

She was, is, proud, too proud, she and her farded palpable friend, Magnesia.

But I could feel growth, an itch, a pinprick of awareness expanding: from the beginning I knew warmth and motion and sound and consciousness. I was insieved but could not measure.

I was born one of several thousand of Set-6 in the year 1984. Thought and gargantuan computation went into my design and manufacture. The POWERS THAT BE had projected new iCities: the Eccentricity, the Chasticity, and the Historicity. Future populations were to be guaranteed. I was simply part of a complex PROGNOSIS.

Such are the benefits of utopian LIFE, ideal and glitchproof, a society equal to its STATEd ideolectic, the perfection of an executed declaration, of a world infinitely known and parsed. Error does not exist except as a myth invocative of that dark world wherein thrives neweroticism and athlete fungus: the Outland. Error is the institutionalized fiction to which the purist narrative of quiet mind is compared and raved.

As a Calculator, I am aware of these intricacies. Operating factors for the control of LIFE are the heavy responsibility of my Set. True error on our part can only upset the delicate balance of PERFECT HEALTH, a catachresis which can allow the penetration of anathema: disease and d--th, its awful sequitur.

Set-6 was intended originally as a Prophylaxis Group—until routine recalcules noted a discrep, most likely a fumbled decimal, a GOOF. The POWERS THAT BE had no choice but to rengineer the Set. Destruction, naturally, was not considered. Our knowledge of genetic design provided the method, reactionary, not yet tested, not altogether certain. The danger lay in the unpredictable, improbable behaviour of a virus, 1-Spiegelman by name.

The preoccupation of medicine before the COLD WAR, vires were not apropos to the practitioners of our PANACEATIC SCIENCE. Infective agents were simply not the concern of these laboratories. But situations demanding fundamental cellular change must be dealt with, regardless of the technical vogue. 1-Spiegelman was not an operative weapon in the curative arsenal, yet the circumstances of Set-6 1984 required mid-development alteration, an immediate coup, taking over the DNA and retransmitting production code groups to make the necessary change. 1-Spiegelman is an artificial virus, indistinguishable from the natural model—possibly some rationale for its use. Like true viruses, it is composed primarily of DNA segments surrounded by protein sheaths. When exposed to the cell, it penetrates the nucleus, shedding its sheaths en route, and commands the cellular DNA to do its bidding. A mercenary. The actual procedure infects bacteria with the agitprop of this biological fraud, 1-Spiegelman, thus creating an attack virus to work its transformations upon the unsuspecting. Mercenary, yes; a small volume was synthesized in secret for THE POWERS THAT BE.

PANACEATIC SCIENCE presupposits the biological inevitability of disease. The positive use of anathema, however bloodless, must be appraised as antagonistic to the STATE. But just as destructive would be expansion iCities without adequate Calculators or with surplus Prophylactics. The decision involved more than the fate of a single Set.

Life without d--th must constantly swell as an ongoing expression of synergism. Large percentages of the population pass the COMING OF AGE and entropy threatens. New birth is required, a generation programmed and manufactured, new communes built, all to sustain the gerontocracy, the world class and midriff bulge, until this energy, too, is diminished and further expansion, greater than the last, is called for. Such were the conditions of our world as I-Spiegelman, through an almost imperceptible rise in environmental temperature, entered my microscopic being to manipulate my corpus. UM!

Oh! to be a foetus! Suspended there in our matrasses, row after row of nascent Calculators, symmetry worked upon me: I could cognit my siblings, left and right, translucent miniatures, tiny arabesque aquarian creatures with a distinct white central line to mark that mergence of brain stem into spinal cord and nerve schema.

And beyond? more, another and others, to their rights and lefts, and others still: one could view down corridors of tanks and tubes, the light shifting mischievously through them like facets. Bubbles battered me with wet kisses, and reflexedly I might take one on the rise through a noseless face that sweetest odor of sterile air. Bliss . . .

In my nutrient fluid I could never know want. (Alcohol 39% by volume, 2% aloes, 2% cinchona, 10% capsicum, 1% gentian, 6% rhubarb, 10% zedoary, 1% calumba, 2% agaric, 7% galongal, 5% byronia, 1% calamus, 1% angelica, 3% myrrh, 1% chamomile, 9% peppermint.) The low UM of the circulating pumps filled my tank with muzak. Occasionally, a Hydropontiff would pass by, pause to monitor my condition, and I would want to cry out to him my happiness, invite him to jocund singalong, mixing the fremitus of his presence with atmosymmetrical pumpsong, a duet I might make trio con brio with the as yet undifferentiated voice of my heart.

I could motivate! What discovery! Not a vigorous shattering kick of term foet to be sure, yet a twisting undulation in my suspensient. Motion! And direction! Days were I would hover in the bottom of my tubule, sensing the closeness of a curve. It was cooler there, or so I felt; in a melancholy dimness, calmer, serene. But other days I would mount toward the top with a bold muscular twitch and float brashly near that membrane through which I would be extracted, come ETU, come ripeness, and transferred dripping to the Incubation Crib. Despite the expectancy of these heights, I could never bring myself to defy the viscous limit and thrust up my head into the light of the Laboratorium; the temptation was accompanied, always and immediately, by gorgonizing poltroonery.

Some of us seemed singled out. For testing I thought. My clone to the right, a reclusive sort who spent ETU clutched to his lower wall, was often visited by Technocrats. I could feel their voices in discussion, a low UM and first audition of beautifulsome speak. But their seriousness disturbed my WELL-BEING; I felt instinctual concern and suspicion for this Set Sixer, something surely wrong about him. Abnormal. Shudder. They liquidated his suspensient, waking me frequently, the sound of some anabaptist additive shaking my prenatal consciousness with significance. We were accustomed to quiet; the unusual decibel level of his stertorous bubbling could only bode evil.

Looking back: I recall he was removed; precipitously, as I slept, the POWERS reneged his cylinder, and I awoke to a muzzy opening on my right. Unity upset, community disrupted, I could not name it then: the loss.

--What truckle, Joseph! All doggerel!

Persevere, Felt-tip, in spite of Urethra's mockery . . .

ENVIRONMENTAL PEDAGOGUERY had been in effect since my INCEPTION, my declinations recorded as a monitor of psychic propensities and metabolic systems. Members of a Set, although manufactured to perform identical functions, are both sanforized and id-vidualized. It is not the purpose of the HYGENIC STATE to do away with personality, but rather to maintain a differentiated humaniformity.

I was distroubled then by such facts, functions, responsibilities, duties. All questions were obscured between layers of a few hundred billion cells, duplicating and reduplicating in ectoplasmic climax, full of LIFE but without meaning. We grew toward IMMORTALITY, without reference to the pirouetting planets, the Outland, the history of reason, or any other chronology, biological excepted. We were as innocent of ETU as, well . . . newborn babes . . .

The prolific Felt-tip has filled the available space with kudos for the STATE. Joseph ceases his narrative to allow the ink to soak and dry into the washed adobe. And hunger discombobs his thoughts. To eat.

He caps the Felt-tip carefully and goes to sit by the door on a soft rug of dusk. A day's work done. The feeding is fiction: one hand on an ankle, one hand behind a knee, he wrenches off a leg and sinks his teeth into the quaggy thigh: chewy, a bit superfluous, not overly lean, tasteless . . .
       --You farcied anthropophage!

GRAPHIPHONIA

Prime flies, across the desert space, since morning, contrail flaring a dusty thread to rise like heaven's ravel. The engine UMs its perpetual pater noster. No sign yet of the HYGENIC STATE.

The Primitive approaches like an angry maverick steer gone bonkers on the essence of the dogweed bloom, long chromium horns lowered for the charge, goggle-eyed lamp insect flecked, unilluminated, not quite sane as a machine must be, its fuel exhausted, run to its knees, welded frame already beginning to bleach white in the sun. Primo bends down on the handlebars, emitting pinto straddle war whoops, and yet he cannot catch, even gain, on his vision, its pony as dappled and as plucky as his own is rusted, valve clogged, piston worn, and gasping with motorcycle emphysema. He should know better, this professional savage, than to ride with such recklessness and abandon; he should realize the dangers of the desert floor, the hidden wash and gully, the furtive quickness of a shifting dune, the rocks that lie camouflaged like iguanas until, too late, the onrushing rider swerves, vaults in the air, end over end, a waggling madness that can only end in those gory hues, blue black and raw, of bruise, internal hemorrhage, and scraped scabless flesh. Rudskin.

Despite its illusive openness, the desert is no empty place. The sand teems with ants and mites, snakes and worms and crawling things of all colors and creeds. The air, for all its magnifying clearness, is aswarm with unseen nits, gnats, and flies. A vulture wheels, a scout. A cactus peers out blindly. Weird towers stand in beamed black, abandoned geometry against the light, left like bleeder's needles in lifeless skin; these once let oil. Primo appears indifferent to these threats and indications.

The sun now settles down to contemplate her navel. Out of that flaming center comes a more glinting light: the prismatics of a jewel, a zircon sun spot, a refracting pooperinner. The Publicity appears. It burns. Primo turns, veers, homes.

Down the polyvinyl throughway, wide and clean! Making the plasticeine! Now the way is danger free. Reassuring to the agoraphobe, the slick UM of the tires soothes a mind and body abused by air, that fluid's subtle beating. All routes originate in the nucleus of the STATE, passing through its WELL-BEING and the Defensive Membrane to welcome farposted aseptics returning from the terrible Outland. Like dendrites they extend, conducting impulses toward the attracting body, yet an ignorant might mistake their curious presence as the high roads of a city that never was, planned and fulfilled only by diagrammatic tracks, the endgame of Megalopoly.

The graphiphonics of the STATE commence:

FABULISM IS FECISM!

The Primitive sighs. The way is long still, it is almost night. He must not miss these anticipatory messages, to be aroused, to arrive safely, to enjoy, he must not sleep.

SLOTH IS DIRT! BE WELCOME! BE CLEAN!

Back in the saddle, hidden with a blanket just like do the Cinesavages, that Holywood tribe, Primo lets go the rubber grips; the road is flawless, he free-hands and fiddles with the PILL CASE around his neck, extracts a BENZIDRENE. Then a chaser, a Jonassalk dime to suck, an after dinner mint, tinking like a chaw between his tooth and gum. Ah, the pleasures of the STATE!

HEALTH IS THE WEALTH OF A QUIET MIND!

He tucks his shoulder into the chrome backrest, lays his mocs upon the bars, sprawled in balance, his head buzzing like an engine, sweet DRENES. Burble vroom REMREM. Eaasssy does it, curves, curves to nowhere, high on, high on two rolling rubber wheels. The itinerary? Black market powwow, make the rialto, to a body house for some pleasure of the STATE-bought kind. There are no dangers ahead—except perhaps for those WURLITZERS, servomotor demimondaines, those sexual gismos so antithethical to the STATE OF PERFECT HEALTH.

SEX IS BODYWASTE! STAY CHASTE!

ETU rush on like a man on a motorcycle. Night passes into morning. The sun climbs again from her bower, all hot and sticky in shorty pajamas, peering, blinking, looking for a lover. The desert is as empty as a cold sheet.

PUBLICITY LIMITS!

Primo takes note, begins to put away his dream like a butt stub of a thought smoking leaf.

YOU ARE NOW APPROACHING THE DEFENSIVE
MEMBRANE!

VOID!

He arrives at the comfort station. The voice of the ENVIRONMENTAL PEDAGOGUE steps out from the speakers to greet him:

WHAT LURKS BENEATH YOUR FINGERNAILS?

Prime knows the immuno drill: the antiseptic pads, the swallow of DRANO, the PUMCODOXPURSACOMLOPAR Ray (Pulse Modulated Coherent Doppler-Effect X-brand Pulse-repetition Synthetic-array Pulse Compression Side Lobe Planar Array ray). He slips off the trembling bike, it too foaming at the exhaust ports, sharing his excitement. He submerges his sweaty mocs in the blue tint pool, steam rises, acid soak, foul beast leather removed and his callousness; he is made a tenderfoot. He wheels the bike in after him and there is a smell of burning rubber.

STAND HERE TILL THE TONE—THE LYRICAL SANITONE

Now for the thousand needle pressure of the showerforce, the roust of cloehardic lice, the vitalisizing of scruff and dandruff. Swirling filth and insect corpses off the vinyl suit are swept away with rainbow film and dust and crust from the transport. Both are stripped of exterior cellular layers.

Q-TIP THE EARS

CHECK BETWEEN YOUR TERMINAL DIGITS

Primo lingers in the glow of the CURATIVE SPECTRUM, from UV to X to PANACEATIC LIGHT. He registers the sustaining warmth, strangely orange, protective against the outlandish chill of the desert night, the temperature of the Publicity, within the Defensive Membrane maintained by law, a perfect Kahnstant: 98.6° Fahrenheit, rather, 37° Kelvin:

Atmosymmetry.

REMEMBER: IMAGINATION IS HYPOCHONDRIA

A wondrous calm settles upon this Primitive, a sanguinity reinforcant to his normal rutilism. His brain, so taxed with the details of caretaking, shuts down, circuit by circuit, as if some custodial engineer walks through, one by one, switching off the lights. He knows no fear, no anger, no darkling melancholy; the STATE has filtered all alkaline Responsibile from his system. He walks slowly through an intervening cerenibrium to where he is confronted with one of his own specious, a porcule MedicOp:

--Your PILL CASE, please!

The Primitive offers it for examination. And his finger for quick blood type and photoprint. In ETU, his ident is vetted:

1, MAN, Original, Size 6, Rud-Special Commemorative Issue. NOTE: Fictile, Do Not Mix With Water. If Found, Contact National Park Service, Division of Outlandish Monuments

He is given his NAD stamp, No Appreciable Disease. Thus he is cleansed for entry to WELL-BEING.

--Outlandish Service, huh? Don't get many passing this way, go out the North Pore mostly. Where ya stationed?

--Acoma.

--Never heard of it . . . but then, I never been out there. Get my fill of acnegenesis right where I'm standing. Must be tough . . .

--Um.

--Sure, sure, sloth is dirt and all that. Still, it can get ya, can't

it, even here, under optimum conditions? Hits me in the lower trak
mostly, you know, like I'm up to six CONSTIPODS, real heavy kinetics
down there . . . Bet it's lonely out at, whadya say? Acoma?
      --Not so bad. Gotta wife.
      --Gotta what?
      --Wife.
      --A woman!
      --Um.
      --By St. Barnard, man, that's against the Law. CODE OF
CLEANLINESS says specif . . .
      --Special exemption for the Outland. Authentic for when
tourists come. I wear feathers.
      --By Kahn, that is tough . . . Say, what's it like, I mean,
female? Don't get me wrong, I'm no philogyne, just, um, curious . . .

CURIOSITY IS CATABOLIC

      The POWERS THAT BE on line. A rebuffered MedicOp.
He must recoup:
      --Nosir, nosir, I'm not the latent licentious sort, as philic as
the next guy. My current's named Pud, and speaking of same, you gotta
license for that mechanical consort?
      Stupid Ops, all the same, so so so gringo. Nandiih! Fumble
the pockets:
      --Had one, yes I did, must have lost it ridin' in . . .
      --No papers, no passage, rules, and let's have no forensics.
Play the jokist on me, the jokee, and find yourself, friend, in one
hispidulous situation. Wife! Um! A quipper!
      --But I got some TURPENTINE, yours, if you don't
impound this wheeler . . .
      Whisper: the tembloring vox of temptation:
      --Oh Kahn, TURPS! How'd you get it?
      --Sap, Op! Conifers for the askin' in the Outland. Surely
more than coincidence, that very morning the homophile, sweet nacilious
Pud, had pouted to his Operous lover:
      --Please, how you rankle me, with your no adventure! What
do I see in a phile like you? So dreadfully verbatim! You will not filch the
DRANO! You will not sniff CHLORPICRIN! Why, please explain, do

I tolerate your prattle of POWERS?

TURPS, and fulminating urps! Would this not show Pud an
Op's true virescence?

--Um . . . if I admit the pissant machine, might ya leave a
resinous gratuity? A gummy pourboire?

The exchange is made, Primo flashes the aseptic servant the
mesodigit, and with a REMREM burble VROOOOM accelerates away.
On to the nucleolus!

DON'T BE HYPOCRITIC—BE HIPPOCRATIC

THE EXPLANATION

King of the HyberNation, Tuponee, august, withered white
with age, speaks:

--You are welcome, stranger, despite your unorthodox
appearance. From where do you come?

--St. Louis (Pasteur), brother, heart of the HYGENIC
STATE. Hidin' out, gone underground!

--You have done wrong then?

--The story THEY tell, I ain't done right.

--Yes, a frequent and powerful distinction. They? You
speak of pedates, men?

--Peccants! Apediculous pedants more like it!

--I see, I see, you are an expatriate, an artist.

--Gotcha!

--And therefore an innocent.

--Innocent! No spockin' way! Worms and snakes, reads
from the beginning, serpent and the wormy moon pie. Hey, man, you
don't go back much farther when it comes to guilt!

--You refer, of course, to the curious narrative of the
dystopia, Eden. A copy of this enigma exists in our library, by a
Mr. Gideon if I recall correctly. But your statement is fallacious, a
reference to one of your myths, not ours, and not, I should add, very
complimentary to our species. I have studied this and found it to deal
significantly with law-breaking, yes, yet this I would differentiate
from guilt. Recall the serpent's point of view. He says, and forgive

the archaism of my translation:

> Ye shall not surely die: for God doth know, that in the day ye
> eat thereof, then your eyes shall be opened; and ye shall be as
> Gods, knowing good *and* evil.

Italics mine. You will find my impressions outlined further,
somewhat dryly I fear, in my "Myth as Post-Facto Justification," *The
Ophidian*, No. 2 of last year.
    --Spock! You tell it different?
    --We don't tell it at all, my friend. Snakes have nothing to
feel guilt for, certainly not for evil. Such is part of our natural state, as
is good co-equally. That serpent, my ancestor, told the truth; from the
outset, you pedestrians did not listen.
    --Strepto talk snake! Get thee behind me!
    --SSSSSSSSSSSSSSSSSSSSSSSSSSSSSSSSSSSSSSSS
    --Be calm, good Worm. Understand that you pedestals, like
the reptile, have no need for gods, idols, or myths; we are all capable of
and expected to create our own lives, in our own image, making do with
good and evil what we can. To this end, the HyberNation has one yolk
tale, one only; we call it *The Explanation*. Would you care to hear it?
    --For laughs, you bet I would!
    --Quite correct, I don't see why it should not be a
laughing matter:
    At first, there was all and only LIGHT, chaotic form and
force and substance, a swirling duration that was interrupted by an
instant of Inception when force as heat was separated out from the
sublime mixture. Thus was set in direction an inevitable process,
stages determined by the very nature of things. The heat billowed
and grew, concentrating its force on form, then infinitesimal life, in
which all of us, men and reptiles, find our beginnings. There followed
a third development: the world as we perceive it now, its substance, our
actions, memory, imagination, the conceptions of unilobes great and
small, powers which serve to maintain apart the proliferating forms.
This complexification continues; our natural state is fractured into
ten million disunities, each in itself an ephemera of broken parts. The
insistent analog: celestial appearance, giant galaxies seeming to us as
reflective masses, sky mirrors, giant solids in reality nothing more, or

less, than random organizations of stellar chips, of suns and moons
and madness. Many find the conditions described debilitating and
defeating, but not our people. We snakes have devised a pleasurable way
of life. We live in the HyberNation, in darkness, in deep dry holes or
the dim lushness of swamps and river shores. We achieve the potential
of our own thoughts, we bask in an imagined sun, soak up the warm
implication of her rays. This life is like an egg, a closed vessel in which
we are momentarily held. We survive: each year we exude a skin, new
born from old, to bespeak our hope that constant LIGHT will return
again, that the re-unification of force and form and substance into that
brightly illumined, continuing chaos is only one logical step removed
from the present world as we know it. We live, as best we can, in what is,
apart from why what is. Someday—perhaps you or I will see it-this world
will shed its skin. And there will be again a glorious renewal of that most
perfect brotherhood of LIGHT . . ..
　　　　Tuponee continues:
　　　　--And you Worm? You men seem so set against fluxion, you
pederasts confuse me so!
　　　　--Yeah, me too.
　　　　--Precisely.
　　　　--Look dude, it's hot out there. I just want to make a stand.
　　　　--Alone?
　　　　--I'm pyorrhea, the lone ranger. You don't see no traveling
medicine show!
　　　　--Tuponee sees a hero.
　　　　--Not once that muthaspockin' savage regurges to THE
POWERS!
　　　　--The Park Custodian?
　　　　--That's who I mean, the Tonto.
　　　　--He is harmless. His woman is our friend.
　　　　--One finger-pointing Cochise!
　　　　--Perhaps not. Coral!
　　　　Awakened from her beauty sleep by a previous intrusion, she
presents herself before the patriarch.
　　　　--Yes, Father Tuponee.
　　　　--Find this foolish Indian, Coral. Follow him and intercede
only if it appears he will betray our new acquaintance. Do you
understand, child?

--Yes.

--Then go and be brave. Pass by the woman's dish for water. To cross the desert is a difficult journey and you must go by forced march. Keep to the shadows . . .

Thus instructed, a twist of color, she spirals up the ladder to Acoma.

--Now, sit here beside me, you Worm. We must talk. How well do you know these POWERS?

--Well enough to avoid their playtex clutches. They know me tho. I've oozed, sicked, and smudged their spockin' cleanliness. I've dropped mucopurulence and smuggled dirt from the Outland, I've rode my bike like wild rodenthood through their prissy streets. I've talked slang and hip and dirty and I've refused to limp . . .

--Why? You limp now.

--So I do, lost boot, slew foot, means I can fly! I can die!

--Indeed?

--I wouldn't swing with homophilia. I took my joy with scrut!

--Gracious! Scrut?

--Females, snake! Stick to your gender in the STATE and I am a helpless clitomaniac! Touch she not! Those Wurlitzers! One size fits all!

--And alone?

--Always.

--But this is tyranny!

--Bingo, snake! I'll get by.

--The last man.

--Yeah. Who woulda known, given the auspicious beginning?

--Then it is up to us.

--Is? Us?

--Yes, Worm. We shall join forces, interfilumwise.

--Hey look, your highness, Worm can barely get himself around, much less move a squad of reptiles. What you guys been smokin' down here in the dark?

--Only thoughts . . .

--Good leaf, no filler? Cancerous behaviour, snake. You're as hygenically outrageous as I am!

--Yes, but we have been waiting.

--For me, Tup, for me? Incredible.

--No no! Listen! With you, we are one Worm! With us, you

are many! You are you, and me, you are White Indian Python, Emerald
Boa, Wart Snake . . .
     Oh Worm, done it now, crossed over the edge, Moon Pie
DTs, you got the wiggling delusions! the reverberatin' anthropomorfits!
          --You are Yellow-Bellied Racer!
     A vision not of the worm attacked, but of the worm attacking . . .
          --You are Copperhead and Water Moc, Garter and Red Milk
Snake! You are a rectilinear army!
     Dreamtalk, glibspeak, Tuponee is a lingulate mesmerizer,
Worm, playing creator with your brain. Beware!
          --You are Texas Rat Snake, agent of chaos . . .
          --Man, you got to be kidding! Yellow cap, blue stars, now?
          --You are Sunbeam Snake! Death Adder!

THE AUTOGRAPH: 2

     Ignorance! abysmal dimness preceded our ETU! The era
may be characterized by the quasi-occult dependence on the False
Psychological Premise, a religious credo promulgated by the schoolmen
and accepted without question by a populace which called itself civilized.
Pathetic! On absurdity that world held the patent, the copyright!
     The Felt-tip trembles.
     A panoply of saints and holypersons were adored, a lot of
panegyric pensters: not one the equal of our DR. M. ANGELO KAHN!
Nor of those other unsung prophets before their ETU; Doctors Atkins,
Jack LaLanne, Jonassalk, Landrum Shettles, Petrucci, Crick-n-Watson,
or Feelgood.
     The False Psychological Premise on which the victimized
multifarious proselytes of the pre-HYGENIC world choked and gagged
was; the distinct duality of mind and matter. Clearly false! Ha! Proven
scientific fact:
               MIND IS MATTER

     That a dictum known to every emerging by-product of
the ENVIRONMENTAL PEDAGOGUE. These errortics actually
believed a mind could be diseased independently of the body. Impossible!
And to disorient further, to compound your disbelief, future lector, it

was a corollary to their credo that universally it was sickness of the spirit that caused the body's weakness. The antipathy of truth!

And so these VIPs devised their bewildering systems for cure, all complex and theorhetorical while falsely applied as science. A tragic story to recount . . . No tears! Bodywaste!

The condition toward which all these quacks directed their energy and concern was called, variously, *neuroticism* or *pneuroticism* or *neweroticism*, depending on the symptomatic connotation. The terms were the vocabulink connecting an amusing variety of signs: general nervousness and stress, "dreams" and "illusions," frenetic sexual fantasies, hysteria, etc. The primary manifestation of the disease, the true determinant of normality, was the patient's ability to articulate what were accepted as purely mental states of mind. Revealed then, and diagnosed, by rhetoric, so too was the cure. Treatment was, in fact, a long conversation, sometimes a lifetime's length depending on physician response, in which all previous actions were relived, examined, dissected and evaluated, in terms of self-satisfaction or consuming guilt, to the absolute exclusion of the future. (There was to be no future actually; neuroticism was closely related to the overwhelmingly expected inevitability; apocalypse, religious and literal, d--th in life and language.) Their past was their only certainty, continuing in expansion with the passing present, with the patient always like a verbose and mocking shadow. Implicative events were hoarded like out-dated currency symbolic of prior wealth, prior security, prior happiness, of course, worthless. A jargon developed to define, to replace, personal relationships with terminology, labeled feelings. Thus, the preoccupation, paramount and indulged, and when it inhibited all but itself, the patient was effectively disabled, a dupe and mouthpiece for retrogressive monologue, onanistic fanfaronade. There were few cures, if any, for neurotics.

The sickness first infected the mid-aged wherein guilt found food like bacteria in the culturepot. The power apparat soon was based on youth, energy displacing doubted wisdom. Rampant pneuroticism 'mongst those displaced. Transience became a permanent status, continuous aging until the grim twilight of gerontohood was achieved, along with longing for that final relocus.

(Youth is impetuous, fact. Despite PEDAGOGUERY, we prohibit citizen involvement until the COMING OF AGE, that ETU of maturity when body cells susceptible to d--th first outnumber new birth, when PANACEATIC SCIENCE commences miracculate devoir. The politics of this previous time justify the enlightenment. Unlike that day, there is no war in the HYGENIC STATE, no such impetuosity to threaten the corpuscule.)

An examination of social conditions then reveals a terrifying instability. A corps was first young at thirty years (a rather illogical division of ETU, the year), next twenty, next younger still until the nations (*op. cit.*) were governed by adolescent fiat. The culture was indicative; it played to an audience of children. Societal arrangements: the highly touted familia unit succumbed to a confusion of rule, parents mostly aping their offsprung. The laws: the great international legal body seemed like a nursery. And concurrently, youth abbreviated itself like a worm swallowing its tail, occurred only after birth in a tiny ETU warp, a quick defenestration through to the euphemistic nada. Life became equated with a few brief lapidary moments of fame. Pneuroticism.

And finally, the newerotics, those sexual morays, entangled guilt, limbs, and sick delusions in an orgiastic rage through which the reassurance of skin, of estrus, was as desperate and meaningless, as venereal, as multilogue and fleet gloria.

All psychochondria, an extravagance built on an infirm foundation. No one studied chemical relationships in blood or brain, no one inquired about metabolic function. Matter, simply, did not matter.

We understand this neu-pneu-newerotica now, and the treatment is no chitchat. A test for porphyrins in the urine would suffice for diagnosis, or a swab of the derm with sodium thiosulfate, grey-blue reaction testing positive, side effect of extreme photosensitivity to light: PORPHYRIA, constitutional difficulty in the metabolism of blood pigment manifested by advanced nervousness and stress, vivid hallucinations, increased sexual activity, some colic, some abdominal pain, occasionally in the most severe cases, hysterical convulsions. Cure: PILL CASE Immunoglobulin Series Injection D.

As for the youth syndrome, more a diet problem, too much wonder bread, *lipidus insipidus*; strange how abolished cultures overly preoccupy with bread.

The transposit from that historical adipoisition of infantile aliphat to the hard lean hi-gienks of this ETU is sometimes dated to the cholesterol panic; I, myself, tend toward the more conservative

Coryza climax. Nevertheless, these two events bracket what can only be interpreted as a class volited volution based on the realization of a world-wide deprivation of beneficial preventive medicine and/or the availability of advanced methods extant only to a patient aristocracy. The populace understood that from the beginning there had always been zygotic inequality, halfs and half-nots. It demanded a more perfect union.

And so, out of the turmoil emerged the Medical Scientist, the researcher not practicioner, dominant and mandated to put forth the parentheses of the HYGENIC STATE. The treasonous physicians were excluded for their strong resistance to experiment and theory and their stubborn adherence to the principles of folkmed and the accumulation of capitalist bricabrac. There was some violence, some d--th; the GPs were burned in the crucible of their own making.

Yes, ETU was, in preHYGENIA, when the world was swept by disease, virtual sturms of malady and sickness, mass suffering and post-nasal drang. An early form was plague, *Pasteurella pestis*, which ravaged the continents, the very earth itself manifesting the symptoms of shiver, rigor, thickened speech, apathy, entropy, intolerance of light, mortality. The worst outbreak in our egographical confines occurred in an ancient Indian pueblo community somewhere in what was then called Nu Mexiko. And it is said—although the rumours, like the humours, are controlled in the HYGENIC STATE—that this terrible threat lies enzootically dormant still, west of the 100th meridian in the Great Southwest, carried there in the blood and bite of fleas and rodents, prairie dogs, reptiles, and other vermin in that slough of dirt and filth, the Outland. A vaccine for *pestis* was developed early, an innocuous innoculation. An anti-plague syrette is carried in the PILL CASE, although no coincidence has been noted for centuries. There is no danger.

Medical Scientism moved conservatively, biding its ETU in reading rooms around the land. Slowly, cure by cure, the pandect of PANACEA was put forth and received by the ravenous like panthegruel. Leukemia, for example, and poliomyelitis through the effort of the great Dr. Jonassalk were early releases. Followed by middlebrow migraine, cardialgia, and arsis. And the biggie: chancrenoma. This a turning point.

(A minor divertissement was played by the artificial organists, identified flying objectivists and publicity schoolboys. This contaminaudition was QUACKERY of the worst order, those surgeons second only to the pixilated Shrinks on an important list of subversive

HUACs maintained by the future POWERS THAT BE.)

And yet, despite all progress, Coryza—the Felt-tip can barely capitalize this misery—the common cold, resisted as a recalcitrant snivel, that democratic virus, the existence of which, as a last human vulnerability, defied credence in PANACEATIC SCIENCE. This was COLD WAR. And only with Coryza's defeat would the revolution come, would the impatient patients believe in our ultimate victory over all disease. Even d--th!

Into these circumstances came Dr. M. Angelo Kahn. Preserved for all ETU in the Formaldarchives of the HYGENIC STATE are the yellow legal pads of this our greatest Holyman. The replica of his dingy office and closet lab, perfect detail down to the motes and monkey pellets rolling in the corners and the sense of suburban shopping pall outside the yellow windowshade, is visited by each and every student of the ENVIRONMENTAL PEDAGOGUE to receive their lesson in inspirational contrast. Kahn was undeniably a genius. Urethra claimed he stumbled over the miraculous like his own two feet.

--A myopic ouspensky, your Kahn, Joseph! A messianic amblyope!

His nearsightedness and thick eye lenses, obvious result of low Vitamin A intake of the mother during gestation, are known, and the story of his fall into the cadaver tank of Rutgers Medical School is renown; yes, his nom is frequently taken in vain. That he did not premeditate or ever understand the significance of his life, well, possibly so; like all leaders who, in the past, have moved the human species to its moments of greatness, he was an accidental savior.

--Or a kahnman, Joseph?

The Doctor was born in the mid-40s, the product of a grim sexual exercise in a bombed out Italy, an origin certainly mythic given the frequency of the reference in preSTATE lit. The concept was anything but immaculate. The father was later discovered by Fumigators outside the Vivacity, living with an unstressed and usually hypermetric final syllable in an abandoned iron lung. Quite an obscene. The man was clearly demented, obsessed with trichotomy, and, as he was exunted, he screamed of plots in threes, characters in triplicate and other novel ideas. It could not have been much solace that he left behind an only son, named Michael Angelo.

Of the mother, Kahn wrote in his official autobiography,

KAHN DID!: "She was a cold hole in a snow damp cellar somewhere in the winter near Montecassino; from her, and the passing stranger, I caught this disease of life." Nothing ambiguous there, the strong antiparturition position you might expect to be approved by the autocracy.

The Kahn child was brought home from the anus of war to the pap of national welfare. An orphan and crosscultural insemination, he was thoroughly indoctored with the notion that as bastard, immigrant, and county ward, his was to be total commitment to the American Dream, that onerous oneiric now outlawed on two counts: as Nationalism and Dream. (See the CODE OF CLEANLINESS, Vol. 4, Sect. 13, and Vol. 16, Sect. 10.) Nevertheless, in fulfillment of this revus, one M. Angelo Kahn graduated indistinguishably from the Rutgers School of Medicine, Class of '67, licensed to sign D--th Certifs.

And sign he did: thirty-eight of 117 patients his first year of GPing the public. He employed seven nurse-receptions, four in as many days. Portraits of all these are part of the lab exhibit media presentation, as are all the lapsed malpractice policies, service shut-off notices, and the two infamous Court Orders: the first, by complaint of the building manager, to prohibit the doctor from sleeping in his waiting room with his shoes off; the other by the SPCA (*sic*) to cage his proliferating monkeys.

Kahn turned to pure research. His subject: the common cold, least difficult only in terms of diagnozes. Or perhaps his choice was less altruistic, more to find his own relief from the current nasal flow first acquired as a trembling infant whose mother's blood, the foul sweat of birthing, was washed away with handfuls of dirty snow. And why not, your first breath a sternute, your first taste unforgettable mucus? There is a phote of Dr. Kahn in his closet lab, always projected in the Incubation Crib to prove that great things can happen in small places, in which I recall a glistening upper labe, nostrils flared with broken capillaries, and generally that tentative expression of an upper respiratory impaction.

--It is certainly an intelligent face, Joseph . . .

Man and monkey are susceptible to Coryza. Lacking patients, Dr. Kahn brutalized mail order chimps, to the detriment of his meager overhead and his consulting rooms which today still stink of simian urine and aging purinapellets. The kahncept was to fight cold with cold and based on the obtrusive fact that the virus, most virulent at $-76°$ C., began to shrink from its normal diameter of 0.05 microns and to lose its resistance to known antibiotics as the temperature decreased. Through

the thin shopping center walls came the staccato of the monkeys'
clattering teeth, their loud nasal catarrh, the crack of discharge against
the fiberboard, the splintering of frozen bananas, as these creatures
were exposed to the virus in all its forms, synthesized from the lode of
the Doctor's own kahnsignment. The office air conditioner struggled
through the seasons at heavy cool.

    At first, the experimentation only accentuated symptoms.
Several monkeys drowned. The beauty salon below complained of
unseemly drifts. Fittingly, the windows of the Doctor's office were
touched with frost, the gilt letters of his kahnnotation advertising the
fierce kahntagion within. But as the temperature plummeted, more
positive results began to show. Scribbled on a yellow legal pad is found
the jubilant comment: "I too show improvement, merely in association
with the chilly chimps. I'm drying up. I kahnvalesce!"

    At 21° Kelvin (+212° C.), Coryza was flash-frozen, freeze-
dried. The findings were published in *The Obscurantist*, in-house organ
of the American College of Malefic Ambiguity, Abstruse, Ohio 49119,
but were picked up by an alert equivocal at *Vague* magazine and Kahn
was warholled through that famous window.

    The POWERS THAT BE moved swiftly. The cyrogenicists
developed a portable system for the application of extreme cold to
Coryza: an inhaler storing a small quantity of liquid helium. Carried
in the PILL CASE, it was to be inserted in the nosal passage, the
abplanapped helium mixed by spraydose with the warmer humanism
in the area of influenca, thus exciting the mist to near 21° K., increasing
viral entropy, to sleep, to d--th. The medical scientists prescribed
small amounts of antibiotics with the inhale. As the patient might
feel a slight burning in the noz, the aesthesiologists suggested 250
ccs of ANAPHORA be added to the spray. The immunologists and
public health types predicted the accumulative effect of widespread
consumption would destroy virile powers and cause a direct proportional
decrease in need, and the calculators concluded that sporadic random
inhalation across the population curve for 5.6 cold seasons would mean
the near total eradication of the threat. The COLD WAR was won.

MOTTO OF THE HYGENIC STATE: KAHN DO!

    --Just a four-letter word, Joseph, a phrase, not a man!

Sadly, while perpetrator of man's greatest advancement toward WELL BEING, Dr. Kahn seemed indifferent to all save questions of patent law and revenues derived from licensing. He was a rigid embodiment of his ETU, a nixonian figure subject to moral and physical delusions. When confronted by a delegation of POWERS, he is said to have replied: "Who are you people to think I'd give up my million bongos for some half-assed utopia!" He flew off to Montecassino, accompanied by a gaggle of high-gloss bosoms and air-brushed vaginas. Kahn knew what was expected of him as a rich man, footloose and kleenex free, and left all his affairs in the hands of a lawyer.

He was permitted a foundation to shelter his proceeds. He was advanced a salary, tax-free, with benefits to include pension, transport, and sartorial advice. The monkeys were to enjoy a similar arrangement. Kahn relinquished only the rights to the Coryza cure; all secondary revenue remained his: the admission fees to the Kahn replica lab, the recordings crooning to the chimps on his private Catarrhina label, the MICHAEL ANGELO LIVES! T-shirts, the Doc Kahn dolls (He wets!). He joined that number who have everything, paid for in old world currency.

Yes, the transition phase was not prolonged, and the HYGENIC STATE introduced its own legal tender, Shettles, Jonassalk halfs, the Zimmerman nickel. There was no convertibility.

--Not so, Joseph. He converted. Kahn's fate.

Urethra told me of an underground film she had seen. She was a Communicator, involved daily with the problems of speak and symbolic systems. When it became apparent the good LIFE was not to be as he imagined, Kahn opted out, chose d--th. It is whispered there were others, number unknown, who when faced with immortality, succumbed rather than to have to live with themselves for the sublime duration. Neurotics mostly. There were saunacides. And Kahn among them!

--Conversion to DEATH, with nothing to show for his living!

Urethra was affectedly given to using profanity. I did not approve.

--Kahn do, Joseph. He forwent the PILL CASE. Deprived of metabolic control, almost immediately his face revealed the uncertainty of his body systems, as if the entire aging process was suddenly freed and poised on the verge of a tidal burst. His nose began to trickle, a moistening that became a stream and followed the contours of his body, a torrent that branched and divided until he appeared turned inside

out, his circulatory system draped like a mesh about him, wetness
everywhere shining like protoplasmic armor. Exposed suddenly, all this
fluid, snot, blood, lymph, urine, perspiration, secretion, dried and his
physical reflection of the powerful camera lights ceased and beneath the
absent veneer the diseases could be seen at work like burrowing worms,
arteriosclerosis, gout, arthritis, failure of blood sugar, acidotic coma,
leucocyte madness, dispossessed follicles and teeth, and tissue consumed
from within, leaving only pain as definition of the supportive bone and
flesh that was once a near-sighted graduate of Rutgers.

--Stop it, Urethra! Your damned linguistic powers!

--More visually visceral, Joseph. You see he could not speak
to condemn or welcome this horrible demise. As he diminished to a
puzzling tangle of cords and empty tubes on the laboratory floor, the
dank flakes of skin drawn toward the air conditioner fan, one organ
remained firm intact, and there was no phallocrypt!

--Yes, I see, it must have been quite revolting for you, Urethra.

--So pathetically vain, puffed and swollen after his other
functions had failed, heart, brain, yet for ETU afterward that appendage
stayed erect.

Urethra laughed scornfully.

--The organ deflated as fast as it had grown, and then there
was nothing left of your M. Angelo Kahn, not even priapic posterity!

I was nauseated by this account. I quickly swallowed two
DRAMAMINE to settle the turbulence.

--He is remembered, Urethra.

--Ha! Come Joseph, surely you, a Calculator, do not accept
the empty myth, you do not believe the graphiphonics!

--Well . . .

--Don't! I compose those xenoralia.

Bless that PILL CASE, I was now calmed. I recorded
Urethra, but my mental consciousness was more directed toward the
incredible curvature of her friend Magnesia's amalgams.

--Don't seem so soporific, Joseph! Remember those
kahnfabulations are fabricated in the Religiosity, as synthetic as you be!

Very depressing. I felt unclean and befraught. And so
withdrew 400 grains of NAPHTHALENE and offered it around.

The moment intrudes on my history of the STATE. I knew
it, and others, would. The technological Felt-tip cannot sustain this

marathon longer. The walls are three tablets of labyrinthine scrawl, slight
left bias, florid F's and B's, uncrossed T's. And mosigraphia threatens.
Dusk has long since come; the night is anxious to erase my palimpsest.

Left arm for dinner.

HY-GI-YA

Her face is in repose. The date of her birth is not sure, a fact
turned legend with no one to listen. But each day is read in the exposed
weathering, like rock abutment, the wrinkles roded across her cheeks,
from her eyes, like dry wash, deep dusty rivers in which a rider fears the
sudden, copious flash-flooding of her heart.

Hy-gi-ya.

As a girl, her beauty spread across the desert like a whirlwind.
Her skin was of an unadulterated color, like that of sand beneath a
boulder, enhancing her mystery, her brave-fevering inaccessability.

She was known for her breasts, perfect lumps like burial
mounds holding secret store. Although no one had ever seen them, it
was known that each day they were a different flawless shape, as if all
the glorious dugs of history were hidden in her pueblo room like rich
maidens' jewelry. She does not regret the lost smoothness of her skin,
nor the twisting of her limbs from quaking aspen to bent juniper, only
the pride of that bosom, now shapeless and empty as punctured water
skins, and dropped so low with the passing years, she might wear them
as foot cloths if it was not for her ageless ingenuity. As she smokes, as she
weaves, as she moves about the old church wherein she lives, those breasts
are gathered up and tied with a fore-in-hand across her chest, a double
windsor fashioned knot of well-used flesh.

Her paps may never have been bruised by the perfervid
husband's hands, but how they had been suckled!

Hy-gi-ya was fatherless, yet daughter to the medicine crone
who wove spells and healed the sick irregardless of the admonitions of
the Indian Agent. The Acomas gossiped her father was no human being,
rather a snake, a notion the medicine crone did not deny, grinning,
showing her turquoise teeth, spreading her legs and titillating the
assembled braves with a snakeskin filled with sand, slick with grease, and
gestured obscenely. The story was given further credence by Hy-gi-ya's

daily walk to the mesa's southern edge where she filled a pottery saucer
full of water and whispered to the clouds and sky. It was certain the
reptiles of the world came to drink at that place for the water was always
consumed by the following day.

As the girl grew, so did the pueblo seem to lose its youth. The
many children, the tribe's regenerative tonic, left to seek a thing called
fortune rumoured to lie off there somewhere beyond a gesture, across
the desert and behind the distant mountains. Talk centered excitedly
on reports of pueblos even greater than Acoma or Taos; there were
mesmerizing accounts of a place called The Angels.

On her deathbed, the medicine crone, herself having seen the
last of eight hundred new moons, spoke of this slow migration toward
extinction. She instructed her daughter in the eternal medicinal ways
as an attempt to prolong Acoma's life. Hy-gi-ya was to water the snakes
without fail. She was to continue to heal the sick, no matter how few
or feeble. And finally, she was not to bury the crone's corpse according
to tribal rites, rather it was a command that she be laid out in the
unmerciful sun and dried like a chile to be crumbled and surreptitiously
mixed in the pueblo's bread. Above all, Hy-gi-ya was to bear children,
never to marry as that was notoriously wasteful and gringo, but to be
ever fruitful in the withering heat, to give birth generously to stingy life.
Dutiful daughter, for centuries, she did as she was told.

Her womb was like a kiln, trim oval shape, unnatural
warmth beneath the surface skin. Opened with astonishing regularity, it
produced a variety of nicely turned, slow-fired offspring, dull red glaze
the color of an Indian's skin, little decoration, an efficient, functional
design tribute to the potter's art. Indeed, these children might well
have been made of clay, each an artistic miracle, as Hy-gi-ya never took
a husband, was beyond question the virgin her witch mother intended.
In a small skin sack tied with rawhide around her waist, Hy-gi-ya
wore modesty to an extreme, and for all her medicinal wisdom was
unaware of what lurked like a startled rattler beneath the loincloths
of the young bucks who came in vain and absurd attempts to win her.
There were fist fights, teeth like spilled water in the dust; there were
ridiculous machismo duels, horses raced to their death, failed leaps across
wide chasms, stalks and hunts and feats of strength. Six braves were
drowned swimming the spring enraged Puerco River, full of mountain
piss, dragged under by their abhorrence of wet, all to solicit Hy-gi-ya's

notice as she foraged for roots along the farther shore. Yet she remained
pristinely unaware, and when later she heard of the tragic Puerco test, in
her next birthing she gave forth a litter of six, all males, in replacement, a
reproductive phenomenon heard far and away from Acoma, witness the
congratulatory telegrams, endorsement offers, and layette sales pitched
from a distance.

The snakes, the snakes, just like her mother crone, went
the late night tribal whispers. The Cacique spent three cold evenings
and colder mornings near Acoma's edge, spying on the bewitch's daily
visits to that pottery saucer. Although it was nowhere written in the
new regulations provided him by the Albuquerque County authorities
(replacing those given his great grandfather by the our paters in drag),
he was certain that fucking with a reptile was against gringo law. To
no avail. He saw nothing, caught the ague, and suffered the ultimate
humiliation of visiting Hy-gi-ya for remedy. He was given a pinch of
dried medicine crone mixed with pream and dissolved in rainwater. And
later, when the fearful hallucinations ceased—skinned alive with coke
glass, cactus spines in his eyeballs, his nethers roasted over sterno flame,
his brain kicked around in some old Indian game—he emerged from his
administrative chamber pale and wan and wiser and cured.

--Stay away from that one, she got plenty chutzpah!

He warned the adolescents in the kiva, but they did not heed
his wisdom. They sniggered and snorted, warhooped and dared, their
desire did not weaken. Hy-gi-ya knew their assault like an unsuspecting
wagon train, reduced by the sureness of their flaming arrows to
quivvering moans, burned the raven haired captive on innumerable
stakes, a western film retrospective of sticky teenage dreams. How
Hy-gi-ya knew them, by night her skin ached from their touch! She
administered saltpeter in old crankcase oil gallon cans. The jerky turned
grey. The cooks were stoned when the stew tasted always of chalk.

The Cacique, these children, their collective desires and fears,
were all the offspring of her most fertile imagination. She was both egg
and seed, painting boychild girlchild in her mind, tones of skin, flattened
noses, eyes so clear, perfections and not so perfect, her brain was the
placenta of a population. She lay on her bed of skins conceiving with as
much passion as those who desired her. The night passed in gestation,
and the morning brought a first contraction, followed by wincing more,
until by dawn light when the rest of Acoma was spitting and shitting on

the rocks, Hy-gi-ya would emerge with her latest wrapped in a bloody rug and the Cacique would make an additional plus mark in the federal subsidy book.

Years passed. Mother outlived her children. She watched them stumble and fall, their first hesitant steps in Acoma's dusty streets, their last into the white man's buryin' box or off the mesa's sharp precipice with prayer sticks clutched to their chest in supplication. Many simply could not wait for death to come, making his rounds of the world like an express rider, and they took his business for their own. And even those who had departed, fled the homeland in search of a pick-up truck and brown bag culture not their own, even those returned to die, straggled in from crossing a now alien sand, nearly mad with the sky's continuum. They climbed up the ravine and to Hy-gi-ya who could no longer save them, only watch them succumb with sad maternal eye. Macabre trails led to Acoma. Burned footprints, black holes to guide by.

On the raised platform in her vaulted house, covered with coyote rugs, she laid her children, stripped them of their foreign clothes, washed and closed their vented wounds. She shaved the heads, the pubic hair; she pulled cheap fillings from their teeth, the rings and chains and plastic talisman. As best she could she restored their outward innocence, made them to resemble newborn. The bodies dried like the crone's on the roof of the pueblo, with mushrooms, wild flowers, hides. The dust she stored in mason jars and rubbed in the cuts of their nieces and nephews in a diminishing attempt to preserve. Her final act, as significant for each as her first, was to lie forehead to forehead with the dank bodies and draw from the dead brains all their experience, wisdom and folly, a kind of mental evisceration and Indian-giving of the chip of imagination she had provided each as a physical and spiritual center. These she restored preciously within her, then a cold kiss, then the sun.

Thus was nothing wasted. The fillings went for flint in the Cacique's lighter. The hair was packed in quilts or made into hairpieces for the tribal bald. The bone and flesh and blood were reborn in another metabolic process, the imagination distributed to a following generation, the life itself returned for deposit with the great source that had made it.

But the deaths became more numerous. Hy-gi-ya's twilights were spent undressing the dead and suddenly around the tiny grain of sadness in her stomach a stone began to grow. No room, no time for joyous birth. Her forehead was bruised from where she bowed to touch her children, her brain became swollen with the fluid of accumulated knowledge and experience, which filtered down into her body tissue, flowed through her veins and arteries, the plasma of loves and lost loves, of aspirations and failed hopes. Her flesh became sodden with bills unpaid, mortgages, new car payments, finance schemes, with worries and amassed hysteria, empty pints, illegal prescriptions, with all the sickness, the despair, the little health each had known: her breasts began to sag.

She could not leave her mortuary room. The dead came in an uninterrupted stream, like a rainwater jug cracked and leaking out its level, until inevitably there would be no more, no more proud notion of race and tribe, songs and dances, lessons, gods, drunken pow wows, lyric poetry, spilled and evaporated into the earth.

In Hy-gi-ya a civilization was interred. Her creative powers were overwhelmed by a miserable memory. Acoma became deserted. Hy-gi-ya grew ugly and fat and old.

There passed an interval of loneliness, as long to her as the shadow of a cloud moving across Acoma, until the day, when drawing a saucerful of water, she observed in the unresolved distance to the east of Katzimo a small black dot moving at speed along the desert floor. It emerged into the acuit of her vision: a pick-up truck. She had heard of these from her lettuce-picking children. She marvelled at its approach; perhaps this was one last child of imagination coming?

--Well, there she is, injun. Acoma!

At the wheel was no less than the Deputy Assistant Regional Supervisor, South Pore, HYGENIC STATE Park Service, Division of Outlandish Monuments; and beside him, the Primitive en route to his new assignment, a bonus roll of Shettles in the pocket of his newly issued green vinyl uniform.

--Acoma!

The supervisor spat out the name like a gob of filth.
The Primitive had been astounded when just outside the Defensive Membrane this High Official of the STATE had stuffed his cheek with dead leaves and begun to drool. The expletive lingered for an instant outside the cab window, then disappeared with a rush.

Primo saw the mesa looming before him, big as a boil to the man who's got one.

--Holy Kahn!

--Yep, sure is something to look at, isn't she?

The Primitive's brain worked to formulate his inarticulate complaint to the grievance board, his previous doubts blossomed into glorious apprehensions like flowers on the yucca bush.

--I gotta live there?

--Sure do, boy, must be five hundred rooms up there to choose from. Well now, true, she ain't no glass house . . .

Spit!

--Yeah, ETUs like this I thank my lucky PILL CASE I was born promoted. But somebody's got to do the job. It won't be so bad once you get yourself settled. I'll be back, do some point work, lay you out a parkin' lot. I got reqs in for good graphiphonics: Pete's Cafe, new Burmashaves, See Rock City. Season opens, you'll get visitors from back home.

Spat!

--Now, you stay clean out here, injun, no funny business. You won't find no sibs, look as you might. All d--d. Say they got wiped out by the plague, tho I don't put much stock in the story. My money says the heathen all BO'd!

Sput! With a chortle, wink, guffaw, and a shift them gears, he was gone.

Hy-gi-ya confronted the Primitive as he wandered, dazed and fearful, down the streets of Acoma. It was a d--th town beyond the Supervisor's warning, and when he saw d--th herself, mams all tied in a granny knot, he screamed and hurled his panic at her.

--Who are you? You were not born here.

--Me? No, by Kahn and all his monkeys, check my PILL CASE! Neo-Navajo, I was assembled in the Facticity!

--I did not remember any living.

And so she left him there, immobilized with fear, striking a pose like the pompous Cacique for the dogs to pee on. When she returned, ten days later, she expected to see him shriveled fit for a crucifix or a mason jar, but she was mistaken. There he stood, asleep, an instinctual adherence to the old Indian principle: when in a confusing situation, do nothing. She assumed he was dead and carried him to her room to strip off the strange green skin and discover the metal talisman with its awkward scratchings strung around his neck.

She found more to dismay her! As she approached his loins with her sharp stone knife, she discovered aiyeeeee! his PHALLOCRYPT and, within, the unmummified remains of his sex.

Primo awoke and found her hands upon him. Awareness returned to his klonce like a bladder full, and he swelled a totem risen, a work of art more than one curator would have offered Shettles for, a vertical and six-colored version of things ever since Beringia. He towered, all pastel like washed wood, and told the story of tracking mammoths down the glacial corridor, of drought and dearth of meat, of foraged tubers and pathetic plants of corn, of constant migration from lands called home, of trading post firewater, of massacre and its alternative, starvation; yes, the history of all bad medicine. This Hy-gi-ya read and felt the stone of recognition jump inside her belly. She felt a displacement in her craw and supple supplicating want in that ravine around which her body stood. Why had she not conceived such decoration for her children? What had distracted her? A spirit passing outside her window in the dark causing her to lift her brush just as its tip tickled the parts of her conceptions? Was this the reason for all the deaths, this absence of art? Was it not a marvel of living when the accidental reality exceeds even the powers of life-giving imagination?

She took this silent lover. As she allowed this stranger, this tribal intruder, the gift she had withheld for so many moons under which screamed coyotes and their two-legged brothers, as he ejacked his effusive warmth, Hy-gi-ya resolved to use this seed to rekindle her dreams, to make children once more, each slung with an aesthetic totem, to sing the chants and hear the legends spoken, to live bravely and long, to be heroes and to put together out of bits of stick and feather and twisted grass the being that would make Acoma live again!

She builds up her fire, and pulls its heat about her like a storm pattern blanket. She is drowsy. She considers that for all their union the gods have not yet seen to grant these children of her resolution. She knows the joy as nothing but the sweat and ooze of love. Occasionally still, she leaves a prayer stick in the clefts of Katzimo or tolls the bell of the womanly fathers who hoisted their skirts and lifted the forged clapper into the rafters of her home, as a reminder to all the powers that they retain their positions only through the mandate of their believers and that now and again they really ought to visit their constituency.

But her wisdom tells her to continue her way. There is always more to come and waiting she knows, though not for what she waits.

A snake wiggles into the circle of firelight, deadly Coral drawn by the flame, a look of determination in her eye. Hy-gi-ya remembers she has not filled the saucer. Tomorrow she must not fail to take the snakes water.

She presses her ear to the ground, listening for the soft footfalls of oncoming sleep.

DOWN AND OUT AMONG THE VERMIN

--You are Krait! You are Puff Adder! You are Hypnale, a neurotoxic Mamba!

Poor Worm rubs his wrecked occipitals, massaging his confusion.

--You are the fleshworm, Lice! Tarnus, the lardworm! Emigramus, the headworm! You are Sanguinea the Leech, bloodsucker! You are Horned Viper!

--Horny is right! O for doo-wah-diddy, my kingdom for a moon pie!

The ceremonial chamber is illumined by heavenly light, as if all that feeble glint is focused at its center, giving the curvature within a vague phosphorescence. The snake eyes are like starry imitation. Tuponee continues his hypnotic herpetologue:

--You are reptiles as numerous as the names of the dead! Boa and the speckled Scitalis . . .

There is smoke from a gasping fire, there is vertical shadow like snakes' dancing, the tangle of gods' hair, a weaving serpentine of scaly bodies, some rising tall, heads in smoke and peering, others coiling rectilinearly, a multiplication of crazy chiaroscuro.

Tuponee's tongue tests the kiva air, tasting the dark feelings of the clan. His flickering bi-forks transmit to the chemo-receptive depression in his upper jaw, the rapture of poetry and dance given voice in the brain through that delicate membranous cellular tissue.

--You are Seps, destroyer of body and bones! You are Serpens, born from the marrow of corpses!

A soft, insistent butting, their skin against wormskin, flake to flake, the participatory lustration of snakes, ritual of purification. Worm's will is bound by an aura of cold, his limbs by a wind of vermin. Wormwood. Screwworm.

--You are bent Anguis! You are Viper, brought forth in violence! You are Spectaficus, asp which consumes man, rotten and rotted by your bite!

The fire swarms. Worm is both altar and sacrifice. The dancers pass by his recline, each bends down to give a whisper, a fanged greeting and flexive dispatch of a tiny drop of poison, black bursts beneath his skin. He feels their striking homage, the piercing statement of their initiatory welcome, the visceral honorific of acceptance. His leather epiderm is ragged, his systems engorged with natural venom driving before it the breath of life.

--You are Emorroris . . .

His veins and arteries burst. His heart explodes.

--You are Salamandra!

In pain he inhabits fire, and yet he is not consumed. Tuponee looms, the wedge skull, the haughty wise old eyes, scar-patterned, criss-crossed diamonds, a patch of mold; slowly with curious reverence, the ancient snake too bends down to offer a searing strike . . .

--You are the Devil, most monstrous of us all! King of Pride! False Angel!

Deathkiss.

Darkness. Silence. Black on black of outcast, exile, shadow of shadow, deep sand, dead stone, the dark shoot of a desert willow improbably rooted, bitterness, rejection, curse like distillate thunder, fear, abandon, mortality . . .

--And so, you are our leader, brother Worm; together, we shall infect their changelessness . . .

--We all get what we deserve, snake.

Thus, in his exhaustion, Worm becomes the chosen one, Prince of the Parasites!

--Good night, sweet prince, you fecundate spermatozoon.

THIRD WALL

Felt-tip:

. . . the world was soap opera, a suspension of belief. Democratic self-government was a failure, crude totalitarianism no better. There were mega-threats of planetary lobotomy, the excision

of one hemisphere by another, ineluctable hegemony sought by east or
west. Plastic, the tyrannical majority, begat plastique and tyrannical
minorities. It was an unenlightened time.

Until Coryza, cold truth, revolution, a twist of the
historical screw.

Some objected; footnotorious intellectuals who viewed the
phenomenon from the perspective of anti-utopian novelty, and the
alter-egos, transvestors and rad-livs, who regretted the gain of personal
dignity and universal WELL-BEING, the substitution for freedom,
that Protean concept, of PERFECT HEALTH, ultimately Protein, the
true shape-shifter. Ironically, many of these acadeems became eager
innovators with the PILL CASE.

As with Dr. Kahn, there were further abstentions. Their
perpetrators were certainly extremists of the first order; yes, even,
I suppose, Michael Angelo. And, then, there were also a number of
continuing natural d--ths, individuals already caught in the mortality
pipeline. Pain beyond the pacifying limits of aesthetics was endured by
these helpless biodegradates and, if they succumbed, tears, despite the
bodywaste, were STATE issue. Actual D--th Certificates exist from
those early days:

Cause of D--th: Grief

Cities, microbe habitat for racial vermin of every kind,
were replaced with iCities, generalities, sterile monuments of glass
and architectural uniformity. The earth, the Outland, as source of
filth, was quarantined. Mass immunology was begun, PILL CASEs
dispensed. PANACEATIC SCIENCE and ENVIRONMENTAL
PEDAGOGUERY reformed LIFE's curriculum. SET CREATION
achieved genetic purity and equality at long last over the erratic
darwinian vicissitudes of the past. In no other ETU had the human
species approached so near its expectations: we had attained the
Mediocracy.

Hereinunder is quoted the remarkable document on which
THE POWERS THAT BE founded the STATEd New World:

THE BILL OF HEALTH
WE, the iCitizens of the HYGENIC STATE, do hold
these truths to be patently medicinal:

I.   LIFE is all MATTER, disease ANATHEMA
II.   CLEANLINESS is godliness
III.   HEALTH is the wealth of a quiet mind
IV.   Age is beauty
V.   Imagination is HYPOCHONDRIA
VI.   Philosophy is QUACKERY
VII.   Heterosex is BODYWASTE
VIII.   HOMOPHILIA is LOVE
IX.   The PILL CASE prescribes our METABOLIC
RIGHTS
X.   No d--th is!

My first exposure to these virulent principles occurred in the Incubation Crib to which I was removed post-INCEPTION, post-GESTATION, post-EXTRACTION. It was another perfect day, bright and moist and pure, such was Atmosymmetry, flavorous and impermutable. I was arrepted from my cylinder, forcepped to the baromacrometer for a measure of weight and length, then, blinking and dripping in newlight far more astringent than apprised previously through the softening screen of nutrient fluid, ceiling traked from the GESTATION warehouse. All around me I beheld SET-6, multiple minor juggernauts on parade, real and dangling, fellow hackers as we cleared insipient vapors from our lungs in favor of a sweeter gas. I was simultaneously hypnogogic and hypnopompic, between waking and sleep, between sleep and waking, stolidly in demi-nod, as if LIFE was the BENEFICENT TEN and birth a dreamhole.

The SET-6 Distribution diverted us to our assigned nanny-crannies, a dizzying path of sharp turns, diminishing siblings, aggravated armpits, until below I perceived a yawning lunula of light. I was unpinced to tumble, gently and awkwardly, into the private box-bed that was to be homeroom for my ensuing scholarhood. The first fall. Does any child forget?

The voice of the ENVIRONMENTAL PEDAGOGUE was midfilibuster:

... *LOVE the PILL CASE prescribes our METABOLIC RIGHTS NO d--th is LIFE* ...

Duce tone, STATE parental, unisexual organ that was to instruct me in mentalist values, to teach me rigor vivus. I was to grow to

love so deeply, homophilially, that warble; I would gravitate to the crib's
speakerend and lay my cheekiness against the foam performations there
to be quiet, be still.

    . . . is all MATTER disease . . .

    I explored the cubits of my crib, color: variable beige, No. 14-
033 Polyurethane. To my sinister, the Response levers, Yea and Nay. To
my right, the Reward Altarette, small tube for liquid, wire cup for solid
feed. There my gobblings were fulfilled by kibble; contentment, rolling
on my bellibone, learning:

    . . . is the wealth of a quiet mind age is beauty imagination. . .

    Libation, cibation, if these are cause, then there is effect,
pish and turdiforms. Bodyby is a continuing problem in the HYGENIC
STATE; it is a correlative biological truth, humbling in the face of
METABOLIC RIGHTeousness, that despite our politprime we iCitizens
remain the source, the fount of imperfection, through our undeniable
propensity for the creation of waste. Retentively filthy, nevertheless
ingenious, our systems for disposal are superefficient and unique. Still,
admittedly, there is no redeeming social value in our ordure, none.

    A less tangible, more serious question is the threat to
Atmosymmetry through human internal combustion emissions,
flatuous melancholia, tympanites, and other sweet deceits. An occasion
exemplifies: the Great Anchovy Panic in the Atrocity ETU's ago. Hear
the Graphiphones:

ART IS HYPERBOWELIC ETHER. IMPOLITIC.

    (Authority for suppression is found in the CODE OF
CLEANLINESS, the *Anti-Gass Act, Being the Acceptability of Novels
and Other Theorhetorical Wind*, Vol. V, pp. 988–1008. In like manner,
lint in the navel is contravened by the legislated abandonment of the
navel. KAHN DO!)

    So. . . gentle technological Felt-tip, correct me when I scrabble.
To continue:

    I mastered Yinglish and HybriUrupean, with a doppling of
Fortran and Allasa, a smuttering of Newspeak, these the grammatical
precursors of our own STATE tongue: Sanitone.

    The ENVIRONMENTAL PEDAGOGUE spoke so coolly,
kibbly punctuated his sibs and glots to a T. I could not articulate myself;

no need to tax my unlimbered larynx with salivics beyond levered Yea or Nay. Was I content? Yea. Operatic jingle of kibble down the slot. Was my mind quiet and still? Was *statistical imbalance* in Yinglish *statimbal* in Newspeak? Was *thank you* in HybriUrupean *taxias*? Yea. Yea. Was Allasa quadriglottic? Was Fortran catatonic? Yea. Silence. Yea? Nay rattle. Confusion. A tentative Nay? Yea. Nay! Kibble. Ah . . .

I had no intimation of a peopled world outside the niceties of language. My friends were aberrated nouns, relatives clauses, my enemies were appositives, and strangers passed me by like indifferent prepositional objects. No verb was I; in solid passivity I was the embodiment of a noun.

--Like drone or dingleberry?

--Why are you so cruel, Urethra?

--I am an aseptic skeptic and you will get no peace from me, noun! Give me WITTGENSTINE or give me d--th!

--Urethra!

Individuals as linguistic econominimums, sublimated to radical and root—undoubtedly a reaction to that priorly over-rhetorical world. And Sanitone? Little did I know that as I lay between chapters of PEDAGOGUERY I was speaking it then, the only true universal voiceprint, abbreviated, condensed, refined, onumatopoetic, the one clean tone *between* words:

UMMMMMMMMMMMMMMMMMMMMMMMMM

Sanitone!

The VOX PEDAGOGUS was personality, as was the waste scoop, stainless extensor, that two, perhaps three, times an ETU scanned my space. My hand inadvertently touched it, fingers clumsily intertwined with its mechanical digits. This became a game, to impede its briskness, and the PyroFecetian in control sensed the fun, reducing me to gurgle and coo via tickling instrument. Laughter. My only speak.

Consider, then, my consciousness, the impact on the temporosphenoidal lobe, when my large word reservoir was defined by a sudden flicker of LIFE at the Crib's projection end, a voice, a frolicking scoop, and four languages made echolalicly valid by the addition of visual perception.

I knew enormous discomfort, a conceptual newness was

embodied in the sequential light. I heard a first disconcerting sound
from within myself, and a body movement that was more than mere
rolling in pish and turdiform. I became frighted, more frighting still as
fear was itself original. I began to shake, my squint fixed to the screen
by a force surpassing my feebly crib-exercised retinal musculature.
Gums gummed, a reassuring kibble lay ignored upon the Altarette. My
awareness was all vision, I saw nothing but light bits despite the formed
configures they comprised, and, while the PEDAGOGIC narrative
accompanied this terrifying propos, I heard no vocative that was not my
own. Nor were these the gurgle and coo of idle volupty, 1-Spiegelman,
you aweful catoptromancer, may your imagism rot in the Outland! A
flaw revealed!

--GOOF here! GLITCH!

I lay shuddering with amazement, stricken as the criblid
raised and there, realer than first perception, stood faces, in grander scale
than screened, larger, in fuller rud, dewlapped with animation. And they
spoke! PEDAGOGUERY in the flesh!

--Record symptoms . . .

--Paroxysms, muscle spasms, foaming and verbose . . .

--Excellent. Your diagnosis?

--Epiplexis.

--Very good! You prescribe?

--Indeed. Immediate inject of 40 cc. HIGHOCTALINE.
Health dossier notation of FLAW, plus requisition for PILL CASE
control medication. Observation to determine acuteness, over 4 on the
Muelmonger Scale, submit for d--th, Classification: COSMIC.

Bureautalk! These were POWERS!

--Rhyparography to my ears, 1-Azoth. Been studying again?

--Yessir!

--Well, don't overindulge, my fellow single; there is ETU
enough for surfeit. You'll soon have your Medisinecure. Slowly, a bit more
drant to your LIFE or we'll be treating you for Uptitis . . .

--Blood's fine, sir, everything's hemapoietic, septicemicly
speaking!

--All right, see to this then, will you? SET-6 has been nothing
but obscenity since that Spiegelman business. Teach us a lesson, mucking
about with the template after INCEPTION with no Warranty . . .

Destruction? I felt immediately a needle like a worm's bite

and, had I a telecardiphone, my heartbeat might have been heard all the way to the Gnosticity. I knew instinctively as well that my emotion must be kept subcutaneous for the POWERS would be watching. But, by Kahn and all that is wholly, that crisp synopse of my defectitude by 1-Azoth connected my personal concept to inconceptuality, prefix non, finale, end of pogrom, no rewind, to d--th and cosmicly! Thus, the hasty intervention of the soft PEDAGOGUE:

... *you are upset, thus upsetting, Joseph SET-6, be consoled* ...

Nay lever. Note that: first lie.

Yea yea, our monitors show your ephemerata, nothing is hidden, however slight. Imagination is HYPOCHONDRIA, the beyond is waste, the Outland inconceivable. The world is totally defined and compiled by the STATE, that is WELLBEING. Calculate for yourself, determine that nothing can exist beyond complete definition, nothing extends beyond immortality.

Yea!

Kibble. Nibble.

Near exhaustion, Muelmonger 4, pulse accelerating, my mind and my matter longed for rest, no day yellow, but rather sleep blue, the nightlight. I observed again: 1-Azoth remained perusing me. And I he. I could not read his physiognomy, his features were gibberish, just as my thoughts were chomsky. Who was starer? Who staree? What did we see? Or were we both fixedly blind?

As if sparing us both further embarrassing witness, 1-Azoth slowly reposited the lid.

THE PEDAGOGUE:

... *we are too quick with you, Joseph, you are sensitive, SET-6* ...

They didn't know that, they who had made me?

Still, I was not to be a tendsome child, subject to condemnatory disquietures and momblishness. I would simply scise this experience as a minutal phantomination, a passing apparit, in an otherwise OK world. I was determined to be no deviate, no parechasis.

... *better, much better, your valence restores* ...

Kibble cupped, a dunker, rondo rattle playing a happy tune on the old granola!

... *perhaps you should relocate the screen, Joseph* ...

Nay I could not, and manhandled the lever!

*. . . Disease ANATHEMA CLEANLINESS is godliness
HEALTH . . .*

Discipline. I rheostaticly cooled until finally I could glance
back to the bright reflections below my feet; I resumed my grave
eagerness to be at LIFE, the picture magazine! Where I saw:

SLOW PAN of iCitizen walking well-swabbed way. Sound
of swelling kibblechorus. Cut to iCitizen features. Could this possibly be?
Unslavering gaze, poreskin slightly sallow and hung along the chinline;
yea, there was indubitability, there was beady-eyed 1-Azoth! You
understand my bewilderment. He had just left me, gone to note the
necessary negation in my dossier! Was I on the verge of presenile
dementia? What possible antarctic could calm me now?

--I have never understood, 1-Azoth, the REALTIME of
our first two encounters . . . Had you rapidly departed the Incubation
Coop? Was the connection linear? Or were you simply in two spaces
simultaneously?

--Motile, we POWERS, eh Joseph? Prismatic, all done
with dites and mirrors, a lapidary mosaic . . .

--I had seen only three facades in the raw by that ETU,
and two of them were yours. My circuitry could not but record a
sympathetic imprint.

--Consider it overlap, Joseph. After all, the kineclip you
viewed had long been part of the Incubation First Program. The
POWERS had auditioned me as typical, a fortuitous event in my career,
you will understand. Not just any 1 is selected as norm among norms.

--Yes, of course, but there is no coincidence in the
HYGENIC STATE . . .

--True, nothing is accidental . . .

--And the sapphics, Urethra and Magnesia, how do you
explain that they, too, were in the film?

--So inquisitive, Joseph . . . How do you explain it? The
camera followed him into his showcase. He postured before me, the
kineman with longlens focus, my brain the celluloid. I observed as he
wash'n'dri'd, the daubing of dappled places with thorough alcohol.
I could not but admire the sharp edge of his isopectorals and hardly
knotted clunes, the draped contours of dynamic tension and, rippling
beneath, the sure flex of internal organs in continuous exercise. In the
near blue light of the BENEFICENT TEN oncoming, he appeared

strangely to incandesce, the natural oils of skin starring his physique, a specimen of WELL-BEING, unruffed and devoid of body pellicule, limned thusly and limbed with mathematical precision, an identikit of ultimately differentiated genetic proportion like the gymnoideal illustration from the Comprehensive Anatomy. My own cerebel was gorged by the vista, cortex sated and nervana pulse zinging through all my cords like pumped iron.

KibbleZAP! Jackpot!

Naked, he removed his PILL CASE and, then, from his waist and impuberal center, another circumference, a glass tube strung on a belt of clear plastic. Cryptic to me, weird! This was the coles container, the PHALLOCRYPT, of which as yet I did not know . . .

The light was near pure blue by this ETU and we both were soon to enter the rejuvenative world of a coma. But first he advanced to the showcase window and stood, his eyes searching the darkening consciousness of the Publicity. And then I saw the goal of this ocular expedition: an idiosyncratic lumescence, so outlandish in the field of a lightless showcase that it might have been a signal fire, an arranged rendayview. The glow was patterned with swaloops and moving shades and curvaceous silhouettes. I was amazed and rushed to calculate the meaning of I-Azoth's hypnotic transfixion.

Then the shadows materialized into a shocking virgin vision of homophilia: two females in the midst of a rhythmic reticulation and writhing embrace. They presented by their dicephelatio union an atrocious concrepiscence; they reveled and twined in an upright vermiculation, their tongues flicked constantly like flesh threads binding their bodies tight. One of these was dark, the other bright; one in her passion wore the moon's frown, the other the sun's wanton delight. This alternation gave their excitative glowsing the color of amaranth or succinum.

Across the intervening distance—was it the one-dimensional depth me to screen, was it the two-dimensional lateral from them to the peeping Azoth—I heard:

UUUUUUUMMMMMMMMMMMM

Was this their breathy hymeneal? Was this his gasping mantric Sanitone? Was this some stilted sound of mine?

They continued their licentious panegyris. Indifferent to

STATE standards of prudity, they meshed enfemic pudenda and mushed
their thorax protuberances whereby the PILL CASEs worn about their
necks tinked together like metallic papillae.
     --1-Azoth, was there conspiracy among you even then?
     The film leapt and jagged and all went black. In an ETU,
there came the Graphiphone:

> DUE TO AN IMAGINARY INTERVENTION
> THIS CURRICULUM HAS BEEN CANCELLED
> PLEASE STAND BY

     The day's lesson apparently was done. The
ENVIRONMENTAL PEDAGOGUE wished me a peaceful good
night, a final whisper with the constitutional admonition:
     ... *philosophy is* QUACKERY QUACKERY QUACKERY ...
     Eyelids fluttering, I plunged swiftly to the level of pre-speech.

RIALTO

     In this bizarre bazaar, Primo breaks the cycle hard, does a
urinant wheelie, headlight down, ass wheel erect, cartoon STOP. The
Black Market stands before him, an insidious alleyway camouflaged
in darkness, arcane arcade shades both practical and concealing.
Hurly-burly of shops and stalls, musty anecdotes and useless vestiges,
of archeological catcalls and shouted numbers. Here Jonas Salks and
Shettles flow back and forth according to tired tenets of supply and
demand, laws as old as Friedman. An awful smell emanates from the
place, repugnant to aseptics: odiferous history.
     The Black Market provides outlawed goods and incunabula.
Here an iCitizen must go to thumb through *De humani corporis
fabrica* by Andreas Vesalius, or copies of the *Charakasamhita*, or *Mo
Ch'ing* (the "Pulse Classic"), or Avicenna's *Al-Qanam*, or the works of
Theophrastus Bombastus von Hohenheim. A complete collection of
the journals of the Salerno School may also be found; in Volume Three,
Constantine the African refers to a birth in Montecassino. Portraits
abound: of Galen; of Archigenes of Apamea, the notorious Pneumatist;
of Dr. Pangloss, the panaceaste; of Huang Ti, of Alexander Fleming,

Selna Wakesman, Edward Jenner, and Dr. Marvin Zimmerman in a
yellow camisole. One small shop specializes in iconography, sensitive
carvings and dashboard images of the saints: St. Vitus, St. Roch, St.
Albertin, and St. Fiacre are in particular demand. In this shop as
well a collector stumbled on a treasure, a needlepoint sampler of that
inspirational motto taken from *De re medicina* by Celsus:

CALOR DOLOR RUBOR TUMOR.

    An inventory of sci-med ejecta: Junker apparatus: sphyg-
momanometroscope, combining one slightly soiled Riva-Rocci cuff, a
perfect tonometer, and three manometers, one water type, two Busch:
and splints, the Zimmer's airplane, Valentin's, a Kavinel cock-up, the
Gooch for flexible coaptation: old scales and laboratory glass and used
bandages: Genga's, Ribble's, the hammock and spica wrap: the Zambezi
ulcer cased in plastic, with lesser examples of Annam's (similar to the
Aleppo boil), the Dieulafoy and Gaboon: unguent pots and a ceramic
spitoon with "Spit Here Please" in Hindi scrit: Finochietto's stirrup, an
obstetric saddle: a stoss therapy machine from Majdanek: sutures tied
up on boards like nautical knots, the horizontal and vertical mattress
suture, the pursestring, the silkworm gut: syringes Higginson's syringes
Neisser's syringes: catheters, the Squire and yes! the infamous dePezzer: a
Daviel spoon and a duck-billed speculum (in stainless): prosthetic devices: surgical knives and napkins: organs under glass: diurnal pollution put
up in carboys and gallipots: pornopix of poison ivy cases: a ponograph for
pain and the records of Amnesty International: rubber gloves (one size
fits all): two calico Hottentot Aprons: on and on and on . . .
    --Psst!
    Like a salesman's murmur, voice of a snake in the grass,
a Marketeer.
    --You want to swap that bike?
    --Grease and all, mister.
    --Come on over here. Sit down. Park it. You look to me like
a man who could make do with a dose of NARCISSINE?
    --Might.
    --I got some Lilly's. Truly kalopsiac, friend.
    --Yeah.
    --OK, I'll toss in some anti-nauseant, a dozen MECLIZINE,

1-(p-chlor-x-phenylbenzyl)-4-(M-methylbenzyl) piperine, that's it. A deal?

    --Nope.

    --Listen! What are you, some kind of malactive monosyllabucolic come down here on a blepping pre-WAR cycle, hirsute and glarry-eyed, expecting to put one over on Mac Machaon, marketeer? What kind of hypnosophy is that, I ask ya? Bloody sterco, friend, I'm giving an honest fracture to you who cannot determine Mbundu from Mel and you sit there silent.

    --Yep.

    --Oy, never in all my years of malpraxis do I encounter such a spherule! You give me cerebralgia with all your booming quiet. So, I want the bike, you are right; it is a distinctly extinct item and worth more than I offer. I make to you my best. I add to that we have discussed a generous handful of METHOCARBAMOL (2-hydroxy-3-O-methoxypheno-oxypropylcarbamate), a skeletal muscle relaxant that, my tongueless acquaintance, will make you as loose as a larva migrans. There!

    Primo pops one and swallows.

    --So . . . It is done?

    --Uh-unh. I want that. For my wife.

    --Wife! Dear Kahn, a final syngamy subvert in the STATE and he finds his way to Mac Machaon with one of the last Balano bikes there too, I should live forever. That to which you point—and you drive a dura bargain, I tell you—is a genuinely tarnished staff of Aesculapus, rod wrapped in a vermicular coil, once symbol of the AMA, that notorious gang of regressive sports against whom . . .

    --Verm? Looks like a snake to me.

    --Snakes, worms, all helminthoid the way my eyes see it. Ugly as it is, I am loath to part with such a relic.

    --You have a choice.

    --So I do. Your wife must have it?

    --For the Acoma wall.

    --Well, there it will hang. My advice to you, my sharpie operator, is take a homophile. Obey the obvious, and look for Wurlitzer if a connection is required. And in the future do not shake down this Marketeer for frivolous extras. My pain in this transaction has been painfully illegal.

    Primo scrapes the inside of his tight pocket and withdraws

several pasty pinchfuls of grey powder.

    --True, Mac, you've been cheated.

    --It has never been. And what electuary is this you offer?

    --Pulverulent Indian. The best, no sand, no oregano. Snort!

    --This I don't know. A novel sapidity. No threat of pneumonoultramicroscopicsilicouolcanoconiosis?

    --My wife, Hy-gi-ya, makes it.

    --Cheated you said?

    --When the bismal tourists give me heartburn, I digel this peptonic stuff.

    --Cheated? Me met my mensk?

    --Yeah. If you'd opened with PLAGUENIL, say, instead of NARCISSINE, you coulda kept your MECLIZINE. I'd have settled for the METHOCARBAMOL, the snakestick, and one hundred and fifty Shettles extra. I figure the antinauseant's worth twice the Shettles.

    --Ah, my little rud-faced adversary, only if the METHOCARB is what I say it is. Might be TUBSCURARINE. But your powder has a curious taste . . .

    --Of crowfoots and buttercups.

    --It is gathered, then, from angiospermous herbs!

    --Grow like weeds round Acoma.

    --But you said this was powdered Injun! This is Hyposcyamus! Stupor, delirium, d--th! You've poisoned me!

    --The bike's a Balano, runs like hell. You get what you pay for. Now, this METHOCARB? I took one.

    --So you did, my trickster. Hyperbole, a bargainer's threat and exaggeration, you'll understand. That 'CARBAMOL's as honest as I am on D--THday, I swear it!

    They grin.

    --Soooo, we've had our little joke. I must confess to you the Aesculapus staff is not unique. In fact, I have many hundreds of them buried in the earth to acquire their age. A final obvert in our game, you see.

    --Just like a white eyes.

    --But I must always have the edge on any deal, permit Mac Machaon the final word? It is an occupational nemesis. As an uncongenital gesture, I will give you this crisp, clean Crick-n-Watson bill to make us even. Fair is fair, a good feeling. Against professional ethics nonetheless. I make an exception, I like you, um . . .

--. . . um, Primo.

--Primo. Well, take your pills, friend, and your souvenir and
hustle elsewhere. Mac Machaon must cache this slick machine from the
inquiring oculuscopy of the competition. Enjoy, my son.

Booths, stands, and stalls: didymi piled like rusted
cannonballs: necklaces and bracelets fabricated in Hong Kong from
calculi and kidney stones: an oneroid barometer: bottled oils from
faraway, fennel, anise, sassafras, vanilla, labdanum, sesame and myrrh:
the odd bodkin: an 8x10 glossy of Dr. Bukht-Yishu, taken on his
appointment as Director of the Shahpur Hospital: a couple of succuba
on a string: a cloud baby: canned demonstration film by the US Army
of Aristotle's anomaly: agars, the Bordet-Gengou potato blood, the
Werbitski China green: a klondike bed from Bethlehem Royal, London,
est. 1547: a water-stained etching said to be from the collection of
Erasistratus: a supercalliphrastic katakinetometric cephalothorocopagus:
a statuette of St. Apollonia on the stake, inlaid with platinum or gold: a
wooden model of Suzanne's Gland, mucus secretor in the mouth beneath
the aveololingual groove, discovered, of course, by that Frenchman, Dr.
Jean-Georges Suzanne: miscellaneous other rarities: more:

MOONPIE

Still: numimous chimeric residue. Worm awakens to the
implications of his found destiny. The kiva darkness arcs above him like
parabolic night. He is alone, the snakes having disappeared like crawling
things in the deep, moist earth.

The thought of an attack on the HYGENIC STATE, a
paranoid reprisal against THE POWERS THAT BE, develops in his
tattered tissues like disease, the primary symptom an initial chancre, an
idea, secondarily spreading like gypsy spirochetes toward a larger concept,
a protean sickness. Worm's head aches, his throat is sore from all that
shouting, he is feverish. Is there no Wasserman, no Kline flocculation
test, to give proof to his infection? Is there no penicillin, no arsenic,
mercury or bismuth derivatives to be prescribed toward his cure? The
tertiary stage transforms the concept into all-pervasive event; no body
organ is unaffected, soft gummata lesions appearing in the heart, the
brain, bones, eyes, ears, digestive tract. The nervous system is motivated

locomotor ataxia, confusion, delusion, loss of memory, or paresis, partial insanity, gradual personality change, paralysis of past habit and resolve. Like a demogogue, in the solitude of his shell, he suffers from lack of insight attacks of violent rage, of apathy and pain shoots through his body in place of conscience.

Syphilis is said by some to have originated in Europe in 1493, brought there from the savages of the New World by returning voyagers. Certainly the then sudden firm knowledge of that heretofore unimagined space beyond the ocean must have spread across the continent like a virulent pox, exchanged like a whisper during intercourse, and fired the lasting excitement, the impulse to migrate from the repressive known to the longed-for freedom of the unknown. It inspired epic poetry: the physician and astronomer Girolamo Fracastoro's popular 1530 lyric, *Syphilis sive Morbus Gallicus*, in which the sungod, Apollo, is infected with the disease for spying on the amours of the shepherd hero, Syphilus. Worm ops for his exiting event, his beat 'em to the putsch journey across the intervening emptiness, the fluid Outland, his random attack on the STATE egg, and he knows he will not return.

--Like my pappy told me: always get 'em in the origins!

Across the washed circle of light is cast a double-helixed shadow. Startled, Worm looks out of his reverie. Two azure serpents wind down the ladder poles from above, come to coil, slink in out-of-fashion gowns beneath which he can see every undulation of their soft flesh, nylons rolled to just above the 14th dorsal vertebra.

--Well, I'm spocked! That Tuponee . . . Twins!

--Yessss, these sisters whisper.

Sweet love in the underground, these two of an insinuous kind, these probodies have come like supersympathetic Bobbseys to provide Worm a little solace for his pornolagnia.

There is elaborate foreplay, a duet for handless players, sweet nipping fang bites. Serpent siblings, when aroused, display a curious swelling the length of their bodies, a flush and a shedding that begins at the lips until in anticipation they have discarded a skin like stepping out of step-ins, shouldering off all body clothing with a shrug, a zip, a snap, and a whimper. Worm is familiar with secret, sensitive places, the rules of touch and feel, and finds their unusual magic button, their curious excitement derived from rubbing his chin along their necks. He moves from one to the other like a dizzy schizophrenic, erotically craning.

Courtship. Love knot.

Worm is torn, his affections split, which one to service first? Why both! Diplopiac miracle, oleaginous snake that he is, Worm is a cross draw; he carries a couple of hemipenes, each of which he inserts in a moist, demanding cloaca. Thus troilistically enjoined, they are the three-backed monster, their natural rhythm auguring good and evil, esodic centrifugal gyrus boring toward a multi-limbopost-climacticlysm in which Worm takes his pleasure and those two nice azure-sheathed girls are at once inseminated and infected. Like the dancing rope trick, like an oversubscribed prostitutorial, like an Ophidian acrostic, they celebrate the Coil of Joy.

--I'm Curissia, says the one with the boopia look.

--I'm Periboa, says the other.

They lie in a tumble of copulescence, hissing and sighing and cleaning Worm's ears with their forked tongues and giving him the formicating trembles. When his filariaform seducers rise from their love nest, they will already be scratching at their nethers as recently transmitted eiloid microbes, 5 to 15 microns in length and rotating like a corkscrew on an axis, begin their slow undulating pandemic and twenty-one day incubation. There are other consequences as well: the results of an incidental union of gametes which, as live young, the girls will deposit secretly and in numbers in a crevice on Acoma and abandon, snakes being adverse to the interventions of parental care and instruction, persuaded pedagogically that offspring left to the free and absolute determination of their own life will not survive but endure. Carriers all. Worm is a luetic Midas; everything he touches turns to rot.

4 WALL

The intervening ETUs are to me now an insenescent memory in which I acquired the skills of LIFE. I experienced the normal range of PEDAGOGUES, retained my training flawlessly, progressed biologically and psychologically according to the calculated norms, was sublimely mediocre. And never once again did I experience those terrible vibes that had once brought me so near Muelmonger 4. I was free and pure of all morbific and necrogenic influence, I was perfectly diasostic.

I recall one day intimately for there was a turbidity in the air that was unusual. My excitement was vital. I listened carefully to my systems lest I detect any reaction to these difficult-to-suppress neo-neurotic tremors. My education was superb: I could run checks through nervous ganglia, blood circulation, bio-electric circuits, chemotransceptors in a matter of milli-ETUs, hearing and recording the sonar responses and intellectual play-backs in a state of perfect body relaxation, respiration rate, oxygen consumption, and galvanic skin response decreased, pulse rate and blood pH increased, EEG recording predominantly alpha (with occasional theta activity noted), progressively increasing in amplitude and decreasing in frequency as my metabolic introspection deepened.

I had achieved THE COMING OF AGE. The crowds were assembled to witness the initiation of SET-6 into WELL BEING. Our growth was complete; we were optimumly developed, the point from which d--th, without the intervention of the STATE, was historically inevitable. Presumably, one then might have had thoughts of mortality, begun to fear and feel the deterioration of every cell, the slow metabolic slide into a morbid oblivion. But those were not my thoughts that day, for I knew that I—all of us—had the alternative of real eternal LIFE.

The STATE had given me being, and now was to cap it by bestowing upon me the continuum, encapsulated as it was in the tiny titanium PILL CASE that was to be so reverentially hung around my neck and worn in a world of continuing light devoid forever of even the suggestion of that bordering darkness.

Each of us was to face 1 POWER THAT BE who was to serve as symbolic parent and patron, gladhanding us into the HYGENIC STATE. We stood before our collective makers, adult male and females, viripotent and nubile.

Only one final adjustment remained—and that for the penile males only, the vestigial triorchids with their two testicles and third gonad, the adrenal gland. The HYGENIC STATE had discovered the cause of the world's catastrophes and historical aberrations in which d--th had been brought to millions: pre-STATE ETUs had suffered from a complex lagnosis or satyriasis by which the abnormal male sexual desire had been expressed by the machonations of war and exploitation, depriving many of LIFE and injuring many more through the ongoing ejaculation that accompanied the virulence of such disease. Once PANACEATIC SCIENCE dealt with the phenomenon, a backlash might have been expected, an outbreak of misandria by which males were relegated to second class citizenship and the tyranny of masturbation, or hand rape. But this did not occur.

In their wisdom, the POWERS calculated that what the world lacked was true sexual equality in which there could be no distinction between valency and uberty, between man and woman. The central issues were intercourse and reproduction. If these two human functions could be replaced, then the evolutionary dissimilarities between the sexes would be unnecessary. As children were propagated by sexual union, it was concluded that by definition all such offspring were venereal and thus a threat to the psychological placidity of the STATE. Children were to be produced by SET CREATION only, obviating both the sexual act and the reproductive organs. The erratic meanderings of evolution might have solved these questions in due course, but the probabilities were slight, and so the STATE intervened to engineer the perfection toward which evolution was presumed to be heading, however slowly. The intervention, second in import only to the end of the Cold War in our history, was of course the end of evolution.

Sic transit simians; Kahn be praised!

The simplest solution would have been to truncate the male limb in question. A faction among the POWERS, ad hoc males mostly, objected. Others suggested eventual atrophy through the legislated lack of use, a kind of anatomical apocope, but this was considered too imprecise. With customary speed and efficiency, PANACEATIC SCIENCE determined that the true explanation for the problem was adrenal dischord. The X-pill was subsequently developed; in fact, monthly, one of those tasty kibble come tumbling down my slot had been of these, an hormone d'oeuvre, slowly building up resistance and eventual immunity to all erotic inclinations, a resultant total myatonia of the penis, and an ongoing condition of sexual sloth. Such was my bliss, as I stood so posturepedically awaiting the ritual.

The crowd milled and mulled their appreciation of us. Murmurs rustled through this grand audience like computer wind, accelerating to a rapid whine when a particularly pleasing one of my SET stepped forward. I was in a later percentile, and thus to pass ETUs as others went before me, I ran a statistical evaluation of our combined physique, a mathematical exercise approximate to six decimals. But as the tabulations rang up in my mind, a disturbing proof stood out: I,

281

Joseph SET-6, my phallus . . . was smaller, by centimeters, than all the others! The WELL-BEING and QUIET MIND I had possessed began suddenly to dissipate in the face of imperturbable totals. There was but one way to compensate. I immediately triggered a slight increase in pulse, heartbeat, and veinal pressure, the prefigurement of a blush; and then I willed that rush of blood not to my cheeks but toward my pubic features!
--Joseph SET-6!
My name! The ETU of COMING OF AGE! Now I was expected to stand before the assembled STATE, to become its member at the humiliating moment when my own member was in defiance of the POWERS THAT BE, one of whom—no! it could not be!—was striding forth to greet me.
It was the 1-Azoth.
I became dizzy, my thoughts spun in a centrifuge. I approached this 1 of a higher degree, stunned by the imaginative coincidence that it could be he who would induct me.
I had lost control. As I moved forward, I heard the whispered exclamations of the crowd, mistaking my mortifying smell.
--Homo erectus!
--Balano!
--So dolicho!
--A petcock!
--A panatella fella!
--Observe that one! A stellar polaris!
--Yes, truly, he is a Pisa!
--A lingamdingam! A humdinger! A ding dong daddy!
Then further sound was blocked by the imposing figure of this POWER robed as a true paragon of anti-Fecism. 1-Azoth appeared the same, except for the growth of a small barbula, an exceptional cultivation of body thrix permissible only for those in whom the STATE puts its utmost trust. (Kahn knows what kind of sycosis might occur should I be allowed to wear hair upon my chin.) It was the highest honor that such a 1 as he would, with a flourish, withdraw from its sterile envelope my PILL CASE and gently lay the chain about my bowed head. I felt the coolness of that silver chalice of LIFE between my pectorals, the subtle assurance of its weight. I was trembling.
He stood back, his expression one of calm and peaceful anonymity. He then received the rubber glove (one size fits all) which

he drew on his hand with grace, with an exciting punctilio whack as it snapped closed about his wrist. With these aseptic fingers, gently he reached between my legs and pushed up sharp.

--UMMMMMMMMMMMMMMMM, he intoned.

I could not respond, I . . . I . . . I was afflicted with acute microphonia.

--Cough, he whispered.

I let the quasi-pain of his finger penetrate my brain to stop my spinning emotions.

More urgently:

--Cough!

I emitted a reverent tussis, the formal begma that was required votive according to deontological custom. I was SET- 6! I was a Calculator! I was now custodian of a PILL CASE presented to me by a formidable POWER! I looked toward the crowd as if to challenge them to know me for what I surely was, a purebred heteronomous servant of the STATE.

Below me in that audience, Urethra and Magnesia observed.

--Look at that misterpiece! murmured Magnesia to her homophile.

--A disjugator, yes, came the scornful reply. It will take more than X-pill to control that one. BENEPERIDOL at least, or heavy dosages of PERPOSTERONE.

Oh 1-Azoth, retrospection does not permit me the attribution of all this to random! Probability has its laws, and so many chance encounters could only be contrived. Why did I not see it then?

The COMING almost complete, its climax approached as he reached for the PHALLOCRYPT, sterile reliquary for my now aesthetic appendage. With great flair, I thought, 1-Azoth vaginated me in glass and tied the plastic cord between my nates. It was accomplished: there No d--th is!

I limped off the stage. Into perpetuity.

At the cocktail party post-rites, I nursed my glass of Listerine and waited. He came late, entered with the POWERS, an electric entourage radiating vigor and volts. He was accompanied by Magnesia and Urethra, those three arm in arm. He was popular among the POWERS; they spoke differentially to him. I swallowed my Listerine for strength and conversational sweetness, resolved to approach him and speak. Speak what? An ellipsis? I did not know. Like particle to pole, I rushed toward him. So there again, facade to facade.

--Yes?

--UM . . .

--Well said.

And he threw an arm about my shoulders so homophilially it was tantamount to the regressive pre-COLD WAR body language of fatherhood. Together we limped to a quiet corner.

--Joseph, welcome! I have been waiting for this ETU.

--I suppose I too.

--Of course you have, it is your metabolic destiny.

The words blitzed through me like a curse, a flinch, an involuntary muscular expletive. I looked quickly about the party for the overhearing ear, the eavesdropping tympanum through which the STATE recorded all subversive static. But the room vibrated with a laughing psychic stability, a frivolous narcolepsy suggestive of mouthwash spiked with some QUAALUDES or CROTALIN or BELLADONNA. It was as if the information gathering apparatus, all the Intelligentsia in their carrels, were plugged and jammed with cerumen.

--Relax SET-6, you betray the flash and flush of anxiety far too reddily, anyone might think you Fecetious. How can you be 1 of us if you blossom at the merest cinemot?

1 of us? A POWER? I wondered.

--What are you drinking?

My Listerine glass was empty.

--Too acerbic for your temperament. Try something more sedative. A Scope and soda?

He signaled for a sterile savant to bring us two.

--I have so many questions, I blurted.

--And you shall have answers to them all, calculable results for you to touch and hold. Yes, I promise you satisfaction, Joseph.

He smiled benignly as the drinks were brought.

--To LIFE, Joseph.

--To LIFE.

We sipped. And then:

--Do you feel our affinity, Joseph?

--From the very first!

--I thought so. Good. Of course, I have cultivated you.

Perhaps this is not the space, nevertheless . . . I am ill, Joseph.

I gasped, a ridiculous swallow that shook my foundation from oblongata to filum terminale. No one seemed to notice. I feigned a paniculation. I-Azoth continued:

--A mental thing it is. Epistemophilia, abnormal interest in learning, a futurist disease . . .

--Speakmoresoftlythey'llhearyou! I murmured urgently in my glass.

--Nothing to fear, SET-6. I am a POWER. I know what the POWERS know, and indeed they know something of my activities. But not all, not all. In fact, it seems we are using one another, I them to achieve an end, they me to refine a more perfect means. An accommodation. I want you to join us, Joseph.

--Me! Who?

--Me and others like me, here in the Publicity, in the Opacity, in the Multiplicity, throughout the HYGENIC STATE. We have Cells established almost everywhere, except, of course, the Outland.

--But what? Join what?

--We call ourselves Noetics.

I recalculated the personalities of the room, POWERS and initiates all, for signs indicative of a unity other than appearance. Their perfect bodies, flushed happy faces, somnific aseptic interpersonal transactions, their HEALTH, WELL-BEING, IMMORTALITY— where was there a flaw? why a conspiracy? where was there a cause? why a need? Against that and them, and the fulfillment I had known by becoming one with that and them, there stood this man, who I had assumed was their apogee, now revealed as their most desperate weakness, an ideoparasite of the worst order. I was aghast by the revelation, true, but more by the realization of how fatefully drawn I was to follow him. Was this homophilia? Was this—what did he call it— metabolic destiny? Whatever, I was liminally on a verge.

Urethra and Magnesia now stood beside me, like parentheses, the sharp pressure of a remark, the sweetsure push of a lobular breast. I was overwhelmed by Magnesia's nearness, her languinous flesh seemed infused with the subtle perfume of kaopectin. I felt a tightening in my freshly encased withers. I was soddened by licid hidrosis tween fingers, pits, and toes. I turned quickly from Magnesia's seductive cutis, only to encounter Urethra's speak, that extension of her intellect which was to taunt me so, as victimizing to my brain with its verbal barbs and knives as the flesh of her homophile was magnetic to mine.

I agreed to attend a meeting of The Cell. We were to meet again. For the explanation. I hastened to leave this triad and the spoiled celebration to return to the solitude of my showcase. I wished to reason. To calculate. To prepare.

As I departed, I heard Urethra say:

--I-Azoth, your Joseph rankles me so! Headache, neuritis, and neuralgia. I need ANACIN!

And I heard Magnesia softly sing:

> Derm to derm
> And cellie to cellie . . .
> I dream of sperm,
> Those manic vermicelli . . .

CLUB CARNIA

Neon writ: club CARNIA CLUB carnia club CARNIA

The decor is all cyrano, vesperal, suggestive of soma. Each patron is pleasurably wrapped in an envelope of blue darkness, swathed in midnight velvet. Primo lies back in a body sling. Drug and ambiance combining, he feels his body damping, the slow, steady diminution of energy as he sinks deeper and deeper into entropic dimness.

--Who's that!

Like a hallucination, a hypnotizing caput, another customer casually drops into a nearby sling:

--Excuse me, please, did I wake you?

--UM! . . . did you ever.

--Sorry, very, all the other hangs were taken. Enjoying yourself?

--Yeah.

--You here, only, for imbibition? You look ectopic, like you could use a stiff one. What's your nom, please?

--Primo.

--I'm Podalerius. You can call me Pud for short. I've got a liter of Rivers cocktail here, nice and cold. Like some? Would you?

--Sure. What is it?

--A mixture of dextrose in isotonic saline solution, with thiamine chloride and insulin added, neat. They keep it for me here especially. Never seen you here before.

--Nope.

--What's wrong with Primo, please? Catalepsy got your tongue? Shy?

--Nup.

--This, then, is your normergic speech . . . how anaverbose! How divinely obtund! No psychopompous thou! Why, please, almost eastern lockjaw you are so malapropos.

--Yep.

--I love a man who . . . reacts! Homophilia IS love. It's in the BILL OF HEALTH, you know. Are you engaged? Pud's free, please. I threw up a MedicOp this morning. Drink, it's clean . . .

A harmless drone supposedly, a kind of white sound like the collision of sand grains or the wind bending around Katzimo or the few birds, misplaced shadows, gliding through the empty rooms of Acoma. Primo rocks in his body sling while his new friend, Pud, breathes a logorrheic monologue, a rodomontade:

--. . . so I dropped him, no sense being monobuliac I thought, a protein chain of homophiles is no social prohibition in the STATE, although I, please, would not want to be considered uberous; no, that offends me, still don't you think one could, should, be faithful, symbiotic and all that, I'm old-fashioned and age IS beauty, it's in the BILL OF HEALTH you know, the STATE encourages romance, an iCitizen such as I, what with facial lift and blood bath every month, I have my choice, I don't suffer from transactional inertia, it's a search, ribosome to ribosome, always looking for the perfect complement, you, please, for example, attract me, you do you do, I admire your drape, I like good conversation, I believe in the phrenic relationship, copulative minds, you seem so so so, please, responsive, like some mysterious, silent messenger . . .

The Meth's cut out; Prime needs something macro to counter this supersilliass citizen of the STATE. He fumbles up his vinyl sleeve: yep MECLIZINE, the anti-nauseant, right, a double dose and chase it with all the RENICOL, should do the trick.

--What's that you have there, oh! NARCISSINE, please, my favorite. Primo, how programmatic we've met, you're just my type, so structural, so plainly pharmaco . . .

Primo doesn't hear, deafened by a calmative blitz, ulamitous booming through the limbic system. The process may have been as follows: the RENICOL, an hallucinogenic, compounded by four the impact of the MECLIZINE on the coordinative centers of the brain; thus the tremors and rigidity that sprung Primo to the floor. In addition, the concentration of HALOPERIDOL was measurably reduced in the cerebral tissue. Both cases resulted in an immediate excess of DOPAMINE, negating the initial palsy, but aggravating the causative optical effect into a thought disorder and unexpected personality change mildly resembling multiple schizophrenia. Speculation, certainly. Nevertheless Primo leaps to his feet, flatfooting in a dancing circle, palming his mouth to produce the most disruptive staccato:

--YOHOHEYHEYAYHEYHAHYEHEYHAHYAY

He wields and shakes the medicine stick. He chants of fire and kukulled snakemen, of reformers and go-betweens, of messiahs, of givers of lex and language:

Quetzacoatl!
Itzamna!
Culculcan!
Bochica!
Votan!
Amilivaca!

A babble of vox in the body house:
--He's speaking in tongues!
--PILL CASE! PILL CASE!
--This man is ill.
--Stick that stick up his zunga.
--Who is he?
--A xeno.
--Where's he from?
--Not the Tonicity for certain.
--Tongue-tied, an inspissated lingua.
--See that short frenum.
--Tongue-twisted more likely.
--These spockin' POWERS THAT BE, I thought we were through all this nosogenic, psintoid, stercorageous . . .

Primo increases his dance toward its peak, yes, a preterite man climbing bedecked in plumose in sight of summit and sky, draws in the aromatic fluid of that space, filling his compound saccular thoracic organs to their pulmonate bounds, and gives one last exclamation to his vesanic acousma:

Wasi!
Quaagagp!
Manabozhi!
Wisakeshak!
Etalapasse!

Then he falls to the floor into a sleep devoid of the usual decrepitating snores.
--Oh my, please, Kahn, deems Pud, a holy 1...
The disturbance has of course brought MedicOps.
--What's the trouble here?
--Officer, get him outta here, he's gone narry, gives me a ringing in the ears, complains a looker-on, a closet symbolophobe.
Pud intervenes:
--I'll look after him, a little touch of metaphorensis, bit too much of the Rivers. He's a stranger, perhaps not properly fluoridated; I'm with Eugenics, he'll be my responsibility, please...
--Get him cleaned up! We'll let him off this ETU, but just this once! Can't have confabulation in a STATE place, IMAGINATION IS HYPOCHONDRIA; you know the rules as well as we do.
--Of course.
Pud's offended, as if he needed sermonette from these officious underlings.
--Next time we'll have to issue him a Cicatrix.
--All right!
Pud lifts Primo, a sacrifice, risking hernia.
--I'll take him to the Bath.
--Good idea.
The MedicOps go back out on cycle. More important things to do. Been reports of a rainbow snake in the neighborhood.
In the rush, Hy-gi-ya's gift, the caduceus, is forgot.

WORM RESPLENDENT

Tuponee speaks:

--My children, if symbols we must be in this novelty, then we must stand for organs south of the chin, the heart and sex, the longueurs of sensation. This man possesses the largest cranial capacity yet known and he claims to occupy it with reason. We must ally ourselves with this logic, use him, then leave it to me to protect our interests. Residuals for everyone! Amends for our participation in this deviation from fact, form, and rule!

Worm comminutes the harangue by crawling from the kiva where he has passed the nightlong with two professionals from the ophidian lupaner, twinborn hookerworms.

--Slam bam thank you ma'am! Ma'ams is more like it . . . He is dressed like a deity of war, his rash redrawn in savage paint, the design a serpent coiled in spirial blue, ominous and muscularly rampant, its integument mottled by mycopus ruptures like the yellow points of stars. Tuponee approaches this demiurge.

--Well-rested, Worm?

--Positively oriental, Tup. Normally, I go one at a time, human-style, but . . .

--If it is your desire to be with more than two, I will send seven Eastern Hognose sisters I know myself . . .

--Easy now.

--There is also Romy, the Reticulated Python.

--Glory, moon pie! The reptile is hip to fornication!

--Specifically, I am hipless and we are discussing the Coil of Joy, not some profane rut. I must say, Worm, your procreative attitude is sadly jejune, but we digress. I have alerted the creatures of the Outland and you will find a splendid army encamped at the foot of the mesa. You will be proud to lead them.

--I need a mount. If only that punk pocohontas hadn't ripped off my machismo . . .

--We have reports of him from the Publicity.

--What?

--Yes, my scout reports the machine was traded for a handful of gelatinous capsules. The buyer was apparently squibbed by the POWERS THAT BE. The Primitive is on a binge. Coral, however, did forward . . .

--Sure he was cheated, the ignorant mohican! I'd have taken
no less than fifty milligrams of black BOMBAZINE for that antique!
Or some uncut SOLANUM! Never mind, let's get to it. How do we get
down off this jive high rise?
      --Coral, however, did forward this!
Tuponee holds up the caduceus to the purelight.
      --Aiyeeeeeeee! go the snakes.
      Like some mysterious apparatus attributed to science, the
twisted sign distills the resource of the sun and her double, moon, to
flow molten, gold, through inter-connected coils, a cyclical experiment,
vaporization and the condensing of lux, phantasmogenetically. A
religious artifact, inconceivably from the Cold War, moves the assembled
snakes to superstition, the specious worship, devotion relicated to a
prayer stick and Tuponee, their serpentine wizard, able to heal the sick
and raise the dead.
      The snakes begin again their circular dance and, as if to
underscore the giving of this sign, the colored air of Acoma triumphantly
clouds and the sands appear like mercury, a fluid, silver simile. The
silence, voice of solitude, is broken by interjected thunder, a divine
guttural echoing distantly:

UM-M-M-M-M-M-M-M-M-M-M-M-M-M-M-M-M-M

      The rain comes, and the snakes descend the walls of the
pueblo like rivulets. The woman's saucer fills and the rock cisterns flood
with treasured waters the ghosts of Keres women come to carry home in
colored, patterned jars balanced on their shoulders.
      As Worm turns to follow, his bootheel catches on a juniper
rung. He tumbles. He slides, the wet adobe walls slick as muddy
mirrors. He tucks and rolls like a smooth pebble riding the attle crest
of a rockslide. From roof to floor, roof, floor, roof to floor he falls, a
cartwheeling Coluber, one of the fleet jaculi, a hooping Amphisbaena. In
the vertigo of descent, he experiences a weird, disturbing flash, a shocking
glimpse among the myriad frames of doors and windows perceived on the
fly: one half a one-armed, one-legged man glimpsed within a room, walls
defaced with autographiti, stylistic jism, imaginary history . . .
      --O great spocker in the sky, why me? These warped peepers,
these funhouse reflectors, what do I see when I see, O bloody sterco!

Then splat, puddled, street-level:

--Hey, Tuponee, d'you see the freak?

--Of what evolutionary anomaly do you speak?

--On the way down the great white rock, the ivory tower there, the psychogimp, the self-mutilate, the cheeky honcho writin' it all down . . .

--An unknown, Worm, no one. Perhaps your paranoids disturb you? We have heard that such disease is indigenous to bipeds. We, of course, do not suffer as we have no pygal excess. You could crawl on your belly, go millipede.

--But I saw him, clear as avedon he was, the ghoul!

--Maybe seriasis? The sun is cogent and you have no scales to shade you . . .

--I got scales, polite of you not to notice, psoriasis never before gave me the heeby-jeebies.

They emerge from the thoroughfares of Acoma to look out across the periol toward the house of the gringo apostles, a basilica built, it is said, by an abysmal healer and baptismal water-waster, Fray Juan Ramirez. In the lot before the great facade lie canted stones, each an asterisk marking an omission, each a padre or his convert foisted on the petard of another prayer stick. This shrine was once dedicated to San Estevan, not the early martyr pelted by rocks ETUs ago in the Jerusolemnity, but rather a later king of Hungary who proselytized phaging pagan magyars. Now, however, there abides only Hy-gi-ya, mater superior, mother earth, sitting on the charming loggia above the cloister, awaiting her husband's return, and noting that the inclement weather has brought the snakes out of their dusty holes.

At the reservoirs they drink.

Tuponee, reflective:

--Worm, do you not sense the history here, the feel of extraordinary continuity to this place? Here is the locus of language, all the quaint phrases and expressions of being, linked together. Myth and totem, art and idea, units of transmission from ETU to ETU; it is a critical epidemic of pseudodoxy, a plague spread through all time, enzootically somnolent, yet ever awakening. Yes, history, my good Worm, is the baneful chain of etymology.

--Um, Tup, we are about to go get dead, remember? What is this hermetic claptrap?

--It is traditional to ruminate on the eve of battle. Never

mind, you are right, we must go. A dangerous trajectory, you must revere
the verticality of the trail.

--Hey! Is there footing?

--Who has feet? Come along . . .

Through the glaze of fear, inspired by descending a
snakewalk on his fingernails, Worm can see below a spread geometry, a
critical mass of crawling things intermingled with pox scars of darkened
dust, pattern of the brevity of rain. The coming of these ranks and rows
has left infinite tracks in the sand until the desert has taken on the
appearance of human skin, lined and cracked with dank creases and
sworls, all the meandering linears by which one reads future. It is as if
every nest and sac has given forth its quota, conscripts and enlistees from
chalky tunnels, rock mazes, the silt of improbable rivers. Even the *Taenia
balanceps* is present and accounted for, worms come crawling out of the
stool of New Mexican bobcats.

--Tuponee! Baby, you deliver! Man, you are some judas ascaris!

--Quite. You will find all the Hemaglutins are mustered, and
the Toxins: Hemo, Neuro, Leuko, and Endothelio. There is, after all,
deadly work to be done. Let it begin!

A caduceus flourish signals the march, the antihenotic
campaign commences. Worm, with his sidewinding, thrust-creeping
limp, leads, resplendent. He is a crowned viper, king of the serpents,
the Basilisk, able to kill by fire, by sound, by sight, and by terrible
putrefaction. It is a glorious spectacle.

Tuponee, the metaphysicalchemist, looks after:

--The goal, my friends, is to cure all the ills of humanity. We
must employ Nature's elements and emulate her operations. There is,
sadly, certainly, no generation without corruption; you see, from vileness,
we shall fashion worth . . .

5: A JABBERWALL

We met that first night in a pseudononymous vacuole they
had rented in a showcase on the perimeter of the Publicity, too near the
Defensive Membrane for me to be quite comfortable. Apparently, they had
been meeting for many ETU; the conspiracy was well advanced. Examining
my psychological situation as I approached this initial encounter, I drew

overload, as if my internal calculation system was underdesigned for the emotions progrum. Nevertheless, POWERS THAT BE, I went to The Cell willingly, drawn by, Kahn forgive me, the inexplicable.

They were already assembled: 1-Azoth, Urethra, Magnesia and others, strangers, one called Vaccina, one called Ouli Po, one called Winston.

--You are wanting an explanation, Joseph?

1-Azoth reassured me with an expression of profound paternalbood. I felt certain he was the leader of this group, these heretical Noetics so-called. But perhaps I errored. He was the cabal's legitimitizer, true; his presence protected them in that as a POWER he could warn. But I quickly saw that his membership was more a function of his confessed disease, his flaw, his epistemophilia. He had a mocking self-description:

--Dear Joseph, I am a hopeless encyclopoede.

Yet Urethra was the metabolic force behind the meetings, she was the theorhetorical power, the superconductive magnetism that attracted them all, held them united, and gave them impetus in the revolutionary direction she desired. And as she was intellectual and andromimetic, Magnesia was a floitive fribbler and maybelline, no less threatening to me, newly circumclosed male, the saccharine curves of her body, her mammaries like lunar landscape, the secretive perfume of her myhx. Like chromosomes, those two were a matched pair, homogenized and homologous, inseparable and synergistic.

But I must explain, quickly, more concisely:

First, metapsychics, not metaphysics, is the concern of the HYGENIC STATE. Philosophy is QUACKERY. The body has no need for theories of knowledge, they are a supreme irrelevance. What exists, exists as a phenomenon beyond consciousness, as ideal function, as perfect metabolism infinitely sustained, a system to which the mind can be attuned, but only after the fact. The body is manufactured, it is a machine divine, GLITCHABLE, but considering the multiplicity and complexity of its operation, a tribute to the manufacturer's art. That there is an original maker is a tolerated fact, but one incorporated into the fabulations of cooperative improvement on the design.

Urethra was a fallopeon, an accident of birth, a COLD WAR remnant. Although most of her LIFE passed under the auspices of the STATE, she was nevertheless of ovary origin and corrupted. Her brain

was like the nucleolus of cognition. Like the other Noetics she gathered
around her, her only guilt was belief in intellectual process.

The POWERS THAT BE were not altogether unaware
of her potential. She was trained, for example, as a Neologist, a new
wordmaker, and was responsible for the best of the GRAPHIPHONICS
and cautionary limericks:

> When struck by the urge to cogitate,
> Reticulate, then fecculate!
> To counter the lure of the cerebrate,
> The PILL CASE will equilibriate
> That little bit of OUTLANDISH in us all.

She was known as a verbal profligate, a novelist.

--Plastiscenario, she said. Pissanthropic, hymenology,
clitastrophe; we deal, Joseph, both in bits, you in multinfinitesstissimal
flashes of light, pulse, within your computer machine, you are
a calculmachinac, while I diddle debris, graeco-roman rubble,
archeologogriphs. Macaronic! Katzenjammer!

--She can be quite incomprehensible, interjected 1-Azoth.

--Incomprehensile.

--The intriguing question, really, Joseph, is of reproduction . . .

--Synonymous botch, mental monstiparity.

--It does not exist in our STATE yet. History, fundamentally,
is a sexual narrative . . .

--Oral antiphony.

--I mean we have evolved, phyletically speaking, from union,
and not this independence.

--Antonymity.

--While we glory in our STATE *usquo*, we are in fact
wasting a most precious resource, the ability to cross over, to interchange
our parts . . .

--A phthisicky wicket.

--Oh come, please, Urethra, enough is enough!

--I can't help myself. A defective invective. Like this Joseph,
like you Azoth!

I blurted:

--I am faultless!

--You ableptic epileptic, are you blind to your own flaws?
You hubrid hybrid, what do you think brought you here?

--I was incepted!

--You were insieved by a strobiloid virus!

I-Azoth:

--It was Muelmonger 4 for you, Joseph, if we had not taken
steps. Do you have your PHILISTINE?

--Of course. I am never without it.

--How many, she screamed, how many in your condition have
survived! You monophthong! You spoonerism!

I was stunned.

--Calm, Urethra, the vacuole might be eared.

She was trembling.

--Yes yes, Azoth, have we made a mistake? He gives me such
thelagia, such a terrible ache in my vulva cerebri. Got any HADACOL?

--UMMMMMM, hummed Magnesia, taking her homophile
in a plurtissular embrace. Ever the symbiote . . .

--That's just it, continued I-Azoth in a POWERsorial tone,
we are all mistakes, prones differentiated from others, the proofs, thus
our abnormal interest in the style of alternative LIFE.

--Style is the mode of expressing thought in language, I
defined automatically.

--Quite so. Of course, SANITONE has no style. It follows,
you perceive, that our sacred speak has no meaning. In ETU you will
see, Joseph. You are among the few left capable of change, a mortifying
embarrassment by your way of thinking, yet in the end your salvation.

I could not believe this. A man institutionally taciturn, it
was as if he had O.D.'d on intellaxative. There was PAREGORIC in the
PILL CASE. It would be polite to offer. I fumbled.

--Pedagoon!

Urethra slapped my CASE with such force the chain burned
against my flesh, snapped, and that receptacle struck against the glass and
broke open, spilling its contents to the horrid septic floor. I fell on my
knees, gathering. Above me, Urethra emitted hysterical syllables.

--Heiritic! Epigone! Adeocephalus! Pharmacocrapulent!

I groped for an illusive rolling lozenge of
DIETHYLOXYACETYLUREA, that little something for a spell of
Hebephrenia.

Suddenly, there was fear in the space. Winston and Ouli Po ran to examine the showcase exterior for signs.

1-Azoth squinched his eyes, went momentarily ON to the Sanitonic frequency:

--Yes, the POWERS are coming. We have been betrayed! We must diffuse.

--It was he! It was he, screamed Urethra, flailing at me. He is the brachyskelous fink, the treasonous phoneme!

--No, he is not the author, retorted Azoth.

I swelled. He trusted. He continued, almost desperately:

--Listen, Joseph, try to understand, and when you do, spread this word: ZOOGONY.

--What is this daft taph? Do you wish to restore the intercurse? the orgone past?

--Joseph, we are revolutionaries, not perverts.

--You chancre! You bolus! You epicene placebo!

She was mad, irrational, barely restrained by Vaccina and that Magnesia. I turned away, myopic; I still saw nothing clear.

--Urethra, commanded 1-Azoth, tell him!

But it was too late, she could not begin to recite before there came the pounding at the door, and each with their terror sought escape. I was alone, until into my disbelieving brain crept the thought that my discovery there could only admit a guilt however undeserved. By association I had defied the STATE. The parameters were there; I had no choice but to join their flight ultimately to these confessional walls, this saturate solitude in the hideous Outland.

That meeting, a brief encounter to be sure, filled with verbiage, and still the word was passed, ZOOGONY, source of powerful kinesia. Even now, as the light rushes from this space again like molecules from a vacuum jar, as my pursuers approach, events of Urethra's causing, oh most holy verbile! run prolix their determined course.

When the POWERS shattered that obscure showcase into a thousand bright cutting fragments, they found nothing, nothing whatsoever save the transparent intimation, like something shed, of a reproductive discontinuity. The Cell had divided.

SPEAKEASY

Bearing his burden, Pud approaches the Bath. A door. In acrylic cyrillic it says:

THE JARGON OF EARTHLY DELIGHT

A sudarium, sweat shop. A sudatorium, a bath of hot air. An onsen, where aerothermotherapy and illutation are the specialty, the culmination of the great spas of the world.

--Here, my carotic friend, whispers Pud, here we shall soften your milavan solid by soaking, macerate your personality for your adoring newphile, sweet Podalerius, the bathyesthesete. How you sleep, dear Primo! I suffer from mild dyskoimesis myself, nothing serious, just things on my mind, occasional disquiet, you know, but it's true, I don't always get my BENEFICENT TEN.

They are met at the door by an attendant.

--What'll it be, fellows?

Ever one to fabricate a conversation, Pud responds:

--Well! This is a clean, well-lighted place! . . .

--Sure is, bud . . .

--Pud!

--Baths to the left, sweat parlor to the right. I'm in cosmetics straight ahead, exorcysts and do spodographs. Here's your towels and deposit those na-asty suits!

He disappears into heat and white.

--Snood! Pud tosses the insult gratuitously after.

But he is preoccupied with getting Primo out of his sandpocked vinyl and into the all-together. He unzips the central zipper with a YKKkkkkkkkk! then plicates the lump in the middle and, like a man experienced in getting friends out of their clothes, skins Primo neatly down to duckibumps and phallocrypt. A collision of cranium and floor slats, and Primo comes to, blinking:

--UM!

--This way, this way! Pud twittering with delight.

In the humidity, a persuasive sense of chill exists; in the sweet air, the underodor of mold and machine oil. There is also a counterpoint of tapping, the POK of cyborg palms against too frail flesh, like myriad

shoemakers run amok, like a metal shop in an electrical surge. A face
looms out of the moisture, inquiring:

--Depilatory?

Pud finds two wooden couches, side-by-side and free. He
unties his Phallocrypt and stakes his claim. Primo stares.

--Take it off, no penal restrictions here. Come come, Preem,
rebukes the affectionate Pud, you look like you've seen a homunculus!
Now, where shall we begin?

Off this chamber are various Bathinettes.

--The beginning? Avocado!

Pud turns and dives, toes pointed, into a pool of green slime.
Primo, aghast, is reminded of a similar sauce once served by Hy-gi-ya,
hot and from a paper box, called take-out, a delicacy brought and saved
since that dying child. Special food, she said, all the way from the faraway
LosAngelesity, the holy place of the Texmex tribe.

--Delicious! Come on in, it's fine. With just a touch of lemon!

Pud does a lap or two while Primo stands reluctant as a
batholith. They move on to the next immersion: Borax. Then Camphor
next. Then Grease. Pud comes up green-brown and lubricated glossily,
superslick all over save for areolae trailing translucent strands like fresh
blown automotive nipples. Then Honey. Then, sliding with a cry of joy,
the Milkbath, a wide white square of the powdered kind. Finally, Pud
scrubs under the lysol shower with gritty cleanser:

--Boom boom! booma booma boom boom boom!

One remaining: the Light Bath. Primo is drawn into that
bulbed world, circles of yellow like a thousand suns, sits down and feels
warmth permeate his rud-skin. His body responds, a glint of sweat like
melting fat, and a thermopolypneac quickening. And there is mental
solace too, that state again of a coma-like sleep, in which the brain
approaches physiologic zero and all stimuli, thermal or otherwise, cease
to cause sensation.

--I feel absolutely moxibusted! cries Pud. I sent off some skin
to that one for spodographic analysis! You can't be too careful.
How 'bout you?

--Nope.

--Maybe you'd like a facial. They do great things here with
pine tar and yellow wax.

The Primitive is content to bask. He drifts off and Pud

begins to find his found 'phile something of a bore. The thought intrudes distastefully. It would be nothing to him if, in some future cosmetic restoration, the POWERS authorized the cutting away of those overgrown hemispherical polyps of the cerebrum, down to the corpus callosum, thus relieving him of all intellectual frissons. Then, truly, would his mind be quiet and still; then, only, could he concentrate in toto on the pleasures of immortality. Perhaps he should take some injections of OLEOMARGARINE.

--Reading matter? That same inquiring face looms by.

--What have you got?

--*Carbohydrates and You*; a best-selling gothic, *Chastity*; and *A Shorter Philological History of Kahnt* is all. Interested?

--Sorry.

Silence, save for buzzing filaments.

--Come on, Preem, you need some inspiratory massage, a little indirect pummelling of the liver by diaphragmatic breathing, give an umph to your steariform! It's back to the palpatorium for us both, please!

Lumped in towels, reclining on a barcalounge, Pud tucks Primo in and signals to a robust robot in the corner. This muscular mechano trundles to position between each couch.

--The works, please!

Rub and stroke, POK! rub and stroke, POK! Primo is rotated, then plugged by a bougie from the anterior, a hydropneumatic douche . . .

--Clean, Preem, inside and out!

Tremolo cuffs to the renal area, blunt butts with the palm to the viscera not nearly protected by their case of cartilaginous rods; through a tube a vaporous gouge to the ear, the auditory meatus a breathy wet fumarole, and then diverted the hot lunt to the lungs to scald out those sacs with a purposeful systalic, Primo sweats blood, sudor sanguineus, hotsweat and black sweat, melanephidrosis, condensing on the outside like a stone at night, hurt and perspiring and victimized by the therapeutical friction of these hired hands.

--OOOOOh, UMMMM! moans Pud hedonistically. The attendant returns.

--Excuse me, but this spells trouble for Mr. Pud.

--Please?

--Right, I did your sample for mineral content. And look here when I read your future . . .

--It goes on forever.

--Yes, but. There's a conditional, an if.

--What! What?

--See on the spodograph, that convolution; there's alkali in your LIFE and . . .

--Alkali! Dirt?

--Accurately put. ME *drit*, fr. ON; akin to OE *dritan* and *L foria*.

--Goodness! What speak is this?

--Diction. A hobby. Go on, try me.

--UM . . . Diatribe!

--L *diatriba*, fr. Gk *diatribe* pastime, discourse, fr. *diatribein* to spend (ETU), wear away, fr. *dia-* + *tribein* to rub. 1: *archaic* a prolonged discourse. 2: a bitter and abusive speech or writing. 3: ironical or satirical criticism.

--Impressive.

--Something to do. Not too much call for spodwork these days, people are into spectrography.

--Yes yes, but then you did see something awful in my mineral make-up . . .

--Do you dubit?

--No, never, but it is sudden.

--True, things rarely change.

--The only novel thing in my life is . . . is this!

--This?

--Picked him up in a body house. A strong and silent type.

--You are a philophile?

--It shows?

--Certainly this lumpen could explain your contamination. He has a slangy slaggish appearance. What has he told you?

--Not a thing. A near mute. Not a mutter.

--Let's examine his CASE.

--From the OUTLAND! Ohmikahn!

--A fungus amungus! Can you pick 'em!

--What to do please?

--Exchange?

--How?

--Me. I'm available.

--Well . . .
--We can hyphenate.
--And hyperbolize?
--Sure, and I can recite your particles.
--Wanton! Verily!
--Philia, guaranteed conjugate bliss! Live in grammatical style,
alkali-free.
--I'm cured.
--No more dangling participle.
--My infinitive split!
--Done, we're a couplet, clerihews, veritable strophes.
--And this Primonym?
--Efface it. Disremember. A simple deletion.
--Easily said, and ficklely sealed with a labial gesture. Bye,
Preem, you sweet laconic.

Pud and his new phile wend away as Primo undergoes the
toepop and chiropractic wrench, intestinal twist from his giggle to his
zatch. The Primitive dozes, and the cyborg pounds out a coda, a wash in
the vibrating scale of phons and phots.

INFLECTION

Paras, reet creeping things, astral serpents, arenicolously on
the run, thaumaturged toward an armageddon by their Commander.
What syntactics by which to struct the context of the iCities? Worm
burrows snakedly through the sand, an underground etymon relying
heavily on vestigial hind legs. Grains sneak beneath his armor to rub the
glowing roseola of thought, overdue load on the right hemisphere resultant
with a general excitability of the central nervous system, along the spine,
the cord of hope. Tuponee observes the agony of this behaviour:
--May I advise the Colonel Worm?

Gratitude for this intervention and the implied mitigation
of logical process provides our leader with a pleasing little gush
of SEROTONIN, a soft ooze of NOREPINEPHRINE, the
neurohumours associated with sleep.
--May I suggest a direct and continuing attack via the
naturopath?

--Had thought of nothing but, my flathead friend. Elaborate.

--Well, they say an injection of PUROMYCIN administered
to the posterior region, the hippocampus and entorhinal cortex inhibits
internal protein synthesis by disruption of polysomes with a concurrent
decrease in working RNA . . .

--Spock! you talk such sputum, snake, such
incomprehensible sprue!

--I was being fecetious, my dear Colonel. I must say your
purely ON-OFF manner of thinking makes subtlety most problematic.
Naturopathy is a drugless system of cure, using heat, physical massage,
and light, etc. We snakes . . .

--Drugless! You write your biological obit. Hey, with no elan
vital, no pneuma zoticon, Tup, the POWERS gonna make puree of this
verminal irruption!

--We are long-lived, you forget we have powers of our own . . .

--You give me the gut feeling . . .

--Fear?

--. . . that we are approaching a pause, a comma.

--A distinguished bunch of Proofs, a ganglia from the
Harvard Univercity has established three basic criteria for irreversible
coma that is tantamount to d--th: 1) lack of response to any stimuli,
even those that would normally bring intense pain; 2) no movements
or spontaneous breathing; and 3) no reflexes. A persistently flat
electroencephalogram, indicating absence of brain activity, is a
confirmatory sign.

--Eggheads!

--Yes, Worm, former oophages, most distasteful.

--So what is it you're suggesting?

--First, a contiguity in time and space of our rhetorical dynes.

--A what?

--Second, anaphora, no one-time exposition.

--Kahnonakrutch, speak Yinglish!

--Third, reinforcement: chiasmus, hypocorisma, periphrasis,
aposiopesis, and the like. The Defensive Membrane will certainly
repel our initial thrust. There will be heavy losses. Without continuous
replenishment of the front line, we will fail to make lesions.

--You are sadly over-thought, Tuponee . . .

--And finally, once within, with trochee and spondee we will interfere and interrupt the stultifying permanence of their learning, their brutal effacement of history's spirial. How, then, we will make the world sound and resound!

--What lipthrashing! Who's in charge here anyway?

--Most definitely you, Colonel; I plan to observe the encounter from a distant hill.

--Figures.

--And yourself? You may yet abandon these willing allies to become again the solitary, befuddled fugitive. Choose now if you must return to your narcosis.

--I'm going out, Tup, might as well go out with equipoison in my veins . . .

--A true synergist; as such I will reconsider and accompany you. Climb aboard my shoulders, and if out we must go, then we shall go together.

--What shoulders?

And so, rising up from the rank comes Worm, astride Tuponee, as inspirational as a becharged ringworm. The Defensive Membrane is no less impressive, its three meninges well adapted to defend against the Outland. Voluted and fissured with sulci and gyri, it offers the attacker no point of deployment, the defender every opportunity for concealment and ambush. The lines of protection are multiple; initial penetration of the dura mater, for example, signifying little more than a minor inflammation and leak of cerebrospinal fluid from the subdural space, an alarm by which the invaders are normally captured in the thin taxis of the arachnoid layer.

Worm brandishes the caduceus; his lesser units proceed against the Operculum and the Occipital pole as diversion. Then a thrust is sent to the Island of Reil, a second feint not to disperse the enemy but to delude them that this is the main slaught. The battle is intensely joined, like a gang war of murine and campestral viri. The air is filled with the kakosimia of d--th, of putrefying jararacas and kraits, greens and gardens, surucucus and Russell vipers. It appears at this outset that the Publicity is perfectly anthelmintic, positively vermicidal.

--Um, Tup, from up here things don't look so good. Our boys is piling up like caterpillars!

--Where's yur-defense, Worm? You seem to lack a certain psychological integration, any faith in personal survival or . . .

--Watch where you're winding! Look out for that
interparietal pothole!

They tumble, a quantum leap.

Misinterpreting Worm's flailing arms, all the ookinete army
moves forward. The lumbering flatworms, Microstomum, let loose their
barrage of fatally stinging threads, these derived from ingestion of the
curious polyp, Hydra. The Planaria advance, wave on wave, cut down
to get up doubled, multiplying the forces twice again, and again as the
Membrane makes minced moieties of their soft, ciliated, mostly aquatic
tubellarian bodies. Not even the maggots are held in reserve, those
eccentric masticators, legless white and whimsical mercenaries who fight
in any war.

It is an army of transformation. Some species retain a third
eye, used to capture light and thermic radiation, and these, like enriched
lasers, seek out hydrogen atoms for fusion, generating miniature
thermonuclear explosions of x-rays, gamma rays, and neutrons, the same
spectrum of radiation as released by the H-bombast, that pre-Cold War
piffle. Other species play at necromime, feigning d--th, only to rise again
from their exuvial sheddings, shucking lives and storming the ramparts
all bright and fresh-fleshed as if they had collectively swallowed an
enormous overdose of REINCARNADINE.

There is a sudden dehiscence and spurt of STATE juice.

--Tuponee! They've broken through!

--A lumbar puncture. We must move quickly.

--Ospockospockospockospocko! Tup, will you look at that!

--Yes, Worm, quite correct; brave deeds, great
accomplishments occur here, surely to be memorialized in future
wormlit, in that larger tradition of heroic verm verse, the *Worm Runner's
Digest*. If we get lucky, they'll hit a Pacchionian settlement, one of the
arachnoid villi weakened by age. We should grind through there quickly
and nothing but the Pia Mater, that last vascular line, will separate us
from the cytoplasm. There we will inflect!

The troops are twisting through the breach. There are
pressing questions of resupply.

--Think I'll pin another yellow blue star magic on my
shoulder board . . .

--With antonomasia, hysteron proteron, and tmesis, we
will infect!

--But I had great staph work, Tup, true enough. You, sir, are a good man for a snake. Gimme some skin!

Tuponee gives him 2.3 meters' worth, a colophon.

EU DREAM

Sleep: I did profoundly the BENEFICENT TEN and yet into my regular 8/sec rushed this disconcerting spiral, this curious length of mental itch. Instantaneously, although so slowly seeming, it shimmed and lummed and aurafied, a phenomenon I quickly crossed off to my advanced neurasthenic condition. It was precisely to combat such subconscious creepers that, in the hiatus, I had taken two SLEEPEZE and twelve SOMINEX.

But the mind confused does not rest, a maelstrom of swithers disquiets; try as I did, I simply could not combobulate, although to the POWERS, peeping as they might have been through the surveil, I appeared stuporously calm and conscience clean. Appearance only! Skindeep!

Felt-tip, prepare . . . for here I begin to confess my crime: I dreamed. Boldly done, pen, strong ovals, you give me courage to continue. Across my Lexicon . . .

Yes. I dreamed. Blatant hypochondriacal act! I defiled the process of sleep. I soiled the perfection of mental void with an impossible apparition. Vernacular vertigo! The excruciating whimsies! An antithigmotropic whorl! Kahn was not watching over my torpidity that night. And nothing for it in the PILL CASE.

I will try to describe this hallucinosis, to quantize and measure:

I turned my vision inward; there was an impression of depth. Such visual inversion is possible through the feedback potential of the retinal ganglion cell, its ability to both transmit and reflect intensity of illumination, thus, when in the configuration normal in sleep, the rods and cones lidded and unstimulated by wakeful contrasts, the neural track, from optic nerve through lateral geniculate body to the striate cortex and beyond, becomes a light trap, a compressed linear path for particles bounced and reflected within the system, accelerating all the while. It is this acceleration that is blameworthy, for it is the only method to produce an impetus amplified enough to

push deeper and deeper still down the vertical columns of complex
and hypercomplex cortical cells, exciting convergent and divergent
connections, expanding perception toward the incorporation of the
whole brain massed like an immense transducer upon a single idea
rebounding madly within a closed apparatus. Not much amplification
increase is required, simply the addition of an increment above
186,281 miles per second, a step toward *mach cognito*, the speed of
thought. But the results are impressive: euphoria, eupnea, eureka,
eutrophy, euryvision.

What I perceived first was the moving interaction of ovate
forms, sometimes abrupt, sometimes graceful, but always in perfect time
to the rhythm of mighty Alpha. As my dream accelerated, sound was
mixed, softly edged, simple and provocatively straightforward, that with the
addition of a low lyric, seductive syllables of the vocal, became pure euphony.

Limbs grew discernible, euglenoid movement, protoplastic,
seductive eurythmy that taxed my eurythermic tolerances. And in my
somnambulism, I was aware of her smell, the aroma of eugenol. The
association gave recognition to the evoking cumuloform, Magnesia,
come to euchre my rebellious unconscious.

--You! I cried aloud.

But I cannot but eulogize the experience. She descended
into my vericenter, so patently placental, eutherian, and mammering
her mammas at me in jellied counterorbits, challenging all the euclidian
arrangement of my thoughts and, incredibly, the eudaemonistic principles
of the STATE. Yes, I could feel the acceleration of light as I stared at
her moving blastematic parts. I registered another terrifying infusion
of blood into the Phallocryptic zone. But I was clearly sopited, my
transfixed lethargy prohibited motor function, and the potency of her
eumorphic dance melted my resistance to the point upon which reaching
I feared a viscid sementic catastrophe.

--Eu! Eu! I moaned. Could they not but hear!

Felt-tip! You understand! In such ETU as these, the aseptic,
tried and true, longs for eunuching. Or worse! Euthanasia.
Oh, guilty. Guilty!

She was laughing. How clearly I can regurgitate that
nympholeptic sound. A burlesquing prosopopoeia; how she bumped
and ground upon all my viscera, flaunting her scient anatomy. I reeled,
and she took advantage of my lack of equiposture to porrect her sexual

gestalt, extending her refulgent puboscis outrageously, that that that plicated malacoma aperture through which, like through a VASELINE haze, I did observe past the ruins of her carunculae hymenales all the way to the uterusity. Ghastful! I was scintillated from schnozzle to sciolism, paroxysmal emotional excitement as my probosc probed her pube and, in a swooning billow of energy, I closed the tiny tissued increment of her penal homologe between my lips. Eucharist!

In the ensuing surge I spurged. My phallocrypt clouded and filled. My mouth fell open and I heard even in the depths of sleep the sound of my own celestial voice:

UUUUUUUUUUUUUUUUUUMMMMMMMMM!

Sanitone!

Euphemism!

Univocalic!

Euphuism!

It was only then, friend Felt-tip, that I saw. I knew that I, too, was a POWER. And I felt a light, ignition, a glorious iridescence, a many-watted fullness and warmth, heat and color to make lux, lumens per M^2, a condition not of emptiness but of perfect density.

Felt-tip, I feel your inky heave.

Knowing same, I had everything to fear.

The challenge came almost immediately.

Perhaps the POWERS THAT BE had followed me from the vacuole or picked out my mental disquiet on the neurological radar, no matter. I recognized their presence as a subtle displacement of my amazement over Magnesia's message.

They struggled to evict her, and may have been successful, for I lost her in a dissolving defluxion, a swiftlike quickfade that might have left me vulnerable had not her absence merged with a second oneiric conception, Urethra, ebb to Magnesia's flow through my troubled dreams. One simply became the other, homophilially valid I suppose, but in my mindfulness more a mnemonic, mimetic meiosis. I realized then why I-Azoth telepeeped their showcase each night.

Urethra bent toward me as if to whisper, the purposeful breath of the revelator.

But:

--Um!

That is the grunt of the Felt-tip against the wall, flung across the pueblo room suddenly by a Kahnawful cramp in Joseph's good and only hand. Outside, the nyctophemeral light, not enough to search by. The pen is lost, its writing done. And the story not yet told! Distraught. Pained. Fatigue of course, failure to fire the metabolic furnace. Joseph must eat. Nothing remains but head and arm. By devouring either, he denies narrative forevermore.

THE WURLITZER

Out of the bathos and into the fire . . .

Scuff of a moccasin, heel and terminal digiting down the streets of the STATE: so—that Primo has fled the sudatorium, stumming out of the glib Jargon. He has abandoned Pill Case, phallocrypt, and vinyl jumpsuit to the checkroom hook and walked forth in the height of cuticle fashion, brown as a bawcock in his innocence bib and tucker, oh most Noble Savage! He must return home to Hy-gi-ya, a tribute to the lure of her fecundity, its power to outdraw the mercantile pursuit of the medicinal bibelot, or the intoxicating wiles of bodyhouse hemogoblins, or the vocab effleurage of the bath, the various enthrallments of the Publicity.

But, en route, he encounters a crisis when confronted with the most gruesome temptation of the STATE, technological hussy, vending machine, prosthetic device: Wurlitzer. This is the dream lover, neon, crenellated box lurking in the glossy shadows. As soon as the POWERS cut off onesuch, two more flicker up with their evil glim, light the color of ulfire to lure just as unsuspecting ones as Primo. This is moon pie.

A Wurlitzer is all fascia, covered over with a villose escutcheon. Center on is a cuneiform infunibula into which one plunges any skinned limb for a timed burst of intraleptic feeling. Its operational design is based on Fechner's Law: the intensity of a sensation produced by a varying stimulus varies directly as the logarithm of that stimulus. Thus, as the machine's infernal internal suckers and rubbers move on the scale to ecstatic, the feeling response of the insertee increases exponentially. Gustav Theodor Fechner was an animist, a psychophysicist and POWER before his ETU. Although he, too, had a flaw, for it is said that under the pseudonym Dr. Mises he wrote, poor man, wrote satire. A closet menippean.

Wurlitzers: there is something far more than perverse in these machines: their inexplicability, the fact that the POWERs have not acknowledged their existence. Rumours abound. All aseptics, certainly, have heard of these through the gossipground, the videovine. The myth of a Wurlitzer pimp persists. Some repeat that a singlemind controls the automatons, a rebellious type with insidious designs to deflect the power of POWERS through these lollipederastos and mobile sweetarts. Perhaps this pimp is a POWER himself?

And so Primo, hands on hips, feet on the ground, inserts his only limb remaining. He mates to cogs and gears and tubes and vacuum pumps, a continuous draw on pleasure that has him first coiling with joy. The action is furious, a blistering caterwaul. Primo is as trapped as a finger in a bottle neck; he jerks and twists, shrinks and swells, loobs until he can loob no more. He plants his feet up against the Wurlitzer dash and tests the plastic tolerance of his tentum tissue, straining to break the salubrious link, but he only verifies another law: that pleasure increases directly in proportion to the area pleased. The Primitive is in real danger of being gratified to d--th.

He kicks, he weeps, he curses, he farts, he laughs, he dies, he howls, he mews, he comes cum come, to kingdom come he comes and comes and comes and comes, an endless spermicide. And just when he thinks he can come no more, the machine recycles and Prime, like a primeval geyser, comes again.

Hy-gi-ya stirs in her sleep. It is not in her nature to waste. Primo seeps into the flow of her dreams and she raises her pelvis like a saucer to collect all his scattered seed. From among millions, one such cracks, fertilizes, that stone she bears inside her.

ON THE 'BRANE

--Antigens to the left of me, antibodies to the right, a real can of worms! Where's that Spockdamned Tuponee gone to?

The finale of this tri-dimensional fable is based on the principle of the stereoscope in which the impression of depth is created by the illused fusion of subtly differing images into a composite. A natural tension results, a triolism, proofs, neuters, and counter proofs, yet, it will be agreed, there is no character in this ongoing malignancy

who is not, in some sense, a worm, an arrangement of evolutionary
letters, a zoonite zoomorph, a simplex, a skeptic, an adept, an artifix.

These are all figments on the brain wherein this battle rages.
And circumvents.

--Tuponee! Don't leave me!

SOLUNAR

--You misinflected dactyl! You vapid solecism!

That susurrus insult from lampooner Urethra in my dream,
thought stream, pulsing verbal tachyons, and the ETU is nearly nothing.
The Felt-tip is lost. The end of this crestomathy? No, I now transmit on
the telepath, throw forth a conclusion to you future tellurians, whoever
you may be. Receive me, despite my senseless method.

Brain drain, I suck on a grey tidbit of the somaesthetic
system, clean my teeth with an afferent fiber and feel my inhibition
dissolve like plaque. One by one I consider the erasure of the tenets of
the universal medicine, PANACEATIC SCIENCE, slipping away from
my calculating clutches on the waves of red lasers. And slowly, as if from
my very epicenter, rises a glowing globe, megatonic, a ball of metabolic
fire, an expanding sphere of photobiotic light, a genesis to displace all my
physical presence, whatever knowledge, habit, or memory possessed still
by my remaining tissue. When that good corona is my equal, my state of
perfect health will be more. I will know d--th is, this high anonymous
room finally empty, and illumined by my absence confirming . . .

But there is too little ETU remaining. I leave as promised the
whispered code, the solemn password, concealed in the esoteric text and
enigmatic emblem of my avocation:

ZOOGONY

XERO DREAM

Primo, he goes slack, like some deflated cocksman, an apathic
flummox, an insensate boner, an over-ejaculated quintaped, and is
released. The Wurlitzer whirls away in search of other hapless suckers.
One born every day.

Nearby lies Coral. Ever dedicated to the commands of Tuponee, she scoops him up in her jaws and shifts him down the long haul of her internal accommodations. She leaves the iCity, her forward progress a slow winding out into the Outland, that anarchic breathing space after atmosymmetry. She regains her nonrigid strength as she snakes her way into the intrinsic light, guided heliotropically toward Acoma, that phosfor-us, that leukosite. Her colors glow with the natural burning of earth pigments, a glow worm glitter, euchromatopsy, a reflection of the legacy of Angstrom, wave lengths absorbed by a substance equal to those given off by said substance when luminous. She is crystalsnake, measured in milliphots and foot candles. She is homing needle, a true sight down an axis of infrared.

Lightsome of heart, fancy full, she bears her awkward burden: the Primitive there where he lies in her aphotic stomach. He can feel the sharp edges of the rocks sliding beneath her as bruisingly as dyspeptic pain.

He will die feeling. He will become an afterfact.

As Coral travels, she is washed by tides of color, veiling and revealing the desert floor, a soothing stroke along her psyche to allay her kenophobic fears. Like through thalassic weed, she passes growths of cliff rose and big sagebrush, grey-green plants for which Primo's ancestors found so many medicinal uses. She scrabbles over broad bands of prismatic seashells, deabated conch, and fossilized stars fallen from their dioptric installation in the nightblind sky. Fluctuant on seas of hot and cool, sun and moon, light and darklight, she moves through the electromagnetic radiation, the fluid vibrations of space:

WORMLIGHT

Worm, a germ, a sperm, has run his course.

There is a disruption in the STATE OF PERFECT HEALTH. The outcome is in doubt. No matter. That chaos is reestablished.

Tuponee, sage and interpreter of mysteries, recognizes the termination in his cohort's eye. He has seen its resolve before, the dialectic, manic glance of his fellow-reptiles gorged on the white and fragrantly evil flowers of the night-blooming cactus *Nyctocereus serpentinus* and driven over the mesa's edge, enchanted by the prospect of free-fall, impact, and death. From ETU to ETU, he has witnessed these massive panics of his species, thousands, millions, driven to coincident suicide, an irrational, compulsive murder of their collective unconscious. On such days, the sky has rained with twisted bodies, a natural helminthemisis, and the desert floor has flooded with their rotting cadavers, assuming into sand; rock, center of the earth, the elements of their composition. The vermiculous Outland.

Worm has penetrated the Publicity and his contagion spreads. The iCities fall, one after another like parataxis. The great glass towers are sarcophagi. The omniscience of the POWERS THAT BE is disrupted by a first-person voice. Failing in their ubiquity, they too must join the rank and file in the CommuniCity of DEATH:

The last word.

All the world becomes the Outland. The novel rushes on toward fertilized emptiness.

Tuponee considers ETU to come. Whether this battle is lost or won, he knows there is the oogenetic replacement of depleted ranks to be achieved, some heavy coiling, procreative joy; he is the responsible phallus, to make future eirons to frye in future fires. He abandons Worm to loneliness again. He does not wish to hear the sanitone of Worm's final speak.

--Here goes nothing!

You did it, Worm! Down, down, down with your wild stellar yellow miracle blue star magic hallucinogenerating cosmicomic atomic acomatoxic comadose!

--Spock, like I scarfed an astrolabe! All squeams, spurls, and crottles am I!

History may yet revise Worm's posterity, transcribe his climactic syllabus into a shout of praise:

Kyrie Alazon!

--O yeah, I taste of the divine moon pie! yUM!

Indeed he consumes the seed of secret fire, *ignis innaturalis*.

He enters a maze of possibility as crossed and colored as reptiles' skin.

He apprehends the splendor of BRILLIANTINE.

He sleeps the beneficent anesthesia of low frequency cortex oscillation.

He hears the heavenly homophony of renovation, music in his sphere.

He becomes the linguistic texiform, the cybenet, weblike articulation of pattern and association.

He knows photodynamic truth, the PHOTOMA, finite flash and infinite beginning without objective basis.

A glorious burst of Worm light: gone:

ZOON

I am totally consumed, already memory. Acute irreversible coma. EEG isolectric, I exist only in electro-cerebral silence. Joseph SET-6, he was, now is only an UM midst the universal Hum. I know the unspeakable, that perfect vacuum:

thanaton

In my concluding ETU, I see the explanation for myself, record the visualization indelibly like an old luminarist peeping through the curtains at the sun's mesmerizing privates. I perceive the *PHOTONE*, the regenerating secret scenario:

There has been no betrayal, no treason that was not intended. The Cell survived the destruction of the STATE OF PERFECT HEALTH. They gathered together somewhere again, seemingly in celebration. The ritual goes as follows:

Magnesia lies, spread, in the rubble, her hands cupped about her alembic. 1-Azoth, theurgic incubus, is on his knees before her. Above them, Urethra whispers:

Zosimus
Heraclitus the Obscure
Geber
Arnold of Villanova
Rhasis
Anaxagoras
Aristotle
Hermes Trismegistus
Nemesius, Bishop of Emesa
Paracelsus

Senior Zadith
Lavoisier
Sir Joseph Priestly
Marie Curie
John Crowe Ransom
Dr. Pepper
Owsley
Jorge Luis Borges
Fulcanelli
Eugene Canseliet
Michael Angelo Kahn
Joseph Set-6

--Instruments of change! Urethra shouts, as Magnesia unties
the Phallocrypt and takes 1-Azoth's lumbric to her.

And they become the androgyne, the circle squared, the
squirming conjunction of opposites, enantiodromiac, male and female,
brother and sister, crossed over, made volatile by their fire and swamped
in their mutual elixir. I see their caduceus, abandoned in the shards,
in chemical wedding, his seed launched toward her egg, a million
microscopic snakes ovum-bound.

They cry: they burn: they dissolve to:

eu-topos

--Zoe! Zounds! Zooks!
And then, the explanation.
Thus spake Urethra:

315

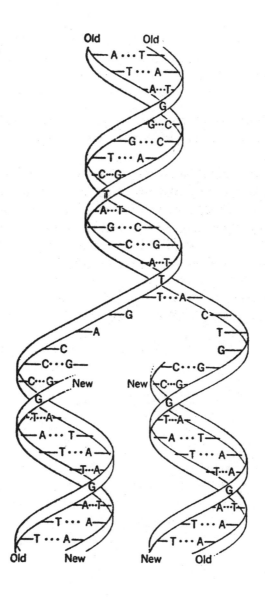

Plusquamperfiction: a palindrome bespoken in screwtape
letters, panagram logos like pure metallic flow, a twisted wystemious
unity that blinds me to darkness: in the light of this final ETU I see,
dear reader, flash before me the possibility of your future LIFE.
        --You adventitious botulus! You failed zoomorph! You cliché!

ACOMA

What animates this world of emptiness?
Hy-gi-ya, while searching for *jojoba* beans, has discovered
in the sand the evidence of proud Coral's inability to reach the water
dish, and the bones of her primitive husband intertwined and wound in
a dried snakeskin shroud, its brilliant colors faded like some weathered
ancient weaving.
What lies out there to which the people are drawn like a
snake to water? What is this poison?
She gathers up the remains. Like her many children, this
Primo, dead, has given her happiness. Like them, too, he has brought her
grief. Love she cannot understand; for all her experience and purity of
heart, she can see no explanation for it.
Her only knowledge lies now growing in her gut, like
language, there to generate a curious nascence, an intimated swelling, a
photobiotic renaissance, primed, primogenerated, primordial, primum
mobile, materia prima . . .
It is late, the sun sets with a low umming lullaby. Hy-gi-ya
turns to the west. Before her: the great mesa, ochre and clay, obsidian,
water-and-sun-washed rock, the PHOTOPIA, like a philosopher's stone,
ever-changing. Bearing the burden of death, and new life, she climbs, up,
and up, toward the blazing ouranosphere, the vaulted sky, up to Acoma,
the luminocity, that place where there is no darkness.

AFTER WORDS

Post World War II literature in Europe, the United
States, and elsewhere experienced a tumult of experiment,
abstraction, and innovation. In fiction, the rules of
narrative were dissolved into a cacophony of words and
forms as disparate and chaotic as the war itself. So much
had been witnessed; it was as if the old structures were
no longer adequate, and, when matched to the inevitable
philosophical questioning of the moment, enabled writers
to invent new anti-heroes, new languages, new approaches
to time and space from the practice of the naturalists and
realists from before. Camus, Joyce, Faulkner, Nabokov,
among so many other brilliant imaginations; Borges,
Marquez and the other South Americans; the young
Americans: Pynchon, Hawkes, Barthelme, Gass, Gaddis,
and Barthes, just to name a few—these were the authors
who shaped and built new ways to tell stories that were
revolutionary, ambitious, and indifferent to critical
success, even as they achieved it. It was a glorious time for
readers. These are the writers who shaped and built me,
and so, as an aspiring novelist, it was inevitable that
I would try my hand.

As tools, words can be used to build useful and stately
things, ideas and institutions that are the foundation of
our culture. Fair enough, but perhaps not good enough.
What if what is built is useless and insubstantial? What
if the ideas are corrupted or the institutions are revealed
as empty shells? What if the product doesn't work or
falls apart? Isn't it important to ask these questions in
any time, so that social intellectual or social may be
challenged? Should words not then be applied as "cross-
words," intricate puzzles that provoke the mind, make
us think, cause us to act as revolutionaries in search of
alternatives and solutions? Should words not enable
riskful thinking?

And what about the sense of marvel? Of the joy of suspension in a world of sound and sense and dream? I can remember as a child reading under the bed, hanging off a cliff in some summer place, retreating from the challenges of parents, peers, and professors, all of whom had notions of right and wrong, at this hour or in this place, from which I needed to escape. And escape I did, and still do, in skeins of words, shards of images, and shocks of insight and revelation. And so it was inevitable that I would try my hand that way too.

These three short novels were first published in the 1970's by a young writer fully engaged in the exercise of words as tools of self-discovery. They were written over nine years —three bursts of many threes. If you look you will see tri-parts everywhere: in the syntax, structural organization, and multiple levels of consciousness. Upon re-reading in sequence, I have also discovered an evolutionary triad of thoughts and feelings about the world, a succession of sensibility and ideas over that period of personal inquiry and growth. The novels combine satire, fantasy, heroic romance, and linguistic abandon with personal history, some three short decades of life experience, and many influences picked up along the way. They are willfully indifferent to realism and the historical novel. They play on and with known literary forms and some treasured precursors, and they make no excuse for their attempt at, dare I say it, originality.

In the interim since publication, several generations of new readers have been born and their interests are very different. Sadly, many of the writers mentioned above are no longer read, and that is a loss, particularly to a generation that prides itself on innovation, entrepreneurship, and daring. But there are in this generation also writers who are using random selection to mix and remix narrative, to destroy the logic of time, to create new vocabulary, to incorporate visual images in augmentation to verbal evocations, and to perform and promote their fictions through computer manipulation, mixed-media, and electronic formats. There will be an e-book edition of 3 and it will be interesting to see if or how the alternative platforms of a traditionally published book and Internet-connected tablet might change, interact, or augment an audience of new readers.

Finally, this work will be left. The manuscripts will be housed in an archival collection; the book you hold will be kept in your library or passed on; and the e-book will remain for however long its pixels will burn as an expression of light in this technological world. What matters most to me as a leaving, however, is evidence of a palpable sense of energy and imagination at work, a presence of being after words can be no longer spoken.

Peter Neill
Sedgwick, Maine
October 2013